BOOKS BY STEFAN KANFER

A *Journal of the Plague Years*
The Eighth Sin

THE
EIGHTH
SIN

THE EIGHTH SIN

Stefan Kanfer

Random House
New York

Library of Congress Cataloging in Publication Data
Kanfer, Stefan.
The eighth sin.
I. Title
PZ4.K1634Ei [PS3561.A472] 813'.5'4 77–90254
ISBN 0–394–41476 4

Manufactured in the United States of America
9 8 7 6 5 4 3 2
First Edition

Grateful acknowledgment is made to the following for permission to reprint the follow-ing previously published material:

Éditions Gallimard: Excerpt from *Plastic Sense* by Malcolm Chazal. © 1948 Éditions Gallimard. Farrar, Straus & Giroux, Inc.: Excerpt from "O All the Problems Other People Face" from *Henry Fate and Other Poems* by John Berryman. Copyright © 1975, 1977 by Kate Berryman. Hawthorn Books, Inc.: Excerpt from *People, Places and Things* edited by Geoffrey Grigson and Charles H. Gibbs-Smith. All rights reserved. Houghton Mifflin Company: Excerpt from *The Long Goodbye* by Raymond Chandler. Alfred A. Knopf, Inc.: Excerpt from the preface of *Ivy Gripped the Steps and Other Stories* by Elizabeth Bowen. Copyright 1946 and renewed 1974 by Elizabeth Bowen. Macmillan Publishing Co., Inc. and A. P. Watt & Son: *Collected Poems* by William Butler Yeats; excerpt from "The Four Ages of Man." Copyright 1934 by Macmillan Publishing Co., Inc., renewed 1962 by Bertha Georgie Yeats; excerpt from "John Kinsella's Lament for Mrs. Mary Moore." Copyright 1940 by Georgie Yeats, renewed 1968 by Bertha Georgie Yeats, Michael Butler Yeats and Anne Yeats. New Directions Publishing Corporation and J. M. Dent & Sons, London, and the Trustees for the Copyrights of Dylan Thomas: Excerpt from "Do not go gentle into that good night" and "Foster the Light" from *The Poems of Dylan Thomas.* Copyright 1939 by New Directions Publishing Corporation. Copyright 1952 by Dylan Thomas. Random House, Inc.: Excerpt from "The Emperor Jones" from *Selected Plays of Eugene O'Neill.* Copyright 1921 and renewed 1949 by Eugene O'Neill.

FOR MY FATHER

CONTENTS

U bar dikhila xoymi, oprundus,
sviymi vastinsa bari armayasa.
Liska ozistar sesi garadu
mangila pali ti inkil ziyasa. . . .

The upright stone stares angrily
with clenched fists and a great curse.
From within a hidden voice
tries to send out a song.

The roads where we still travel
wait to hear it.
The Gypsies await the call
together with their horses.

But they are quiet, all are asleep.
Our brothers lie among the flowers
and no one knows who they are
or on which road the victims fell.

Hush, Gypsies! Let them sleep
beneath the flowers.
Halt, Gypsies! May
all our children have their strength.

—Gypsy chant,
Dimiter Golemanov

As the Middle Ages knew it . . . each sin
came in human shape, identified and
described: Wrath with the whites of his eyes
showing, snivelling with his nose, and biting
his lips; Avarice beetle-browed and bleary;
Gluttony with his rumbling guts, drinking a
gallon and a gill . . . Accidie lying in bed in
Lent . . . till matins and Mass be done.
These examples are from *Piers Plowman,* but
others as vivid might be taken from Dunbar,
from Stephen Hawes, from Marlowe or from
Dekker. Not merely the writers, but the
preachers gave their imagination rein: "Lust
consumes the body . . . It destroys the
tongue of confession, the eyes of intelligence,
the ears of obedience, the nose of discretion,
the hair of good thoughts, the beard of
fortitude, the eyebrows of holy religion." The
Ancren Riwle gives each Sin its attendant
beast: the Lion of Pride, the Adder of Envy,
the Unicorn of Wrath, the Scorpion of
Lechery, the Fox of Avarice, the Sow of
Gluttony, and the Bear of Sloth. Nearly four
hundred years later, the Sins are still riding
their beasts through Spenser's *Faerie Queene;*
but Avarice has now a Camel, Lechery a
Goat; and Envy, riding a Wolf, carries the
Serpent in his bosom.

—Geoffrey Grigson and
Charles H. Gibbs-Smith, eds.,
People, Places and Things

I: SURVIVAL

WRATH. AVARICE. SLOTH. PRIDE. LUST. ENVY. GLUT-tony. And the greatest of these is Wrath.

You can beat back the others. Or they can wear themselves out. Lust has not taken hold of me like a virus since Inger.

> What shall I do for pretty girls
> Now my old bawd is dead?

As Yeats used to say to me, Pride? No longer enough to qualify as Deadly Sin. Envy. Of what? Money? Possessions? The acquisitive instinct dies hard. But I have stolen enough things. So much for Avarice, then. Gluttony: underweight is better. I had good actuarial possibilities, the doctors said. And would have yet, if it were not for what I have to do. Sloth: no more, thank you. I have lain in enough hammocks, taken enough vacations from the will, spun in enough backwaters, had enough sleep.

Wrath is another matter. Anger has a systolic beat. I cannot get rid of mine; even the business of Eleazar Jassy could not kill it.

Murder. Means nothing to the ear. I prefer the word of my old Romany tongue, of my people: the Gypsy term *morteur*. At least it contains death the way an apricot contains a bitter pit. Murder in English means nothing. It could even be glamorous: Murderers' Row. Murder Inc. The Simple Art of Murder. Murder, She Said. Ah, God, language is a zoo. The words bark, slither, snap, devour, copulate: animals in a menagerie. But there is always some goddamned moat between them and the onlookers. And the keepers.

Murder.

And there are worse substitutes for feeling: Passed Away; Just Reward; A Long Illness (meaning cancer). And the most inadequate of them all: Holocaust. A nothing category; a eunuch of a word.

A Jewish term, anyway. To them it has significance. To the rest of this numb world it means fire. To the Gypsies, even less.

This is why I became a painter. In my denial I thought: suppose God had decreed that words were insufficient. That from now on we were to paint our prayers.

In my denial I did not speak for three months after the English liberated the camp.

ITEM: The [Gypsy] children were all skin and bone. The thin skin rubbed on the bones and became infected. The sick children would drink the washing-cup water as there was often no other water. Sometimes the children's blankets (in the sick barracks) were washed and put back still wet on the beds.

—L. Adelsberger, *Auschwitz*
(Berlin: Lettner, 1953)

ITEM: The [Gypsies'] children were suffering from Noma . . . which reminded me of leprosy . . . their little bodies wasted away with gaping holes in their cheeks big enough for one to see through, a slow putrefaction of the living body.

—Rudolf Höss, *Kommandant in Auschwitz*
(Stuttgart: Deutsche Verlag, 1958)

They helped me at the Center and probed tentatively and asked questions. I had no reply. There was a prevalent theory then that the children were resilient and needed principally to be fed. Accordingly things were expected, in the words of the directing physician, to "zigzag back to normal." But fathers and teachers, what is normal? Why do these children resemble their grandparents and why are they afraid to sleep?

Someone discovered our value. We were labeled detritus of the war, living proof of atrocities. Witnesses. We were photographed, interrogated, "debriefed" they would say now in yet another repellent euphemism. We were palpated, injected, tested for reflexes, heartbeat, brain waves and kidney, spleen and liver functions. They left our minds alone to forage at the outskirts of sense. Our bodies begged for help.

ITEM: The imprisoned Gypsies were often shrunken to skeletons. I went into the kitchen and found that the food did not contain the prescribed 1,680 calories. I wrote a memo immediately but Hartjenstein (Commander of Birkenau) said, "Oh, they are only Gypsies, after all."

> —Evidence given by Dr. Franz
> Bernhardt Lucas, in H. Langbein, *Der*
> *Auschwitz Prozess*, 2 vols. (Vienna:
> Europa, 1965)

Then without much warning we were packed up and sent on a great drab roaring transport plane to London. As we took off, a one-armed Jewish boy sitting next to me shouted, "*S'hma Yisrael.*" He looked pale and green; a nurse marked it as fear; but I recognized the color of valediction and repeated the phrase. It was the first time I had talked since the liberation. No one noticed. We landed heavily, yet there was no terror for me, nor, I think, for the others. We stepped into another latitude, a place of other people's memories and structures. I was immediately struck by the powerful buildings and the pinched faces, by England's stubborn and mysterious nod to the bulk of lost power. Everyone seemed to look skyward constantly, determined once and forever to demolish the ghost of the *Luftwaffe*, to banish dread, to stare through particles of loathing and resentment, to blink away nightmares of captivity and bombing and uselessness and all the residue of conflict. The air was stained with the odor of bituminous coal burning in every Englishman's castle. To me it had the compelling aroma of dinner or perfume.

There were only a few Romanies in the Center. The Cambridge men in lab coats were anxious to examine us—particularly me because I was the youngest. We were the distillate of an old and broken culture. Curiosities. Wanderers. Who could

blame the scientists for their curiosity? I was the first Gypsy
boy they had ever seen.

—*Do you know what happened to your father, Benny? (This in
    enameled French.)*
—*Benoit.*
—*Benoit, then. Do you recall what happened to your father?*
—*I don't remember my father.*
—*Surely you must have some memory. How about your mother?*
—*Difficult to comprehend.*
—*Your mother or your father?*
—*My memory.*

ITEM: Until far in the night I heard their cries and knew they were
    resisting. The Gypsies screamed all night . . . They sold their
    lives dearly.
                        —Evidence of Diamanski at
                          Auschwitz trial

Consultation. This in English. I had picked up some of that
elastic lingo at the camp, waiting around in the infirmary. Two
doctors were Scottish, I think, or Welsh—accents meant nothing to me then—and one of the surgeons had taken it into his
head to teach me prehensile grammar. But his hours were long
and many of his charges were dying of the results of long
starvation and there seemed to be nothing anybody could do
about it and he used to fall asleep with wet eyes during our
conversations.

—*The boy is obviously attempting to forget.*
—*Given what he has probably experienced, perhaps that is for
    the best.*
—*No, no. Don't you see? What does not come out must ex-
    plode later, perhaps in puberty or worse.
    (Come now, Dr. Aaronson, what could be worse than pu-
    berty?)*

ITEM: Afterwards Boger and others went through the blocks and
    pulled out Gypsy children who had hidden themselves. The

children were brought to Boger who took them by the feet and
smashed them against the wall . . . I saw this happen five, six,
or seven times.

> —B. Naumann, *Auschwitz* (London: Pall
> Mall Press, 1966)

*—You must try. A boy does not forget. He has not had enough
time to forget. He has not lived long enough. He only pretends to forget.*
*—I am not pretending. I am trying. (To destroy my memory, you
soulless quacks, to erase the years.)*

ITEM: We heard outside cries like "Criminal, Murderer." The
whole lasted some hours. Then an SS officer came whom I
didn't know and dictated to me a letter. The contents were
"Special Treatment Carried Out." He took the letter out of the
machine and tore it up. In the morning there were no more
Gypsies in the camp.
    At dawn I noticed the scattered pots, the torn garments.

> —E. Heimler, *The Night of the Mist*
> (London: Bodley Head, 1959)

—Let me try a new approach, Benny.
—Benoit.
*—Benoit, then. You're a growing boy. Do you ever think about
. . . about girls?*
—What about them?
—Do you ever think, you know, about being with girls?
—Never.
—About being with boys?
—No.
—About animals. About loving animals?
—I like to think about them with their clothes off.
—Animals?
—Girls.
—I thought you never thought about girls.
—You got me interested.
*—Benoit, I think you are malingering. That is quite enough for
today.*

After the shrink, the English lesson. I saw this agreeably, as the vestibule in a new house.

—*Very well, Benny.*
—*Benoit.*
—*Benoit, then. We will converse in English.*
—*Wery vell, Master Jessup.*
—*No, not wery vell. Very well.*
—*Yes, yes. Very well, Master Jessup.*
—*We will have a conversation. Shall we go to the theater tonight?*
—*I would like to march to the tragedy of* Hamlet. *They praise him very much. Yes?*
—*Go on, Benoit.*
—*It was played with applauses. Is good?*
—*I'll tell you when it's over.*
—*The actors make wery vell their parts. Us are—we are—enjoy. Thank you.*
—*Are you finished, Benoit?*
—*Yes, Master Jessup. How it was?*
—*Let us try a new approach. (New approaches were the rage in London that year.)*
—*What are you doing, Benoit?*
—*I am combing my her.*
—*No, you are combing your* hair. *Hair. To sound as fair. Or pair.*
—*Sorry, Master Jessup. I am combing my hair.*
—*Very good. What are you sitting on?*
—*Mr. Jessup, I am sitting on my ass.*
—*(In a voice the size of a needle): What-is-the-wooden-thing-you-are-sitting-on?*
—*Oh. Master Jessup, I am sitting on a cher. A chair. How I am?*

After school, I was allowed free time. St. Luke's amounted to a minimum-security prison. It was not hard to scale the low wall and make your way through the back streets to the Number 2 bus, and thence to London. There was no bed check until eight o'clock, the place was crowded with refugees and no one kept close track. I had no friends and talked to no one except when I had to. The handling of the psychiatric conquistadores and the English instructors was simplicity itself. Those idiot ink blots, those fundamental free-associative traps. Did they never learn that if one man could invent a code, another could crack it? My mind was marked *Not for Sale or Rent;* my English was better than anyone knew.

When I got to Oxford Circus I customarily leaped off the red bus and wandered in a prescribed and personal manner, touching certain lampposts and walking over specific manholes to the Embankment. There I removed a stone behind which I had secreted a metal box. It was full of pastels shoplifted from Harrods and a blanket taken from the school. In various neighborhoods I took off my cap and turned it upside down, showing the threadbare purple-satin lining. I threw in a few sixpences and threepenny pieces, spread the blanket, knelt on it and became a sidewalk chalk artist. The people did the rest. Good coins there were in those days: huge coppers with the fat Queen Victoria scowling. Churchill ruled in name, but the powerful dowager on the penny hovered like light itself around the Georgian façades, on the old squares that exhaled melancholy and in the storefronts, blinking back the motes of war. There was nothing and there was everything. No eggs, no meat, no jobs, rationing, queues. There was also the London light pulled in and held by the city's gravity.

London: has there ever been constructed a larger emblem of masculinity, one that spoke so directly to the fatherless? Like Albert's ghost I haunted the vast, cold museums. There was no room in my eyes for non-English painters. Blake glowed with lunacy; put up your hand and you could feel the mad heat. Turner announced that the sun was God; Constable constructed a world of space and leisure where I could vanish for whole afternoons. The walls of the Tate and the National Gallery whispered and beckoned. My heart accelerated as I walked those dusty, echoing corridors. I did not know then that I was walking in the tomb of art. Once outside, I knelt on the sidewalk again and drew. I pretended to be dumb and even deaf when people tried to start conversation. The chalk murals favored Rumanian countrysides—cows, chickens, pigs and the like—but passers-by confused them with scenes of the Lake District. Often they gave me shillings. There was a tall, horsy lady who once gave me a ten-shilling note, an enormous amount at that time. Only much later did I find out who she was. She wrote in her book *Ivy Gripped the Steps:* ". . . All the time we knew that compared to those on the Continent we in Britain could not be said to suffer. Foreign faces about the London streets had personal pain and impersonal history sealed up behind the eyes. All this pressure drove egotism underground, or made it whiten like grass under a stone. . . . You used to know what you were like from the things you liked, and chose. Now there was not what you liked, and you did not choose. Any little remaining choices and pleasures shot into new proportion and new value: people paid big money for little bunches of flowers."

And chalk bouquets drawn on the sidewalk. I like to think that Elizabeth Bowen was writing of the group from the Center with sealed eyes. The specter of this century is the unwanted child; its character is the displaced person. We were both. I always meant to write to her. Now she's gone, now she's gone. Well, I can draw another picture for her. I have done four through the years. Another may help. Who knows what God responds to. Gypsies take the long view.

ITEM: Even hardened prisoners were deeply moved when the SS in the fall of 1944 singled out and herded together Gypsy youngsters. The screaming, sobbing children, frantically trying to get to their fathers or protectors among the prisoners, were surrounded by a wall of carbines and machine pistols and taken away to be sent to Auschwitz for gassing.

—Eugen Kogon, *The Theory and Practice of Hell* (London: Secker & Warburg, 1950)

At St. Luke's I was marked as a tough but not uncrackable nut. One of the masters saw me drawing on the pavement and concluded that what I really needed was not a chance to be away from school, or to have a sidewalk of my own, but art lessons. With four others, two sour adult Hungarians and a lame French girl of seventeen who had a number tattooed on her arm, I was sent to the Robsjon Art Academy. We learned fundamentals, which I already knew somehow, and refinements, which I did not.

Two classes made it all worthwhile. In oil painting I stared at the hues. I had not even known their names, much less their range: cerulean, ocher, chrome yellow, burnt umber, cochineal. The little tubes lay before me in a maple box like a series of illimitable options. I was not to be given so much choice again until I came to America.

The other class was the drawing of the nude.

Here again I was the youngest, always the youngest. Above the students, near the molding, were a series of statements made by painters: "He who pretends to be either painter or engraver without being a master of drawing is an imposter." William Blake, etc. One leaped out at me and I was certain was put up there solely for my humiliation: Yet why was it gray and dusty? What other child had it meant to embarrass? "There has never been a boy painter, nor can there be. The art requires a long apprenticeship, being mechanical as well as intellectual." Constable.

But I was more embarrassed by the nude. Her name was Birdie, a metallic blonde with close-cropped hair, and she appeared before us over a series of weeks, pulling her brown muslin shift over her head and presenting an overweight and collapsing body for our inspection. The frankness of her pudenda, the enormity of her freckled thighs and pendulous dugs seemed to lie upon my skin in plenitude and utility, like wool upon a sheep. She made the air heavy and sometimes I could not get enough oxygen and felt the early strains of panic. When the instructor said "Birdie, if you're cold you can put the shift back on for a while" and she refused with a small shake of the head, I understood. I was warmed by her. Couldn't Mr. Gregory see that she was a source of heat, like Blake?

Early on, Mr. Gregory took a pointer and toured Birdie's neck and shoulders, reminding us of curvatures and anatomy.

"Remember," he said, going southward as my mouth constricted; her torso seemed ornamented with pears, apples, grapes; "remember: the breast is only a bag on the chest." But her aureoles were as large as Victorian pennies, and I could see past her skin. It seemed to me that her body echoed all the primitive inventions. The wheel was the circle of the eye; hinges, the joints. I could understand geometry deriving from the planes and angles of the nose, the teeth, the elbows, nails, genitalia.

On those afternoons the world centered around Birdie; around the freckled thighs, the stretch-marked paps wrecked by gravity, around the swells of her belly. At the same time, I had no true conception of lust. I thought in terms of restitution. If only I could get close to Birdie, if only I might manage to place these coppery hands against her English skin, everything might be all right again. And by everything, I meant every thing.

It never happened. One day Birdie was gone and in her place was a Shetland pony. "We have studied the human form," said Mr. Gregory. "Now let us go backward in time to examine the animal." I could not draw horses then; I cannot now. The announcement about the boy painter came home to me with the force of ether. I took to falling asleep in class and was soon transferred to a series of lessons on portraiture.

These altered my life. I had a knack, it turned out. I could draw faces, even at that age.

It was a matter of proportion. What is the face but a landscape? Map the planes and elevations and the likeness rises from the paper. Dusty, empty, two-point perspective was all I offered. It was enough. Constable was right, of course. My portraits were only accurate; there was no insight. But I was fourteen. They thought I was a *Wunderkind.* The instructor, Mr. Drake, bought my first pastel portrait of himself. He invited me to his home and I drew his dark, cross-eyed wife and their two glowering daughters. Mrs. Drake patted my head, gave me shortbread and tea, and put her arm next to mine to compare coloring.

"They say my grandfather was half Gypsy," she told me.

"That's where I get my coloring. I understand you're a full-blooded Gypsy."

"Just a full Gypsy," I said, patting my stomach and indicating the emptying plate of cakes.

It was my first English riposte. She laughed and patted my head again. When I left, Mr. Drake saw me to the bus, and as it pulled up, shook my hand. I felt something crackling in it, and when I looked down I found a pound note. My first commission.

There was a succession of them. Forgetting became, instead of a career, a bodily process. Only the dreams persisted, and these diminished through my own will. I forced myself to dream of prismatic colors, hues, tints. And of money. I dreamed constantly of money until the pound notes and bright, silent cascades of shillings became a scrim through which hardly any evidence was admitted. Hardly any.

ITEM: [The Gypsy] was locked in a large box with iron bars over the opening. Inside, the prisoner could only hold himself in a crouching position. Koch the Camp Commander then had big nails driven through the planks so that each movement of the prisoner made them stick in his body. Without food or water, he spent two days and three nights in this position. On the morning of the third day, having already gone insane, he was given an injection of poison.

> —E. Kogon, *The Theory and Practice of Hell*
> (London: Secker & Warburg, 1950)

In a palimpsest month, when summer and spring and fall and threats of winter all lay upon each other, when the colors screamed on the paper, Mrs. Kaufman entered the classroom and altered my life.

There is a theory among many artists that each person is destined to blossom at a specific age. Mediterranean girls at eighteen, reedy French intellectuals at fifty, Scandinavian women at thirty-five, English clubmen at seventy, and so on. It is my own belief that certain people were born to be animals, and that through some genetic quirk they became instead—to their detriment—humans. My fellow student Risa Kaufman was, in the grand design, meant to be a mare. Her features were so equine that one half expected her to be shod. Her teeth, displayed in occasional whinnies, were intended to bury themselves in a bag of oats, and her long body, with its sturdy, sensible hips and shoulders and astonishingly good legs and narrow ankles, bespoke epochs of breeding for Ascot.

I see now that this makes her look a caricature. In fact, she was something of a self-parodist. But like many another woman who radiates decency and affection, she convinced you within ten minutes that she was beautiful. It was only after you left her company that you realized that she resembled no person so much as Citation or Man o' War.

Risa had the habit, once associated with the ionospheric reaches of certain British classes, of merchandising a semistutter until it became a virtue.

"One one one feels," she might say, with a wobbly lilt, "looking at yellow that it is the the the common denominator of colors." Or "The the the eye's pupil is—as it were—at at at eternal noon."

She had been studying the work of a French artist much given to aphorisms about the physical world, and she would parrot these sentences in class and afterward, driving the instructor bonkers. However, I found her repetitions helpful for my autodidactic instructions in English. Moreover, I found them valid. I told her so.

Thereafter she began to hover over my work, stopping to correct some stylistic inadequacy and interjecting phrases that she had read or heard in Paris.

"Garnet is is is, as it were, the apoplexy, the *ap*oplexy of mauve."

"Purple is the the the embolism of blue."

"Deep red is is is the *hea*viest color of all. In a red dress the bust sinks sinks sinks to the hips, the hips to to to the legs."

Later I was to hear this artist, Malcolm Chazal, on subjects other than color. For example:

"The act of love is the only entertainment without intermissions. Love-making is always a one-act play, no matter how long the performance or how drawn-out and complicated the production."

But I would not hear such things from Risa. She acted, as many highborn women do, as if she were well past love, the way a minute hand is well past the hour hand. She would encounter it once again, the intimation was clear—but not here, not now.

A month or so after we became acquainted and chatted during and after class, she invited me home to draw her husband. I don't know what I expected. Thirty years later it is difficult to recall. I suppose, as I stood nervously before the green door of their flat in St. John's Wood, box of pastels in one hand, bouquet of violets moistly clutched in the other, I thought that the door might be opened by a horse—should I have brought sugar lumps?—or perhaps a centaur, someone who had taken Risa's tendencies all the way into a vanished Grecian world.

I was not totally off. Max Kaufman was a fur-bearing mammal who had blundered into the species *Homo sapiens* by mysterious means. Hair grew on the back of his fingers and hands, out of his nostrils and ears, the back of his neck, the portion of chest that peeked through his shirt—everywhere but on his head. There, a bald teak-colored rock showed through, surrounded by a circle of iron-gray fuzz and interrupted with follicles, the way a seaside rock is decorated with a few stubborn lichen.

"In or out?" was his first demand. I thought him inhospitable until I looked at my feet and beheld a mongrel of indeterminate age. This was Lenin, whom Max regarded with the solicitude normally given to children. He motioned both waifs inside and began a monologue. I thought Risa had stationed herself in the kitchen to give us time to get to know each other. I could hear the clank of china, but I later learned that their portable gramophone was put offstage somewhere, and that a twelve-inch record featuring the sounds of dinner being prepared was put on by Max himself while Risa went out to the local pub to buy some steak-and-kidney pie. She could not cook at all, it turned out, nor could Max, who taught modern American poetry at London University.

Max, I was informed straight away, was a Marxist, a hater

of the Empire, of England in general and of those sonofa-
bitches Churchill, De Gaulle and Franco specifically. Much of
what he said went by me. I was too busy looking at his walls.
I had never been in a library in my life, except the children's
one in the Center filled with John Buchan, Conan Doyle,
Edgar Rice Burroughs, and the like. Max's dark-green sitting
room held three thousand books of varying sizes and colors.
One entire shelf was devoted solely to the subject of chess, and
below it were two tables set with pieces, black against white
and green against red, both frozen in mid-battle, as if time
itself had broken down upon my entrance.

I had a sudden feeling of cavernous inadequacy, a knowledge
of my own ignorance, of the books whispering behind their
bindings, of information denied me, that would always be
denied me, of concepts, phrases, secrets only this man knew—
but how could any human being read all these books? He must
be a hundred and fifty years old . . . I sat down, my head empty.

We spoke of dogs, and of the school and of the Center. Max
only nodded and put in a question from time to time. I got out
my pastels and he found a piece of paper and I sketched him
in profile. He had the nose and lips of a Neapolitan, but he was
a Russian Jew, an American who had served in Intelligence
during the war, come home to find his wife in love with a
neighbor, stayed long enough to sever connections, and then
returned to London, where he had some left-wing connections
at the university.

While I drew him he opened the newspaper and fulminated
again, this time at Lord Beaverbrook and Harry Truman. "Fascist bastards," he growled. "Making the whole postwar world
a goddamn prison." I kept my face down and sketched. I was
an ignoramus, a greenhorn, a DP, a guest. Nevertheless, I
thought him a fool. What did he know of fascism, of prison?

I was wrong. Max, Max, it took me years to know what
searching, what an infinitude of longing swam beneath that
fury. It was not until you sat griping and dying of diabetes,
wondering, If Stalin was your God, where do you go for absolu-
tion? that I had more than an inkling of who you were.

And there was this: except for that first day, Max never once asked me what I had done, who I was, where I had been before he met me. Only that evening he said, perusing the *Telegraph,* "Look at that. 'Germany refuses reparations.' How do you feel about reparations, hah? You think the Krauts can give you back what you lost?"

ITEM: A Gypsy woman tried to escape and was caught. The others had to stand and watch as she was beaten and had dogs set on her. Then the German guards put her in the punishment block and told the other prisoners there they could do what they liked with her as they had to stand there in the freezing cold because of her. Some prisoners in the punishment block beat her to death.

> —Testimony of Lina Steinbeck at Ravensbruck, D. Kenrick and G. Puxon, *The Destiny of Europe's Gypsies* (New York: Basic Books, 1973)

"Max?"

"Hah?"

"Can't you see the boy's practically practically perishing before your eyes? Honestly. I mean, honestly!"

Max stirred himself. "Well, hell, Risa, I couldn't very well offer him a drink."

I must have appeared chalky. Abruptly they were all over me with ginger beer and Cheshire cheese. I ate and drank and had another portion, and another one, and resumed sketching.

The beer was homemade and of uncertain alcoholic content. I remember little more except that Risa changed the record of kitchen sounds to one more appropriate—Cockney music halls —and after a dessert of trifle I lay on their couch and slept until morning. Risa had called St. Luke's and obtained permission for me to stay. It was the first in a series of sleepovers, nights as strange and fragrant as pomegranates, ostensibly to study the technique of portraiture, but principally to be away from school and to find a world I had never experienced or known about.

St. Luke's was a good place to be away from. It was the same school beloved by the stately genteel, satirized by the envious and exposed by the knowledgeable. The uniforms were traditional blue with a round bold crest on the jacket, proclaiming an illegible tradition of Right and Crown. The masters were, without exception, men who had been too old for the war; scraps of quaint, grotesque, receding culture; instructors in whom ambition had been stunted or slain.

St. Luke's was proud of its sandstone buildings, its clipped boxwoods and limed athletic fields. And prouder still of its graduates: ministers, captains of commerce, scientists, exhibits produced at assemblies to refute the school's third-rate reputation. Its present scholars were the customary bunch portrayed in every picture of English life from the Pleistocene epoch onwards: the small knot from reputable families and mellow backgrounds; the identical twins whom all the students could tell apart but none of the masters; the fat boy who piped his answers in an indulged, eunuchoid voice; the mama's boys who wet their beds; the bluff athletes with their wake of sycophants; the meaching tattletales; the brooding incipient homosexuals; the sadists; the genius who would get a first in history at Oxford and never be heard from again; the nonstop vulgarian who knew everything about sex and who would prove it one day by becoming a film producer; the shabby genteels who would say "ectually" and talk about the country going to the "demnition bow-wows"; and the small crowd of misfits—boys with limps or stutters, Jews with money and no background, scholarship winners from mining villages or East End slums, and little Benoit from the camps, coveting the acceptance he was never to have, the little beast with his peculiar accent and un-English color and wild, internal aspect. Almost all the others treated the place as an Elysium, and their intimacy, their ease with language and place put me in scholastic misery and gave me a kind of disgrace I was never to shed. I have since been claimed as a schoolfellow by some of them, but I was so estranged that I could never recall a name, only a face, usually yoked to an insult ("Gypsy, Gypsy, father's tipsy," etc.).

Through no specific fault of its own, St. Luke's sometimes appeared—as schools will to outcasts—a prison. The difference in my case was the recollections that lay immediately beyond

reach, so that when I got into a fugue state I could not bear
to look at the barbed wire above the harmless hurricane fence
bordering the cricket field. At such times, my well-nourished
fellow students seemed victims with sentences of execution
written down and filed with the authorities.

To the other boys I was as rare and strange as an albino crow.
There were accents worse than mine—usually from sons of UN
officials or diplomats. But I was the sole refugee, planted there
by the indulgence of His Majesty's government. With the
callousness that only the undeveloped can show each other, my
fellows wanted to know how much punishment I had received,
what it was like in the camps, what I had seen. I affected a
general ignorance of the English language for a while and
threw myself into my schoolwork, my tongue sticking out of
the corner of my mouth as I drew maps of the Roman con-
quest, or attempted to understand the deployment of loga-
rithms and the innards of a frog. The difference between
loneliness and solitude is the difference between *a* cold and
the cold. I suffered from one and enjoyed the other. I endured.
I survived. Then I made the awful mistake of idly sketching a
fellow student in a slow moment. Another student spotted the
portrait, and soon the boys crowded around me, asking for their
pictures in charcoal or pencil. Pride came, privacy went.

With it came feelings of envy. I remember coveting a big
turnip watch owned by a boy named Philip Simms. I agreed
to paint his portrait in oils for the watch. The painting was to
be done on approval; it was, after all, a present to his parents.
After a holiday he told me that the painting was accepted, but
that his father had forbidden him to trade the watch. A group
of boys gathered round us. "He says a guinea will do," Simms
informed me.

"But the watch costs far more."

"What does a boy like you want with an English timepiece
like this? It's a hundred years old. It winds with a key." Then
in grand style he slapped my face.

I threw myself on him. I think I had always known that I
would never have the watch. Even as I lunged I had the
repellent notion that there was something unmanly about at-

tacking Simms, about not walking away with the stoicism of the contemptuous.

ITEM: One has to admit that the Jews are very composed when they go to their deaths—they stand still—while the Gypsies cry, scream and move constantly, even when they are already on the spot where they are to be shot. Some even jumped into the ditch before the firing and pretended to be dead.

> —Report of junior officer, Nuremberg
> Document #905

They pulled me off him as I banged his head continually against the wire fence. I had remembered nothing but the slap and then being separated, Simms's head dripping blood onto my sticky hands. Although Simms was not generally disliked, the assault made me a bit more acceptable. I became known as the boy who would take a dare. I put stink bombs in the Commons, let air out of the director's bicycle tires, asked the biology master what a steer was when I already knew, inquired about the grammatical difference between "lie" and "lay."

Hence the interviews.

—*Benjamin.*

—*Benoit.*

—*Just so. Benoit. I see that you are a refugee.*

—*Yes, sir.*

—*You should count yourself as fortunate to be here.*

—*I do, sir.*

—*Most boys your age are not in so good a school. Nor do they have your chances. I see by your card that you are from Bucharest. Do boys like you go to schools like St. Luke's in Rumania?*

—*No, sir.*

—*With all due respect, I imagine boys like you in Rumania are working at a trade by now.*

—*Sir, with all due respect, boys like me in Rumania are dead.*

—*Yes. Well. That may be so, Benoit, but we are not in Rumania. We are in England. And we are at St. Luke's. Here*

you are no different from the son of a duke or the brother of
a dustman. You are expected to follow the rules. Do you
understand?
—*Except when you speak too fast.*
—*Let . . . me . . . speak . . . slowly . . . then. A St. Luke's boy*
does not make stenches in the chemistry lab. A St. Luke's
boy does not put margarine on the end of his ruler and propel
it to the ceiling where it drips down hours later on the masters.
A St. Luke's boy does not make water bags and drop them
off the roof onto other students. Am I going too fast for you?
—*No, sir. Am I for you?*

This followed by the standard lectures, black marks, and,
finally, the one thing that hurt: detention. This prevented me
from seeing Max and Risa, and eventually made me less willing
to take dares, but did nothing to erase my conception of the
world as a conspiracy, overlaid with a chaos of rules and stand-
ards I could never apprehend.

I had only one bad evening at the Kaufmans'. Max had
bought a guitar from some impoverished student and was
noodling on it when I arrived. When he released it I put it on
my lap and began to pick out a tune by ear. I sang low, out of
earshot, piercing only my own skin, I should have thought, and
Risa and the flat dissolved like kettle steam before me and I
heard black strains of the unkillable past riding the G clef like
notes.

> *Andr oda taboris,*
> *ay, phares buti keren,*
> *mak mariben chuden . . .*
>
> In that camp,
> O they work hard,
> they work hard and they get beaten.
>
> Do not hit me, do not beat me,
> or you will kill me.
> I have children at home,
> Who will bring them up?

It was difficult to get to sleep that night, and no hot milk, no ministrations, no glowing coals in the fireplace or lullabies upon the gramophone could save me. Risa got up at midnight and sat in a chair beside my bed and told me the story that too many English people tell: of the husband dead in the trenches, the hours of despair, the contemplation of suicide, the long, boring sacrificial months at the Red Cross or the canteen or the Salvation Army, the colorless evenings listening to speeches and light, optimistic music until finally the future was foreclosed and the war tumbled to an end. Max had found her in his classes, the only mature woman in a roomful of unwashed adolescents. "I will sleep with no more students," he had told her. "I will no longer wake up beside a person who looks up at me and asks, 'Who was Mussolini, anyway?' " Max had a daughter whom he professed to adore, but he had not been back to see her since the month after V-E Day.

With every childless couple, one of the pair becomes the child. But Max and Risa had not been married quite long enough for that, and Lenin would not do. I was by way of becoming the child, and Risa acknowledged it that night. Still, feeling her long fingers over my hair, full of the aftertaste of the rum with which they had laced my milk, I could not sleep for the strength of an ineradicable melody.

ITEM: At SS Major Rodl's command a camp band was formed. Most of the musicians were Gypsies. The Gypsies had to pay for the instruments themselves. It was ghastly to watch and hear the Gypsies strike up their marches while exhausted prisoners carried their dead and dying comrades into camp, or listen to the music accompanying the whipping of prisoners. But then I remember New Year's Eve . . . suddenly the sound of a Gypsy violin drifted out from one of the barracks far off, as though from happier times and climes—tunes from the Hungarian steppe, melodies from Vienna and Budapest, songs from home.

—E. Kogon, *The Theory and Practice of Hell* (London: Secker & Warburg, 1950)

The rest of the times were like a pack of cards—all different, all the same shape: the difficult, awkward presentation at the door, the ritual of Max and Lenin ("in or out?"), the sketching and the punctuation by Chazal's aphorisms.

"Green, garnet, purple and mauve are all suspended in space by blue straps."

"We seek out blue; yellow comes to us."

"Gray is the Styx of color, the boundary line between white and black, the frontier of all colors."

Etc., etc., until I no longer heard them, or until Max put them down with a post-beer belch and a "Let the boy alone."

There was also, most importantly, most vitally, the intense and fragile sense of warmth radiating from the coal fire that was the sun of their room, and from both Risa and Max.

Sometimes they had a guest or two from the university, lean Oxbridge types, or pallid poets, or students in love who held hands ostentatiously through dinner or drinks while I sketched them. All of them seemed to me breakable, carved of ivory or molded of paraffin, exquisite but not quite alive and wholly foreign to my darkness and ignorance. To me they spoke slowly and warily, as if I were a cannibal who might at any moment revert to his native diet of long pig. But they talked to each other in stately polysyllabic periods that left me far behind and outside, with my nose pressed against a window, looking in with begging, hungry mind.

The only guest who did not belong in this category was a man I knew for years only as Mr. Mordecai. He was a vigorous old Jew of undisclosed origin, a denizen of the East End since just before the war. Mordecai, discovered by Risa's mother at some charity benefit, was a carpenter by trade and a tragedian by inclination, forever smiting his forehead and muttering *oy veh* and *gefehrlach*—"danger"—at the least sign. He had the face of a melancholy shovel, brilliant teeth that had obviously rested all night in a glass, and hands no larger than catcher's mitts. But he had a sculptor's feel for wood grains, for tongue-and-groove fittings and the rightness of specific lumber for specific tasks. He was the only man I have ever known who could make bar stools that would not wobble and doors that clicked shut like a mind made up.

This refugee was billed as an old family treasure, followed, when Risa spoke to other English people, by the phrase "It's *so* hard to get good help nowadays." But in everything except carpentry, Mordecai was antimatter. If he tried to help with the dishes, he smashed them to jigsaw-puzzle bits. If he passed a plate of Stilton and biscuits, it was as if by appointment with Lenin, for they invariably landed on the rug where the dog, his tail galvanically twitching in gratitude, swept them up with his black tongue.

Mordecai had one enthusiasm besides wood, and it was as contagious as cheap music. He saw himself as what he called the Johnny Appleseed of Yiddish. He took it as his mission to spread the language throughout the *goyishe* sections of Britain, perhaps in hope of tolerance, or maybe just out of the universal itch to communicate. Our host refused the carpenter's efforts. Max saw himself as wholly secular; any residue of Judaism he regarded with the same repugnance that the Catholic renegade views the Latin mass. All else fell before Mordecai's will. The local Chinese restaurant offered Low Mein: a *michaga*. The French launderer had a sign: *shmatte* in by 12:00, out by 6:00. Risa herself would look down her long nose at Max and say, "I I I absolutely forbid you to *nosh* on any more *chozzerai* before dinner." The Irish landlady downstairs, Mrs. Higgins, took to referring to the Saturday visits of her brothers, both priests, as a call from the *mishpocheh.*

Mordecai had some effect on me, but not much. I was wearing a groove in my brain learning English, trying to catch the winged phrases that kept strafing me on the streets, in school and at the Kaufmans'. Mordecai and I were yoked together not by language or by tragedy, or even by manual skills, but, as we exchanged ambiguous smiles across thresholds and over dinner tables, by the secret understanding that this little flat, with its shelter of clothbound books and kindness, was our lifeboat, our Rachel, the thing we must cling to or drown in the postwar tide of recollection and sorrow.

There came a time when even this was not enough. It would be necessary for me to go on to some other school. I was past fourteen and difficult at St. Luke's. My English was better, but I could not make my mind work at the events of history—what history mattered except the events that had just befallen Europe? Nor could I get interested in the principles of mathematics that were cold to the touch, or those of biology and chemistry that were irrelevant to drawing or feeling. Even English might not have worked except for a peculiar Saturday afternoon when the four of us went to Regent's Park Zoo.

Mordecai was a deciduous Jew, shedding proverbs. "Don't esk de doctor, esk de patient" was his advice when I inquired of an attendant what the gazelles were feeding on. And later, when I stretched out, drugged with the unseasonal heat of early May, the walking and the everlasting ginger beer, I heard him instruct me: "Sleep faster, ve need the pillows."

When I awoke, the three adults had gone off somewhere. Our picnic was set just outside the zoo gates, and with unfocused gaze I tried to determine for a moment where I was. I felt the assumed world receding, the old one superimposing itself, like a fever dream, against my will. I fought it with song and conversations with myself. I tried to draw something, a sketch of a nearby couple entwined on the grass, of an elderly drunk preserving his dignity by twisting the ends of his mustache until he fell against a rubbish container and upended himself in it. Nothing helped. Memory stained the present like a testamental curse.

ITEM: We faced something terrible. Heaps of unburied bodies and unbearable stench. When I saw the surviving Romanies, with small children among them, I was shaken. Then I went over to the ovens and found on one of the steel stretchers the half-charred body of a girl and I understood in one awful minute what had been going on there.
>   —Testimony of British serviceman
>   Fredrick Wood, 6th Airborne
>   Division, which overran Belsen

I took up a book, one of several that Max had heaped in the picnic basket.

> The loss of his clothes hardly mattered, because
> He had seven coats on when he came,
> With three pair of boots—but the worst of it was,
> He had wholly forgotten his name.

Wholly forgotten his name. I read *The Hunting of the Snark* through once, and then again. And then again. I had not known that there was a literature of nonsense. Here was a whole anthology. None of the bluff and reedy instructors at St. Luke's believed in the absurd. Sometimes an acrid humor broke through their chalky fatigue, usually in sarcastic form. The liberation of nonsense, never. I suppose you had to experience absurdity to have faith in it. "Do you believe in ghosts?" asked a cockroach of a cat in the same book. "No. I have seen too many to believe in them," the roach answered. I felt my blood respond. Page after page I consumed, of cats and fiddles, pigs who married owls, of dishes that ran away with spoons, of articulate whitings and snails and eggs who could rhyme.

In a dazzle of light I thought I saw why Max read; of course: it was to lose himself. The eye jogging along that black street of letters, that row of images and terms, would have no time to look back or to the sides. I devoured the whole book, lying on my stomach or my back, holding the volume up to block out the sun, feeling the little dry tongues of grass on my nape, watching myself read the way an alcoholic will watch himself drinking, measuring his capacities.

Once back at school I began to take books from the library for the first time. I had no system, no desire for information, no sense of seeking escapist literature—only an appetite for what was not the stuff of today: books about the safely distant past, novels of other epochs, other men. "Is it true?" the child wants to know when it has been told a fairy tale. I was the polar opposite. Is it false? Did it happen long ago—a war or a peace, a condition that would be impossible to repeat? An occurrence, say, in the Congo, or in the England of villages and post chaises, of swirling fogs and detectives in hansom cabs, or the lunatic Russia of the czars or the gilt and stinking courts of vanished France or Spain? Or, even more remote, on a raft in the Mississippi or a whaler in the Atlantic? If it did, I was content.

Max used to gripe about my sudden and indiscriminate reading. "In a baby that's called pica," he told me. "They often find kids with something haywire in the system eating wallpaper and library paste along with the zweiback. That's you. You don't discriminate. Chekov, Margaret Mitchell, that Imperialist warmonger Kipling—all the same to you."

I opened my mouth to protest.

"Good thing you're an artist and not a thinker is all," he said, terminating the discussion. Yes, I thought, but didn't say. That *is* good.

Still, he nourished a secret pride that this unformed boy with the narrow and still-forlorn face, with the wild eyes and unkempt hair was switching helplessly from *Mitteleuropa* stray to English lit major. Max knew, as all teachers know, that once a student is truly hooked on reading he is hooked for life. Thereafter, the victim will read candy-bar wrappers if they are all that is available, and will stock his bathroom with everything from Kafka to Raymond Chandler. Even a thirty-second urination will be accompanied by a sentence or two, or a couplet from some poetry collection. You never get away. You are marked, a hermit crab living in the shell of received ideas and descriptions. You cannot step into certain rooms and gardens, certain squares and streets, certain conversations and arguments without seeing things for the second time: Dickens's characters and James's scenes, Tolstoi's aches or Conrad's ports, just as you cannot look at certain women without feeling the tug of Renoir or perceive the geometry of apples without remembering Cézanne. Yes, it is a secondhand world, and it became my world, and I thought—no, I hoped—that experience would be no substitute for literature.

And yet . . . and yet. We are what we were born, Mordecai used to say. Also God gives with one hand and takes away with the other. Along with my new fidelity to print there were still the vestiges of memory, memory that is the editor of one's sense of life. These new days with the Kaufmans, this new enchantment with reading was built over a sleeping volcano.

I knew it; I think Risa and Max knew it. I had no proper defense against the world in which every tale of someone else's suffering—from the Blitz, say, or from those veterans who had fought in the war—seemed to me a pretext for talk instead of silence. Max counseled patience and proper reading—i.e., political texts. Risa said nothing, only listened when I asked what I should feel. I could not be numb; I did not know how to operate the apparatus of hate. I was an alien not only in England but in myself. There was a ground of sorrow even to my drawing with chalk on paper. Books of philosophy were opaque to me; Max's political pamphlets were strident orders, as elaborate a waste of intelligence as chess. Poetry I could understand only in a musical sense. It had no moral appeal. "We must love one another or die," Auden had written. No wonder he had expunged that trashy quatrain later. We must love one another *and* die would have been germane. My father had loved my mother. My parents had loved my brothers and my sisters. We had all loved one another in the caravan, and we had all died. No, they had died; I had made it.

There had been some facile palaver about survivor guilt by the shrinks at the Center, who had doped it all out. I had flattered them by taking it seriously. Guilt. *What* guilt? I had no guilt. The Germans did not feel guilty; why should I?

I had come out of it because . . . I did not know. A roll of the cosmic dice? Because God had chosen me as Ishmael; I alone have come back to tell thee? Lies. Theological shadow play. Bullshit. I would tell *no one*. I would never say what I had seen. I would not assume the burden for my people. I would not sell my memoirs or conceal my contempt for a planet that could permit what I had seen.

If there were moral laws, they were in suspension. I had seen enough history and read enough imaginative works to know that no matter what I did or how vilely I behaved, I would never touch bottom. That had been done by others, in the camps and even before.

ITEM: The appearance of Gypsy bands is a major threat to the pacification of the territory, as their members are roaming the country as beggars and render many services to the partisans, providing them with supplies, etc. If only part of those Gypsies who are suspected or convicted of being partisan supporters are punished the attitude of the remainder would be even more hostile towards the German forces and support the partisans even more than before. It is necessary to exterminate these bands ruthlessly.

—Evidence given at Nuremberg trials

ITEM: The Police commanders will decide in cases of doubt who is a Gypsy.

—Order of Himmler, December 1943

Well, let them decide, I thought. The way of the transgressor is hard, proclaim the white movable letters on the churches. But not hard enough. The BBC regularly announced that the Germans were blinking their way back into the sunlight. The Nuremberg trials had punished no one I had heard of. The common citizens who tortured us were free.

In my desultory reading of that period I came across a list of the seven deadly sins: wrath, avarice, sloth, pride, lust, envy and gluttony—the transgressions of a naïf. Even the Middle Ages, with its leprosy and public executions, its plagues and ritual degeneracy, knew nothing of sin.

"Don't pollute your mind with that religious shit," Max said when he saw me poring over *The Medievalist.* "Read something that sticks to the ribs or go back to drawing faces."

I think it was this misinterpretation of my interest in religion that finally turned the tide. Max was terrified that I might yet become a Christian convert, mumbling petitions and crunching wafers, succumbing to the blandishments of Jesus instead of shouting slogans of brotherhood at the First Church of Karl Marx. And Risa, the foalless thoroughbred, saw me as a way to save the world and herself, to combat the erosions of time, to assuage God knows what longings and losses. They filed adoption papers with St. Luke's, which was glad to see me gone.

"A grave responsibility," said the headmaster.

"Good riddance to bad rubbish," said the mathematics master, against whom I had released a sulfur and charcoal insult earlier in the year, but who had not dared to whip me.

"Good-by," piped a little third-former, delegated to say a collective farewell on behalf of the student body, "which is an abbreviation for God Be with You." Good-by St. Luke's, good-by Romanies, good-by England, good-by memory, good-by. . . . Hurry up, please, it's time.

I was not merely leaving the school, I was leaving the country. For Max, through his always cloaked and involved connections with the Left, had been offered a situation at New York University. He had jumped at it. "Maybe in England there's a chance now that Labour's in," he announced. "But fascism is coming to the United States unless there are enough of us to turn the whole thing around. We have to populate the newspapers, the radio stations, the classrooms, the unions. Organize." Yes, of course, he was spiraling in the lights like a moth, whirring with the same dogmatism of the hated religions. What did I know then? Nothing. It was all noise, verbs. I was only pathetically, uncritically glad for his sympathy and Risa's. When I heard that Mordecai would be coming later, ready to convert the United States to his Yiddish standard— he had received some sort of visa from the Jewish Welfare Board—I was beside myself.

Kafka once wrote that he believed that everyone in America smiled. (This from that premonitory doomster, that ghost who cleverly avoided the camps by succumbing to tuberculosis. "My head and my lungs conspired behind my back," he told me.) If Franz believed that well of the United States, how was a fourteen-year-old boy to know any different? I saw the life I would lead there as a series of recognitions, a long row of books that would keep me from myself, and an endless progression of portraits that would make me famous and wealthy. I know, I know. But that is the way refugees thought in those days. Our senses, our souls were caught by the symbols of Yankee skills and appetites. By the huge soldiers of liberation with their omnipresent raucousness and chocolates. By the great silver airplanes, and the vast white bedrooms and purring orchestras and monumental plains of the American movies. By the incalculable combinations and permutations of making money and losing it and making it again.

As I stepped aboard that long white boat, my chalks and paper in hand, I looked down at the sun hitting the brackish inlet and saw gold coins. That night, as the ship pitched and rolled and Max cursed the capitalist ocean in the bunk overhead, I dreamed intermittently of extravagant colors and of Birdie and of money. Unending heaps of it. I heard, or thought I heard, in the whine of the engines the half-forgotten song:

> *N'avlom ke tumende*
> *O maro te mangel*
> *Avlom ke tumende*
> *kam man pativ te den.*

> I did not come to you
> to beg for bread.
> I came to you
> To demand respect.

American money was green. It papered the walls of my dreams.

II: AVARICE

Into the porch at Bethlehem
have come the evil Gypsies.
From the newly born babe
they have robbed the coverings.

—Spanish carol

We are three Gypsies who tell good fortunes
We are three Gypsies who steal wherever we may be.
  Kind child, so sweet, cross our palms with silver
  And each will tell you all that is to happen to you.

—"The Three Wise Men," Provençal carol

The Gypsies went and ate the wheat and oxen,
then after a year came with pale cheeks. The Shah
said, "Was it not your task to plough, sow and
reap? Your asses still remain. Load them up,
prepare your harps and stretch the silken cords."
So now the Gypsies live by their wits. They have
for company the dog and the wolf, and tramp
unceasingly.

—Firdausi, *Shah Namah*, Persia

HEAT. HEAT IN THE ELEVATOR, RAISING THE ODOR OF urine to the status of plague. Heat in the lobby, mixing with dust and the smell of Sullivan the doorman, who gave off a peculiar amalgam of lima beans and sour mash; heat in the hallways, where the dime-store perfume of the fat lady mixed with the damp-wool aroma of her poodles; heat on the asphalt, where the heels clung to the liquefying tar; heat on the iron sedans that were dangerous to touch. Heat sucked in by the windows and shimmering off the Hudson River with the force of mirages. Heat in the candy store, where the gum balls were annealed; heat in the Chinese restaurant, where the water glasses sweated more profusely than the chain-smoking waiters; heat in the bedroom, where the wandering mind suffocated and the wallpaper stuck to the cheek. It was a primal picture, evoking elemental things: furnaces and sand, salt and anger. The smell of hot iron and tar seemed not to rise from the pavings, but to slide downward on the rays of the treacherous sun.

Alone, entering a dark room, most of us shut our eyes to grope for the light switch. I came to New York as if blind, and made myself blinder. I felt the heat rather than saw it, tasted and inhaled the streets instead of observing them. I sensed the city in black and white; the rods and cones of my eyes were out of order. These were the now inconceivable days before air conditioning, when a fan slowly shaking its head from side to side, as if in disapproval of its owners, provided the only relief to sullen weather inversions that drove couples to belt each other, off-duty policemen to fire their sidearms at a loud, harmless drunk with a load of rye under his belt, and pushed kids out on the fire escapes and into the streets to force open hydrants and bathe in the rusty flood. I was one of them, soaking my undershirt and lying in the ninety-degree shade of Riverside Park. I had experienced nothing like this heat in the worst summers of Europe. Every day I oscillated between the delights of being in the promised city and the certainty that I would melt and run down the pavement and into the sewer before the end of summer. Max used to sit in the living room for hours, scratching his shirtless chest, slapping at the war-mongering mosquitoes, reading his moist and cranky *Daily Worker* and pamphlets, excoriating *The New York Times*, drinking beer and soda and belching angrily.

Risa, who seemed to function at a body temperature of forty degrees Fahrenheit, knitted or read, or played her wind-up gramophone. She had found a set of Fred Astaire–Ginger Rogers records and provided hours of amusement by harmonizing with Mordecai, who had joined us. He lived in the rear room of our nine-room apartment, which cost the Kaufmans, if memory serves, $100.18 a month. Risa would begin haughtily: "We should be laike a couple of hawt tomahtoes." Mordecai would join in: "Bot you're as kalt as yestiddy's mesh pedades."

Max, choking on his soda, would applaud mightily. Neither Risa nor Mordecai quite understood why; you could tell by their dazzled eyes they were off in Cloud-cuckoo-Land, a place where the telephone, the walls and the butler were all white, where Edward Everett Horton would wait forever to dispense loony counsel and sympathy along with the martinis.

"Get out and make friends," Max advised me when I spent too long in the living room in rapt admiration for the Risa-Mordecai duets. I went out to the streets reluctantly, book in hand and praying that I would meet no one. The rich kids were away at camp. The poor closed ranks, playing street games whose rules were elusive. I observed from the peripheries until I understood the elemental romantic laws of stickball, and then edged my way into the games. Like all converts, I became possessed by baseball, by Red Ruffing's fast ball and Tommy Henrich's clutch hitting. On the asphalt turf I was Dixie Walker as I hit, Hugh Casey as I pitched. But I was tolerated, not accepted; I only participated when the teams were short of a player. Others could hit the longer ball and make the one-hand catches that still escaped me. Nor could I compete at baseball-card flipping, or at basketball in the baking cement schoolyard. No, my best sport was thievery. No one could touch me at it.

Ruben Gutierrez and Charlie Abruzzo were the companions of that first dissonant summer. Like me, they were barely coordinated; I doubt if Charlie could have put his pajama tops on without help. We sat on the curb, soaking from dips in the hydrant, and jawed. Occasionally Risa would look down from the apartment on the 89th Street side of our Riverside Drive building, and say something intimating disapproval. When Max observed us it was always with great approbation, applause, cheers, and an occasional shower of coins. This was his idea of democracy in action: a Cuban, a Romany and and Italian shoulder to shoulder. You loved them in World War II, now here they are again in Manhattan Street Scenes.

He might not have been so sanguine had he heard our idiot conversations:

ABRUZZO: You tink dat Bawston has a chance against Bvook-lyn?

KAUFMAN *(for I had taken my new parents' name and jettisoned still more recollections):* I dunno. I guess so.

GUTIERREZ: Booooo-shit. Dodgiz gonna take it awl.

ABRUZZO: You tink dere's gawnna be anuddah waw by de time we're draft age?

KAUFMAN *(parroting the home line):* Unless the warmongers stop making trouble in Washington.

GUTIERREZ: Booooooo-shit. Ain't gonna be no maw waw. Used up awl de bullits.

ABRUZZO: Yeah? What about duh adam bomb, stoopid?

GUTIERREZ: We de oney ones got de bomb, ass. Who's gonna make a waw if we de oney ones got de atom bomb? Ansa me dat.

ABRUZZO: Boy, it's hot.

KAUFMAN: I bet it's a hundrid degrees in the shade.

GUTIERREZ: So who says ya gotta stay inna shade? *(Dissolves in mirth.)*

ABRUZZO: Ya know de Apthorpe?

GUTIERREZ: Caws we know de Apthorpe. You know the Apthorpe, don't ya, Kaufman? *(As in the English public schools, New York street life considered the use of the first name to be effeminate.)*

KAUFMAN: Course I know the Apthorpe. *(I had no idea whether it was a building or a movie theater. It might even be a disease.)*

ABRUZZO: Well, I was in dhere de uddah day. Ya know the d'vorseee. Da one I whistled at yestiddy down at Bohack's?

KAUFMAN: Yeah . . .

ABRUZZO *(in a husky, confidential sotto voce no louder than a cement truck):* Well, yestiddy I was delivin' groceries. At the apartment.

GUTIERREZ: Yeah, yeah.

KAUFMAN: Go on.

ABRUZZO: So I'm standin at the door. I hear a voice. "Come on in," it says. So I go on in. She says, "Leave de groceries in de bedroom." Ya know what I mean?

KAUFMAN: Yeah, yeah, so?

ABRUZZO: So I go in de bedroom and 'ere she is, lyin' on de bed. In nothin' but her bzeer.

GUTIERREZ: Her bzeer?

ABRUZZO: Yeah. So she says, "Come here, kid." She means me, see?

GUTIERREZ: So den?

ABRUZZO: So den she says, "Say, kid. How'd ya like ta take a tvip avound de world?

KAUFMAN: So?

ABRUZZO: So den I humped her nine times.

KAUFMAN: *(Pause.)*

GUTIERREZ: *(Longer pause.)*

KAUFMAN AND GUTIERREZ: Booooooooo-shit.

ABRUZZO: No, I swear!

Dead silence . . .

ABRUZZO *(shrugging):* Let's go glom something.

ITEM: The accused bicycle thief, Gypsy Zacharias Winter, has no previous convictions and during the time that most of the offenses were committed he was not quite eighteen years old. In view of his general development, however, he must be considered an adult. As his innumerable thefts prove, he is a criminal who represents a constant danger to others. For the protection of the public, the death penalty is necessary in this case.

—Nuremberg Document NG 456

Oh, but when they took you away, Papa, and we heard you had been shot and my disordered mind wrestled with the powers of death, I wondered: What did Papa steal? And I, I who had watched old man Ivor's cart overturn, I who had grabbed the copper bowl and hidden it under my coat and buried it beneath the fir tree, how long would it be before I would join Zacharias Winter and my father in the stone courtyard ripped apart by German bullets? If a bicycle was enough to die for, what punishment would a copper bowl earn? Would I be tortured, like old man Taras, given castor oil, or branded or whipped or mutilated? What had they done to Papa before they shot him? Maybe it was only bicycles the Germans killed for. If I could only be a German and know about such things. Thievery would not be a problem to a German.

We three developed a technique for thievery: Charlie stayed at the door while Ruben moved around the middle of the store. I asked the proprietor about merchandise, lingered for a while and eventually bought something.

While he was ringing up, say, the purchase of two candy bars, I passed along three or four boxes of model airplanes to Ruben, he tossed them to Charlie, and we were out of the place before anyone was wiser. We often returned to the same store to see whether our purloining was noticed. Our impudence grew. We stole food from the A & P, pairs of socks from a Broadway shoe place and flashlights from two hardware stores.

The others did it for the dare, or possibly in Ruben's case out of need. His father was the superintendent of our building and there were seven children in the family; every piece of clothing made the trip from Ruben's back downward to the baby, who wore old shirts as swaddling clothes. In my case the thievery was a disease.

Can you possibly appreciate what New York was like in those postwar years? To a boy caroming from Central Europe to London to Manhattan the city was a market left unguarded. It cost a nickel to go anywhere by subway and there was no danger—or if there was, we three adolescents, with minds like jungles, shambling, undefined gaits and spermy, lying conversations, constituted that danger. People got out of *our* way when we walked down the sidewalk. Black, shiny cars were everywhere, roaring like braggarts, a sign of rude American health. Women were forever having their hair done and buying dresses and stockings that looked like silk but were of some miracle fiber that was supposed to outlast dynasties. And food! I ate single dinners that might have supplied a hundred Benoits only a few years before. Rappaport's on Second Avenue decorated its tables with mounds of rolls and pyramids of butter pats. Butcher shops were redolent of plenty; fish stores stank of waste. I ate constantly: hot dogs, Mello Rolls, Clark bars, gristly hamburgers, moist cashews from glassine bags, Cokes—plus the three standard, balanced meals at home. My stomach was always hungry; my body burned the calories and asked the stoker for more. I appreciated the merchandise in this rich, oily, cacophonous town and wanted to consume it all.

To allay the appetite I spent afternoons in movie houses, sometimes with others, mostly by myself. It was so hot, said Sidney Smith, there was nothing for it but to take off my flesh and sit in my bones. I was familiar with that sensation. "Forty Degrees Cooler Inside" yelled the cheesy green sign on the Riviera Theatre. I climbed to the balcony and sat in my skeleton, watching anything that moved on the screen. I was John Garfield and Richard Conte and Dane Clark, as battered and uncorrodable as a zinc bar, home from the Big House, out of the Army, returned from the Coast, back in the big city ready to reclaim my girl and clean up the mess that had been made. I lived in a black-and-white world, where the hair of my girl friend was so blond it illuminated her face in the closeups, where the villains had faces like fists, where things would always come right for me. Or I would die. Either way it would be all right. The guilty would not go unpunished.

ITEM: The Germans began to kill the Gypsies. There were two houses full of Gypsies. They threw small children out of high windows onto the cobblestones and there was a lot of blood.

—J. Fikowski, *Ciganie na polskich drogach* (Cracow: Wyd/Literackie, 1965)

ITEM: [In refusing claims of restitution] it should be borne in mind that Gypsies had been persecuted under the Nazis not for any racial reasons but because of an asocial and criminal record.

—Circular, Interior Ministry of Württemberg, May 9, 1950

Neither Charlie nor Ruben read at all, except page three of the *Daily Enquirer* with its litany of interesting crimes of violence. ("Hey, Kaufman: lookit this: 'Rapist Kept Black Book on Blondes'; 'Florida Judge Calls Her Kind of Dog-Walking an Unnatural Act!' Get what they mean?") My own reading was confined to nights when sleep came with great difficulty and I read the tales of Poe and Le Fanu and Bierce, anxious to be distracted, voracious for tales of unreal dread.

Things were better in the mornings. They often are. The three of us would meet on the corner of 96th and Broadway and take a subway somewhere, anywhere. Sometimes we were surprisingly benign: we wandered the Museum of Natural History, wondering at reconstructed dinosaurs or gaping fatuously at star sapphires and the great quartz acquisitions of the Morgan gem collection. Other times we continued our thefts, lifting clothing and razors—Charlie and I had begun to shave—from department stores. It was the stolen watch that put me on the police books.

Like all those hovering on the rim of experience and looking down, Charlie and Ruben and I affected enormous boredom. We confected individual situations, scenarios in which we separately starred. In my own drama I moved like Garfield through dooms of hate. Threatened by the Mob, I made my bantam swagger cover my terror. "Everybody dies," I muttered, clutching my stomach where the bullet had entered; "everybody dies," I spat at the head gunsel (played by Lloyd Gough), "even you." In this tragic, defiant mood I asked the saleslady at Franklin Simon if I could look at a tray of metal expansion watchbands. When she opened the case and slid the tray out, Ruben carefully knocked over a small standing mirror on the glass counter. Under his torrent of apologies—I can still see him blushing on cue, the red flushing under his umber skin— she bent down to retrieve the looking glass. In doing so, she rested the case before me. Some of the more elaborate bands were affixed to watches. I chose the one that seemed the most expensive and looked for Charlie, intending to toss it to him. He had vanished without the whistle that signaled trouble. I pushed the bands around so that they covered the space marked by the missing watch. The saleslady didn't alter expression. "Well?" she said after a while. She was fat and her perfume was neon for the nose and something about her manner seemed even more furtive than my own. Maybe she stole from the cash register, I thought. I bought the cheapest black plastic band she had, watched her ring it up and then pop it into a little paper bag. The Fifth Avenue exit beckoned. Ruben, and Charlie if he was still around, would meet me at a prearranged table at the Automat. I got outside the door and turned downtown. There was a hand on each arm.

I had the sensation of having my blood pressure taken on both sides, then of being lifted from the ground and around the corner before I could manufacture an excuse. There was something muttered about arrest, the watch was plucked from my pocket and I was suddenly inside the store again, admitted by a large brass door marked Deliveries. My captors were two men in their forties, both in raincoats, both running to fat with plenty of gristle left under the adipose. They had the large, noseless faces of retired patrolmen, men with pale-blue dispassionate eyes, eyes that had seen too many boys like me, and rich kleptomaniacs and dice hustlers and pimps and maybe killers, eyes that had looked for evil and never failed to find it and then were disgusted with how easy the hunt was, eyes that were small and made everything small with them, bright but not intelligent eyes, steady eyes, unafraid eyes, bored eyes, cop's eyes.

The men took me in an elevator to the top floor. No words were exchanged and my few mutterings were ignored. I was taken before a wan, narrow man of about fifty in a dark suit. He was seated behind a metal desk. He had wispy sparse tannish hair, and judging from the pictures of his family on the desk, he had married his sister and they had produced three girls with the identical hair. "Name?" was all he said.

—*Name?*

The official with the leather gloves also sat behind a desk but the desk was on open ground, tramped down by boots and bereft even of weeds. The sky was sullen and it hurt the backs of your eyes to look up at it.

—*Name? he asked again and the blond young trooper pushed the gun in my mother's side and then they made her spell it while the man behind the desk typed slowly. They had let us take the pushcart as far as the gates, but now it was gone and we had to carry our clothing and possessions in our arms. I rested my satchel on the ground and a man in uniform pushed me with a stick and made me hold the satchel up again. My arms were tired and I felt like crying. I began to breathe through my mouth to force the tears back in the ducts. I looked down the line in back of us. I could not see to the end. I knew everyone in the queue. We were allowed to pass into the barracks area. The voice came from behind me now.*

—*Name?*

It was old man Nikulaje. He could not understand.

—*Name? the man on the desk repeated. We could hear the rifle butt strike and a cry. I looked back and the old man was on the ground, retching, a line of saliva and blood issuing from his small mouth. My mother pulled me by the neck and I heard nothing else but some cursing in German.*

"Ben," I replied.

He typed Benjamin. I did not correct him.

"Last name?"

"Kaufman." I shook free from the dream. I even felt a kind of ease. This time I was genuinely guilty. I had done something for which there was a prescribed routine, possibly a legitimate punishment. This was not Europe, after all. I had nothing to fear from these monkeys.

"You admit to stealing the watch, Benjamin?"

"Yes," I said. John Garfield could not have been surer.

"Do you have parents, Benjamin?"

"Yes."

"What would they say if they knew you had stolen something?"

Again the test. I affected great remorse. They would be ashamed, I told him. Here was a boy who had been given everything and who had stolen a watch. (I was never to have much luck with watches.) But it was because I had been given a watch like this for my birthday and I had taken it off to play basketball, sir, in the schoolyard and when I had returned it was stolen. I feared the hurt, sir, the sorrow of my parents, and wanted to replace the watch I could not afford.

The man behind the desk tried to frown his way through my story, but he was moved. Hell, *I* was moved. I shambled around a little and the men behind me at last backed off a bit, convinced that I would not make a run for it. "I'm sorry," I assured my audience. "It'll never happen again. Even if I had gotten away with it, I would have saved my allowance and sent the store the money." By now I was beginning to warm to my tale. I had half convinced myself that yes, I really was a sportsman, performing for the kick of it, happy to toss the fish back in the water.

They bought it. Oh, they fingerprinted me and checked the label on the back of my shirt—on which Risa had inconveniently sewed a name label for the laundry in England. They also checked my address with the Manhattan telephone book. But they made no call, and after a lecture of the go-thou-and-sin-no-more, ending with the I-have-children-like-you-at-home coda, I was allowed to leave. At the door, one of the raincoats told me I was lucky, and who knows what stealing could lead to; he had seen death descend from the simple act of rolling a drunk. Yes, well, if once a man indulges himself in murder, very soon he comes to think little of robbing; and from robbing he comes next to drinking and Sabbath-breaking, and from that to incivility and procrastination. De Quincy, gentlemen. I hear he was a lawbreaker, too.

I found myself out in the sunshine, alone. I was not angry with Charlie or Ruben for lamming. It was incumbent on them to save themselves. On the other hand, if I alone was to be caught, who needed them?

That evening I told my co-conspirators what had happened, laying it on a bit thick. This allowed them to stifle their attempts at collective thievery for a while, and left me free to operate on my own.

Alone I worked Macy's and Gimbels, the Army surplus stores, and when I was dressed in a tie and jacket that matched my pants, Abercrombie & Fitch's and Brooks Brothers. I stole ties and socks, watchbands, toiletries, compasses, knives, notebooks, vitamin pills, costume jewelry, paint brushes, magnifying glasses, cans of ravioli and sleeper yo-yos.

There were two pawnshops on upper Broadway that received this swag. They paid cheaply but with no questions, even when I came in once with a gold locket lifted from an antique shop on Third Avenue. The money was received in small bills. I seldom took away more than twenty dollars—always locked in the same metal box I had used in London. This time I secreted the box behind a loose rock in Fort Tryon Park, down from the Cloisters. That reconstructed castle had become my retreat, a place where I could pore over my holdings and read Poe. When I felt down I opened my private safe and thought, like Timon, that money makes black white; foul fair; wrong right; base noble; old young; coward valiant. I would redeem it some day for a purpose as yet undeclared. Often I would walk around the parapets and stroll in the interior garden to the low music of Gregorian chants, imagining myself to be as insubstantial as a ghost, and like a ghost, capable of every theft, any vengeance.

In the crowded substantial world downtown I was caught not once but several times—always, it seemed to me, by the same two men, as hard and varnished and alike as night sticks. The first few embarrassments went my way; the man—and in one case woman—behind the desk listened to my remorseful-lad-replacing-a-birthday-gift with patience and indulgence. I was let off with warnings, although on one occasion I was photographed and I was always fingerprinted. What I could not know was that all department stores shared an information service on shoplifters. It took a few weeks for the data to shake down; then one afternoon when I was caught for perhaps the seventh time, the security department did a quick check and found my references in the files. I was taken downstairs to a police car and driven to the 55th Street station. There was no conversation in the car. Pushed along, I spun through the heavy glass doors and clumped down a corridor opening onto a blank room smelling of carbolic acid, fatigue and twice-breathed alcohol, a room redolent of low-grade power. It was not a bad room; the walls and the benches were old and peeling. The people, black and white, who waited did not even hint of ill-use. The policemen sitting and typing reports or emptying the water cooler or going off and on duty were men in their thirties and forties, aggressively underpaid, neither angry nor friendly, American civil servants who had, because of family or ethnic tradition or indifference or perhaps some vague moral sense, gathered in a place as uninhabitable as an alkali desert, and set down roots.

But I looked down at the cracks in the floor and saw flames. A forge of hair and gold rings. The plain, stained garments of the dead. Straps against the soul. Spikes and wires. I heard guttural black laughter. Fireblind, I stumbled forward, weals on my hands. Oh the chimneys! Children who never saw butterflies. Or flowers. Or the primary colors of belief. My mouth dry and white against my sandpaper tongue. The vinegary fiddle notes of home. Uniforms and boots bringing severance; motive hunters: What is the reason for this boy? Send him to the punishment block. No, don't send the boy! He means no harm. The scrapes of pain. Tears only at night, by owl-light. Barbs of Satan snagging souls in midstream. Ruined eyes. Yellow screams in the courtyard. Men like upended beetles. A flood of stones. Choirs of lost faces. "The moon is more important than the sun. It glows at night. The sun glows in the daytime when no one needs it." O Christ decreased, diminished in sin. Petals tumbling from the rose of the Holy Ghost. Thorns and prayer. *Und Schweigen ist ein neues Land.* Inside that silence: fire. And inside that fire: choirs of Abednegos. Pioneers of dying, explorers of torment. The coffin lid of night decorated with cold constellations. Faces wracked with agnostic sobs. Why hast thou forsaken faces? Tears are orphans. Stacks spitting cinders. Smoke holding souls. Airborne flesh branched like antlers. This senile child begs bread. The stockade of teeth barks back. The gaunt pursued, rounded up, lanced by the unicorn pain. And home is only the rooted sorrow. And rescue only a mask, like music. Bodies rubbed raw by the salt of torment. Motive-hunters: *Pourquoi? Porqué? Perchè? Warum?*

ITEM: The old French Gypsy told me her story: they were itinerants, making the rounds of fairs and markets with some very good games and amusements, inherited from relatives. They were fourteen in all: she and her husband, their grown children, a son-in-law, and a married brother. But when the season was over they always returned to a nice little apartment in Paris, with radio and all the conveniences. One night the Germans arrested all the itinerants at a fair (in Lille, I think) and deported the dark-skinned ones. They were taken first to a prison in Belgium, where they learned they would be going to Auschwitz: *The others told me, "Poor woman, that's hell where you're going." But what could I do about it? When we got to Auschwitz they put us in a big wooden hangar with black gravel for a floor, and nothing else—no straw, no blankets, and nothing to eat or drink for two days. And we could see huge red flames through the cracks in the walls, but we didn't know what they were. After two days the order came that we would not be killed; then they gave us soup and tins of water and sent us somewhere else.* Then came the beatings, the executions, and they died one by one, until none remained but her, and perhaps her youngest daughter in another camp; she didn't know. But why? What did we do? she asked over and over. Why?

—G. Tillion, *Ravensbrück* (Paris: Éditions de Seuil, 1973)

ITEM: About 4,000 Gypsies were left by August, and these had to go into the gas chambers. Up to that moment, they were unaware of what was in store for them. They first realized what was happening when they made their way barrack hut by barrack hut toward crematorium I. It was not easy to drive them. Schwartzhuber told me that it was more difficult than any previous mass destruction of Jews, and it was particularly hard on him, because he knew almost every one of them individually. They were by their nature as trusting as children.

—Rudolf Höss, *Kommandant in Auschwitz* (Stuttgart: Deutsche Verlag, 1958)

"Throw water in his face."

I awoke to Max standing beside me, helping me to my feet.

"He's all right now," Max was saying to one of the plainclothes policemen, or perhaps to a policeman not yet on duty. The cop seemed to know Max. He lit a cigar and gave Max one. "Bill, you're not like the rest of the Cossacks here. Do something."

I sat down again slowly. Risa was there, seated beside me now, and was that Mordecai off in the corner? Yes; good old Mordecai, book in hand, with scarcely a look at me. He had come to spread the Yiddish word and even now was leaning forward, speaking in a low voice to the black policeman at the desk. *"Goniff,"* he was saying. *"T'ief,* it means. Say it. Like *gone if.* My money's *gone if* I don't put it in de benk."

"Gawn-iff," said the cop.

"Excellent. Fine. Now you speak two lenguiges. Now try *faygeleh.* Means a sissy, a nency-boy, a pensy."

"Fay-gu-luh."

"One one one feels *some*thing ought to be done," Risa said, half to me, half to the air. A white-haired captain who had spent a lot of time in squad cars eating carbohydrates came out and motioned with his head. Two patrolmen met him and began to talk in low voices. They were obviously talking about me, then about Max, who was still consulting with his friend Bill. Time seemed to be turning from a liquid into a powder. If I moved at all, even breathed, it was with the slow fatigue of a narrow-gauge train making its way up steep grades, through arid country. I was parched; my thoughts broke apart when I moved them.

Risa handed me a sandwich. I don't remember what it was. I chewed mechanically. "Salt fills up the cracks in food," she said, another aphorism offered with her usual bad timing. We watched Max gesturing, his voice just out of range. "The the the throat broadcasts the voice in capitals." Risa handed me the other half of my sandwich. "The lips in lower case."

Max and Bill joined the captain and the two men who had brought me in. "We we we speak with our lips to explain, but our throats to persuade," Risa went on. And by God, that is precisely what her husband was doing, riding his rolling bass, smiling with a bogus confidence, even cracking some sort of joke that broke up the captain and then his men.

There was some talk of "release in the recognizance of his family" and probation. I could only follow parts of it. By then I had contracted a fever, the temperature had taken over, and for the first time in months I could not eat. The sandwich lay unfinished on a paper plate. I was told to rise. Echoes bounced in my head, blood jumped in my chest. The lecture was brief and incomplete: "Lucky . . . with your background some things can be overlooked . . . any repetition means detention in juvenile home . . . Kaufman promises to make good on all stolen goods . . . if the stores agree . . . Messy business . . . no prosecution . . ."

I was sick for a week and delirious for half of that. When I could sit up Max came into my room, offered me half a grapefruit and gave me a swift talk. "Listen," he said, "what you've been through you could multiply by a thousand all over the city. Fault of the capitalist system: dangle the goods before you, then deny them to any but the bourgeoisie."

"No, listen, Max," I tried to explain. "I didn't steal those things because I was poor. It was like a game. I'm as guilty as hell, I really am."

"Guilty? What do you know of guilt? Here." He cracked open a little book. Max was forever opening Marxist guides for the perplexed and reading stories of Western exploitation. But this was only *The Emperor Jones*, its passages carefully underlined with blue wobbles.

" 'For de little stealin' dey gits you in jail soon or late,' " he read in a vaudeville Negro dialect that he would have found racist on any stage but his own. " 'For de big stealin' dey makes you emperor and puts you in de Hall o' Fame when you croaks.'

"You're a victim just like all the disenfranchised, the poor, the locked out. Your rob a banker, you land in the slammer. But let the banker rob *you* and he ends with a mansion and a yacht in Long Island Sound. So if you're going to steal, steal big. Wait until you're twenty-one, get into business and rob the little people blind. But lay off the penny-ante stuff."

I listened to this transparent psychology, looked again at my vital, sorrowing guardian and felt—if ever I was capable of the emotion—love. I nodded and resolved, Garfield style, to go straight. School would be starting in a few weeks. I owed it to myself, to my new parents, to whatever I had left behind and was about to assume. Max saw the decision in my face, nodded, and left me alone.

Then I was visited by Mordecai, who must have been on his hands and knees at the keyhole.

Mordecai, like me, had no faith in the power of fresh fruit. Every day he massaged his bridgework with caramels and nougats, *mandelbrot* and macaroons. Occasionally he tapered off with Fig Newtons, then, when his weight assumed the proper proportions, went on halvah orgies. He entered with a boxed assortment from the neighborhood bakery, a place called Galicci's, but which under his influence now offered *"nosherai* and other Neapolitan dishes." I crumbled a cake in my fingers and ate small pieces of it, washed down with lemonade, while he talked.

"A nice-looking boy like you." He shook his head. "You should be, you know—"

"Ashamed," I offered.

"No, det's not it."

"Sorry?"

"No. What's the word I'm lookin'?"

"Apologetic?"

"Hongry. Det's the word. Femished. For one wik you been lying like a dishtowel. Look how thin."

He provided a hand mirror for the purpose. I stared back at deep, hollow eyes that reminded me of other faces I did not want to confront just then.

"Sit down on the bed and teach me some Yiddish," I said.

"*Abi gezunt—dos lebn ken men zikh aleyn nemen.*"

"Meaning?"

"Your health comes first. You can always hang yoursalf later. Have a mecaroon."

I chewed slowly and asked Mordecai if he had anything more my size.

"*Di eygene zun makht layvnt vays, un dem tsigayner shvarts.* The same sun bliches linen and bleckens Gypsies."

I liked that. It made me a little easier in my skin.

"*A toytn beveynt men zibn teg; a nar-dos gantse lebn.* A dead man is mourned seven days; a fool, his whole lifetime."

He gave me a face loaded with blanks, but he might as well have written it on the ceiling. I looked down at the covers and breathed through my mouth.

"Listen. I want to rid you sometin'." Mordecai opened a little book.

"What's that? Another of Max's pamphlets?"

Mordecai was suddenly the rabbi stricken at the altar. "Vot? You tink I need to get political lectures from dot *momzer*? I was redical when he was peeing in his pents. I vos organizing in Poland thirty yiss ago. I led strikes in Liverpool in nineteen ondered and thirdy-eight. Semuel Gompers wrote me five ledders. You want to see?"

Thank you just the same, I told him. A houseful of radicals, and me as political as a bullet. I went on chewing macaroons. Mordecai gave me the book, *Ten Rungs*, with Hebrew on one side and English on the other. He too was fond of underlining in little wobbles, but for some reason he favored Waterman's blue-black, which on this cheap postwar paper ran on the pages like furry caterpillars.

"Rid," he demanded.

I read:

THE TEN PRINCIPLES

Said the Great Maggid to Rabbi Zusya, his disciple: "I cannot teach you the ten principles of service. But a little child and a thief can show you what they are.

"From the child you can learn three things:
He is merry for no particular reason;
Never for a moment is he idle;
When he needs something, he demands it vigorously.

"The thief can instruct you in seven things:
He does his service by night;
If he does not finish what he has set out to do in one night, he devotes the next night to it;
He and those who work with him love one another;
He risks his life for slight gains;
What he takes has so little value for him that he gives it up for very small coin;
He endures blows and hardship, and it matters nothing to him;
He likes his trade and would not exchange it for any other."

"So-O," said Mordecai in his singsong.

"So-o. De idea is: from a child you learn. *After* you no longer a child youself. Whan you grown up. From a tief you also learn. *After* you no longer a tief. *Farshtaisht?*"

"Yeah," I said. "I understand."

"Good. Now go to slip."

"I just woke up."

"So? I just inhaled. That means I don't have to inhale again?" And he was gone.

After a decent interval, during which I tried to read "The Gold Bug" and found the meanings sliding under the words, Risa came in accompanied by Lenin. I searched her eyes for the lecture and her hands for the book she was going to offer. Why should she be the only one without a moral lesson? But Risa had no book. And after smoothing the covers, she turned and started out. Then, calling me so thin that I looked like two profiles in search of a face, she paused at the doorway. I lay back, prepared. Sure enough, she began: "You know what the English proverb is about boys in the summer?"

"No," I replied.

"Neither do I," she told me, and exited.

Risa had mastered that most difficult art, the ability not to say the right thing at the right time. I lay back, grateful, my eyes full of grains, and slept for four more hours.

What betrayed that sleep? Why did I unravel the trust of those who had helped me most? I have so little idea even now. Who is the child in the dime-store frame on your piano? What do you have in common with him? Except for the fact that you are the same person. Would you get along with him if he were to spring from the picture and sit across from you in a chair, asking questions, demanding answers? I was that boy; I lived his life. I felt with his flesh and thought with his cerebrum. But I can only hazard guesses as to his behavior, his confused and vagrant acts.

Yes, certainly, the maimed Gypsy child running from his blood, his heritage sticking to his life like the shirt of Nessus. Neat, facile, Freudian rationales. It could just have been temptation in a hot summer. Or bad genes. Who can tell after thirty years? Who can tell?

When I rose, recuperated, I went to the old places, the touchstones of street life. The metal box full of stolen treasure offered no pleasure; the metal no longer glistered, and the toys seemed the property of the little brother I no longer had. The

Cloisters were composed of dust and dead religion. The music was aged and stale. Only the streets offered solace; they rang with vitality. I rejoined Charlie and Ruben. It was the last day in August when the humidity, thoughts of imminent school and the urges of puberty all struck at once.

GUTIERREZ: Wanna grab some school supplies?
ABRUZZO: Too smawl.
KAUFMAN: How about an electric fan?
ABRUZZO: Too smawl.
GUTIERREZ: What ain't too smawl for you—Grant's Tomb?
ABRUZZO: A cah.

A car. Ruben and I regarded Charlie with an amalgam of trepidation, fear and awe. Here, clearly, was a young man on the way, no longer satisfied with cheap goods. Max's Big Steal.

"What if we get caught?" I asked the question Ruben was afraid to state.

"We won't get caught," said Charlie. "I done it befaw. We'll ride around half an hour, then we leave de cah a coupla blocks away. Evvybody has a good time, nobody gets hurt. You chicken? Or you coming?"

We came, of course, down to the drive with Charlie leading us, palming the handles of convertibles and coupes in that still-innocent city. Door after door opened to his touch, and in several cars the keys rested in the ignition. He chose a prewar Plymouth roadster, ancient but well kept. Of the trio, only Charlie knew how to drive. Ruben sat next to him and turned the radio up full blast. I sat in the back, my sneakered feet thrust impudently out the window. With some fits, starts and double-clutches and backfires, Charlie moved us out to the Drive and north to Harlem. On the way we did all the *shtick* beloved of Warner Bros.: hairpin turns with squealing wheels, imaginary gun battles with pursuing wrongos and rogue cops, dying with a bullet lodged off camera. "Sure I'll give you a chance," I grunted over the voices of the Andrews Sisters, "the same chance you gave my brother." And, "Go on without me. Make sure my share goes to Ma."

Charlie shouted, "We're being tailed." And gave a pretty good imitation of a siren. It was too good. We *were* being followed, and the shrill, metallic sound of the siren issued from a police car that was gaining on us. Charlie pushed the accelerator, and the trees and walls of Riverside Drive began to merge into a brown scrim. Going down toward the Henry Hudson Parkway at 120th Street, I looked out back and shouted that the police were less than two or three carlengths away. I felt the car swerve—Charlie must have planned an evasive U-turn—and then there was a loud impact and a brief crescendo of shattered glass and dented metal, overridden by the continuing sound of the siren.

Some sharp chrome had ripped the skin of my thigh and forehead, and there was a good deal of blood. I could scarcely see because of it. But there was more fright and confusion than actual pain. People seemed infinitely tall and made sounds beyond my aural range. The white ambulance came and took us away, and in a few hours the accident was reconstructed. We had hit a parked car broadside. I was thrown more or less clear; the wounds were the result of impact with a curb and hydrant. The worst I would have was a small scar that disappeared into my hair and a broken valve in a vein that would disfigure my leg. Charlie had been shaken up, one of his ribs was cracked, and he lost a front tooth; that was all. Ruben's head had gone almost through the windshield. The glass had been scattered so far that for a week motorists were picking up bits of it in their tires. He was alive when the ambulance picked him up. But the hospital had signed in a corpse.

To stare at the dead requires the most intense concentration. Ruben's coffin lay open at the services, and I looked at the rebuilt head, reposing in whitest silk, the body outfitted in the one suit that would not slide downhill to the brothers and sisters who now lined the front row at Our Lady Queen of Martyrs on 137th Street. The church was filled with other Cubans, handsome and melancholy people who jostled one another and spoke darkly in sibilant Spanish. The services were in their native tongue and incomprehensible to Charlie, who kept asking me what was being said. I gleaned some meanings from words that were shared in French and Rumanian, but in truth I was too conscious of the nods in our direction, indicating that we were the boys in the car with Ruben, that the tall one was behind the wheel, and consequently the killer. Nothing was said to us; Charlie's huge father was there, overweight, breathing angrily, restive, disturbed, suggesting the violence he had continually administered to his son, hinting of further punishment. Charlie's mother, a woman as pale and worn as an old wedding ring, wept throughout the entire afternoon. Max and Risa were on my right, dressed in black, silent and isolated. Two policemen were in the row behind us, ready to take us back to the Tombs, from which we had been sprung for the occasion.

The liquid music of the mass poured forth. The baseless vision of eternal life was articulated by a Spanish priest with eyes like anthracite and a voice that recalled guitars. The sorrows of life were repeated by carillon; the ritual told of pity and redemption; the rustle of hands crossing themselves across shirts and mantillas was amplified by the fieldstone walls. Voices broke, and the language of tears was more audible than I could bear. But for me crying was impossible. Try as I might, responsible as I felt—what if I had refused to go along? Would the others have taken that final ride?—I could not bring myself to melt. I would not unlock. Let them have their formal consolation. Let Ruben move through the lips of novenas and run along the surfaces of the rosaries. Tradition is the democracy of the dead. Let the deceased boy vote. But I would not release my pain, or let loose my sacred rage. I still responded to the undertow of older mournings.

The church bells pealed with the sound of O. Low. Groans. No's. Goads. Blows. There was no way to stop the ears.

—*Mama, why can't we go to see Anna?*
—*She is gone.*
—*Couldn't we at least see her body?*
—*No. They took her away.*
—*Where? Where did they take her?*
—*To the place where they burn the dead.*

—*Why do they burn the dead? Why can't they bury them?*
—*The ground is too hard.*
—*But I could dig in the earth. See? With my foot. It's not so hard.*
—*It is too hard for Anna.*
—*Will it be too hard for me, Mama?*

ITEM: We were within easy earshot of the terrible final scenes as German criminal prisoners using clubs and dogs were let loose in the camp against the [Gypsy] women, children and old men. A desperate cry from a young Czech-speaking lad suddenly rent the air. "Please Mr. SS man, let me live." Blows with a club were the only answer. Eventually all the inmates were crammed into lorries and driven away to the crematorium. Again they tried to offer resistance, many protesting that they were Germans.

> —O. Kraus and E. Kulka, *Death Factory* (Oxford: Pergamon Press, 1966)

ITEM: I cannot forget the cry of one Hungarian Gypsy mother. She had forgotten that death waited for all of them. She thought only of her child as she pleaded, "Don't take my little boy from me. Don't you see that he is sick?" The shouting of the S.S. and the weeping of the children awakened the occupants of the neighboring camps. They were the horrified witnesses of the departure of the trucks. Later that night the long red flames flashed from the chimneys of the crematory building. What crime had the Gypsies committed?

> —O. Lengyl, *Five Chimneys* (New York: Ziff-Davis, 1947)

The following morning Charlie and I were remanded to juvenile court for sentencing. The judge, moon-faced, heard our case and the pleas of two lawyers. Charlie's was a young Italian who got lost in his argument and ended by throwing the client onto the mercy of the court.

Max and Risa sat in the back of the courtroom while my attorney ventilated the bromides of the Left: the crimes of the capitalist state, the struggles of adolescence in a repressive socioeconomic system bent on crushing the potential of the deprived, the criminal as victim, etc., etc. He was beaky and crested like a jay, caparisoned in blue like a jay, oily, noisy and full of argument like a jay, and his worn words swirled to the ground like feathers. The judge frowned a great deal and yawned upon conclusion.

We were sentenced that afternoon to not more than two years or less than six months in the Mondale State Reformatory in Connecticut, then considered a model correction facility for the young. Risa's tears surprised me; even Charlie's mother was soundless. Her husband made a lot of angry noises, but in fact both parents were anxious to get the delinquent off their hands before he did worse. Risa was the only one to cry. Before I was taken away Max shook my hand, and Risa hugged me and handed me a narrow white box from Mark Cross. It held a thin pigskin wallet, and when I opened it I found three five-dollar bills. I had forgotten that the next Tuesday, when I would be away, I would be celebrating my fifteenth birthday.

III: PRIDE

HOW CAN THE ECHOES OF A FUNERAL DEPART? HOW DOES guilt recede? Attention, adolescents: Are you being held back from fulfillment by your past? Why not become a basket case? You can't beat the hours . . .

I know the durable image of juvenile detention homes. Derelict humanity, beached souls; the sneering warden, the confluence of pederasts, muggers and rapists despoiling the young; brutal trusties, little conspiracies and corrupt screws. For that we may thank products of the Brothers Warner and the other bottom-of-the-bill crime epics—plus the decent muckrakers who came after, ripping the walls off small-time prisons and cheap-jack facilities. All that had nothing to do with the place they sent me. Mondale was major league from the minute you entered its white brick walls to the day they kicked you out with ten dollars and a used suit. Its dominant characteristic was a colorlessness that the mildest depiction could overtint. Chalky walls, ceilings, roofs, floors. Peeling sycamores and oaks provided the only contrast as they leaned over the walls and fences, looking down at the fields parched past rescue and stony paths worn smooth by dawdling feet.

At Mondale you got up at five every morning and in the beginning you ached in every joint because you did calisthenics for half an hour before breakfast: sit-ups, push-ups, a run across the cinder track, bending, stretching. Breakfast was served on long tables where you sat with your cabin-mates and two proctors—men assigned to the rehabilitation of five boys each. After breakfast you returned to your bunk for bedmaking—hospital corners, blanket so tight a penny could be bounced on it—followed by sweep up, window polishing, latrine cleaning. Then on to school. The instruction was simple and lucid, scaled up or down to fit the individual. At about ten there were private sessions with counselors and analysts, then more exercises, then lunch, then brief retirement to the cabins for inspection, followed by relaxation for an hour. Before the school session resumed, we were given physical education.

The athletics instructor was a short, wedge-shaped homuncule, Napoleon without brains. All he knew was his subject—but he knew that backwards. His job was to find the right exercise for the right boy, and by God, he located every customer in some activity—even horseshoes for those who were lame or disabled. Analyzing me (accurately) when my leg healed as no team player, he assigned me to track. I learned to run. Around the cinder oval I crunched, finding the finishing kick I could never master back at St. Luke's or on city streets. "Sport is a war," he used to bark through his megaphone. "War against fact. Every baseball player is running against Babe Ruth and Joe DiMaggio. Every swimmer is going against Johnny Weismuller's record. Every runner, every jumper is going against some record. Now, nobody expects you to break no records. Your war is against yourself. If you ran the mile in seven minutes yesterday, you're gonna try to run it in six minutes fifty-nine seconds today. That's ath-a-letics. That's life."

The English instructors had another interpretation of life. These were a group of indistinguishable young ex-sergeants who had taught English to Japanese prisoners. With characteristic osmosis they had absorbed Japanese poetry in the process of transmitting English verse. Haiku was quoted everlastingly; we heard about grasshoppers wavering at the ends of reeds, circles in ponds and snow obscuring lonely men, until our eyes glazed over and our pulses grew as feeble as the seventeen syllables. Anemic, fragile, we did not respond until Longfellow and Henley were served. "Life is real! life is earnest! and the grave is not its goal . . ." "I thank whatever gods may be for my unconquerable soul." These were our beefsteak, our calves' liver after weeks of water chestnuts and bean curd; anthems could not have moved us more.

The mathematics instructors had yet another diagnosis of

phenomena. A tall, cadaverous teacher named Barnes, whom of course we dubbed Bones, offered us the theory of the Fibonacci numbers. This is an elegant mathematical progression echoed in nature—in the arrangement of certain pine cones and the leaves of bean plants. One number is added to the next. The result is added to the preceding number. $2 + 3 = 5$, $5 + 3 = 8$, $8 + 5 = 13$, $13 + 8 = 21$, etc. "This," testified Bones, "is life."

Intimations there, Mr. Bones. Absolutely, Mr. Interlocutor. If only I had penetrated mathematics, it might have taught me how to live, after all. Question, Mr. Interlocutor: Why does we celebrate men of letters but not men of numbers? How come we resents being digits—as in bankbooks, insurance, social security, employee numbers—and not letters? Mr. Bones, I submits it is because the combination of letters is something else entirely: a transubstantiation. An "o" may hope for a career in "holy" or "noble." A number, even in conjunction with other numbers, is always itself, enlarged perhaps, but without a prayer of change or alteration. (Music up.)

After 6 P.M. you could play Ping-Pong or pool in the dayroom, or half-court basketball on the outdoor macadam. Or you could lounge on your bed and read, or stare up at the cracked plaster ceiling to find the outlines of animals or faces. Smoking was officially frowned upon by the authorities, but not actually forbidden. There was no Surgeon General's report then, just as there was no public analysis of the dangers in automobile exhaust. Ignorant of these killers, we inhaled luxuriously and loved big cars. Guilt was not so general as the century halved.

Aside from masturbation, smoking was about the only activity one could enjoy without sharing. In all else—or so it seemed to me—we were in the company of proctors. They were in the cabins, on the ball fields, in the classrooms. They drilled us, instructed us, guided us to the various examinations for physical, mental and spiritual health. Most of them were Army and Marine veterans in their twenties, men with short fuses but unable to bear grudges, in superb physical condition but essentially witless. The mathematics proctor thought toads caused warts. The physical education instructors could do one hundred push-ups without losing a breath or sink foul shots from mid-court, but sorry, they couldn't remember the name. Perhaps with good reason. We were all given crew cuts upon entrance, and the crowd of adolescent prisoners—"trainees," as we were called—must have looked like an indistinguishable collection of velvet doorknobs.

The course of our lives was, in fact, brilliantly conceived. Not because of the instruction or the fact that we were never alone, hence unable to concoct new criminal activities. No, it was simply that we were always tired. By the time the proctor snapped the lights off at about nine o'clock we were too weary to think. Any child can blow up a dream to be larger than the night, but it was weeks before I could begin to pierce the blue-black of exhaustion.

It is said that boys in mid-adolescence are approaching their sexual peak. We might have been in our sunset years. On the bunk to my left was a narrow, pockmarked boy named Joe Tower, much given to braggadocio. I remember his shout several days after his admission to Mondale, rending the darkness with distress: "Hey! I can't get no hoddon!"

"That's 'cause they put saltpeter in the food," said some voice at the far end.

The talk of girls diminished, dwindled, guttered and went out. Instead, in the moments before we ourselves were extinguished, we spoke of our previous adventures and what brought us here. Like me, Joe Tower was a thief. He was, I thought, motherless—he never talked about her—and his father was a derelict. That was all any of us knew until one evening when both of us woke up in the middle of the night. I went to the john and came back to bed and couldn't fall asleep again. I turned around in bed like an animal. Joe got up, visited the urinal and came back. He also thrashed and punched his pillow. I heard him snuffling.

"Can't sleep?" I called in a thick voice.

"No."

"My mind keeps bouncing like a truck."

"Me too. I keep thinking about home."

"Where you from, Joe?

"Kentucky."

"What're you doing up here?"

He hesitated, snuffled and then unloaded. His father had been a jockey, built, from the sound of him, along Joe's lines: small, lean and sallow. He was never a front-line rider, but he had worked Belmont, Aqueduct and Hialeah. At one of the tracks he had been involved in a horse-doping scandal.

"Naturally, Pop took the fall," Joe said. "He and a couple of other jocks were barred for life. But the owners, that knew about it, what did they get? A warning. Money protects money. Never a rich man died in the electric chair."

"What happened to your old man?"

"After they broke his heart? What could he do? All he could get was assistant trainer, which is nothing but a glorified exercise boy, riding the horses around, you know, and getting them used to a human being in the saddle. Until a real jock can take over. He begun to drink more and ride casual when he thought nobody was watching, but somebody was always watching and we moved on."

"Where'd you go?"

He sat up and counted. "Hell, where didn't we go? Massachusetts, Maine, Tennessee, Kentucky, Georgia, New Jersey. Eleven different farms and stables in ten years, all of us."

"How many is all?"

"Me and Pop and my brother Dave. And," he added as an afterthought, "my goddamn Ma."

Mothers were usually taken as semisacred by distressed prisoners. Other than the generalized and meaningless conjunction "motherfucker," it was the first time that I had heard maternal sacrilege at Mondale.

"How come you talk about her like that?"

"Because of what she was. Somewhere in the time we was moving she started going to church. She was raised a Methodist, but none of us ever went except at Easter and Christmas."

There was a shout of "Shuddup!" down the line. We waited a few minutes, then walked to the window and smoked and resumed.

"All of a sudden she found God," Joe recalled. "In Macon,

Georgia. Of course she'd started drinking too, and the preacher was good-looking and smooth as Vaseline and she fell for him and his line."

What kind of line, I asked. I never did get the name straight. Something like the Tribe of Nazarene. Joe spoke in a stage whisper that made the light sleepers shift in their sheets. "They have a book," he said, *"What to Do Until the Messiah Comes. It tells how to convert people, how to work on your parents or your kids. The scariest garbage you ever saw."*

Max would have been proud of Joe as he fulminated against his favorite villain, organized religion. Voice of the people.

"My mother used to work on my brother Dave and me and Pop again and again, telling us how Jesus was the only way out of this mess and how since she had found him she had peace of mind, though I notice people who tell you that generally don't give *you* any."

He began to snuffle again and both of us were embarrassed and waited for the sounds of the night to fill up the corners. After a while he started whispering again. "Ma said history was one long horror movie, and that if we wanted to get out of the theater we had to read the Testaments and join the church. She shoved the Bible at us so many times I *had* to read parts of it. You ever read it, Ben?"

"They used to read it to us at St. Luke's. The school I went to in London."

"Well, hell, ain't *that* one long horror movie? The Bible, I mean. All that revenge and death?"

"Some of it."

"Oh, there's some psalms. I know them. And one or two interesting histories, but the rest—if I had a son like Dave that isn't old enough to make up his own mind, I'd ban that book the way they ban books in Boston. I would. I don't care what anybody says."

"I didn't say anything, Joe. I'm not religious."

"Neither was Dave—at first. Jesus, he was a nice kid. Used to write me post cards. I mean, I lived in the same room with him and he'd write me post cards. 'I have borrowed your red undershirt. Yankees will take the pennant by 15 1/2 games.

Regards.' Stuff like that. But then the Tribe got hold of him."

The duty guard began walking around, and we doused our cigarettes and ducked down and waited for him to crunch by. Joe said nothing for a while. I didn't know whether to pry or let it alone. I asked him what happened to his brother.

"After a year or so Dave was completely under the spell of those people and began to feel that he was living among devils. That's what happened. The devils being Pop and me because neither of us would go to church, although I used to catch Pop praying when he had the shakes. Pretty soon Dave would start preaching at us, repeating what they told him in church that Sunday. It got so I couldn't stand to sit at the same table with him. He was all thunder and oil. One afternoon he told me I was nothing but a hound of hell. I said, 'That makes me a son of a bitch, I guess,' and he said, 'Yes it does,' and I said, 'Then what does that make Ma?' That's when he hit me with the cat."

"With the *what*?"

"The cat. It was the nearest thing to his hand, is all. There was two big yowls, one from the cat and one from me. I still have the scars, see?"

His four cicatrices were like my single one, light and running into the hair.

"Blood started to come down over my nose and eyes and I went for Dave and got him around the neck and Pop started banging me over the head with his open hands and Ma started in screaming I was a criminal type and there was never anything like that on her side of the family and must be given training or I was bound for jail and hell. Pop said the only thing wrong with me was her, and several days later the marriage was over. Officially. Unofficially it had ended years before at the clubhouse turn. Funny thing, though."

"What?"

"Ma was right. I *was* bound for jail and hell. And I still am. I started thieving right after that. Like I was cursed. The very first armed robbery we all got caught, and here I am. Hell. We're one of those families you read about." His eyes filled up. "The fuckin' *Daily News* ought to run a story about us." And so they did, a few years later, but it was a story that belongs to another time. I don't know if I can bear to read the clipping right now.

To my left was a black boy, Otis Hall. "Otis the Lotus" he called himself, or "Hall the Tall." It was my first exposure to this sort of palaver; the only black people I had known were those committed few at Max's cell meetings, dark, intense men in suits and ties who spoke tersely of the Class Struggle and Comrade Paul Robeson. They were indistinguishable from the whites at the meeting, except for an occasional richness of voice, not vocabulary. Here was Otis, free of Southern diction and spouting what seemed to me a liberated verse. I couldn't get enough of his riffs. "Why are you here?" I asked him, after I had entered my own plea. "Hell," he said, "for decoration. You get yourself a bunch of night, what you want in it is a few bright stars, right? You get yourself a white piece of paper, what you want on it is a few black letters. Consequently, when you got a recipe for Caucasian stew, the appetite says too much white, what you do? You add a drop of melanin, throw in a Negro, and beat well. Serves two hundred."

I never did find out what he was in for. But he was bright and fast and I figured him to be dead or famous by the time he was thirty. I was off by a few years.

With these companions I made it through three months. The depression lifted; so, slowly, did the exhaustion. On Sundays Max and Risa came up to visit with cookies or salami. We lay on the grass in the visitors' field, exchanging silences. Max never asked how things were and Risa looked sad, wondered how the food was, brought books that I tried to read but never finished, and told me to take it a day at a time.

One day Max looked at the bulletin board at the end of the field. "I see they got chapel here," he remarked around his cigar. "Protestant, Catholic, Jewish, Other. Which one do you go to?"

"Other," I told him.

"What's that?"

"They let you go to a place and read if you don't want to attend services."

"What kind of place?"

"It's sort of a room at the back of the chapel."

"Has it got a cross in it?" Max asked suspiciously. "Or a star?"

"No, nor a hammer and sickle," I said.

He didn't like that. "What's that supposed to mean?" he demanded.

"Max," Risa interrupted him. "Let the boy alone."

She changed the subject, or maybe he did. No more was said about chapel. The next time, they brought Mordecai up for leavening. He spent the entire two hours teaching one of the guards to say *"macher"*—"minning de boss," and *"fashiderne"* signifying various. "Like you got *fashiderne* boys here." And *"schvartzer,"* which the black guard already knew.

I had bristled at Max for a devious and wrong reason. The week before, the warden—or Uncle Howard, as he preferred to be called—had sent for me in the middle of a track meet. Peculiar, I thought, retracing my week mentally, wondering what infractions I had committed. It was the first time I had been in his office since my entrance. Uncle Howard was a bluff, two-hundred-pound specimen of the football-coach persuasion, complete with crew cut and the kind of jaw you could hang a lantern on. He had been smitten years ago, when he first looked into a mirror, and he was smitten still. It was a great love story.

"Boy," he said, in an introduction calculated to warm *fashiderne* cockles. I wondered if he began that way with Otis. "Boy, I understand that you do portraits."

Max, I thought, and felt betrayed. "I used to," I replied.

"A boy fourteen—"

"Fifteen."

"A boy fourteen, fifteen, whatever. A boy doesn't 'used to' do anything. If he used to do it, he still does. Boy your age doesn't have a chance to forget. Tell you what. Like you to do a group portrait of the family. Pay you for it, of course. Pay you well." He lingered over the last sentence. Whether it was the idea of money, or just the sound of his voice, that he enjoyed I couldn't tell.

"I don't think I can do that, sir," I said.

"Why not?"

"Well, in the first place, I *have* forgotten a lot. And then, every time I do draw people, something bad happens. So I thought I wouldn't do it for other people. Just for myself."

"Pretty selfish attitude, don't you think? World doesn't revolve around you, you know."

"Yes, sir, I know that."

"Sooner or later you're going to walk out of here. Like it to be sooner."

There was silence while I stood there. The proctor, who was seated at my left, covered a yawn with his hand, but it leaked out of his eyes.

Uncle Howard tried a confidential approach. He motioned me to a chair, then stood up and strutted around with his hands in his pin-striped pockets.

"Ben," he said. "Listen. Know what I did yesterday? Played hooky. Something you can't do. Went to a baseball game. Brooklyn versus Boston. The last time I went I took my son. He was seven. Now he's nineteen. Senior at Colgate. Twelve years ago we sat in the same place, behind third base. Took a look at the third baseman. Checked the program. He was twenty-eight."

The guard got interested at this, and even I tried to anticipate the point of Uncle Howard's anecdote.

"This time I looked at the third baseman again. Then I checked the program. He was still twenty-eight. Different third baseman, but the same stance, same uniform. Same age. Don't you see, Ben? The spectators get old, the players stay the same. For two decades I've been sitting in this office, watching. You guys are always fourteen, fifteen, sixteen maybe. Boys licking their wounds, boys bearing grudges, boys with angry looks, boys who can't keep their hands still" (ah, there, Uncle Howard, what an eye for detail) "or their brains. Boys looking to get even with something or somebody. Seen them come, seen them go. Now, how fast *you* go is up to you. Why don't you think it over and report back to me? Tonight."

"Sir, I'd rather tell you now. I don't want to draw while I'm here."

Silence. Then: "Very well. Dismissed."

And I was taken outside. I had reason to regret my refusal the next morning, when my bed was found unsatisfactorily made. I received a demerit for that, more for goofing off during various classes, and more for uncooperative attitudes in gym, English, chemistry and French, a language I could speak with greater fluency than the instructor, with his two years of stationed-at-Rheims accent. The result was a weekend without privilege—sans the visit of Max and Risa.

"They gone wear you down, soldier," said Otis. "Give them what they want. Shit, they want to see a bucktoothed, smiling, blue-gummed nigger, I'm going to give them something make Stepin Fetchit look like Anthony Eden. What I want is out. Why not you?"

How could I explain that obduracy is not susceptible to sense? How could I say to anyone that I had no power except that minor denial: the ability to withhold a single scrap of ability, a little gift of drawing flat and seeing round? How could I speak to Otis of detention, of isolation and the theory and practice of hell?

—*You wish to see your family again?*
—*Yes, sir.*
—*You will then answer all questions, you understand?*
—*Yes, sir. If I can remember.*
—*A boy your age has not had time to forget.*
—*No, sir.*
—*You and your family traveled a great deal, yes?*
—*Yes, sir.*
—*How many in your family?*
—*Seven, sir, including me.*
—*You* Zigeuners *breed like flies.*
—*Yes, sir.*
—*Yes, sir, yes, sir. Do you always agree with everything?*
—*I don't know, sir. I only wish to—*
—*You only wish to please the nice Kommandant.*
—*No, sir, I only wish to live.*
—*Well, now. It depends on how badly you wish. Do you wish as hard as our friend Eleazar Jassy?*

—*Yes.*

—*Yes, but?*

—*I don't like to do what he does.*

—*Sometimes it is necessary to punish people. If you wish to live, sooner or later you will have to do that too. Can you do that, do you think?*

—*I don't know, sir.*

—*We will find out fast enough. Right now, tell me what you saw when you traveled. Did you see partisans?*

—*Excuse me, sir, I don't know what partisans are. You mean soldiers?*

—*I mean men in ordinary clothing. Men with guns.*

—*Yes, sir, I did.*

—*Ah! Good boy. Good boy! How many did you see?*

—*Ten or twelve, sir.*

—*Where did you see them?*

—*Outside the village of Tanbourg, sir.*

—*There are possibilities in you. Distinct possibilities. Are you hungry?*

—*Yes, sir.*

—*Have this apple. Here, come outside. I want you to hold on a rope and pull it.*

—*No, sir. I cannot.*

—*Don't tell me you cannot. There is a disobedient man at the end of this rope. There will be three obedient men at this end.*

—*I'm not a man, sir. Please don't make me do this.*

—*Come on, Ben. Don't spoil it for us.*

—*Pretend to pull. Eleazar will do the real pulling.*

—*No, I cannot.*

—*Damn you, pretend or we all die.*

—*Oh, God, where is God now?*

—*Pretend, Benoit.*

—*Pull! Slowly now! Don't let him up too quickly!*

Dangling black puppet twisted against the white clouds. Gypsy like me. Death, we are only your orderlies. I lied about the partisans. My hands lied upon the rope. I let it through my fingers. When would the Kommandant find me out?

ITEM: First the [Gypsy] girl was forced to dig a ditch, while her
mother, seven months pregnant, was left tied to a tree. With
a knife they opened the belly of the mother, took out the baby
and threw it in the ditch. Then they threw in the mother and
the girl, after raping her. They covered them with earth while
they were still alive.

—R. Bubeničková, *Tabory utrepní a smrti*
(Prague: Svoboda, 1969)

With measured caprice, my proctors stopped distributing
demerits toward the end of one week, and I found that I would
be allowed visitors after all. But Max and Risa had already been
told that their son would be unavailable that weekend. I wandered into the visitors' yard on the autumnal Saturday, alone,
feeling sorry for myself, watching and hearing the families
reunited, the knots of people sitting on the lawns and benches,
the sounds separating and meshing into designs of sharp, concentric laughs, into convoluted mazes of plans and the blunt
and elementary shapes of gossip. All this against a background
of sparrows and crickets announcing that they were no longer
in charge, that the chill of death was shaking the leaves.

"*Shmuck!* What is with you?" came a voice at my ear. I
turned around to behold Mordecai, dressed in crisp nine-
teenth-century black, complete with homburg and silver-
banded cane. He looked as formal as a document. "How can
you do dis?" He used the cane as a gavel against the grass.
"You're breaking everybody's heart vit dese demerits. Vot's de
matter you couldn't do a sketch? Costs you something?"

"As a matter of fact, it does," I returned hotly. But there was
no way to stay angry or resentful, not at Mordecai. Standing
there in his only suit, having come, I knew, by rattling prewar
bus, and without anything to read, he was only exhibiting
concern. To him I was a stubborn lunatic adolescent without
enough sense to come in out of the rain. He opened his CARE
package—a delicatessen ranging from smoked whitefish to
kreplach—spread a blanket on the ground, and resumed his
lecture.

"Pretty soon we'll have to do dis inside. You got inside
here?"

"Yes, when it gets cold they set up visitors' tables in the gym."

"You gonna stay here until next spring. Till next Tishubov. Maybe you never get out."

"I'll get out."

"Gadles ligt oyfn mist, farshtaisht?"

"No. You know I still don't speak Yiddish."

"That's you trouble. If you onderstood Yiddish, you'd onderstend Benoit. It means: Pride lies on the dunghill. Also: *Far der velt muz men mer yoytse azyn vi far Got aleyn.*"

"Translation?"

"The world makes more demends than God himself. Believe me, Benoit, a proverb is five thousand years in a fortune cookie. Listen and learn."

"A proverb is a band squeezed down into a drummer."

This from Otis, who had drifted by. He occasionally had visitors. Aunts, as far as I could tell, plus a couple of little nieces; there were never any men in his company. But today he seemed alone and looking for companionship. I introduced him to Mordecai.

"If you want to know how story go, wait till quarrel come" was Otis' opening line. "African proverb, by way of Lenox Avenue."

"Not bad." Mordecai reached for a reply. "How about '*A kluger farshtaisht fun eyn vort tsvey.*' A wise man hears one word and understands two."

Otis fired another salvo: "When a man say him do not mind, then him mind."

Mordecai, with a nod to me: *"Der vos vil gayve traybn, muz hunger ladn.* He that stands upon his pride keeps starvation by his side."

"Precisely: When heart and mind collide, the reason is always pride."

"Yes, right, *exactle.*" Mordecai put his arm around Otis and they began a discussion about stubbornness. I left them conferring like two predators gnawing on bones—my bones—and wandered the grounds. Maybe they were right, I thought. Maybe I should do a few portraits—what was so difficult about scratching resemblances on paper, after all? Should I pay in weeks and months for some irrational distrust? Could it all be because of those years in the camps? Because of what had been done in a dread place, a grief ago? Wasn't it time to get past all that?

But I could not. Pride is no exclusive of the orphan. In the middle of the night the whitest, most privileged child can imagine more hells than Dante and reaches for possessions. The only thing in the world that was mine was the capacity to draw faces. I had been promised recovery by my rescuers. But time had really healed nothing. It never would. I would not capitulate. When Mordecai left, I think he knew that. He had no more proverbs, only a melancholy shake of the head and a surprisingly powerful grip of the shoulder. "You know best," he said. Then, as I unwound, he added, "Also worst." An exit not calculated to put the soul at rest. Otis came up and wished him farewell in Yiddish, which was all I needed.

That night my dreams were designed by some *New Yorker* cartoonist: Black men paraded with signs translated from the Yiddish. One said *The world will end tomorrow;* the other, *The world ended yesterday.*

When I woke up, the world had stubbornly refused to conclude, and it and I got on with the rest of our sentences:

> Pride, envy, avarice—these are the sparks
> Have set on fire the hearts of all men

as Dante said to me. I never did paint a portrait of Uncle Howard and his family. Pride. Every dog has its day; Benoit would have his.

Unfortunately the calendar specifies another 364 other days in the year, and these did not belong to the dog and had to be got through. I crossed many of those days off as they occurred, and one evening it was revealed to me that since we were rounded up in 1940, and I was not adopted until 1946, and was now, in 1948, in Mondale, I had spent more than a third of my life as a ward of the state—the state varying from German to English to American. That was enough of that, I concluded.

The notion that an ability to draw was so powerful that it could
—by negative application—keep me imprisoned worked in my
skull like eye of newt in a cauldron. The next evening, when
my fellow prisoners and proctors were asleep, I tiptoed past the
snores and broken sentences of the oblivious and made my way
to the toilet. Behind the closed but lockless door I sketched
Mordecai from memory and in great detail. It was not difficult;
his features were as simple as a fist. Even the glistening ambition of his eyes was so pure and fundamental that it could be
rendered with a crayon. I furled the picture to the thickness
of a pencil, and since our ingoing and outgoing mail was inspected, handed it the next day to Otis Hall along with a
five-dollar bill. Otis was due out in two days, sprung on good
behavior and the promise of a place in Performing Arts High
School. I wanted him to take the message direct to Max and
Risa, along with a note asking them to invite him to dinner.
It also informed them that for me attendance at a traditional
school promised catastrophe; that above all I hoped to attend
some art academy. There I could make my way with the sole
blessing that had not been taken away by force.

"You a fool," Otis informed me the morning of his release.
"You a swamp chucklehead. Or, if you prefer"— and here he
switched from his Mississippi-buck put-on to a wrinkle-free
Brooks Brothers Caucasian intonation—"a willful, stubborn
and ultimately self-destructive character is what you displays."

I admitted same.

"And you won't change?"

"No."

He extended a palm. As we shook hands he looked down at
our grip. "Listen, Benoit. You're not a black man. And you're
not precisely white, either. You're the only creature I ever met
I feel sorrier for than me."

He began walking around, throwing off ergs like a man
dropping change out of his pockets, exhibiting the same sort
of manic bounce that millions would get hooked on one day.

"Ben. Look at me. Last week I was working in the records
office, you know? And when the old man went to take a leak
I snuck a look at our charts. You know you and I got the biggest
IQs in this hole, you know that?"

Intelligence Quotients. Another racket. Another con.

> Rain is to steam as
> 1. Ice is to snow
> 2. Night is to sun
> 3. Cloud is to kettle
> 4. Sorrow is to laughter

Number two. Because one falls and the other rises. Small minds inventing tests; what one man can concoct, another can dissect.

Otis stopped prancing. "Look at this," he said, and showed me his watch. "One hour I'll be free. But that's not why I'm showing you this." He switched to his holy-roller ministerial tone. "Brother, they is a hour hand, a minute hand and a second hand. The hour hand is wisdom, and the minute is calculation. And the second hand is foolishness, runnin' around like a chicken with his haid cut off. You can see de second hand run, but you can't see de minute hand move, 'cause it's too clever. And de hour hand is the smartest of them all, 'cause it's learned to move slow and accurate; no hurry at all, but it gits there. You dig?"

I dug.

"Stop bein' a second hand, Ben, 'fore you hurts yourself."

"I can't, Otis. I'm sorry, but I can't. I guess I'll always be running around—"

"I don't know what they did to you, Ben, back in the war. None of my business, right? But, you know, there are millions of kids right here in this country getting the lives choked out of them. Every now and then one of them climbs out and makes his way because he won't quit on himself."

"I'm not quitting, Otis."

"And because he stops fighting for dumb reasons. You got a battle here against the wrong folks. I remember when I was in court: 'The State of New York versus Otis Hall.' I didn't like them odds, Ben. I figured I'd change them, and here I am on my way out. Why don't you rig them odds your way? Come out and we'll go to school together. I tell you, there's a new day coming. I can feel it. Gone be all right for us not-quite-white citizens."

But he knew the answer before he had put the question. Otis shook his head, offered his hand once again and was gone out of Mondale, Mr. Chameleon on his way.

A month later even Joe Tower was free, aiming for California where, he told me, there were rackets undreamed of back East. Joe had no mental stuff, he lacked all but the fundamental skills of crime, but he knew himself. "They told us this story in chapel," he said. "Where everybody gets to put their troubles in a sack? And they put the sacks in the middle of the room? And then God says okay, pick up any sack you want, and everybody goes for their own sack. Well, not me, Ben, not me."

"Whose sack do you want, Joe?"

"Yours. Anybody's. Except mine. Shit, man, they got my number the day I was born, you know? Probably got yours, too. People like us, we travel under a fuckin' curse."

Otis wanted me to be his brother under the IQ. Joe wanted to yoke me to his own despair. That left only Charlie. After Joe got out to thumb his way to page four of the *Daily News,* I tried to see my old pal. We had been separated early on, under the rule that no members of a "gang" be allowed to associate in prison. Of course we saw each other at track meets and assemblies, but Charlie lived in a different cabin and his proctor kept a close watch on him—as did mine on me. Visitors' day I saw him with his miserable family. He always wore his depression on his face for days after the visits. But unlike me, Charlie had been receptive to the counselors and the talk sessions known today by the repulsive title of "rap groups." His grades were low but his deportment was flawless. He was getting out two months ahead of schedule on exemplary behavior, and on the last Friday before his release, Charlie was allowed to visit me.

I was lying on my bunk, visitorless that weekend for some infraction or series of pecadilloes; I no longer remember. There were a couple of other luckless sprouts on their bunks, reading or playing some desultory card game. The dust motes caught the sun and made me sleepy, and for a moment Charlie's face seemed to be a component of some dream.

"Whuddya say, Ben?"

No, it was no vision. There was only one voice with that cloudy, moronic good nature. "How ya doin', good buddy?" it said.

Good buddy. Southern Army rash caught from his teachers. Charlie was whoever he talked to last.

"I'm fine. I'm first-class."

"You don't look first-class, ya know that? Ya look peekid."

"That's because it's my period."

Wild laughter from Charlie. A model prisoner, an ideal audience. "At least ya haven't lost ya sense of yuma."

"Not me, Charlie. I'll always be Mr. Laughs."

I scrambled around looking for cigarettes, but Charlie told me ostentatiously that he had given them up. "I'm free," he said. "No more oral dependencies, ya know what I mean?" The voice of Dr. Klein; support your local specialist in the psychiatric problems of adolescence.

"Tell me more, good buddy. Lay it on me."

"There's nothin' more to tell. My criminal behavior was really a cry for aid. I was exhibitin' asocial tendencies. I was becomin' part of society's lowest common dominator."

"De*nom*inator."

"Yeah, that too. You oughta talk to Dr. Klein. Do ya a lotta good."

"I've talked to Klein. It worked wonders. Thanks to him I'm reborn."

"Well, there ya are. Just probably works slower on you, that's all."

"You're a ray of sunshine, Charlie, you know what I mean?"

"Yeah, well, I do my best. You'll integrate wit your peer group soon enough, take my word for it."

"Oh, I will, I do."

Charlie was satisfied. Mission accomplished. He got up from the edge of the bed. "Hey, can I do something for ya when I get out? You know, answer some needs?"

"Charlie?"

"Yeah."

"Do you ever think about sex?"

"About what?"

"Sex, s-e-c-k-s. Sex."

"What's that supposed to be, funny? Of course I think about erotic drives. Pubescent males constantly think about that. It's normal."

"Okay, I just wondered."

"You really oughta talk to Dr. Klein again. Your libidinal impulses are probly what's holdin' you back right now. You're not achievement-oriented. You're gratification-oriented. Tell him about your fantasies. He'll understand. He's very good about the superego. No shit." And he was gone.

Now I was truly alone. Tell Dr. Klein about my fantasies? That fountain of jargon, that mellow Answer Man who turned boys into textbooks? Thank you just the same.

ITEM: The official Polish estimate—the most conservative and not universally accepted—is that approximately 52,000 Gypsies (children made up at least one-third of this total) were killed in four camps.

—Gitta Serenya, *Into That Darkness*
(New York: McGraw-Hill, 1974)

Lost in the eternal pity, we were not to be regarded as young humans, even as humans at all. "The airplane as one of the elements of modern negation and abstraction. There is no more nature, the deep gorge, true relief, the impassable mountain stream, everything disappears. There remains *a diagram*— a map.

"Man, in short, looks through the eyes of God. And he perceives then that God can have but an abstract view. This is not a good thing."

No, Monsieur Camus, it is not a good thing. Suffer the little children to be brought unto me. At eye level. Let God be here to watch, to see the fires stoked with little souls. Let him not look down the chimneys as if they were microscopes focused on circles of anguish.

—*You keep yourself astonishingly clean for a Romany. How do you do it?*
—*Please, sir, I wash in the rainwater. I waste no soap.*

—*Did I say you wasted soap? Besides, the soap is made of Gypsies. We waste nothing here. Benoit?*

—*Yes, sir.*

—*Bring me that bottle. This one is empty.*

—*Yes, sir.*

—*Did you know that I have children?*

—*No, sir.*

—*You think we Germans have no children?*

—*I don't think about it, sir.*

—*You think we have no feeling? I simply obey.*

—*Are you sick, sir?*

—*The world will never understand the design of this machine. Fine-looking people, you Romanies. The last group: beautiful women, lovely children; stocky and strong-looking men, marvelous specimens. It took three days to kill them all. And ten days later we had processed all their belongings. Imagine, at fifty kilograms a person—that is what they were allowed to bring to this "resettlement." There were 720,000 kilograms of belongings. Incredible how the machine proved itself in those ten days, Benoit. Incredible.*

—*Yes, sir.*

—*I am alone. I am absolutely alone.*

Frogs eat butterflies. Snakes eat frogs. Hogs eat snakes. Men eat hogs. Conscience is consumed by duty, duty by obedience, obedience by weariness, weariness by self-pity. I would always have to watch weariness and pity. I would have to watch that, too, watch it the way a ballplayer regards himself, seeing if he can still get around on the fastball, observing the reflexes and the measure of his deterioration.

What is your favorite movie method for illustrating the passage of time? Check one:

A. Leaves showering down from trees, snow falling, blossoms.

B. A train cutting through America with terminals dissolving through it: Tuscaloosa, Chicago, Minneapolis, New York.

C. A colt lengthening his stride, becoming a yearling, then a stallion.

D. A house rising in rapid stages from a blueprint.

Mine is the bottom of a vaudeville bill: Benoit Kaufman, The Gypsy Mentalist. Then the middle of the bill: Featuring that Genial Gypsy Fortuneteller, Benoit Kaufman. Then near the top of the card: Master Mentalist Benoit Kaufman in his only Philadelphia appearance. Finally, heading the program: The Pantages proudly presents the one and only Benoit Kaufman, direct from his European engagement. For one night only. Followed by a man in overalls with brush. Over the sign he sploshes a paper: *Sold Out.*

Or in my case, Let Out. Good-by Auschwitz, St. Luke's, Mondale. Farewell to another institution. Handshake. Lecture. "This is not a period in your life, but a comma. It's up to you how the rest of the sentence goes, etc." Max and Risa waiting and the short voyage home.

Like the heroes in those forties movies, I came out into an altered world. Politics had about the same appeal to me as kohlrabi. But I was immediately aware that there was some fear and anger that lay just out of reach. Everything seemed the same: Max was just as hairy, Risa just as equine; the apartment had not altered in appearance—still book-lined and dark-green, still underlit with bridge lamps and redolent of a semi-retired fireplace. But there was a tenebrous undertow to dinners and the conversations I heard from my bedroom. Something to do with the State Department, the college; something to do with Max taking the Fifth Amendment at a Congressional investigation; something to do with progressives and red herrings and takeovers.

The blue air of early evening was filled with shibboleths: "comrades," "struggle," "the people," "oppressed class," "labor," "youth," "barricades," and that greatest of all rallying slogans, "history." Then there were ominous rumblings: "witch hunts," "loyalty oaths" and "security clearance."

As much as possible this was kept from me. Max and Risa concerned themselves with my attempts to leave high school for art school, and with some finagling they got me into the Lasch Institute.

Risa had taken a job downtown, something to do with the administration of a Negro charity. She came home drained— Max was to discover how drained in a few months—in the evenings, and buried herself in her studio, ostensibly to sketch and paint, but often to spend hours on the telephone. The words she spoke were inaudible, but the whinnies and declarations were unmistakably those of a person absorbed in something more intense than gossip, darker than rumor.

Max for his part was either attending protest meetings or hosting them. The fury of those gatherings was so palpable that way off in my room, where I tried to read or draw, I could feel the hot plush apartment air crackle. A truck-faced, rawboned man with red hair on the back of his knuckles shouted about the need to aggressively oppose fascist hooliganism. A perpetually smiling black man from Connecticut (who had only two jokes: referring to his house as "the old plantation" and saying that he had a touch of the tarbrush) rose continually to speak of Brother Robeson and the fact that Russia alone was colorblind. La Passionara's line, "It is better to die on your feet than live on your knees," was trotted out like a dish of tired canapés every few hours. The pledge of allegiance was, Max said, to a shroud, not a flag. Repression, his colleagues allowed, was in the saddle and rode the universities. Like the Germans, who were ignorant of what went on in Nazi concentration camps, said a fat contralto who was later to become a nun, the Americans were unaware of the facts of moral life. It was unanimously agreed that U.S. citizens were living in a reign of terror.

Resentment was aimed at employers, at senators, at the duped American public, at capitalism, at the state. But loathing, hate in its distillate form, was reserved for the lifelong enemies: socialists, liberals, aesthetes.

> For you
> History prepares a shameful grave
> A nameless spot burned under weed and stone
> Where creeping jackals shall come to howl
> Stirred by ancient kinship with those bones.

Alfred Hayes contra the Austrian Socialists. Repeated with approbation by the voices at the end of the hall. Apocalypse beckoned, and was there a sense of thrill in it? A sense that together they might find what they could never before experience: martyrdom? Was there a sense that those ancient battles, the Spanish Civil War, the defense of the Moscow trials, the Stalin-Hitler pact, might somehow be mere stations on the way to this cross: the trial of the teachers who would take the Fifth Amendment versus the faculty senate?

For, after all the roiling and backbiting and warnings, that was what it came to. Max Kaufman sitting down in front while the other professors reviewed his case. This gathering was closed to the public, and theoretically out of the ken of all nonacademic civilians, but Max had insisted that his "families" be in attendance—possibly to influence the judges, but more likely to increase his sense of martyrdom. His ex-wife Ellen, a bohemian *baleboosteh* with severe ballerina hair and a body that might have taxed Gaston Lachaise ten years previously but that was now relaxing into a dirigible; his daughter Sara, nine, who read *Ferdinand* over and over again; Risa and I—all sat courteously and on exhibit while the charges were pored over, denied and affirmed.

It went on for days. Outside, the newsmen from the *Times, Post, Sun* and *Herald Tribune* waited patiently and smoked. Occasionally they asked me something, but I protested ignorance and went on to my new art school. I could scarcely believe that Max was on trial for anything; people were endlessly polite and scrupulous. No one at the Institute had the slightest interest in what was going on downtown; academic freedom did not concern anyone above Fourteenth Street. I felt an alien on the outside, and stranger still in school, where no one bothered to talk. Artists were an inarticulate bunch at best, anyway. At the "trial" I looked at my family. Risa was not my blood, nor was Max, nor were Ellen and Sara, to whom I was in some technical way related. I was only Benoit again. This was the way it was and always would be: the mutant with neither a past nor, as far as I could tell, a future. Perhaps the future resided right here, in the rumblings of trouble renewed. God, would the probing never stop? When would history pause for breath?

—*History will vindicate us, Benoit.*

—*Yes, sir.*

—*History will show that we did what we must. Do you comprehend?*

—*Sir, I am only a boy. I cannot comprehend very much.*

—*Yes, yes. Of course. You're tired. Go to bed.*

—*Yes, sir.*

—*Before you go, give me the files.*

—*Which files, sir?*

—*Of those to be sent to . . . of the Z files.*

—*Sir, they are destroyed.*

—*What? By whose order destroyed?*

—*By your own.*

—*I ordered no papers destroyed. You little beggar! You burned them, didn't you? You hope to save these prisoners? I can have duplicates of those files sent on from Belsen.*

—*Sir, last night you asked me to burn them. You were crying, sir. And tired.*

—*I, crying? You little liar, you fool—*

—*You had perhaps had too much to drink. Don't you remember?*

—*I should have sent you to the ovens with the rest. Human garbage, that's what you are. Get out. I don't want to look at you.*

—*Yes, sir.*

—*Benoit. I feel a wreck tonight. Benoit. Count yourself fortunate when a man who means life and death to you feels a wreck.*

The faculty senate heard all arguments: Max's, his colleagues' and the opposition, whose attacks rested on a single syllogism: communism is a conspiracy. A Communist is a conspirator. Therefore a man who refuses to answer whether or not he was a Communist is a Communist. A man who invokes the Fifth Amendment is a conspirator.

Two questions were put to Max by Dr. Molenhoff, the investigator for the university:

1. Do you reject the teaching of Lenin that a party member

should, when it will serve the interest of the movement, resort
to any ruse, cunning, unlawful method, evasion and conceal-
ment of the truth?

2. If you reject these features of the Communist doctrine
and practice, are you willing to give proof that you do so by
resigning from the party?

"A catechism to catch heretics, rather than a program to
test the truth," said Max's defender. Max himself respect-
fully declined to go along at all. He told us privately that
he was doomed, that these attempts at judicial fairness were
a repressive crust, that suffocation was at hand. "Just look
at this crap they use to destroy us," he said, waving an edi-
torial by a vigorous old Trotskyite turned Red-baiter. The
column quoted Justice Holmes's remark that a policeman
may have a constitutional right to talk about politics, but
that he has no constitutional right to be a policeman. By
analogy a man had a right to be a Communist, but no constitutional right to be a teacher.

In the end Max waved aside his counsel and spoke for
himself. He took up Macaulay on the Jews. "If it is our duty
as Christians to exclude Jews from political power," Max read
in a solid voice, stained with tobacco and the remembered grit
of his boyhood Bensonhurst, "it must be our duty to treat them
as our ancestors treated them, to murder them, and banish
them and rob them. For in that way, and in that way alone,
can we really deprive them of political power." He walked the
room silently now, and the boards creaked beneath his feet.
Papers rustled and then stopped. Max might have been Tos-
canini waiting for the Carnegie Hall crowd to settle down for
Rossini. He dove back into his volume: "If we do not adopt this
course, we may take away the shadow, but leave them the
substance. We may do enough to pain and irritate them; but
we shall not do enough to secure ourselves from danger, if
danger really exists. Where wealth is, there power must inevita-
bly be."

This sarcasm vanished into the interstices of the library, into
the heads of the listeners, whose minds were already made up,
into the prose of those sympathetic and hostile reporters, who
at last had something to print.

The week that the newspapers reported the summaries at Max's hearing, a congressman named George S. Dondero promulgated his devil theory of modern art. He had beefed about some State Department show of paintings in 1947, and now the papers reported his revelations: "Communists Maneuver to Control Art in the United States," "Communism in the Heart of American Art—What to Do About It," and "Modern Art Shackled to Communism," mostly because "dadaism, futurism, constructionism, surrealism, suprematism, cubism, expressionism and abstractionism" were all foreign isms representing "weapons of destruction" destroying "our priceless cultural heritage." Ah! Here was an attack to which the art school could respond. Let them burn heretics at the stake or drive spikes into the hearts of children, and there would have been no cry from the artists. The prevailing wisdom there was that the creative soul had no responsibility save to itself, that it lay outside conventional moralities. Politics were for the geeks, the unwashed or the sheep who were born to be fleeced, those moneyed parvenus who might buy one's paintings, but who would never understand them. But when Art and Artists were attacked, that was another matter entirely. Dondero called for the "hard-working, talented, reserved, patriotic proponents of academic art to organize themselves and fight these traducers [i.e., modern artists] of our American inheritance with their own weapons if need be."

Riots outside the school. Pamphlets produced overnight. Petitions circulated. Suddenly a connection made between Benoit Kaufman and Max Kaufman, victim (so it was said in one wall newspaper) of the university's kangaroo court. Abruptly I was recognized, my drawings fussed over, my opinions solicited. I had nothing to say. What did I know of all this Red stuff, this "witch hunting" or "housecleaning," this chant of subversion and degeneracy? Max gave me Carey McWilliams's book to quote, and I tried to be wise when I read his analysis of the security crisis enveloping the schools: "The failure to understand that it is the Devil, not the Heretic, who is the real architect of social disaster is one of the major delusions of our time." The heretic being Max, the Devil played by Congressman Dondero, the isolationist senators, and all those professors who voted Max out of office.

Pride revisited me. I pretended to be knowledgeable and deeply affected by these undercurrents. In fact it was all opaque. Resuscitating it now, I feel only those old strivings of vanity, the itch for recognition at any cost. All I really knew, all I could be certain of, was that the Devil lived in another country. This American incandescence struck me as artificial light; I knew the real phosphor, the authentic thorns—or thought I did.

ITEM: Gas-chamber plans were discussed at daily luncheons at headquarters in which Ohlendorf, Schellenberg and Nebe participated. The extreme cynicism of these meetings apparently exhausted Nebe so much that he had to go on sick leave twice. In July, 1943, he became a "human wreck suffering from a persecution mania," but less than a year later, he felt sufficiently recovered to offer his "Gypsy half-breeds" for seawater experiments.

> —Nora Levin, *The Holocaust* (New
> York: Schocken Books, 1973)

Do you see, Daniel? Can you possibly peer that far back to the dry history of my adolescent years, or before? Or does it crack in the hand like old paper? Can you appreciate what it was like to enter the New World only to find that it was the Old World refracted in some odd, unreadable manner?

Persecutions, accusations, names thrown around, "fascist," Communist, terrorist, what could these greenhorns of terror know about *real* sin? And what could I tell them? My own besetting sin was going around with my lips turned inward, holding my cigarette like Bogart, suffering unostentatiously (which is the greatest form of braggadocio), half wishing to be the son of a martyr, even while I wished Max free.

> 'Tis pride, rank pride, and haughtiness of soul;
> I think the Romans call it stoicism.

As Addison said to me. Well, but what else was there? Merely sinking in the heartland of that little anguish, that silence inside a silence inside a silence. Providing an envelope for the noise of the present. I fought to keep a toehold on my mind, a grip on my own hand, but the past fought with teeth. I recalled the fevered arena where I stayed alive through the indulgence of the Kommandant. I saw Eleazar Jassy, the Kapo, killing the members of our caravan, working with the Germans. How could I hope to expunge that? My memory, my curse, stirring in the dust of ground bones. We choked on it, cracked open with coughs and warnings. Beseeched our God to spare, pled with Him to save. Streaked with light in the back of our sockets. The moon stared blindly at the back of the child.

I remembered October 14, 1944. I watched Eleazar Jassy and swore, as he marched four men, fathers all, to be hanged slowly in the dense, crackling morning, that one day, if I lived, I would dress myself in the black of mourning and find Eleazar and spill his soul into the dirt. I had no idea that it would take me close to three decades. But perhaps the Rumanians are right. Revenge is a dish best eaten cold. Why, then, can't I lower the temperature after all these years?

IV: ENVY

N EXT SLIDE, PLEASE.

There is no passion so strongly rooted in the human heart as envy. So Richard Brinsley Sheridan tells me. Inaccurately. One passion could chew the roots of envy for breakfast.

But lacking the unicorn of wrath, the viper will suffice.

Max was fired, of course: dismissed by a majority vote of the faculty senate. With exquisitely phrased euphemisms that made the school appear to be picking some lint off its jacket, he was pronounced unfit to teach impressionable minors. By invoking the privileges against self-incrimination he had revealed himself as a dedicated pawn in the Bolshevik conspiracy, anxious to pollute the minds of his charges with propaganda scattered through the works of Dryden, Pope and other radicals who were in Max's curriculum that year.

This was merely the beginning. My father's *tsuris* came not in single spies but in battalions. Risa waited as she must have waited through the blitz, with prim and gallant fidelity to her ideals. But once the rubble was cleared she chose to run off with Fred N. Deever, a very large, very self-important, extremely ebony functionary in or around the party. It was, according to Max, a crime of passion, "a twist of the knife in my already murmuring heart."

"I know, I know, she looked like a horse," he would say, looking up from his Swift, groaning broadly from his chair, never directly at me, sometimes at Mordecai, sometimes at a colleague, but mostly to the air. "I had a dozen better in bed. Fourteen, counting the French whores. Two of them used to give it to me for free, if you can believe it. I knew fifty wittier conversationalists. A hundred superior cooks—a thousand. The woman couldn't squeeze an orange, for God's sake."

"She was a nice dresser, however," Mordecai reminded him once.

"Torquemada was a nice dresser," Max exploded. "Lucrezia Borgia was a nice dresser. Tojo was a nice dresser. What the hell do I care about clothes? She had—pheromones. And she winds up with a *schvartzer*. All right, opposites attract, but I thought I was opposite enough."

Pheromones. I had to find that one. It helped explain a good many things to me later, almost all of them concerning the women I was to seek, women who often had little appeal for others, or whom some men could take or leave alone while I was obsessed by their liquefying walks or inveigling voices.

Pheromones: chemicals exuded by insects and other wonders. One particle of the female Cecropia moth's essence can affect one million parts of dead air, pull in males from five miles away, set them panting to arrive with bouquets, boxes of bonbons and theater tickets. Non-Cecropias pass it by like a sign in a foreign language.

Risa was Max's pheromonal female. What she had broadcast he had required. And now she had run off, the second woman in his life to discard him for another lover. This on top of the sudden placement of ex-professor into the dust bin of history. Sometimes Max would emerge steaming from the shower and peer at his girth in the looking glass. "Okay, I'm not the answer to a maiden's prayer," he would bellow, reddening. "I'm bald, I'm fat."

"Eisenhower is bald," Mordecai would call encouragement. "Churchill is fat."

"Those corrugated boxes. Those *alter kockers*. No wonder Risa ditched me." Then Max would look down. "Ah, well, the bathroom mirror only tells half the story. Maybe I didn't love her right. Maybe it wasn't my head or my stomach. Maybe it was my tool."

Actually, it did look like a tool sometimes. Like hardware put out by Sears, to unscrew and disassemble into shaft and head and hang up on a pegboard in the cellar. Mordecai wondered if the knife had gone there and not in the heart.

Yet I could never imagine Max and Risa as a sexual couple. Perhaps I didn't want to. Ah, there, Doctor. What could be worse than puberty?

—*The boy must be handled with extreme care. Who knows
what he has seen?*
—*The group was without such evident shock, except for
him.*
—*But he was, after all, the youngest. His mother. His father—
brothers and sisters, perhaps, killed. Who can tell? The rec-
ords were burned. He refuses to talk.*
—*There is always a hazard with people like this. They come to
believe anything that they love may be taken away.*
—*He was found in block R. Criminals, some of them. And
women used by the SS. Plus a few malnourished adolescents.*
—*Who can tell what he has seen?*
—*Or how much of it he understands.*
—*Thank God he is too young to understand much of anything.
Particularly the camps.*
—*Tell me, Doctor. Do you understand the camps?*
—*We have no room for sophistry at the hospital, Doctor. Kindly
pass me his charts. And be grateful he can't speak or under-
stand English.*
—*All the same, I would like to see him five years from now. Or
else I would hate to.*

Thank you, Doctors. Five years from then I thought myself blessed. A good though ailing father, some local celebrity, a place to stay, no conformist manifesto disguised as
academic schedule, and art school all week long. True,
every Thursday I had to report to Mr. Lemmon, my parole
officer, who operated from a metal desk in a frosted glass
cubicle with last year's oxygen and a copper ashtray full of
L-shaped cigarettes. But to him I had no identity beyond
the last incarceration. Mr. Lemmon's walls and blotter were
of a green not attractive enough to be considered bilious.
He himself displayed a froglike tint, although that may
have been the reflection of surrounding color. He was, I
suppose, forty-five, but he seemed ancient to me, his authority bled out long ago. He had grown tired of waiting
for the kiss that would turn him into a prince, and now
whispered with great fatigue the sort of sagacity in which
he no longer believed. A Whitehall Street Polonius.

"Life," he told me, "is a river. You can't swim upstream. Tide's too strong. But you *can* choose what bank to land on. Now, which bank do you choose?"

"Chase National."

"That attitude is what gets people talking through a wire screen, Benoit."

"Sorry."

"Accepted. Have you been attending school regularly?"

"Yes, I have."

"Any problems, things I can help you with?"

"What sort of problems?"

"I don't know—money, that kind of thing. You need a job? Boy of your intelligence ought to get something commensurate with his—"

"I'll get money when I need it."

"Yes, but it says here your father is now unemployed."

"I'll get money when I need it."

"Don't be too proud, Ben. That's how we get repeaters, if you understand."

"I understand you, Mr. Lemmon. I'll be all right."

"Fine, fine. Next week, then."

So much for the in-depth probe.

Lemmon's cigarette was discarded with the interviewee. As I left, an assistant called, "Keeson, Jack." Keeson usually followed me on the roster, a pallid hunchback in his twenties. I had no idea what his history had been; prison, probably. He had a tattoo on his arm that read "Death Before Dishonor" and another of a heart that read "Jack Loves Myron."

Who could fathom the by-roads of affection in those days? Half of me wanted to stand at the door and eavesdrop; half wished to flee down the stairs and into the bright ungreen world. That half always won.

As I left I invariably heard the scrape and hiss of a match ignited. New client, new cigarette. I used to wonder about Lemmon's lungs. They must look, I thought, like Joe Louis's punching bags.

But it was the constant references to money that stayed with me when I made my way uptown. I had only Max's word that we had no financial stress. There was some sort of compensation that schools offered to the sons of professors from other schools. Max, however, no longer had a position. In New York, then as now, your status was defined by your job.

Never mind, I used to prod myself. You're here, for Chrissake. Until they kick you out, enjoy it. Who, me? Enjoy anything? Yes, you, you adolescent *shmuck.* You have some talent. Get to work. But Max, Risa . . . Never mind Max, never mind Risa. It's Benoit we have to worry about now. Remember him? Get to work. Draw. One line means nothing. Put in a second to emphasize. Now a third.

The Lasch Institute was a grid of vertical egos and horizontal achievements. The teachers had all of the attitudes of the genius, some of the instincts of the artist, few of the talents of the hack and none of the delight of the professional in his work. The undergraduates all imagined themselves to be Picassos and Lipchitzes, except that both of these artists were continually raked over for their excesses or pretensions. Our palettes were inadequate to our phosphorescent, light-dazzled visions of ourselves. We wished to arrive without a trip, to learn a language without bothering with the grammar, to receive recognition without payment of dues. In brief, we were art students. Drag a net through New York today and you will find the same relentless quarrels, the same fatuous theorists, the same unripe sophistication, the same eager, unfinished faces and canvases. Follow the embryo Maillols, Jackson Pollocks, David Smiths, Rothkos, Rauschenbergs, Warhols, and in five years see them peopling the cubicles in advertising agencies, polishing the graphics for NBC and Universal made-for-TV movies, churning out rabbits, nudes, vases, canny abstracts—buckeye for Originals, Inc. Galleries, *shlock* stores to the parvenu since 1968. All of the attitudes of the genius, some of the instincts of the artist, few of the talents of the hack and none of the delight of the professional in his work. O my America! my new-found-land.

As Donne tells me. Only in his case America is his mistress, and he is talking about humping. Yes. Well.

III

"Amateurish," said my oil-painting instructor. "Rudimentary. Your light suffers from too little halation. Look for color on the edge of light, not just the center."

He was correct. But I went on painting landscapes or bowls of flowers or something else in my old and stubborn manner. I remember suddenly a cartoon of a painting in which nude ladies leap over stiles and hedges and bend over to nibble grass. Two upholstered matrons regard the picture. "I still think," says one, "that he was at his best as a horse painter."

I was doing portraits of a field as if it had a face, or a bowl of fruit as if it had a nose and eyes. Only I couldn't find the eyes. All I could detect in the eggplants and pears and peppers were haunches and breasts, shoulders and the planes of the belly.

The universe lurked in my pencil. I drew—badly—a planet of women. None of the girls in my classes or the models on the podiums conformed to the proper specifications. They never would; I would see to that. For the real ones frightened me. No, terrified me. This was the early fifties, and they clung together like parasol ants and made uniformly acidulous remarks to the boys, except for one or two older and patently attractive lads who smoked pipes and affected massive indifference. Lawrence Pettit, for example. He was a big, tall dreamboat washed out of Yale Art School and soon to be a master of the target-and-flag *scuola di* Jasper Johns. Full of theories about the morality of the artist. "Take Ezra Pound," he liked to say, in a rich chocolaty bass that you could box, wrap in foil and take home for Mother's Day. "This man is a genius. A source. He had to obey the dictates of his own conscience, not the world's. He gave us Eliot, Joyce, *The Pisan Cantos.* It more than compensates for a few broadcasts for Mussolini."

I would learn in time to let stuff like that go. But I was still unfinished, still raw from the barbed-wire dreams, still harrowed by the flash cards I would deal myself involuntarily.

"No," I said. "No! Nothing compensates for that. Nothing can give back honor to those who capitulated. Even insanity is no excuse!"

"Now, Benoit," Pettit said with his mellow radio voice, "indiscretions hardly qualify—"

"Indiscretions! If helping Mussolini, if aiding Hitler is an indiscretion, then what is murder? A small error, a mistake? These men were major demons."

I saw my classmates exchanging embarrassed looks. Pettit assumed the role of conciliator. "Well, of course, no one is *proud* of what Pound did. Least of all Pound himself. And of course no one disputes the horrors of fascism for a minute. But equating propaganda with murder—really, I—"

"Propaganda is lies. And lies are a kind of murder, a killing of sense. Don't you see that? Don't you see if you say impurity one day you will say prison the next, and death the day after that?"

"No, I don't, Benoit. Just as there are degrees of good there are degrees of evil. If Pound committed a sin, I assure you it was a very venial one."

"What do you know of evil?" I caught a long shot of myself in the model's mirror. A mask of rage. A stranger.

"I know what I read. I know what I think. And I think any of us would be capable of committing evil under certain circumstances. Who of us has the right to judge Pound? Who has the right to condemn him?"

"More important," I said, "who has the right to forgive? The mother whose child bled into a mass grave? The soldiers disemboweled in the streets? The witnesses who survive, like Pound, with half their wits gone? They have no right to forgive. That would be the greatest sin of all!"

Here the teacher entered, and staring at my disarranged face, asked us to sit down and turn to our work. After the class there were a few who had the temerity to agree with me and give Pettit some backchat. But most of the students never read anything deeper than the side of Grumbacher crayons. The brighter ones were put down by the Pettit surety. I envied him that—and his looks, and his wardrobe. Hell, I envied him his dandruff. I always wanted a tone like that, an aura of certainty; they gave them out at prep schools with the diplomas. For the rest of us there ought to be correspondence schools. Dogma correspondence school for the unsure. Attic Wit correspondence school for those who think of stinging replies in the subway home. Erogenous correspondence schools fo · those like the present deponent, who would have had trouble seducing a girl in a brothel. Military correspondence school for those who lack discipline in their lives. Drill by mail. Receive demerits in the privacy of your own home. Honor system bayonet practice. Pennies per day.

I never said another word about Pound, and very few at all to Pettit. The problem of evil was an uncrackable egg, anyway. Maybe he was right. Maybe nobody had a corner on vileness or cruelty. Maybe the artist was immune to moral criticism. I liked to think that I would have made no broadcasts for Mussolini. Who is so low as to reject the role of martyr in the imagination? But after all, good people had done worse. Eleazar Jassy killed. Perhaps I might have killed. I was too young then; I would never know. The hell with Pound. And with strident theories about the liberty of the composer, the writer, the artist, the citizen, the Jew, the Gypsy.

I concentrated on my work. Also on Jean, Marilyn, Patricia, Joan, the girls who attended classes in sculpture and oil painting, perspective and architectural rendering. From whom I received a series of cold, albeit bare shoulders, draped in the peasant blouses of the period, garments that were demurely fixed about the neck until the wearer left Mama in the morning, then on the IRT were lowered to the fashionable limit. The swells and valleys used to drive me up and down walls, but neither hints nor the straight Harpo Marx onslaught ever won me acceptance as a human being, much less a suitor. I was only Max Kaufman's son, a curio. Until Laura Zimmerman. Jewish girl. Very large hazel eyes, disproportionate irises, beaded lashes, lots of peculiar tie-dyed shirts a decade before their time, voluminous skirts, good legs hidden by yards of cloth and stained smocks. Laura wanted to be a weaver or a textile designer. Hence the antique, not to say bizarre cut of her clothes, all homemade.

One afternoon when we were turpentining the stains out of our skins and smocks, I asked her if she would like a cup of coffee.

She finished wiping her hands. "Why not?"

It was as if a lifer had been granted a pardon. I felt my skin warm and then tighten. I must have fallen all over my feet getting her downstairs and steering her to one of the local coffee shops that scattered a few tables on the sidewalk Deux Magots style. I had rehearsed a few opening lines. Her sculptures resembled the work of Bernard Reder, whose whimsical bicyclists and idiots playing cat's cradle still exert a lunatic appeal. When we sat down I burbled a few bars of praise for Reder and waited for her assent.

"Facile," she said.

"Me or Reder?"

"Him. Ackshully both of you. You both have facility."

"What's wrong with that?"

"Nothing, except that facility is so . . . facile."

I asked her about the latest paintings of Max Ernst. He too was facile. So were the recent movies of De Sica and the final architecture of Frank Lloyd Wright. As well as all the instructors. I omitted to ask her about the cave paintings at Lascaux. I figured we all knew how facile *Pithecanthropus erectus* was.

Still, I couldn't help telling her that she reminded me of my stepsister, who, the first time I met her at the faculty senate, announced: "I learned a new word today. Try to surmise what it is. I'll give you three surmises."

Laura gave me a smile without any teeth. But she consented to go to a movie. I forget what we saw. John Garfield on a boat. *The Breaking Point*, probably. "Sure, sure, push me around." Slum kid on his way up and down. She watched the film; I watched her, part of the time. There is much to be said for the reticence of that period. In this epoch, when licenses are distributed for all behavioral extremes, when you can step into a massage parlor and get anything you want—dogs, chickens, little girls, black, white, yellow hookers, little boys, cantaloupes, catchers' mitts, troilism, daisy chains, fellatio, cunnilingus, whips, high heels, chains, leather goods, rubber, sadomasochism, hard-core, soft-core, gang bangs, personal vibrators, French ticklers, foot, knee, nape, nose, navel fetishists, fag, dyke, straight rapes, perversions of all nations—there is something to be said for the hand resting upon the upper slope of the brassiere.

At the Institute we were a little more fortunate than most other adolescents. We could, after all, attend a figure-drawing class and see all the flesh—usually about four acres per model —that we wanted, much as medical students can always take a cervical smear if curiosity gets desperate. But these models were rendered almost asexual by the instructor, and by their own overripeness and superannuity. They did little for the mind and nothing at all for the organs. I was subject to more fitful erections on the Fifth Avenue bus than in class. Masturbation fantasies centered around Rhonda Fleming's Titian boobs, Joanne Dru's and Jennifer Jones's bright overbites and the tapered legs of the Goldwyn Girls. Locally the female students did us—most of us—no good. I was told that Anne Feretti spread for anybody with the price of two orchestra seats to any Sinatra appearance, but I never tried. She seemed to be walled in by a throng of sniffing classmates. I guess they all had aisle seats at the Paramount. But that evening with Laura, with my arm first around her waist, then with my fingers in her hair, then on her blouse, I felt as excited, I am sure, as any poor john now on Eighth Avenue getting his brains blown out.

The edge of the bra was the perimeter of Eros. I was not allowed to explore any further, and like any well-bred soul of the period, I refrained. There was lots of time. My opening had not been the gaffe I thought; obviously she was still attracted or all this would not have happened. I would turn the conversation away from art to literature. When we walked out into the night air I spoke of plans to create a new kind of art and a world free from angst; then segued adroitly to Romeo and Juliet, mocking my own fantasies with a slight Garfield turn of the head. "True, I talk of dreams,

> Which are the children of an idle brain,
> Begot of nothing but vain fantasy;
> Which is as thin of substance as the air,
> And more inconstant than the wind . . ."

"It stinks like a gas stove outside," Laura said nasally. Con Edison was, as usual, working the street. "Dig We Must for a Greater New York." I held my tongue with my teeth. We walked on in silence in the oppressive afternoon. After a pause she said softly, "Could I ask you a question, Ben?"

Ah, now the Bard was reworking his erotic magic, slowly, fatefully . . .

"Of course," I said, matching her tone.

"You won't get mad?"

"No."

"Are you part Negro or what? I mean you're always tan. But you never go on vacation or anything. You *are* angry."

I wondered how I could use this to my advantage. Should I refer to my skin as an off-color joke? Or tell her that she wanted everything in black and white? Or ask if she dated by percentages of melanin, in which case I could ask if she had change for a quota? But no. I told Laura that I was a Gypsy. I thought that this might intrigue her. Dark flashing eyes, tales of romantic caravans, Carmen and Don José . . .

"You mean like those people in storefronts?" she asked me.

"Sort of."

"I thought they were dark because they didn't wash."

"Maybe they don't. Or maybe they descend from tribes back in India. Anyway, there's all kinds of Gypsies. The English ones are fairer than Van Johnson."

"Yeah, huh?"

"Yeah."

She chewed that one for a while. Then she asked, "What language do you speak?"

"English. What language do you speak?"

"Don't be so thin-skinned. I'm just curious. I never talked to a Gypsy before. You sure you're a Gypsy?"

"You want to see my kennel papers?"

"Don't be facile. Your father doesn't look so dark. Judging from the picture in the *Times.*"

"He's not my real father. I'm adopted."

"That's a switch." Laura liked that. "I thought the Gypsies always snatched other people's babies."

"You're a regular information booth, you know that?" I told her.

"I used to feel sorry for you," she returned as we moved to

the subway kiosk on Fourteenth Street, "because I heard you were in a concentration camp."

"Who told you that?"

"I don't know. Roger."

Roger Kinsella. With whom I shared some self-hardening clay on Thursday afternoons. We had split a sandwich one evening, and the cashier had a number on his arm and Roger asked what the numbers meant and I told him. He asked how I knew. I told him that, too. Fucker couldn't keep his mouth shut. Well, Laura had cared enough to ask about me. Before tonight, anyway.

"But now," she went on, "I mean, you're no different from all the others. In spite of your background, you're just a smart-ass."

"Not smart. Just facile-ass."

"See what I mean?"

"You ever think maybe *because* of my background I'm a smart-ass?"

"Don't hand me that." She lingered at the top of the Up-town The Bronx and Queens entrance. "However many Gypsies were in the prisons, there were more Jews."

"I know," I said. "I saw them."

"Well, so did I, afterward. And some of them were screwed up, and some were sad, but most of them were nice. And not one of them was a smart-ass."

"Well, I guess that was lucky for you."

"I guess it was."

Was that the year of the New Look? I seem to remember too much skirt, an excess of surface so that even the calves were hidden. Yet I seem to remember them bidding an impudent farewell. I knew nothing of sexual tension in that blue time. In Laura's wake came a cloud of perfume or body powder that had entered my nostrils earlier. Plus something else. Pheromones. The sheep mask fell away and I wandered Fourteenth Street like a rank and skulking predator, adding my sweat scent to the malodorous night. The solidity of the fierce dark commercial street was insulting, cacophonous, profane. The memories were coming back, the bad times. I felt undone, bent backward like the ribs of a reversed umbrella. The place was redolent of exhalations. Storefronts looked like yawns. The night itself was some kind of aperture, a passage to despair. A drunk wove up to me, vertiginous, thick-maned, stubble-jawed, mumbling something from a fence of teeth. My nerves burst from my fingers as he collared me. I pushed and lost my footing.

There was a garbage can lying on its side, and tumbling over it, I thudded to the sidewalk, splaying fingers on the cement. As I rose I could see the passers-by regarding me as the drunk, and the drunk as someone who had been wronged. I stumbled eastward, a bleeding and scarified loser.

There were a series of hookers who used to ply the peripheries of Union Square. One by one they called at me from doorways, "Want to come up?" "Hey, handsome, got any time for me?" "Whaddya say, sailuh?" This from a black-haired chalky girl who could not have been more than eighteen. Her face was older, but her hands—always the giveaway—were a child's, unlined and still rounded with adolescent fat. My head and loins smarted from Laura's dismissal.

"How much?" I asked.

"Twenny dolluhs, sailuh." Georgia, sounded like. Or Alabama.

I looked toward the Square, where in those days knots of men would gather to argue about God or politics, or to wheedle and beg, or to pick up women, or to cruise, or to panhandle, or to start fights, or to tease the whores.

"If He exists, why is there murder?" one of them was shouting. "Why are there poor?"

"Awright, honey, fifteen," she said. "Because you're you."

"Why is there pain?"

"Because you're not alive without nerves. Nerves cause pain. You want no pain, you got to be dead."

I felt in my pocket. I had four fives. My allowance for the week.

"Come on, sailuh. You kin affawd it."

"You got change of ten, sister?"

"Hey, Aggie, you got change of ten?"

"No!"

"Then keep the whole dime."

"Besides, what you consider evil, God may consider good. Conversely, what you consider good—"

"We're still suffering from the Depression, ya know that?"

"We're still suffering from Roosevelt, is what we're suffering from."

"I blame Eleanor. She made the bullets and he slung 'em. Caved right in to the Reds. Red himself, you ask me!"

"Your average Commie, he lives worse than a pig in Iowa."

"You got it, sailuh. I know you got it."

I could get by on hamburgers with the remaining five, if my art supplies held out. "All right," I said.

She gave me a ceramic grin. "What's the name, sailuh?"

"Freud."

"Okay, Fred. Le's go."

"He gave us war, he gave us taxes. All for what? For the Jews is what! Franklin D. Rosenfeld."

"Take away suffering, you take away existence."

"Hey, I don't mind that Agnes only made twenny dollars and twenny-five cents las' night. But who gave her a quarter?"

"Everybody."

Up the stairs. Why is it hookers always live up the stairs? The height of passion? Elevation of mankind? They used to take the girls and bring them to the second floor—no, the third. We could see the lights. Sometimes the shades were drawn, sometimes not.

ITEM: Tens of thousands of defenceless Gypsies were herded together in Transadniestrin. Over half were struck by typhus. The gendarmerie practised unprecedented terror; everyone's life was uncertain; tortures were cruel. The commanders lived in debauchery with Gypsy women and maintained personal harems. Approximately 36,000 Gypsies fell victim to Antonescu's fascist regime.

—J. Schechtman, "The Gypsy Problem," *Midstream* (November 1966)

ITEM: SS Officer Broad got up an orchestra in the Gypsy camp, and once a full-scale concert was arranged. But this was inter-

rupted by a curfew during which the SS came to fetch many
hundreds of Gypsies to be gassed. Later all instruments were
taken away, and this spelled the loss of interest for many. The
SS men came sometimes in the evenings and took girls off to
dance in their barracks. Through this contact the Gypsies knew
of their coming annihilation.

—H. Langbein, *Der Auschwitz Prozess*
(Vienna: Europa, 1965)

—*Who is that? Anna?*
—*Yes, Anna. With two men.*
—*I recognize one. Lieutenant Straus.*
—*What will they do?*
—*Listen to this, boys, will you? Repeat what you said, Benoit.*
—*I only asked what they do.*
—*They sleep together, what do you think they do?*
—*I don't know.*
—*You don't know. Of course you don't know. You're too young
to know anything.*
—*Look, they're doing it. You can just see the shadows on the
wall.*
—*Why do they move when they're sleeping?*
—*Will you listen to him? You think they really* sleep *together?
Snore and fart like your Aunt Lela and Uncle Jan?*
—*How do I know?*
—*Yes, how do you know? How should you?*
—*Let Benoit alone.*
—*But he knows nothing. He's an ignoramus.*
—*He's only a child.*
—*I am not only a child. I am a young man. Papa said so.*
—*Papa said so. Papa said so. Listen to him.*
—*Melchior, shut up! No one who is here is a child.*
—*I will not shut up. Listen, Benoit, you want to know what they
do up there?*

Up the warped, protesting stairs. Ululations from the courtyard, or from the other rooms. Black girls looking out from two
of the doors.

"Agnes got a live one."

"Hey, Agnes, look like he under the legal limit. Better throw him back till he git bigger."

"Never mahnd them nigguhs, honey. You come in and get all comfy, y'heah? Lemme take off your shirt. Don't back away. Y'all been a sailuh long enough to know how to treat me."

My damp hands on her dry thighs. Her body all shadows heaped on shapes. A humid, inescapable malaise. Would it be possible, with it beating like that, to have an extinguished heart? Sixteen years of knocking against the walls of the hairless chest. Always the youngest. The others were always hairier, had veins, while my arms seemed juvenile and narrow. Charlie would know what to do here. Or Ruben. *Ruben's dead, Benoit.* Oh, Ruben, hear me. Make it all right, Ruben. I want her. No, I don't want her. Yes, I do. But can I do it? The thin shift over her head and the etiolated flesh, the red-eyed breasts staring. "Don't shake so, honey. Let me take this off you. Tha's right. You jus' lemme wash you with a little rubbin' alcohol. You're so hot, sailuh. You just a walkin' radiator. You prob'ly runnin' a fevuh, honey. Agnes gone cool you off ri' now. This gone be a night to remembuh."

Anger stirs in my carnival skin.

"Oh, my, looka that! Lemme lie down, honey, you get up and ride."

"Agnes! I got a trick. Out here!"

A coal voice, with the scrape of sore authority. The sound of a black pimp.

"Nemmine what you got. I got a trick right in here. Ah'm doin' fine."

"Well, git him finish. Man wants you. Got no uthu fays out here."

"Bettuh hurry up, honey. Hurry! Goddamn it. Move! Tha's just so fine. Now go git clean up."

—*Listen, Benoit, he doesn't just sleep with her.*
—*Shut up, Melchior.*
—*You shut up yourself. He sticks it in her cunt, in her ear, in her throat, in her ass. All over.*
—*Does it hurt? She says he hurt her.*

*—Like hell it hurt her. She loved it. They all love it. All whores
love it.*
—Look at this little fish hit. Stop it, Little Fish.
—Benoit, stop causing a fuss. The guards will come.
—I'll kill him.
—You minnow, you couldn't kill time.
—You insulted Anna.
—Anna insulted Anna.
—Don't listen to him, Benoit. Anna has no choice.

No choice. Who can select in this barbed-wire republic?
Suppose we are what Grandfather Piet says, parts of a snake
eating its own tail. Then the world will consume itself, is
consuming itself now. Maybe this is what the ovens mean, the
mouths of those engines, the driving, prodding guards. Mama,
I want to be a dog, I heard a little red-haired girl cry. Because
the sentries like dogs. Well, I want to be a snake.

Our bodies are to be devoured, then. And my body not
even formed. A hatchling, I feel myself, newborn, wriggling
into morning. The other boys are older, bigger, hirsute, talk
in terse, opaque sentences. There is a connection I cannot
make between contempt and sex. Women are virgins or
cunts. But what women can they know besides the ones in
the caravan? And there is no promiscuity in the caravan.
How can there be? Even a dancer is protected by her musicians. Flirtation implies betrothal. Violation is punished by
banishment. My father remembered a woman screaming
when they cut part of her ear off for sleeping with a man not
her husband. Was the caravan a lie? Am I dreaming now,
looking out the window at my sister's shadow moving in the
fan of light?

"Okay, sailuh, leave the money on the desk."
But I wanted more; I wanted Agnes again.
She sat up in bed in the half-light. The pimp kept banging
on the door.
"Awright," she snapped. "Don't git your bawls in an
uproah." More banging. Agnes slowly put her shift on over her
head, like a curtain coming down on a play. Through the cloth

she shouted at the pimp, "Up your rosy-red rectum with a red-hot railroad ramrod."

"Gone cost you" came the reply.

She opened the door and blinked out into the hall. I thanked her and she laughed. "Nobody ever done that before." She touched my hand. Then she saw them and winced. The pimp was not large but wide, with the mouth of a truck grille. The john was my height, but about fifty. Both were dressed in dark pleated suits. The pimp pushed Agnes back, and I said it was my fault; I was the one who wanted to stay. He looked away, then put his open palm against a loose fist and drove his elbow backward. A shrewd piece of business; it went into my solar plexus and for a while there was no air and no hope of getting any. I sank down against the wall, my mouth open, retching for breath.

"How they hangin', sailor?" he asked.

I said, "I'd like to return the unused portion and get my money back."

The door slammed and the men went inside with Agnes. There was an undertow of grunts and inaudible chatter. A slap. The door opened and the pimp came out alone. He stood over me. "Git up," he said. I found it hard to rise. "I only stand for 'The Star-Spangled Banner,' " I grunted.

"Ah mawn give you fi minutes to shove off back to ship. Nen you gone be one sick sailuh." He hesitated at the head of the stairs. "Question of mind over mattuh," he said. "I don't mind. And you don't mattuh." He went on down, galumphing. "Gon git a cop," he said. He probably was going to get one, too. Always the offender, I forced myself to my feet. The midsection was sore but nothing was broken or pierced. I heard giggles from behind the door. A night to remember.

The trip downstairs was a little shaky, but I had eaten very little and the nausea was easy to put down. The envy was another matter. Everyone was more at home in the world than Benoit: the citizens crossed the Square, the whores and their customers operated with marked ease. Everyone had a destination, a sense of self. Except Benoit. I felt stateless. Exhaust came out to meet me. I rubbed my gut and felt the slow return of appetite. I still wanted Agnes. And the money was gone. Christ! For that furtive hustle. The arena of the glands was still filled.

"What is history?" A black-haired, cadaverous man on the order of John Carradine was addressing a group. "History is a cage in which we prowl like tigers. The bars are built by capital. The zookeeper is the state. And the meat—the meat, my friends, is you and me, all of us feeding on each other. To bend those bars, to break them requires strength. The strength of a group, a party."

He waved some pamphlets and raised his *Daily Worker*. There were two policemen near him, and it occurred to my primitive social sense that I would never find a better definition of irony. Here was my father railroaded out of his position while some half-cracked zealot of the same persuasion was carefully afforded the protection of New York's finest—probably on orders from the governor. But a few minutes later, when the speaker began to hail passers-by and one jostled him and knocked the papers to the ground, the cops were nowhere in sight. The man stood his ground and two beery, overweight trucker types who had pushed him around stared back with hot, pink-rimmed eyes. I prayed that the confrontation would go no further because I knew something in me would be forced into the fray and that this time I would not come off with a mere bruise of the lower digestive tract.

The evening assumed a phosphorescence, the outlines of the men too brilliant and the dark very charred. I sat down on a bench. It was full of splinters and several cut into my arm as I leaned back, but the wood seemed part of me, or I seemed part of it, and the notion that thin shards were entering my body seemed irrelevant, as if pieces of me might just as easily enter into them. Agnes was right; I must have been running a temperature, but all I felt was heat and envy of all the surety, even that of the anti-Semites and the Communists and the degenerates who knew who and what they were.

And now the men did fight and I had to go forward, pitching into that tiny gyre of the black-haired man and his adversaries, pushing into it with lunatic strength. The victim of the truckers could not fight at all and caved in when they hit him. I was fast enough to avoid their first punches, and cut one square on the nose. His friend caught me on the side of the head and the speckled ground came up to meet my jaw. I was out for a time, not long, and when I sat up they were gone and the police were back, looking down at me.

"He's awright," one of them said.

"You want witnesses? You wanna prefer charges?" another said. "We have one of the perpetrators in custody." They had the Carradine man. His eyes looking down at me narrowed in contempt or—who knows?—hate, perhaps. Maybe he wanted to get beat up. Win him a lot of points at headquarters. The cops narrowed their eyes when they looked back at him. I awarded the evening to the police on a slit decision. I told them I would not prefer charges. Go explain to those blunt guardians that the man they had in custody was the most innocent of us all.

Max, thou shouldst have been with us in that hour. You would have loved it. A paradigm of your capitalistic corruption. Except that when the cops had gone the dark-haired man began lecturing me on liberty à la Lenin: "It is true that freedom is precious—so precious that it must be rationed." That was all I needed. Had I aided the wrong side? When he launched into history I pushed on. Maybe history was the nightmare from which we were trying to waken, but for me nightmares were the history from which *I* was trying to awaken. And I could not seem to do it.

ITEM: I was kept six weeks at the police station and then sent to Auschwitz . . . Two Gypsies tried to escape but were caught, beaten and hanged . . . Once I was given twenty-five blows with a whip because I had given some bread to a new arrival. One day I saw Elisabeth Koch kill four Gypsy children because they had eaten the remains of some food. Another time we stood for two hours in front of the crematorium but were sent back to the barracks. I was given lashes a second time for taking bread from a dead prisoner. Dr. Mengele injected me with malaria. I was then in the sick bay with my uncle. Some Gypsies carried me to another block just before all the patients in the sick bay, including my uncle, were killed.

—Barbara Richter, Auschwitz *matriocola*
Z. 1963 (Padua: Lacio Drom, no. 2)

E Block.

The outer limits of faith. Afternoon, steam in the brain. A bleak, pinched man with wire-rimmed glasses below the sign: *Arbeit macht frei.* Work liberates. He holds a trembling sheaf of notes. I should be grateful to escape with my life, he says to Eleazar Jassy. But I must keep this manuscript, too. At all costs. It is my life's work. Mathematical theorems. Do you understand? Eleazar comprehends. A grin moves across his face, then mine. But then a piteous look takes its place, then amusement, mockery, insult. He bellows the German national anthem: "Shit." The man's face changes in a moment. He becomes another of the phantoms. There is no life but this one. Pity is for the living; envy is for the dead.

"When we say the state, the state is We, it is the proletariat, it is the advanced guard of the working class. Comrade Lenin speaks to us all."

"Look around you, my friend. Who owns the *Times*, the radio stations? Sulzberger, Ochs, Paley, Sarnoff. Who owns Hollywood? Cohn, Goldwyn, Mayer. Hebrew is at the base of all our troubles. And I have not begun to mention the banks."

"Just enough to eat is what I want. A quarter, a dime, anything."

Voices from the knots of people, the gatherings of men. Only men. Not even any couples. The women out tonight are hookers.

"My friends, if there are laws of gravity, laws of chance, why is it not possible that there are laws of affection, anxiety, rage, envy?"

"Listen to me: the rational mind is a knife capable of murder or suicide when it is not opening packages."

"Antecedents mock without intention. Monkeys parody men, movement makes fun of words. Capitalism caricatures progressivism."

The algebra of discourse. The geometry of fanaticism. I tried to rise from my body, to convince myself that I felt nothing. The wounds in my fingers still stung, matched by the scrapes on the side of the face. But my brush-fired mind made them fade. At the edge of the Square, near where the artists maintained studios and looked down on all this, I saw a new group of prostitutes, and when they looked at their bruised, disreputable target they turned away. All but one. She was a light-skinned black girl, a victim of vigorous hair straightening. About my age, I would guess. But she had absolutely no Southern overtones. This was someone off the asphalt. "How about it?" she said. "You got the price? Fifteen."

I supposed that made it bargainable to ten. But all I had left was five. I told her that and turned my pockets inside out for proof. "Sorry," she said. "Not enough. Not near enough." I had nothing to offer but my watch. This was, in truth, a present from Max and Risa. A Benrus worth maybe fifty dollars when new. I took it off and held it up. "I'll give you this," I said. "But I want to stay all night."

She looked it over like a pawnbroker casing an antique gold wedding ring through a loupe. "I dunno," she said. "Wait a minute." And consulted with her colleagues. The three went over to a car where a sluggish, veal-faced man in a Panama hat sat lounging in the passenger's seat smoking a cigar. He took the watch and held it up to the streetlight, then lit a match and examined the back. The engraving read, in minuscule script:

> *"The Future is something which everyone reaches at the rate of 60 minutes an hour, whatever he does, whoever he is."*
>
> Always Love Max and Risa

C. S. Lewis. Whose Christian conscience Max loathed, even though he dog-eared Lewis' *Seventeenth Century English Prose.* The quote was put there to teach me to put on the brakes. Mordecai preferred "Death is nature's way of telling you to slow down." I preferred Lewis' idea about the road to

hell being without milestones or signposts; a ramp, I concluded, and not a stairs. I thought about that, watching the
man twirl my watch by its metal expansion band, then nod to
the girl. "Come on," she said and grabbed my arm before he
could change his mind.

Her place was not as depressing as Agnes' in one way, more
erosive in other ways. It was freshly painted, and looked lived
in. The bed was wide and the sheets looked fresh. There was
incense burning on a bookshelf, flanked by a volume on either
side. One was *The Prophet* by Kahlil Gibran. The other was
a *Reader's Digest* condensation of four books. On its side was
a Bible. A Gideon, stolen from some hotel. I began to feel tears
at the side of my mouth. I don't know why, but that Bible
wiped me out. I kept looking at it, and then I started to cry.

"What's the matter?" she said. "What's your name, anyway?"

I told her the truth.

"What's the matter, Ben? You can tell me. We got all
night."

"I couldn't tell you if I had all week, all month." The tears
kept coming up in my eyes and I couldn't blink them back.

"You crying about your watch?" she said. "Because if you
want to change your—"

No, I told her, I wasn't crying about my watch.

" 'Cause you got hurt, then? I can see you been in a fight."

"No, I don't hurt from that fight. I don't know why I'm
crying. But I feel hurt in my throat. In my head."

"Take off your clothes." She went over to the window and
lowered the shade. "I'll fix it where it hurts. I'm not putting
this down so folks can't see in. I'm fixing it so I can't see out.
We'll make a little world here. Right here."

I asked her not to do that, to leave the shade alone. She
blinked at me and said nothing. I went to the window and
raised the shade on the violent tenor of life, humanity in its
own redoubling filth. Love has built his mansion in the place
of excrement. As Yeats tells me. But all I saw was excrement.
And love, that degraded fantasy, hawked by troubadors,
boomed by groups who ironed their hair and babbled of green

fields on the blackened cement—love was a rite without basis, a convention to keep people from liquidating their neighbors. I would never have any except for this caricature, this purchased variety, and even that only so long as the bills and watches held out.

When both of us had taken our clothes off, she pushed me down and lay on top of me and then sat up suddenly, holding her arm against my shoulder.

"You partly black?"

"You're the second person to ask me that tonight," I said.

"Well, are you?"

"Does it make a difference?"

"No. Yeah, it does." She got up and walked across the room to the refrigerator and got out a can of beer. She poured it into two glasses. "I never laid a quadroon before."

"I'm not colored," I said. "Not that it makes any difference. I'm a Gypsy."

"A Gypsy!" She handed me my beer and sat down on the edge of the bed. "No shit? A Gypsy. I never laid one of those before either. Well, here's to firsts. You ever laid a colored girl before?"

"No," I said, and drank up.

"If you were colored for one hour you'd never want to be white again. If you are white."

"It says Caucasian on my papers."

—*Let me see your papers.*

—Zigeuner. *Over to the right.*

—*Your attention. Criminals will wear a green triangle; Jehovah's Witnesses purple; shiftless elements such as Gypsies, black. Feeble-minded will wear an armband with the word* Blöde.

When will this stop, this ceaseless revolution of the cerebrum, always backward, backward to the recesses of obscenity? The future is something that everyone reaches . . . Well, let me reach it then, let me go from this swamp of my childhood. Let me go, God, release me, give me a passport from these sins.

Oh, Daniel, if I could have severed my head from my shoulders that night, I would have done it, submitted myself to the executioner, the hatchet man.

Dena came out of the hut at the end of the quadrangle, limping. She cannot have been Negro, she must have been pure Gypsy, a throwback maybe, or was M. Proust right when he told me that there are distortions in time as well as space, and do they include the shading of skin? I seem to see her as brown, and she exits, her dress wet in the middle, with blood running down one leg.

She collapses on the ground and two heavy clumping soldiers come toward her, one on either side, and get her to her feet. I recall Dena from the caravan, much younger than my sister Anna. Only a year before she was wandering through the fields dragging a rag doll with her wherever she went. The soldiers try to pull the girl back toward the hut. She is whimpering quietly, incoherently, pushing her bare feet in the powdery ground, kicking up small yellow clouds. Once they get her in the hut, her screams continue, now muffled by wood and by hard sounds from the men. In the very early morning she is thrown out, cold and broken. Something inside Dena is punctured; she bleeds from the nose and ears and an hour later perishes in her mother's arms. Her mother is named Olga, a fierce, argumentative woman once; as she holds her dead child she becomes a dark, shaking figure incapable of speech. She can only wail until they call formation for attendance. Olga starts for the place where we always assemble, then breaks away and dashes in the direction of the fences. Some women attempt to restrain her but she is like a demon. Thrashing around, breaking their holds, Olga ascends the steel-chain fence. Several infantrymen raise their rifles. A dog barks, pulling against his leash. The major holds up his hand to keep his men from firing. Dena's mother climbs higher, higher, until she is just below the electrified portion. There is a low chorus of "No," until she seizes the wire and then there is a clamorous silence. No breathing. No wind. No machines. Nothing. Her body gives a galvanic twitch, then another, and drops down like a gunshot bird. The major gives a mirthless laugh and walks away. The women come close to the body and touch it gingerly at first, as if it still harbors electricity. Then they take it up in their hands and bear her back.

Somewhere in that night the candles guttered and we went to sleep. I seemed to scorch the sheets, and dreams projected themselves even when I opened my eyes on the screen of ceiling. The girl slept next to me, but when I put my hand on her brown back she jumped and gave a painful little moan, as if she had been scalded. My heart leaped in its case and I felt at once chilled and soaking. There was not enough air in the room. I put on my clothing, my mouth clattering and my hands shaking. I could hardly stand on one leg to get my pants on. I undid the three locks on her door and went downstairs. Was Max still awake? Should I call in case he was sitting up, worried? What time was it? My watch was gone, there was no clock in that little room, and no timepiece visible on the street. It must have been three-thirty or four, just after the little rush hours of cleaning women and lobster shifts; immediately before the early truck deliveries, the fresh new patrolmen and the pugnacious sunrisers who like to get a three-hour start on the world. It is the only time of day when the city catches its breath, when even the pushers, even the muggers are asleep.

There was no one out; I was alone in the Square. A wind came up and searched through my clothing. I got chilled again and felt in my pockets for change. I wandered toward the subway. At its entrance there were a few people coming home, and down the block I could see a man, about thirty, bouncing on the soles of his feet, walking with manic purpose, almost running. There was something about him that looked half familiar, but my eyes were not focusing well and I looked away. There was an all-night cafeteria nearby, and I thought for a moment of going in and having a hamburger or a cup of coffee, but nausea intervened. I hesitated at the subway entrance. The bouncing man crossed the street. He was perhaps fifty feet from me when a cab came by. In those days before crime-inhibiting bulbs, headlights were the only device for illuminat-

the temporary glare. His image was clear, then obscure. The walk, the expression, the steady, unmoving eyes had survived. It was Eleazar Jassy, out of context but still alive. Still living, while my family was dead. I felt a new chill and opened my mouth to speak. The cab stopped; Eleazar must have hailed it; it was gone before I had enough presence of mind even to look for the license. I ran up the street to a telephone. My heart seemed unable to keep up with my movements, and I was stricken with sudden harsh, crippling cramps in my legs and stomach. I dialed home. It rang a long, long time before Mordecai answered. I must have said something to help him locate me. All I remember is the heavy *pissoir* smell of the telephone booth and my legs giving way. I awoke to the white, neutral walls of Beth Israel Hospital and the equine voice and steady stare of Risa.

"Well, here we are again," she said. "Me in in in transit and you lying down on the job. As usual."

"Habit," I said. "Irresistible. Like gravity."

"Or being in love," she replied. An odd thing for her to say. "Benoit"—she sat on the edge of the bed—"now now that you're stuck in one place, I want to talk to you. Seriously."

"I'm too weak to talk."

"I'll talk. You listen. There's nothing wrong with you but but but extreme fatigue. Now, Max will be here in a few minutes and before he comes I have some some some things to say. Please pay attention to me."

"Okay."

"You're new at this business of sex, Benoit. Don't look away. You are. We know where you spent the night. The police found the man with your watch."

She handed it to me.

I said nothing. I was too weak, and, yes, too full of whatever passed for shame in my raisin brain that fall.

A nurse came in, dropped off a tray and glanced at me. Boy trades watch for night with hooker, her face said, is found senseless in phone booth. She walked out, inhaling loudly through her nose.

I said, finally, "I'm sorry, Risa."

"I'm the one who should apologize, Benoit. I'm the one who's done the most wrong. I—oh, how how *how* shall I put this?"

I shrugged and wished for the nurse to come in again with a pill, an injection, a bedpan, a dirty look, anything.

Risa went on: "Love, affection, sex, whatever we call it. It's like like the measles, Benoit. I mean to say, the older we get the harder it goes with us. I tried for a long, long time to stay with Max. He's a fine man, a concerned man, a good teacher. I like him very much."

"But you don't love him?"

"I thought I did. Then we came here and I met Fred. It has everything going against it. He's black, he's wrapped up in his mission—he's married, Benoit. Did you know that? But still we we we fell in love. Just like in the books. You try not to. You really do push against it. And then just when you think you're over it, when you make up a list of everything that's wrong wrong wrong with him and you and it, you're in it even deeper. I don't expect you to forgive me for leaving Max. And certainly not for leaving you. I I I only expect you to remember me. And remember this. Because one day it may happen to you. Then perhaps you'll understand. Perhaps not forgive, but understand. That's all I can ask."

She stood up. "Is there anything I can get you?"

She reached out her hand and I took it and looked up at her and I could feel myself shaking. "Risa," I said, "listen, don't worry about Max and me. You do what's right. You're not my mother. He's not my father. I have something worse to worry about."

She sat down on the bed again. "Benoit—" she began. "What you did was was was in its own way perfectly normal. After all, a boy your your age is practically a man. And in these times—"

"No, Risa, listen," I pleaded with her. "Last night, just before I made the call, I saw Eleazar Jassy. From the camps. You know who he is?"

"How could I know? You never talked about those days. And we never asked you. Max and I—"

"He was a killer. A Kapo. He murdered for the Germans. He killed Gypsies like me. Younger, even. He hanged them, shot them. He liked to hurt. I know he did. He was Gypsy himself. And yet, and yet . . ."

"Benoit, stop that. Nurse!"

God knows what I looked like. Probably something out of Gogol, with chalky skin and hollow glaring eyes and a mouth that would not quit. But I felt all right. I really did. I was certain that last night's glimpse was not a hallucination.

The others were not buying. Max had been outside the door, waiting discreetly with Mordecai, and now, upon hearing Risa's alarm, they burst in. Max with a "Whassamatter?" and Mordecai with a "What are you hollering? For a *meshugge*, de boy looks perfectly normal."

I told them all what I had seen. Disbelief stared back at me. Charitably, of course. Indulgently. The boy has been ill, the faces testified. Who can tell what's kicking around in his system: fever, syphilis spirochetes, sulfa pills, recollections? He threw up all morning, the doctors said. Now his brain is vomiting the agonies of the past.

"No," I protested. "I saw him. I know it was Eleazar. It couldn't have been a mistake. You just don't make mistakes like that."

There was a hasty conference.

"Ben, Ben," Max began. "All right. Maybe you saw him. But isn't it just possible it was someone else? It was late. You were sick, running a high fever."

"Also," added Mordecai, "how good could the light have been?"

"I saw him, Mordecai. I swear I saw him." My head was light; at that moment, I doubted for the first time.

"Boychick, I don't know; maybe you did. Only sometimes I see my sister from the beck, *shlepping* up Broadway. Vit her fet enkles, carrying a shopping bag. I run up—it's not Sophie. Sophie died in Poland, like your family. *Nu, a tserisn gemit iz shver tsum heyln.* A vounded spirit is hard to heal. Maybe there *are* ghosts. I think so sometimes. Jews see Hitler in cefeterias on de Vest Side. Fathers fifty years dead advise old men in de morning. Devils live in pillows and vhisper at night. Maybe you saw a dead man."

"No. If I saw him, he was alive."

"*If* you saw him," said Max. "*If*. But what if you didn't?"

"Could you check, Max?" Risa asked.

He refused to look at her. "How can I check? You think he's listed in the Manhattan phone book? When Benoit's well we can go to that corner. We'll stake it out and hope that—what's his name, Eleazar?—returns. What else can we do?"

"Meantime you've got to get well," Risa said. "And go back to school."

"Right," said Mordecai. "Listen, you're a good sketcher, a painter. You draw a picture of this guy like de police do. I'll esk around. You never know."

We did both. My indisposition, as Risa called it, was over in a few weeks. I returned to school, and for two weekends, Max and Mordecai and I sat in that cafeteria, casing the street like plain-clothes detectives, swilling tea and hamburgers and looking out the window onto a neon Reginald Marsh atmosphere. Mordecai quoted proverbs; Max gave me a sex lecture consisting of fifteen dirty jokes about someone named Speedy Gonzales, and a real performer named Superman who did his act in Cuba, screwing four ladies a day seven days a week and dying at twenty-seven; and of Max's adventures in Paris and what would happen to my vas deferens if I contracted gonorrhea.

I did make several charcoal sketches of Eleazar Jassy as he looked that night, amplified by my memories of him several years earlier. I gave the pictures to Mordecai, who told me that he had distributed them among his friends, with no result. I learned much later that assuming I was still among the walking wounded, and wishing only to do the right thing, the old man had tossed them in the incinerator.

Neither Max nor Mordecai ever saw Jassy. And it took years to realize that the man I saw the night of my collapse was not an illusion, that he was as real and as dangerous as the flames of Germany's crematoria.

V: GLUTTONY

A Romanian tale recounts how Gypsies built a stone church and the Romanians one of bacon and ham. The Gypsies haggled until the latter agreed to exchange buildings—then promptly ate their church. Hence today they have no religion and little regard for that of others. Another, recorded in Bulgaria and Turkey, said that when God was giving out the different religions, the Gypsies wrote theirs on cabbage leaves. A donkey came along and ate the Holy Book with the same result. A Turkish proverb says that there are seventy-two-and-a-half religions in the world and the half belongs to the Gypsies.

—*Journal of the Gypsy Lore Society*

THE DIGESTIVE TRACT, LIKE THE EYE, CAN FALL IN LOVE. Indiscriminate and voracious, mine developed crushes on, had affairs with roasts and poultry, with crustaceans and crushed almonds, with salmon mousse and chocolate mousse, with *chozzerai* and *nosherai,* with *trayf* and *kosher,* with *milchedig* and *flayshedig,* with the lowest cuisine—Mallomars and Drake's Cakes, or as Mordecai called them, Drek's Ceks, plus whatever menus the pooled resources of Max Kaufman and Son could afford. Max had obtained a paltry and galling job at a private college in Bronxville, teaching the joys of the Lake Poets to the daughters of the privileged. No connoisseur of irony could have chosen a more embittering assignment for a used radical. But salary checks were regular, rent was low and Max cared neither for clothes nor the theater. There were no women in his life. He had chosen the Freudian withdrawal from sexual competition: overweight. First food, then ethics, as Bertolt Brecht told me. So we ate. We chewed and swallowed our way across the West Side: steakhouses, French dives, Mandarin joints in Chinatown, hostelries, short-order diners, pancake houses, Sabrett stands, mixed grills, steam tables, Japanese places where you sat on the floor and watched account executives and their inamoratas, delicatessens where you stood and chomped with factors from the garment center. I was perpetually foodstruck, but the intake still burned off in an excess of yearning. With Max it settled in, losing itself in his increasing girth, adding to his specific gravity and dense melancholy, the powerful stomach now a Falstaffian sack of guts. He began to amuse himself with small diversions. He grew a beard. He learned Spanish so that he could gossip at the new bodegas along upper Broadway. He bought a piano from the Salvation

Army and resumed the lessons he had abandoned at the age of nine. And he ate. Principally he ate. Max sometimes gave off the faint aroma of acetone. I should have sensed trouble, but I knew nothing except the techniques of art. Nothing.

Mordecai kept pitching low and away. Still Johnny Eppleseed, he had succeeded in getting the Cubans of the Habana Restaurant to advertise *cuchifritos noshes* and the Great Shanghai Restaurant to offer sweet and pungent sizzling *lokshen.* But some force had overtaken him as it had undone Max; age, perhaps, or America. Mordecai was getting knobbly in the knuckles and joints, bending in unaccustomed ways like a ginseng, the root that looks like a man. Still, he went out each day and took two subways to Varick Street, where in some obscure factory he made butcher blocks for the trade. For a long time he brought samples home, but after we had installed butcher-block doors, drawers, floors, chairs, desks, bathroom cabinets, toilet seats, bookshelves, benches, lamps, and on one ceremonious occasion, a butcher-block butcher block, it was decided that too much was sufficient. From then on Mordecai confined himself to offering the stuff to his dates. Other elderly men brought their ladies a bunch of daisies or a bottle of wine. Mordecai took wood. "Vot de hell," he said. "Booze you drink, it's gone. Flowers vilt. A butcher block lays on the sink till you're a honderd. Or you can chop op put in de fireplace. For lanyap."

"For what?" Max asked him, and demanded a spelling.

"Lanyap. L-A-N—yap."

"You mean lagniappe."

"Dot's vot I said. Yiddish for extra."

"Lagniappe is *French.* It is not Yiddish."

"It is now."

Max breathed through his nose and glared at the ceiling. "And another thing. It's lo and be*hold,* not lo and behind. And a thing is either immense or tremendous. It is not tremense."

Mordecai smiled tolerantly. "Yiddish forgives averyting," he proclaimed. "In mine lenguige is no mistakes. You should learn."

"I am learning. I'm speaking Yiddish now. I just *think* I'm speaking English."

Scenes like this would go on five, six times a day. They began
early in the mornings. I often awoke to linguistic skirmishes
down the hall or in the kitchen. At other times I responded to
dirty, broken light bouncing up from the river or the metallic
buzz from the hive of southbound traffic. What do we first see
when we open onto the day? Ceilings, I guess. There was a map
of the constellations on mine. I had tipped the stars with
luminous paint and in the dark I could contemplate the gods
like a Phoenician. I could even move them around on my own:
Pegasus lying down with Gemini, etc. But in the mornings the
omnipotent astrological figures, the illuminations of myth,
receded into follow-the-dot puzzles and lost the power of enchantment.

Invariably I then looked to a sheet of fiberboard on the east
wall. It was covered with small reproductions, cut from *Life* or
Art News or from magazines superstitiously preserved from the
London days. Turner paintings, mostly. "Rain, Steam and
Speed," with the rabbit scuttling from the train. Snowstorms.
Venice. Sea fires. And a copy of his groping poem, "The
Fallacies of Hope": *the fierce archer of the downward year.*
Whatever the hell that meant. But the sound was right. And
I liked the title.

There were also pictures by another Englishman. The drawing for "Ghost of a Flea," for instance, because Max looked like
that sometimes, and "The Man Who Taught Blake Painting,"
because I had learned that the Man had never existed, that he
had come to crazy Blake in a dream. I used to try to conjure
up that vaporous instructor; dream me and win a free 10-course
lesson. Below him was a poem and picture of Yeats torn from
a book and presented to me by Risa long ago in one of the bad
times:

> He with body waged a fight
> But body won, it walks upright.

The rest of the verse was not so encouraging.

If there was no light and no traffic we three bachelors all still
rose at seven-thirty sharp, when Mordecai descended
from his bed and farted. B-dap! B-r-r-r-ack! B-dap! Who

needed an alarm clock with those sound effects? After contemplating the board, I looked west, out and down at the estuarial neglected Hudson moving with ponderous regularity, the earth's least mysterious river, an elephant of water, giving back the umber of the Jersey factories and the secondary palette of the city, lurching toward some appointment at the end of the world.

We tried for a while to make breakfasts compelling, and dinners, but Riverside Drive was not the place to indulge appetites. Any appetites. Occasionally Max brought students home and they would cook for us. But they always looked at him as if they expected their professor to write "A" on their plates and scribble on the side of the roast "See me after class." The girls I sporadically invited were all from art school. They could *paint* a good meal, but they could cook nothing; I was never lucky that way. The women Mordecai introduced—ah, that was another matter. The widow Sadie Liebowitz, for example. She was a star of the Yiddish theater, still acting ingénue parts thirty years after her flowering. She and her art form were fading institutions, yet on occasion both could kick high. Whatever the lady's roles, she never gave off a whiff of grease paint or spirit gum. Sadie was redolent only of delicatessen. I think she worshiped at Zabar's, a place whose air you could walk on: fresh bagels, whitefish, Nova Scotia salmon, dill pickles, chopped liver. I used to imagine Sadie taking essence of chopped liver, dabbing some of it behind each ear and the rest down her magnificent bust.

"The edible woman," Mordecai used to call her, without erotic implication. He simply meant that she could have been another item on the deli menu. She was in her fifties, but her great globular breasts were high and opalescent, riding above her scoop necklines. Her haunches were ample but tapered, and stretched the satin of her skirts. The legs were those of a chorus girl. And her skin, freckled and light as wheat flour, had the aroma of hot yeast. Sadie kept promising to bring her daughter, and for weeks I had visions of a reduced version, kind of an hors d'oeuvre with much the same, though proportionately smaller, dimensions.

But in that epoch, the daughters of prepossessing women had about the same chance of inheriting beauty as rich men's sons had of receiving character. Dyanne was as pale and angular as an ibis, with a weather-vane neck, disproportionately long legs and narrow, undernourished calves. Her sorrowful face was nearly as equine as Risa's, furnished with overbite and a chin that frequently trembled. This was framed by lank, hair-colored hair. She blushed when she spoke, and sometimes stammered. She was the kind of girl to whose teeth lipstick naturally adhered; whose slip straps always rode outside the confines of the dress; who took her shoes off at the movies only to find an hour later that they had mysteriously moved two aisles distant; who cried equally at *Wozzeck, Leave Her to Heaven,* and the time her cat snagged a pigeon on the window ledge; whose stockings bagged at the ankles; who could only neck in the dark and who referred to her period as "getting unwell" or "the curse"; who wore padded bras of different contours so that she seemed to rent different torsos for different occasions.

I fell for her at once.

She seemed to me caught in some noose of consciousness, or trapped by an awareness of the fragility of mere existence. It was as if she took it upon herself to display the whole human burden of sorrow and inadequacy. Some penalty is said to attach itself to beauty, but what are we to say of the distraints and forfeits clinging to the state of homeliness? Where are the lute songs in celebration of the lame girl or the cross-eyed boy? Who wrote the sonnets for the disturbed and shabby, for those swallowed by their own weight or too fearful to come out from the shadows of custom or tradition; whose terrors compel them to touch lampposts and mumble special recitations to the dead; whose affections are diverted to smug felines or Lhasa apsos; who sit on benches and talk to strangers about God; who are smothered by families or denied any at all—the stunted and grieving citizens for whom the world is as whimsical and pitiless as dice? What are we to say to them?

Off guard, her face turned away, Dyanne seemed a woman I had only imagined, someone whom I, for a change, might teach. She was a student at the Mannes School; her instrument was the cello. On those occasions when we returned to her mother's mirror-walled apartment on West End Avenue before Sadie herself arrived, always radiating disapproval and suspicion, Dyanne would take the cello from its corner, bow her legs around it, and release the melodies resident in the womb of that most female instrument. The long notes filled the hollow nights with a dark, sexual voice. Watching my reedy player, her narrow ribcage pressed against the wood, her wide eyes opening onto who knows how many rooms of disappointments, love flooded my own house and I was undone.

It was interesting to watch Sadie at that time, Sadie the edible woman who had written off her child as a loser, an embarrassment shaped like a girl. The baroque spelling of Dyanne's name broadcast Sadie's wish to trade up. And then the daughter had turned out like this; it was *too* stifling, Sadie said with one of her lofty, disdainful gestures. Still, Dyanne was not without her uses. The girl was scrawny and somehow old, and this lent her mother an artificially green, robust air.

The fact that Dyanne had acquired a suitor did not elevate her in Sadie's eyes, but reduced the man. Sadie, who once used to pat me on the head, then grab my arm and walk down the hall to the dining table, her capacious balcony advertising itself against my elbow, who used to open her private stock of Jewish stories about old couples ("Doctor, mine husband don't make love like he used to." "When did you notice this, madam?" "Three times last night and twice this morning") now held me in contempt. What kind of person could possibly be interested in her daughter, a known *meeskite?* Besides, I was a *shagitz*, and yet not the usual threatening goy, all horn-rimmed glasses, narrow lapels and self-satisfaction; I was in some social limbo, a *Zigeuner*, three or four steps below a pushcart peddler or rapist.

Dyanne and I fled our homes; we went to little restaurants on the West Side, where her incisors later testified that we had consumed spinach salad; we attended plays where she coughed at the denouement (once, at *The Great Sebastians*, Alfred Lunt gave her a special look, a glare duplicated by Alexander

Schneider at a recital of the Budapest String Quartet). We cheered on the Dodgers and brought our Chianti bottles to the Mannes School parties; we attended rallies for blacks imprisoned in Mississippi or to aid the Civil Liberties Union; Max took us to hootenannies, where pallid blondes wailed about Elizabethan disappointments and the resurrection of Joe Hill, and where Pete Seeger affected his jest-a-hick-with-a-banjo-and-a-pick manner and chanted of injustice and the House Un-American Activities Committee.

At these gatherings I kept trying to shake off something, to arise from Max's thirties scenarios. Ghosts of that epoch, decent and profane, had clung to the lines of my father's face, and to the folds of his deliberately unpressed proletarian suits. Now they tried to get hold of my own face and coat. Amid the folk chants, under banners inscribed with the cabala of Equality and Peace, I sat silent and unbelieving, as cold as the floor.

—Deutschland, Deutschland über alles. *What's the matter,*
  Zigeuners. *I know you have voices. I heard you shouting.*
—*We don't know the words.*
—*Then we'll teach you the words.*
—*Please. There is no need for this. Some of them are children.*
—*Give them a quick lesson and leave them with the pamphlet.*
  Gypsies! When we come back tomorrow, every one of you will
  know the words.

One evening after we had heard Rubinstein play an all-Chopin concert at Carnegie Hall, I could see tears in the corners of Dyanne's eyes. I said nothing. We took a subway in silence to the Village and sat in Rienzi's, where they played classical music and gave you a pot of tea and left you alone over your chess table.

I inspected my black army. The soldiers were as elegant and bloodless as mathematics. "Pawn to king's four," I began.

She pushed her king over in an attitude of mate and started to cry softly.

"What's the matter?" I handed her my napkin.

"Thank you, I have one of my own." A hot, hostile voice.

Mentally I catalogued my remarks for the evening. Nothing. "Dy, for God's sake, what did I do? What did I say?"

"Nothing. Everything. I'm crying because I'm going to be unwell soon. I'm crying because the concert made me sad. I'm crying because when my mother left my father he died. I'm crying because I have dreams of what it was like for you when you were a boy. I'm crying because the only reason you stay with me is because I'm someone you can feel sorry for."

The conversation around the room was in one of its periodic lulls. The music of Bach fugues on the harpsichord settled on us, covering the Chopin with dry leaves.

"You're a talented musician," I told her. "And a wonderful companion. And you attract me as a man"—which was true—"not because I feel any sensations of pity." Which was untrue.

She snuffled into her teacup. "You know what I wish I had?"

"What?"

"Tits. I wish I had enormous boobs like my mother. Men turn around on the street to watch her. And she's fifty-three years old."

"Your mother's a Thanksgiving Day balloon, not a woman. Besides, men who like big breasts are just looking for their mother."

"They're looking for *my* mother."

"You want a lot of men, is that what you want? Isn't one enough?"

"He isn't when he's got lots of women."

"I haven't got lots of women. I only have one."

"For now."

"For Chrissake, Dyanne—" People looked up from their games. I feigned deep interest in my Oolong.

She said, "I see you check over the merchandise when we come into a restaurant or a party. And I see them checking you out."

"Sexual tennis is all that is. I serve to your court, you serve to mine. Everybody plays it."

"I don't."

"You will."

She suddenly took hold of my wrist. Her thumb and long

forefinger encircled it. "You know what this means? You can find it in old paintings; a girl circling a man's wrist with her fingers. Benoit, you're the only man I ever loved, and it's not going to work out."

"Can't we just have what's here now?"

"What's here now is a pot of tea and a chess game. Incomplete."

There was no reply to that.

When sufficient time had gone by and she had sat looking down into the bottom of her cup like a storefront fortuneteller I said, "You're the only person I know who suffers from *pre-coital tristesse*." She threw me the kind of look she sometimes gave her instrument when a string severed. I apologized. We had never been to bed together. Now we never would.

> Then he struggled with the heart;
> Innocence and peace depart

As Yeats told me every goddamn morning. I reached out and tried to take her hand. She rose and took her cardigan from the points on the back of her chair. Like Ginger Rogers walking out on Fred Astaire. I thought of those shimmering old moments with Mordecai and Risa. "We should be laike a couple of hawt tomahtoes," I sang. "Bot you're as kalt as yestiddy's meshed pedades." And through a glaze of tears Dyanne laughed. I kissed her on one wet eye and then the other, and we took a cab uptown without saying anything, without touching.

The Liebowitz apartment was dark. The only light in the place was a triangle of zinc white emanating from Dyanne's little room. She never turned that light out except to sleep.

Daniel, you above all should know the singular feeling that occurs when you enter a room in which an explosion of temperament has taken place—particularly between husband and wife. Even if only one of them is there, even if *neither* is there, hostility crackles from the walls and the rug. But there are other sensations that linger after people are no longer there: bitterness, for example, frustration or melancholy.

Something terrible emanated from that cube, something different from the sexual jangle we had just experienced, or the adolescent blues that hang around the retreats of every excluded youth. I thought for a moment that it might come from the framed picture of her father, a spaniel of a man standing before what was obviously a warehouse. A girl's father: a mystery always, a maze.

The picture next to him was another matter. Dyanne also had a bulletin board covered with clippings, poems, snapshots. But in the center was an atrocity photograph, one I still cannot contemplate squarely. Neither the sun nor death can be looked at steadily, Rochefoucauld reassures me. It was not the candid shot of the bulldozers in the death camps stacking up cordwood bodies, nor the images of soap rendered from human fat, nor brass nozzles in the ceilings of cement bunkers. No, this was only the celebrated glimpse of a little Polish boy with his hands up, walking through some forgotten cobblestone square while helmeted German soldiers round up families to send them in cattle cars to hell. The photograph screamed. I tried to shut it off, then felt perhaps I could stare straight through to the captured essence of things, like a savage. Photographs: our contemporary household gods. Children in frames, cousins and ancestors, bodies leaning against summer cottages, preserved snapshots of discarded lovers, possessions of youth, glimpses of the procreative years. These are the creatures we truly genuflect to, that we really summon in distress or melancholy.

—*Take their pictures, Lieutenant.*
—*The children's too?*
—*Of course the children's. Quickly.*
—*Brothers line up here. Sisters here.* Zigeuners *with dark eyes over here. Gray eyes here. Blue here. Why he wants this is beyond me.*
—*Genetics fascinates him. Doesn't it make you curious?*
—*No. Aliens look more or less the same. What a shithead assignment this is.*
—*Better than the Russian front.*
—*Just barely. Quickly, all of you. The train is waiting.*

ITEM: It is impossible to educate them. All Gypsies should be treated as hereditarily sick. The aim should therefore be elimination without hesitation of this characteristically defective element in the population. This should be done by locking them all up and sterilizing them.

—Dr. L. Behrendt, "Die Wahrheit über
die Zigeuner," *Nazi Parti:*
Korrespondenz (NSK) 10, iii

ITEM: . . . Gypsies came from Sachsenhausen, Buchenwald and elsewhere to a center in Dachau for experiments involving injections with a solution of salt . . . Beiglböck, who was among those conducting the research, found some of the Gypsies had been drinking water and he flew into a rage . . . Franz Blaha, an eye-witness of these experiments, says that in the autumn of 1944 a group of forty to eighty Gypsies and Hungarians were locked up in a room for five days and given nothing except salt-water . . . Gypsies were [also] used in Sachsenhausen for experiments with mustard gas . . . One of the survivors was killed and dissected for an autopsy. At Buchenwald twenty-six Gypsies received injections of spotted fever virus on the orders of Pohl . . . Dr. Mengele . . . killed some Gypsies because their eyes were of a certain color. He sent the eyes to a Berlin institute. We also know he used Gypsies in experiments at Auschwitz for injections with phenole, and was particularly interested in twins and blood groups.

—Donald Kenrick and Grattan Puxon,
The Destiny of Europe's Gypsies (New
York: Basic Books, 1972)

"I saw him."

"Saw who, Benoit?"

"Oh, God, I don't know, Dyanne. I don't know." But I did know. I walked out of her room and she followed me. Her mother, who had obviously taken classical and flamenco lessons in narcissism, had sprinkled the apartment with looking glasses. Little round numbers with Renaissance trim, huge full-length golden ones with antique backing, bright metallic opposing mirrors that threw back an infinity of selves.

Dyanne put her arm on my shoulder. "That could have been me," I said.

"He was you. He is you. That's why I keep him there."

"And I'm the one who's supposed to feel sorry for *you*?"

"It's not pity, Ben. It's something else."

"What?"

"I don't know. A sound. I don't see that picture any more. I hear it."

"What does it sound like?"

"Your voice."

"Take the picture down, will you? It makes your room a morgue."

"All right, Ben. All right. I'm sorry."

She retreated. I waited a minute and came in, passing a crowd of Benoits lurking on the walls. Enter Gypsy Chorus. The room was suddenly dark and her back was to me. I turned her around and kissed her wet face and licked the salt tears again. I'm sure Dyanne could taste my own sorrow. Her clothes came off like dandelion seeds; I could have blown them away.

We made long, slow, grave, serious love; fervor moistened our thin bodies and humidified that little shelter. The only perfect climate is bed, Mark Twain cackled. I thought at first Dyanne might be put off by my scarred and veiny leg, but she just ran her fingers across the places that were always warm to the touch and cried again. I wanted to say nothing, just to lie there and let her know what her flesh might mean, let myself know what might be possible in the name of affection. But in a while, when I closed my lids and rolled my eyes way back in my head it seemed to freeze the frame of the moment, and there came a series of other frames, other moments, and to dispel them, to keep the smell of the chimneys at bay and the caravan from moving, I told her what I could of Eleazar Jassy.

When I was through she said in a jittery voice, "I believe you."

"Which is more than Max does."

"He doesn't want to believe. But I know Jassy is alive."

"Know he's alive how?"

"I just do. I read a lot of Holocaust literature. Anything is possible. Any*one* is possible."

"I don't read any of that any more."

"You don't have to read what you lived."

I got out of bed and went to the window. There was nothing to see but an air shaft and nothing to hear but the pastel strains of Viennese instrumental music. Strauss, it sounded like. WQXR was very big on the Austrians in those days. Proof that the German-speaking peoples weren't all bad. After all, they gave us Mozart, didn't they? And Hitler. For lagniappe.

"Stay away from that stuff, Dyanne."

"I can't. I don't want to, and besides, I just can't. I read it all the time. I'm part of the Holocaust. We all are."

"You haven't paid enough dues to say that."

"Not physically."

Her eyes looked like those of a hunted animal. It occurred to me that she might be mad, like the rest of us. Only without just cause. Making herself sick.

"What are you trying to do?" I asked her. "Experience it all over again? Wasn't one time around enough? Forget it. It doesn't belong to you."

"Who does it belong to then? Only you? Or to the dead?"

"There are committees appointed to remember. There's a a guy in Jerusalem who does nothing but chase ex-Nazis. Some of Europe remembers. Israel remembers. Gypsies remember. It's enough."

"No, it's not enough. You know it's not enough. Stop trying to protect me. It's too late for that. I've read all about the burning babies and rabbis spitting on the Torah and the people lying in their own . . . excrement."

"Shit. Say it, shit."

"Shit, then."

"That's what it is. The whole thing is the shit of civilization. You should be looking at black dots on lined paper and playing melodies, not reading about concentration camps. Why should anyone sane want to read that?"

"Because it's our duty to remember."

The cant of the Hebrew. If I forget thee, O Jerusalem. And not only Jewish. What does the ghost of Hamlet's father say? Take care of yourself? Ripeness is all? Find a way? Try to understand the unnameable? The meaning of life is invention,

not discovery? No, he says, "Adieu, adieu, remember me."
Remember. *Me.* Perfectly understandable. What the hell is a
gravestone but adieu, adieu, remember me, remember me? Or
a photograph? What did my own father tell me?

I looked hard at her. "Dyanne, if we remember the dying,
we have to remember the murderers. Don't you see? If I bring
all of that back, I have to resurrect the Germans. I want them
dead. I want *it* dead."

"You can't kill it, Ben. If you could, you wouldn't wonder
about Elezear."

"He's a physical thing, not just a memory. *If* he exists."

"He exists." She turned and pulled me around and looked
up at me. The eyes no longer looked deranged. I wondered
what mine looked like. Exhausted, I suppose. Burned out. This
was a subject that could kill you if you let it.

She took a long, deep breath. "Look. I know a woman, a
French lady who used to be a friend of my father's. Eleanor
Clair. She has personal files from Auschwitz and Buchenwald
and Belsen. Lots of places. They're her own papers. She's the
one who gave me all the Holocaust literature."

"Remind me to thank her."

"Don't be so hostile, Ben. She's a little single-minded, is all."

"Single-minded. Is that what they're calling obsessive this
year?"

"Stop it. Stop picking it all apart. All right, she's obsessive.
Damn you, can you name a better obsession?"

I took the piece of paper Dyanne handed me without comment, for once. I wonder now what might have happened if
I had come up with a smart-ass reply and she had taken it back.
Or if I had lost the name and address. I suppose the thing
would have played itself out some other way. But with the same
characters. *Damn you, can you name me a better obsession?*

Cooled down, Dyanne asked me what I did when I wanted
to forget.

"I eat," I told her. "I eat all the time."

"Why aren't you fat?"

"I don't know. Metabolism, probably. What about you?
You're skinnier than I am."

"I don't eat. I have nothing to remember, remember?"

"Come on, I'll give you something to forget." I carried her back to bed. She felt as light and dry now as a box of matches. A small body, full of hollows and suggestions.

She played the cello afterward, naked. Bach transcriptions. I recalled my Uncle Zanko, who gave up playing tunes on his violin to concentrate on the single note of A. After several afternoons this began to grate on my aunt's nerves, then the children's, until in a few weeks time he was left all alone. Finally my father asked him, "Zanko, for God's sake, that one sound coming from your violin is driving us all crazy. Why do you play it and nothing else?" Zanko looked up with a face of purest innocence. "Others of you are looking for this note," he said. "I've found it."

In time we repaired, on my insistence, to the vast and gleaming kitchen. On the far blue wall was a lithograph poster advertising Sadie as the radiant lead of *Mirele Efros*—the Yiddish Queen Lear—back in the forties. Let the record show that absolute vanity preserves absolutely. She was dramatically unchanged.

Dyanne set up a spread from the refrigerator that looked like a branch office of Zabar's. We were anatomizing the whitefish and a series of toasted bagels when we heard Sadie at the door with Mordecai. "It's been a wonderful evening," she was telling him. "Now let's not spoil it." There were some token protests from the old man, then the sound of an elevator. Sadie called out: "Is anybody?"—a favorite mock-Jewish line of hers. Her own offstage speech was that kind of tony locution favored by actors who grew up in homes where English was not the first language. "How was it, Mother?" Dyanne shouted.

"A good crowd," Sadie answered back, still invisible. Doubtless she was checking her manifold reflections. "I always work best with a good crowd. You know, same as a musician. Only with me, my body is my instrument. That's why I—" The disappointment loitered on her face for an instant as she caught sight of Dyanne's gentleman. The expression was displaced by a stage smile. "How very nice to see you, Ben. If I had known I would have asked Mordecai to come in. You could have ridden home together."

"I was just leaving," I said. "Perhaps I can catch him."

"Now, don't let me chase you. Although it's the small hours."

Sadie looked down at the items on the kitchen table. "I believe I'll just join you for a morsel," she told us. "Even if I am on a crash diet."

"Oh, Mother, you're always on a crash diet," Dyanne said.

"Well, I'm not lucky like you two. Look how emaciated. You can eat anything you want. Not me. I have one grape, I swell up like a tire. I must be five pounds overweight right now."

This was trolling for a compliment. None was forthcoming. Dyanne and I chewed quietly while Sadie nattered on about the zenith of the Yiddish Rialto, when the audiences called for the author, only the play was *Romeo and Juliet*; and the great, fading days of Jacob Adler, who had fathered so many illegitimate children that when a boy came to the back door demanding a pass the old man squinted at him and announced, "Let him in for half price. You never know."

There came a moment when even Dyanne and I were full. But Sadie the dieter kept doing her locust impression. At about one-thirty, concealing a series of *grepps* and yawning with flourishes, she wrapped up the remains of the feast in white, oil-stained paper and signaled the close of the business day.

But between her entrances and exits, Dyanne's mother must have found something redeemable in her guest. I was invited back. I thought at the time that I must have done something appealing—listening with bogus attention, perhaps, or staring in spite of myself at Sadie's torso. But no, it was only that I liked to eat. So did she, it turned out, but like a social alcoholic she would not do it alone. So on the evenings when Dyanne and I sat at the kitchen table munching, Sadie joined us "just for a *nosh*" and remained to see me out the door, thinking, probably, that she had also saved her daughter from the depredations that had, in fact, taken place when she was Queen Learing on Second Avenue.

Dyanne never returned the picture of that kid to her bulletin board. It must have been two or three months before she raised the subject again. I was sketching her portrait as she sat at the base of the Soldiers' and Sailors' Monument on Riverside

Drive. The planes of her face had begun to change. Her color was higher, and the concavities looked less dire. The severity of her mouth and eyes had started to soften, and her body, now several steps up from the stick figure, had assumed a different series of contours. She looked like the cousin of her cello.

"Ben," she said, squinting away from the sun. "Did you see Eleanor Clair?"

"Who?" But I had not forgotten.

"The lady with the Holocaust records."

"Do me a favor and don't use that word, will you, please?"

"Holocaust? What's wrong with Holocaust?"

"It doesn't say anything. It's just a word."

"Everything's just a word. What would you rather have me say?"

"Nothing."

Which is exactly what I got for most of the evening. She liked the portrait, though. Even Dyanne had to admit that it was a decent likeness. I had reacquired old skills, the ones first claimed in London, plus a catalog of technique from art school —the method of letting the eye complete what the pencil has only suggested, for instance.

Chazal claims that the face collects echoes of the body; the female mouth, he says, is an idling vagina. Maybe, maybe. Certainly the collection of features proclaims the world below. But it also reflects the universe outside. The pupil is a sun at perpetual noon. The shadows of the nose hide the color of wood grains; the white of skin and the black of hair create blue, not gray. The eyes of a race write what its historians cannot. Women reveal themselves with their eyes; men with their mouths—particularly with the lower jaw, set, through the years, in attitudes of denial or indulgence. Not only the mouth but the eyes (like Dyanne's) can stammer. Indeed, I was to find that stammer in many prominent subjects; it was something a portrait painter could reproduce with a canny series of lines, like unimproved roads on an ordnance map. Just the way he could make the space between the forehead and the neck an archipelago of features, related or isolated, the eyes sometimes lying to the nose, the chin at war with the mouth. Or sometimes, in the rare cases of very beautiful women, linked by bridges and wholly at peace. The nose, as Proust tells me, publishes stupidity more readily than any other organ; beware the man with an inadequate one, or a woman who crinkles hers. The face is a calendar and a medical chart. Look at the nose to see how the health has been. The eye's white tells about the nights, the margin around the eyes, the days. Examine the hair to see the current state of health, skin tone to find out the future, the mouth to see how things go from day to day. My instructors indicated their dissent to all this by drawing concentric circles around their ears with index fingers.

But that catalog was all I had. Plus the ability to reproduce what was in my eye. And although the school faculty held me at arm's length, they saw the possibility of a new ornament. I had already sold a few portraits to students and even to the dean. Horace Chase, who taught portraiture and caricature, introduced me to an agent who had taken my portfolio and asked me to see him in a month or so. Like every student with half a gift I imagined I had a whole one and thought in cinematic terms of career, money, a place of my own and, I regret to confess, a social advance. What garbage that was, and how much it meant to me then! Dyanne meant something more—and also something less. The beauty I had seen resident in that waif, the way an Eskimo "sees" a sculpture in a piece of uncarved soapstone, was becoming apparent to the world. This step up from skeleton, this anthology of shadows, was acquiring true substance. Her figure through the months was filling out. The beauty of her bones bloomed in her skin. Her capacity for love seemed to grow, and this was at once enchanting and perilous. She started to talk of her married friends, every one of them seedling *yentas*, saddled with husbands on the periphery of the professions, or second-generation manufacturers, all of them with matched Drexel furniture sets ordered *en bloc* from some eight-floor department-store display. It was as if the concerts on unacompanied cello were illusions that I had mistaken for soul; as if I had confused the shimmer for the structure. But she *had* talent; she *had* something worthwhile. Those evenings, watching the beauty leap from woman to instrument and back, like a spark gap, I still remember them as unassailable evidence, fact uncolored by eros.

Dyanne's greatened appetite for viands, for affection, for life itself were diminished by her quest for permanence—a husband, a life. In the beginning I had courted her in the classic manner, with lyrics, as she had come to me with music. We read Emily Dickinson, mostly, and Elizabeth Barrett Browning and the unfailing aphrodisiac lines of cummings: "The voice of your eyes is deeper than all roses." Sometimes we read the Song of Solomon, maiden and beloved. For the first and only time I entered that book without seeing Absalom bled to the dogs, or firstborn perishing in a little choir of sighs, or Saul and his three sons killed in the same afternoon.

But as we grew from the sexual flush to something more serious I could feel the snares. I read the Yeats aloud from my bulletin board in hopes of breaking the enchantment:

> Then he struggled with the mind;
> His proud heart he left behind.

But Dyanne took it all for love lyrics and prattled of a future together.

The ways to erase an intense, sad and carnal affair are varied, and useless until the enchantment has passed. I talked it out with Risa, who agreed that I was too young to marry, or to do anything more complicated than tying my shoelaces; with Max, who thought I ought to wait until I was fifty: "Marry money; if there's one thing an old Lefty knows, it's the value of capital and the fiction of love"; and with Mordecai, who read me the canniest Yiddish proverb of them all: "Not only are two people in love one, but one person in love is two."

Make that a dozen, Mordecai. A score.

Another way is to sleep around in the hope of diminishing the beloved, but there is no obliterating one bed in the bed of another. I sought, if one-night stands can be called pursuit, a couple of slovenly models and one art student, Judith Cheney, who whispered to every male in sketch class the same jape:

"You're all right in my book. And my book was banned in Boston."

Which, in those refrigerated days, it was. Full of exuberant postures: anal, umbilical, oral and sometimes genital, illustrated with more positions than you could shake a stick at, if stick-shaking was your idea of a good time. Twenty-three, thirty-four and a half, sixty-nine—it was all one to Judith, calling numerical signals like a quarterback, and offering about as much yielding, feminine appeal. I don't know; maybe she was dynamite in bed. So her other lovers claimed raucously, over beers at the Cedar Street tavern. I kept thinking of Dyanne until one night Judith shouted, "Go, and never darken my towels again," counseled me to reread my *Kamasutra* and presented a mail-order catalog she had received from the Sex Shop in Kobe.

I gave the catalog to Mordecai for a joke. He pretended to be embarrassed and made a great show of throwing it in the wastebasket. The packages that arrived thereafter, in brown envelopes and with Japanese stamps, were marked for a Mr. Moishe Pipik but grabbed by Mordecai. "Textbooks. Friend of mine," he would explain hastily. I thought, briefly, of introducing the old man to Judith, but in the end I didn't think her heart could stand it.

And all the time I had imaginary negotiations with Dyanne. When they became actual, they never went as scripted.

"Why?" she asked on one of our nervy, tortuous walks along the upper Drive. "What makes you think you'd suffocate?"

How could I answer her? How could I say that the future she wanted loomed as white, tidy and noxious as a diaper-service truck? That the procession of domestic acquisitions of stainless and wineglasses, of carpets and graphics were claims on the spirit; that the Rek-o-Kut turntable and throw pillows, all the hard- and software of domesticity were snares for a Romany?

How can I tell myself now that I ran from affection like a stricken deer, my eyes red from the fury of my own hurts, convinced still that whatever the promise of the world, when you reached out, thorns scratched your skin to the muscle. That what you loved was always taken from you, or cracked irreparably, like a glass or a mind.

You're lucky to escape said my *shlong* in the mornings, free to seek its own adventures in new channels. But the dreams summoned Dyanne's spirit from the vasty deep, and I heard her cello echoing in unlikely subway tunnels and in the throaty barges along the Hudson. The erotic world is as round as the solid one: we always wandered away to meet each other somehow, and to resume.

But things altered. At art school undergraduates could no longer affect the atelier life. Korea. We strove to maintain our student status—frivolous, according to draft boards. To them, art students belonged in the infantry. Some of us took more acceptable courses at N.Y.U. or Columbia. A few got married. One guy went to a psychiatrist and obtained a deferment. I was examined, surrounded yet again by those green walls, and allowed to continue. My disfigured leg granted me a stay, not a parole. Who knows, perhaps it saved my life. In those days, knowing the war could not last long, we played for time. Time was kind to me then, and kinder to Dyanne.

Her figure arrived. When we made love in the dark I could feel it, rising and falling with my own skin and fingers. But on some evenings she burned dime-store candles and the body did indeed seem to be a miniaturized solid-circuit version of Sadie's. And Sadie? The eating binges that she had enjoyed with her daughter and with me, and certainly with her theatrical colleagues, had done wonders for her figure as well—wonders if you were an Assyrian and liked your women to check in at two hundred pounds avoirdupois. As Dyanne had become supple, then nubile, then voluptuous in a minor key, her mother had gone from a Rodin sculpture to Gaston Lachaise to the Venus of Willendorf, all breasts and thighs and belly, chins working at all times, upper arms jiggling in hemidemisemiquavers of the necklaces, the mouth as busy chomping as it was complaining about stairs, the disintegrating quality of white bread, the collapse of the theater, the Bomb, etc. Onstage, she was a Grosz caricature of herself, still dressed in fabrics that accentuated her size; after a long speech she grew out of breath and puffed like a grampus, and when she bowed to the orchestra her buttons popped. One weekend the mirrors disappeared from the walls of the Liebowitz apartment. The place was being done over in Biedermeier and Empire. Out went the furniture, out went the glass, farewell to posters, so long, memorabilia, now assigned to a backroom studio. Hello croissants; greetings banana-cream pie, Brie, Lithuanian rye; hello Carlsberg, baba au rhum, salted almonds, whipped butter.

I ran into her once waddling along Broadway with another equally large friend whose legs overflowed her ankles. Sadie's calves were still astonishingly perfect, but widening into God knows what cellulite folds as they headed north toward freedom. She was emptying the contents of a greasy kraft-paper bag into her mouth, and gave off hints of garlic.

The two gorgons stopped at Zabar's. Sadie entered, nostrils flaring, mouth in a rictus of delight. It was her final, her most theatrical transmogrification: Dyanne's mother had turned into a delicatessen.

One evening as I whuffed and brushed my lips down Dyann's thorax over the little hillock of belly to the woolen welcome mat, there seemed to be the aroma of warm yeast. The metamorphoses were complete: Dyanne had become the Edible Woman.

The wretchedness of forsaking what I wanted, of ducking the unavoidable, lingered too long. I tried to lose myself in my work, but Dyanne used this as yet another reason to marry. I was going to be able to support not only myself but a family. "Look what's already happened," she said. I looked. Who could deny the signs?

Every year the school offered a prize, the Chase-Allison Award for Portraiture. As it happened, no one was found fit for the award the year before, so when I won it a hoo-ha occurred, resulting in a picture in the *Herald Tribune* and a brief story about my origins, "No Gypsy in His Interests," plus a few commissions, one from Whitelaw Reid, who owned the paper. Most assuredly, I was on the wing. The agent called the following week with two jobs, one for the *Saturday Evening Post*, which wanted a portrait of Louis Armstrong; and the Lansing Company demanding a mug shot of its outgoing president. I also received a message from a man who called himself King of the Gypsies. I did not return the call.

These offers seemed to indicate a long, remunerative career; so the school said, so the agent burbled. What reason could there be, save for our youth, not to become officially engaged? Clearly it was a moment for decisiveness, a time to declare ourselves in or out, willing to be together for all time or never. There was no excuse for hedging any more. It was yes or no, on or off, in or out.

So we said maybe. For years.

Fade in. Fade out. She grew. I grew. We slid into our twenties. Almost a married couple, except that we still lived apart. This went against her ethic, and, more important, against her friends' expectations. Quarrels disfigured every negotiation, even after love-making. And then there resurfaced the insistence on my visiting Eleanor Clair, a name that I had almost forgotten, or thought that Dyanne had forgotten. The mere mention of the Holo————, the black past always fell on me like a sort of radiation, sickening the body, making the brain seethe. Until one afternoon I could stand it no more, broke off an argument in the middle of a sentence, and sought Mlle. Clair, with the air of a man who has tickets to an execution. *His* execution.

The lobby of the Glendower looked like the mouth of some animal that ate light. Two electric fans gathered strings of brown dust and barely discouraged the flies from mating in midair. Shadows appeared five- and sixfold from clusters of naked incandescent bulbs whose ceiling covers had long since been broken. The place shook periodically as the subway passed underneath it, oscillating grainy dust on the scratched granite floor, covered here and there with mock-Arabic rugs in shades of reform-school green. Elevator passengers could hear trombone retchings and snare drums from studios as they ascended in a vertical rickshaw that promised every claustrophobe the ultimate in angina.

On what would have been the thirteenth floor but which was labeled 12-X I stepped out, along with a tight-lipped Sikh in a burnoose. I followed him down the hall. Every green metal door had frosted glass and black-and-gold lettering. The theme of the downstairs rug varied in the hallways; here the decorator had chosen dried-blood red, interspersed with souvenirs of cleaning fluid. It served chiefly to remind the viewer of a time, twenty years previous, when he could walk in buildings like this on maroon runners past solid metal doorways without the sensation of running errands for an abortionist.

Twelve-X was my kind of floor: Misery, Obscurity, Exotica —Mr. Kaufman's attorneys. Exotica is out to lunch; would you like to speak to his assistant? This way; Misery will see you now.

Dr. Klein. Tuesday–Thursday—8:30 A.M.–7:30 P.M. Hints of chloroform. Yes, Mrs.—ah—Johnson. This is your daughter, Gretchen? In this room, Gretchen. Disrobe, please, and put on the smock. Leave the money with the nurse. There's no reason to be afraid. Many girls like yourself come here in this situation. An hour later it's all behind them. A follow-up visit is extra. Leave the money with the nurse. Ah, yes, this is your daughter, Mrs.—Simon . . .

Inwood Collection Agency. This is your third notice. That's right, by tonight. Otherwise the furniture goes Monday morning. In front of the neighbors. Illness is no excuse. You weren't ill when you bought the bedroom set . . .

James Greenhalgh, LL.B. We can get you off with a fine, but you got to come in wearing a black parochial suit and a dark thin knitted tie. You got that? A dark tie and a white shirt. Judge Lindell likes white shirts on niggers. She started to paw you in the car and you obliged her. You got that? You obliged her because a chauffeur don't refuse a passenger. It don't matter how fast it was . . . Any penetration, no matter how slight. You're just lucky she was a Chink, pally.

Marlyn Music Publishers; The Burlap Council—the Sikh got off at that stop. Czechoslovakian War Relief: Mrs. Ida Wyzcylcski. Hours: Daily 1–4. Same as a baseball umpire. The Willwyck Fund. Clair Research. No hours posted. My stop.

The door was locked. I announced myself and mentioned Dyanne's name. It took a lot of jiggling to release all the catches. Once inside I could hear a small fan, but it was out of sight, possibly below desk level. Two ladies sat at separate metal desks as gray as their hair. Both were dressed in black so severe it would have made a nun's habit look frivolous. The first, the older of the two, seventy, maybe, never looked up. She was copying something in longhand out of a large brown book. The book was German. She was writing in French. The other was closer to the door. She looked up with very alert, disturbingly youthful black eyes and said in a heavy accent, "How may I help you?"

Before I could reply she motioned me to a chair under the window. That aperture looked out onto a brick wall—or would have if it hadn't been so smeared with age and neglect. I sat there with my hands in my lap, waiting.

"You have taken rather a long time to come."

"I was nervous about it," I answered her in French. "Anything about this business makes me nervous."

She defrosted enough to tell me her name. Eleanor Clair. The other lady was her sister Jacqueline. I nodded. She didn't look up.

"Jacqueline lives for research entirely," said Eleanor. "She has a very active life of the mind. But here on earth . . ." She made a *moue*.

"And you?" she asked. "What kind of life do you lead?"

"I live here on earth. I don't have much life of the mind."

"Yes, you do." She went to a filing cabinet. "I can see it in your face. You were in the camps."

"Dyanne filled you in, then?"

"One or two words. You wanted to know about a man, possibly a survivor. A Kapo. Eleazar Jassy. A collaborationist. A killer. You were several years with him."

"Is that Dyanne's idea of one or two words? Or yours?"

"I have here the file on a person, Jassy."

"Can I see it?"

She ignored me and lit another cigarette off her stub. The front of her dress was marked with the residue of other ashes. A chain-smoker, brown fingers.

"You were under Jassy?"

"In a manner of speaking. I was very young."

The air was heavy. God, let me think no longer of myself when young. Let me resist all the manifest signs given off by the sight of this ministry of despair.

"You were a Gypsy, yes?"

"Still am."

"Jassy was also a Gypsy?"

"Yes."

Why should Dyanne do this? She knew what Clair research was like, what it would do to me. In what name did she persuade me to come here? Love? The appalling mysteries of affection are indecipherable, and it might be that in the name of love hellish things are done. Or it might be that in order to understand love I first have to hate, just as for some people, prisoners mostly, the experience of hell leads to the acceptance of paradise.

There is a phrase, "Why me?,". that cancer patients are said to utter upon first hearing the bad news. But fathers and brothers, there are other ways to die, and the same question occurs to the mental patient, to the child in the ditch, to the hollow eyes of the near-corpse, to all of the century's witnesses.

ITEM: With a view to freeing the German people of Gypsies, and
with a view to making the eastern territories which have been
incorporated into the Reich available for settlement by German
nationals, I intend to turn over criminal jurisdiction over Gypsies to the Reichsführer-SS. In doing so I stand on the principle
that the administration of justice can make only a small contribution to the extermination of these peoples.

—Otto Thierach to Martin Bormann,
October 12, 1942

ITEM: Item item item item. Item, for Christ's sake, item! Death, atrocity, what difference can it possibly make now? You in the back. Yes you. Behind the mind. Stop whispering. Close the books, shut the doors, bar the memory before it bars you. I have to *live*. I can't sit here and remember with two old ladies.

Living well is the best revenge? The hell it is. Revenge is the best revenge. But I don't want it. Not at these prices. Please God—

|||

"I'm sorry. We never let our clients see the folders."

"All right, you keep the folder. Just tell me whether Jassy is dead or alive."

There was no such thing as time in that office; no hours, no days, nothing. The Clairs lived for their research, you could see that. A piece of paper was life to them, and life was a piece of paper. They had both been in concentration camps, that I knew from Dyanne. But why? They were not Jews or Gypsies. Communists, maybe.

"Nuns," she said.

"What?"

"Nuns, we were nuns. I don't read minds. I read faces. You wonder what we were prisoners for."

"Yes."

"We helped children escape after the collapse of France. Our beloved nation was the only one to collaborate fully."

My eyes were fixed on that folder. I needed no lecture on the moral lessons of the occupation, thank you. But I couldn't say that, not to her. She had a formidable mouth, even when all it emitted was smoke. What do you get when you cross a parrot with a lioness? the old story went; I don't know, but when it talks I listen.

"The Church, to be charitable, had an ambiguous role. We were captured outside of Cherbourg, in a stone farmhouse. Five of the children were with us. The rest, I am happy to say, escaped north. One of them still writes me. Others were not so lucky. It was a dangerous business. It still is."

It was only then that I noticed on her desk the most incongruous of all paperweights: a 38-caliber black-handled Luger. Well, I thought, the Church and its portrayed martyrs could give lessons in self-dramatization to the most lurid imaginations. Yet surely these ladies had lost their faith; there were no crosses on the walls; nothing except for some framed photographs of men's faces. I didn't recognize any of them. The sisters displayed no beads, no religious artifacts.

But then Eleanor said, "That winter we learned that God was no longer important in the sensual world. He would only be important in another world. We saw too much suffering even for those equipped to suffer. And some are better equipped than others."

She looked to me for affirmation. I nodded. And tried to force her attention back to the folder and away from the confessional.

"The mundane grew in importance. We survived the camps and the war, but not undamaged. Do you understand?"

"I think so. I don't know many lapsed Catholics, but those I know seem—"

"There is no such thing as a lapsed Catholic." She clutched the folder with the grip of a gargoyle. Well, you've blown it now, I thought. But who can deal with the renegade mind? Certainly not another renegade.

"We still believe in the truth of the Faith. But we discovered another mission. The finding of people, the uniting of families. The punishment of the guilty."

"There are governments who do this. Why are you on your own?"

"Naïf," she said with a little smile. "Governments are not interested in truth. Governments are interested in governments. We give information to Israel, to Poland, even to the Soviet Union and the United States when it suits us. But when the information gets too embarrassing—if the Nazi is still in office, if the ex-Kapo is highly placed, if the data is too embarrassing—it often disappears. We prefer when possible to deal with private clients. Or government agencies willing to make a contribution."

Silence. Another cigarette. Another cascade of ashes on the black linen.

"You would be amazed at who comes in here." Eleanor's eyes were staring inward, watching her customers pass in review. "Avengers trying to trace medical experimenters. Federal investigators. Private investigators. People like yourself. And of course the agencies. Repellent, I suppose, but they pay the most. They and the ex-Nazis."

"You sell to ex-Nazis?"

"To the minor ones, yes. Sometimes a man has a job; he was a minor functionary. He wishes to eradicate what was. He has atoned. My sister and I discuss it; you can see this requires the most delicate moral judgment."

I nodded. I would have agreed to the Spanish Inquisition if she had permitted the folder to fall open.

But why should she relinquish her captive audience? Eleanor Clair watched me with my hands digging into my knees, ready to rise from my chair, anxiety in convenient, ready-to-take human form, and she went on, "We found, after the war, who were the greatest aids to the Resistance. You know who they were?"

"No."

"Whores and priests. It was the middle who corrupted."

And how about you, Mlle. Clair? How untainted are you here, poring over the dossiers of the victims and the culpable? Maybe like Dyanne you want to live it all over again; maybe she caught it from you. Maybe you are like those shades in the *Odyssey*, anxious to lap up blood.

She was still talking when I opened my wallet and took out every dollar I had in there. I had just been paid for a small sketch of a master of ceremonies—Robert Q. Lewis, I think— for an NBC promotion. Fifty dollars. I put it on the desk and said, "For God's sake, just tell me where he is, is all. I don't have to hear the lecture, I was there."

I might have told her that wheat closed mixed and soybeans were off in sluggish trading; she just spoke of her clientele. She didn't even look at the money, and her sister kept on writing. It occurred to me then that the office was missing the one object that every other office in the world had: a telephone. No outside influence; just the recording angels in black getting it all down. And selling it back.

Before my mind was about to leave its moorings, and my seat its chair, the speaker looked down at the dossier on her lap. "Jassy," she said.

"That's right."

She rustled through the papers. I tried to read some of it upside down but she moved too quickly and held the folder at various angles, perhaps to prevent me from discerning too much. It looked like photostats of prison-camp records, but a few of the papers had the Reich stamp. They were old and written in faded blue ink, and must have been stolen from the camps or from government offices.

"How much?" I asked with my patented subtlety.

"You can pay whatever you like. We have no set fee for individuals. This will do." Her stained fingers snatched the bills away and tucked them in a sleeve. Nuns. They were not used to pockets. She sat there looking straight ahead, smoking. Behind me her sister scratched letters on lined paper with a red margin. I had as much effect on them as a smear on the window.

"The folder?" I almost hated to interrupt that silence; it had a sculptured, finished quality, like amber.

Then she was all business. "Jassy. Cell Block E, is that correct? Armbands of Z, under Kommandant Werner?"

She had the goods, all right. How she got them I would never understand; I remembered Werner burning the duplicate papers one by one before me, just as I had once burned the originals. Incredible. Nothing is lost. Presenting the traveling Clair sisters in their unforgettable role as the mind of God in which nothing in this world is destroyed or forgotten.

"No identifying scars or disfigurements. Born 22 September, 1915. Eyes brown. Hair black. Skin dark—well, of course dark. A *Zigeuner*. Record of total cooperation and collaboration. Health excellent. Died 1945."

"Died?"

"A suicide. Testimony of Officer Leland L. Carr, December 3, 1945. Death certificate signed by Major Neil Armbruster, Army Medical Corps. Death was by hanging in Cell 55, Allied Prison Barracks, Berlin."

What do I do now, I wondered. Laugh or cry? Whom did I see that night? Was I just too fevered? Was it hallucination? He had seemed so real, far more authentic than these black apparitions I was now consulting. I rose and left while she was still talking. She yelled "Wait!" after me, but I just walked out and down the corridor and no one followed me. One more memory exorcised. No more items, no more recall. Maybe now I could get on with my work.

It was good work. Good diversion, anyway. The first assignment I had after the Clair interview was the rendering in charcoal of one Louis Armstrong.

It was far easier than I thought, but that was because of the sitter, not the artist. "I read about you," he said, and showed me a clipping someone had neatly sliced from the *Tribune.* "You a true Gypsy?"

I said I was. I had already begun to sketch.

"Put that down a second," he said, indicating my charcoal pencil. "We gone get to know each other."

I retired the pencil to my jacket pocket and watched him. Everybody remembers the incandescent teeth and the wide brown smile. But his was a sad face, really. There were hard lines under his right eye, and his lips were very heavily calloused; almost black in some spots, with layers of skin built up into scar tissue. The amusing sandpaper singing had done terrible things to his throat. When he spoke his large eyes watered. He talked about my skin, though, not his.

"You know that thing they used to say when I was a kid: If you're white, you're all right. But if you're black, git back."

I had not heard it.

"Well, you look white, but somewhere in the background you got something not quite white. But you're not colored either. I don't know what you are, do you?"

"No."

"Well, hell!" he said. "Who cares? You got women?"

"One," I told him.

"One is enough. At a time, I mean. You religious?"

"No, Mr. Armstrong."

"Louis. Well, I am. I'm a Baptist, *and* a good friend of the Pope, and I wear a Jewish star for luck. See? You got money?"

"No." (This was to be my accompaniment to Louis's riffs.)

"Me neither. I made it and I blew it. You don't see me with no big estate and yachts—that ain't gonna play your horn for you. When the guys come from taking a walk around the estate they ain't got no breath to blow that horn."

The eyes were very melancholy now. His horn was up on a shelf. I asked him to hold it, just finger it a little while I drew him. He took it down and looked at it gleaming in his fingers. I sketched again very lightly. He put the horn to his lips, squirted out a bar, maybe, of something I didn't recognize, and then rested his lips. He wiped them with his red kerchief. "This gonna be in color?" he asked.

"Black and white."

"Very appropriate. Like notes on paper. I'm the black notes. Man says in the *Times* you can't play jazz without the black notes. You can't play *life* without the black notes."

Then without warning he flashed his famous billboard grin on me and held it.

I took breath and then chanced it: "Mr. Armstrong—Louis. Don't do that."

"Do what?"

"Don't give me that big commercial smile. Any photographer can get that."

"You want the real Louis?"

"Yes."

"You don't think this is the authentic Satchmo?"

"No."

"You know too much. We gone have to rub you out." And he increased the perimeters of his smile.

"What the hell I got to be sad about?" he asked. He took his trumpet in his hands and examined it, and looked at the distortions of his reflection in its burnished surface.

"I could be sad if I wanted, kid. The stuff about the detention home and the hookers, the two wives. No children. I could give you stories." For one instant the smile receded. Then it returned twice as wide, three times as false. A persona, coated with cochineal and ivory. "I been lucky. Why should I complain? All that traveling don't wear a man out if he keeps in the right frame of mind." I started sketching before he stopped me, trying to duplicate the vanished face. "I don't vote, you know that? I haven't voted since I lived in New York. Ain't no use messing with something you don't know anything about. A cat came up to me once and asked about the Big Four, I said I just hope that combo has a good time."

I hadn't the wit to say, "Louis, Louis, stop putting on the

African mask." I just listened, sketched and departed, flashing my own put-on grin.

Neither could I tell my next subject, a businessman of tran-scendental self-inflation, to discard his harrumph disguise so that I could see the man beneath. I slowly realized that I would have to start from the skull outward—something Munch knew and Giacometti learned in his cradle. Something that took me too long to find out.

Armstrong was what you would take to get rid of Lamont Lansing. This was the first of those two-last-name types— Putney Guest; Courtney DePeyster; Whitney Soames—whom I was to meet constantly in the next decades. I would learn from such people how to greet an anecdote with "You can dine out on that" and how to deprecate the competition: "Lieber is the best portraitist there is, *if* you want a photographic likeness"; where to buy clothes and where to eat; how to take a client to lunch and see to it that the thing he held most dear could be revealed to my painter's discerning eye—his bankroll; how to find something to admire on every society dreadnought, even if it were only her earlobes or her shoes; the different smiles for doormen and headwaiters, for sitters and their wives; how to arm myself with dust-jacket prose (there came a time when I had dust jackets sent to me so that I could speak knowledgeably about my subjects' books); how to espouse the new American credo: that the Mafia is run by kindly white-haired men with houses in the suburbs; that Los Angeles is now what the whole world will be someday; that the children of psychoanalysts are the most neurotic kids of all; that gambling is a disease, like malaria; that the stage musical, the Western movie and jazz are the only authentic American art forms; that girls with deep-brown suntans will have skin like rhinoceros hide one day; that you never hear a good joke any more; that the Russians want peace as much as we do but their leadership forbids it; that the crushing burdens of the presidency make it the loneliest job in the world, etc., etc.

Shibboleths. Jargon. Bullshit. I learned it all. I never wore garters or rep ties. I never faked a prep-school accent; that was beyond my ear. But the patina, even on the scrawny Gypsy boy, started building up; I was getting free of the past. All it cost was a few brain cells.

Still, those early portraits were the goods; Louis's was in his house in Queens when he died. He must have liked it. I felt a gratitude so profound that I could not work for a month after I read about it in the *Times*. I offered to buy it back, but the will was inviolable and the portrait now sits on a wall in a museum in New Orleans. Doubtless, Lamont Lansing's picture rests on the walls of the corporation that bears his name. Smiling down upon his employees, he reflects the complete absence of conscience that I was subversively able to capture and that he was unable to see.

Within two years the commissions came in with the regularity of a company pay check. I had my own bank account. I took Max and Mordecai out all the time and picked up the check. "When the father gives to the son, both laugh," Mordecai said. "When the son gives to the father, both cry." If we could have, Max, we would have. Instead we both ate. Risa's studio was turned over to me. I had my own place within the old apartment, and sometimes Max would telephone me from three rooms away. Sometimes Dyanne would call me from *one* room away, but those were rare occasions.

For, as my career consolidated, the affair deteriorated. Until one afternoon Dyanne and I had our terminal argument. I forget about what. No, I don't; I remember. I recall everything. My memory, my curse. There was a lady sitting for me that afternoon, the wife of some branch manager from Cincinnati. I was not spending the whole afternoon painting. Dyanne had a key to the place and decided she would drop in and surprise me. An old story, an old story.

After that, she would not even come to the phone. She crossed the street once when she saw me coming. My letters came back unopened. I heard from one of her friends that she was involved with an oboist in the NBC Symphony. Then I heard that she had become engaged to a young dentist.

Reader, she married him. One weekend Dyanne and Myron "Mike" Selz eloped to Maryland, a *shanda* to his family. They had planned to have him marry the daughter of a department store.

I sent a note and a silver tray from Jensen's. The gift was matched in innocuousness by its accompanying note, a quote from someone safe. Father Hopkins, I think, in case her husband should happen upon it. A sterile note came back in acknowledgment: "Mike and I were thrilled . . . The tray has tons of charm." Jesus. Tons of charm. We exchanged no more words until one afternoon in March when I was working in the studio. My subject was the twelve-year-old daughter of some Detroit middle-management type who had been instructed by her parents to sit absolutely still, as if she were posing for Matthew Brady. I was attempting to loosen her up by telling her palindromes *(Able was I ere I saw Elba; Straw? No, too stupid a fad. I put soot on warts)* when the phone rang. It was Max, calling from back in the apartment, ringing me on the unlisted number. "Max," I said, "couldn't you walk down the hall and save yourself ten cents?"

"I don't think so." The voice seemed far away. From another country, another epoch.

"Why not?"

"Because I think I'm having a heart attack."

It was not the first time this had happened. Three months ago the same thing. Only then it was gas.

"Max, I don't make house calls unless it's real. You sure this is the goods and not onions?"

No answer. I belted out of the studio as if my sitter, whose face had unbent enough to be painted, was a plague carrier. Max lay on the floor of his room. There were bubbles around his lips and he was barely audible. I called for Mordecai. No response. Out with his cronies at the Broadway Cafeteria. I dialed a hospital, dismissed the kid, made an appointment for next time and got my father comfortable, the way they showed in the first-aid books. To make a long story unbearable, the men in white from St. Luke's came with a stretcher and carried him out. I rode in the ambulance. *And you, my father, there on the sad height.* I held his hand. An astonishing grip seized my fingers. Above our heads there arose a high, insistent keening as there always is from an ambulance, only this time others were wondering about the catastrophe and I was riding. Max raised his head. His eyebrows worked like caterpillars.

"Death is nature's way of telling you to slow down," he assured me. Max closed his eyes and murmured something inaudible. I bent down and thought I heard *"S'hma Yisrael,"* but I wouldn't swear to it. The siren was very loud.

Once settled in his bed, Max was ordered to be alone. I walked out into the street and met Mordecai coming up the stone steps. He had found my note. In his wake was Risa. I told them what Max had told me. Risa was pale, with eyes and mouth painted in exaggerated gestures, like a Japanese mask. Guilt? Memory?

"Well." Mordecai put his hands on his narrow, stubbly cheeks, "If the rich could get somebody to die for them, the poor could make a nice living."

We went back into the hospital so that Risa could inquire about visiting hours, and then left again and shared a cab uptown. "You got a call," Mordecai told me. "I wrote it down. From a Mrs. Selz."

For a second no slide was projected. Then I saw Dyanne and Mike, figures on a wedding cake.

"She seemed very anxious to talk to you. Left a nomber."

"She say what it was about?"

"You should have married her."

"She said that?"

"I said dat. She said nottin'."

Risa patted me on the knee. "I hear you've become very successful."

"I'm making a living."

"—for your age, I mean."

Mordecai sighed. "Risa is like God. Gives vit von hend, takes avay vit de odder."

The apartment was dark when we got back, and full of echoes.

I think we all knew that Max was not going to make it, although he was to fool us by a year. I left Mordecai and Risa at the kitchen table reminiscing and walked down the hall to my studio. My father was dying and there was nothing I could do about it except hope that he could survive long enough for me to say thank you. Fathers seem to be objects that grow

larger as we get away from them, and what would I do now
when I just wanted a beer and to listen to someone grumble
at the consumer society and shout the lines of Lewis Carroll
out the window: " 'But wait a bit,' the Oysters cried, 'Before
we have our chat. For some of us are out of breath, and all of
us are fat!' " All the things undone and unsaid. Who else would
have taken in such a pocked and hapless discard? Who else
would have held on in the face of such anger and misdirection?

Ah well, I thought, ah well. Too old to cry, and anyway, who
would I cry for? Me, that's all.

The message was pinned up on the bulletin board next to
the telephone. I dialed the number.

Her voice sounded remote. I'm sorry, the lover you have
dialed is not a working lover.

"Dyanne?"

"Ben. How is he?"

"Pretty bad. He had diabetes. Did you know he had diabetes?"

"No."

"Neither did I. I lived with him and I didn't know."

"Don't blame yourself."

"Of course not. I'll find someone else to blame."

"Ben, I meant to call before this."

"It's all right. I've been out of town a lot."

"Eleanor Clair has been trying to reach you. Through me.
She's been calling for a week. Ben, will you go?"

"How do you like married life?"

"Please don't answer a question with a question."

"All right," I said. "I'll see her. For you."

"No, not for me. For you."

The hell with it, I thought. But two days of sitting at Max's
bed, watching him stare at the ceiling with creased and stu-
dious eyes, having squeaked by the midterms with old man
Decrepitude and now cramming for the finals with Professor
Death, plus Risa's awkward chatter and whinny, plus Mordecai's crackpot advice ("He that would avoid pain must hang
himself when young") was enough to push me back to visions
of the New Order.

Now playing, three nights only, *The Past Encapsulated*, plus selected lights in the brain, joint aches and low fever.

In the morning a great sensitivity in the throat and eyes, an inability to confront light. Pain in the roots of the hair. All sounds too loud and furnished with a faint echo. No relief granted by pills, or from Mordecai's formula: wear a necklace of garlic and go around the house trying not to think of a white bear. The ache persisted in waves until I hailed a cab and returned to the Glendower Building.

In the elevator I could hear the voices of disturbance and terror. I would always be in the trajectory of someone else's fury. The loony bin is where I belonged, the nut house. Coming to see these harpies. With one more Clair sister you could open *Macbeth*.

"Can I help you, sir?" Thirteenth floor. A behemoth in a camel's-hair coat, full of greasy bonhomie. He would have played halfback at an undistinguished college and they would have called him Meat.

"Clair Research."

"You wished—?"

"I'm here to pick up some eye of newt."

Zero response. The closed face had an implacable shallow seriousness that indicated plain-clothes man. I told him the truth.

"This way, sir," he quipped.

There was a group around the door of the Clair sisters. One cop held a Speed Graphic and kept squeezing off pictures. The others were a nattering gang of journalists and officials mixed with the curious who come with every catastrophe.

Jacqueline peeked out, pallid and full of terror. She said something to one of the cops. Up to then the only sound I had ever heard her make was that of a pen scraping on foolscap.

"This gentleman said you had called him." The camel's-hair coat jerked his head in my general direction.

"Benoit Kaufman," I told her. "Your sister had a message for me."

"Oui, oui!" Words at last. She nodded to the cops, and they let me in and closed the door. Now there were three of us in the office: Meat, Jacqueline Clair and me.

"Ma soeur—elle a distrait—"

"In English," said the cop.

This was very hard for Jacqueline. Almost every word came out by itself, naked and alone. "My. Sister. Eleanor. She died."

"I'm sorry." I sat down in the chair opposite her desk.

"She was. Killed. Just before."

"Who by?"

"We don't know who by," said the cop. "I'm Captain Scully. We thought maybe you could help us."

She looked at me or through me; it was hard to tell. "There was also. In the camp. Another. E. Jassy? Emil Jassy?"

"Yes, yes. An Emil Jassy."

"The brother of Eleazar?"

"Yes."

—*Benoit, I thought you had escaped. They told me you had.*
—*No, they caught us ten kilometers from Bucharest.*
—*All of you?*
—*I don't know. Eleazar is the only one with me now in E Block.*
—*Stay away from him, Benoit.*
—*He said he would protect me.*
—*Eleazar is* Mulo, *a walking curse—death's double.*
—*He says he can help all Romanies.*
—*Listen to me, Benoit. He has a bad character.*
—*You two! Take your gear and move!*
—*Kai jaz ame,* Emil? *Where are we going?*
—*To hell, Benoit. To hell. Good-by, Little Fish. Remember what I said. Stay away from Eleazar.* Mulo, *death's double.*

"My sister," Jacqueline went on. "She had. Papers. Many people. Would kill. For the. Papers."

Captain Scully offered me a Life Saver. Friendly gesture, page 16 in *The Patrolman's Manual.* "Why did you want to see her?"

"It's why did she want to see me, Captain."

"Okay, why'd she want to see you?"

Jacqueline looked at him with obvious loathing. "We had. Records. A man named Jassy." She pointed at me. "He wants. To know. Whether this man. Is alive."

"Well," Scully asked, "is he?"

"He died after the war," I said.

"No!" Jacqueline's bright-green, mad eyes opened as wide as she could get them. Very *sanpaku*: lots of white under the iris. "Eleazar, you asked. My sister looked. Under the wrong. File. *Emil* Jassy she had." Emil. Back in 1946 I heard that he had perished in the camps. They neglected to say it was in the victor's camp.

I took hold of Jacqueline's wrinkled hand. "What about the other E. Jassy? What about Eleazar?"

"The results are. Incomplete. It looks to us. To me, now. As if he was living. Still."

"Where?"

"I don't know."

"Let me see the records." I took hold of her shoulder. Captain Scully didn't like that. He moved toward me in a solid bulk. A standard method: you don't pull a gun or pull back a fist or anything, you just loom. Chapter 9 of *The Patrolman's Manual*: Looming at the Perpetrator.

"No records. They are all destroyed now. Or stolen."

I looked down at the floor and at the ashes. The place had been thoroughly searched and looted, I could see that now. The blood was still sticky on the floor. The patented B. Kaufman timing. The door opened.

Jacqueline was looking over the office blankly. A police matron came over to her and talked in French. Captain Scully asked me to step outside.

The reporters moved into the room. Nobody questioned us as we went down the hall. Scully said nothing all the way down in the elevator, and as we crossed the lobby all he did was hum tunelessly under his breath. When we got to the curb a squad car came out of the traffic and pulled up.

"Drop you somewhere?" he asked.

I was going to ask him whether that was an interrogation or a command, but I had once been told not to answer a question with a question. I got in.

It was a brisk, uneventful ride uptown. To Captain Scully all red lights were green.

On the way, he asked for my wallet. He looked through it,

at the credentials, the parole card and the picture of Max and Risa and Mordecai from London, and the certificate from art school. And the money.

"I think you're clean," he said as we pulled up to my building.

"You have good instincts," I told him.

"I hope so. You have any idea who did it?" he asked.

"Somebody who could be hurt by the records, maybe. I don't know."

"There are a lot of crazy people came out of those concentration camps." This from the driver. A squat, fortyish lad with boil scars on the back of his neck. "I apprehended a woman the other day with a number on her arm. Walking down Lexington and setting fire to every garbage can. Said Hitler was garbage, so garbage was Hitler. So she was burning Hitler. Can ya imagine?"

"Yeah," I said. "I can imagine."

"So this guy"— Scully referred to his notebook—"Jassy. You thought he was dead and now he's alive, that right?"

"I don't know."

"You were in a concentration camp together?"

"Yeah."

"You thought he was dead and now maybe he's alive."

"Maybe."

"You want to see him again? Get reunited?"

I would not answer that question with a question. Or with an answer. I went upstairs to the silence that had been a companion in my adolescence, and that I would now welcome back as a savior.

I looked over the first self-portrait that I had made since school, and then scratched it out until all that was visible were eyes. How much of myself I had exposed in these fat years— especially the eyes. I took a cloth and erased them too.

You want to see him again? Get reunited?

For what purpose? To prove that it had all really happened? To loose all the rage that I had so carefully buried? To satisfy a lady? To avenge the dead, who could not care, and the living, who could not remember? It was decades now; what difference would it make? Vengeance is mine, saith the Lord—with a little help from the screwballs. Was I some nut like the Clair sisters to imagine myself an instrument of avenging heaven? I have so much to do I am going to bed says the Gypsy proverb, so back I went, to be greeted by the bulletin board with the conclusion of Yeats's mocking prophetic couplet:

> Now his wars on God begin;
> At stroke of midnight God shall win.

VI: SLOTH

THERE ARE SILENCES INSIDE OF SILENCES," MORDECAI
liked to say, "inside of silences just de way dere are rooms inside
of houses and vardrobes inside of rooms and tronks inside of
vardrobes, and boxes inside of tronks. And ven you come to de
next to lest silence, vatch out because inside *det* silence is de
biggest silence of all because it's God."

Well, I could not again be that half-child, that sullen remnant of his tribe, sworn to testify only to himself. All the same,
on the things that counted quiet prevailed. Few words on the
Korean War. Less on the past. None on love. That was gone,
displaced by the itch for recognition and arrival.

Yeats had vanished from the bulletin board. In his place, the
words of Chazal: *All words ring hollow in the well of silence.*
And silence is your champion against evil. Offer it the leverage
of your words and it uses them like a bridge to enter your
stronghold, but throw your words into the pockets of its silences
as you would dynamite a wall by laying sticks in its fissures. Arm
yourself with silence, the supreme sword of justice. Words
wound, silence kills.

Every morning Kafka reminded me: "The Sirens have a still
more fatal weapon than their song, namely their silence."

These were my *horae canonicae*, the nones, vespers and
lauds of my new life. I used them to cut loose from the traplines
of Romany, from the diseases of childhood, from the terrible
energies of the dead.

"Why why why don't you call any more?" Risa was whispering. It was one of her sporadic visits to Max, who snored
luxuriously in his ancient stuffed ottoman. The tweed threads,
loosened long ago by the depredations of Lenin, hung slack and
hapless, like their owner.

No answer.

"Come come come *on,* Benoit" came the demanding English neigh. "When you were distressed last year I I *couldn't* shut you up. Now I can't get you to *ex*hale in my direction. Are you cross with me?"

"No."

"Well, you're you're not yourself."

"Who am I, would you say?"

"I don't know. Nobody *I* know."

"Well, you've been away."

"You still still hold that against me, don't you? Don't you. Ben, Ben, for God's God's God's sake, *say* something. Blink your eyes once for yes, twice for no. Do *some*thing to indicate you're still still still in there."

A smile. A fatuous exchange. Don't mind me, Risa, I wanted to say. No, I *should have* wanted to say. I'm overworked, I've been worrying about Max. The screen between me and death. I had an unhappy affair. Anything she wanted to hear but the truth. That I have no other weapon against the things of vengeance except this. Words wound. Silence kills.

I lived in dread that the fugue sounded in European cadences was to be developed and orchestrated in the American idiom: That which you love will be taken away from you. The evidence sat before me, cutting z's, slowly taking his leave of the earth while I watched the breaths shake his beleaguered soul.

And Max could tell his own stories: two wives, both of them gone, one with his child, to other men and other places. His daughter now how old? In her teens, somewhere. I saw her occasionally in the living room when I came in. She called him Daddy and decorated her greeting to me with braces, but I think she had trouble recalling my name. A nice girl, heavyish, thick eyebrows, sad eyes like her father, but with a good mouth. His mouth.

And Dyanne. One brief communication about the Clairs. Then gone. Vanished.

The sense of home gone, and those days, those funny hours cracking books without classroom demands, and the guys on the street and the crazy girls, all gone. And New York crystallizing into a hard place with nowhere to hide or nourish sensations of sadness. And the green feelings, the staring innocence, the ability to be wounded. Finished. *Fartig,* in Mordecai's term.

"You couldn't tell?" Mordecai was asking. "He's filling sorry for himself. Only gonna make tvanny-tousand dis yir, dot's all. Before texes. Ve should be so sorry. Believe me, I'd sell the shirt off mine beck to be rich."

If I hear one more proverb from this gnarled loudspeaker, this wandering Jew's harp, I will personally take him and—

And what, you *shmuck?* He's right. That's what hurts, not the proverbs. Self-pity, that blue mask of vanity.

"He only only only does it to make me feel . . . culpable," Risa told him.

They began talking about me while I sat there, the classic doctor's gambit, a signal that the subject is considered beyond reach, that any remark to or about him is a condolence call.

I didn't care; I was numb. Who knows what clashes might have ensued if we had talked? At the minimum, a shrink. Risa suggested it in my presence, and Max, awakening to this affront, blasted her with a mirthless laugh. "You know what Rilke said? 'If you take my demons, you will also take my angels!' "

"So? He'll invent new angels," said Mordecai.

"The expert," Max said to the air.

"I don't need a psychiatrist," Mordecai returned loftily. "I got a rabbi tells me what's wrong vit me."

"Really?" Max leaned forward in his chair. "I didn't think there was anything wrong with you. I thought you were perfect."

"It just so heppens I'm onted."

"You're hunted? Who would want to hunt you?"

"Not unt. Ont. Like a onted ouse."

"What's ont—what's haunting you?"

"Ghosts of de pest."

"Like Scrooge?"

"More like nails. Being hit by little hemmers. Personal, I

think it's davils. Little davils in mine knees and albows."

Max howled. "Mordecai, do you have any idea how superstitious you are? You, a believing Jew, with devils in your joints."

"Okay, you're right. You're right, it's not davils."

"That's better."

"It's vempires."

"Jesus, vampires. Mordecai, you're an *old man*, for God's sake. Didn't you ever hear of arthritis?"

"I'll hev you know I'm not yet saventy. Vot ve in Poland used to call de prime." He sulked for a moment, twisting in his chair. *"Old*, em I?" he demanded abruptly. "I can still cot a rog." He started to jig on the carpet. "Come on, Risa, like olden days." He and she did a turn, and for a minute I found myself transported to the silly afternoons of 1947. Max and I applauded and the performers joined hands and took two bows. "See?" Mordecai reached for breath. "I'll dence all night. I'll dence all day. I'll dence on your gra—"

A mistake; a gaffe. Mordecai knew it, and showered us with proverbs and Yiddishisms. He knew that he would indeed dance on Max's grave—and maybe on Risa's and mine. The eternal Jew; country of origin lost, language likewise, secular and holy and irrepressible. One foot in vaudeville and the other in Jerusalem, seeking converts to a tongue not really his, able to make things, to find associates, colleagues in cafeterias, sexual partners on the crosstown bus, and friends everywhere.

"And you," Risa was saying. She broke through whatever speculations occupied my head. "You make make make people dig their own graves with their mouths, and you keep keep keep still. What gives you the right to sit in judgment?"

Had I missed something? In these fugue states were whole arguments constructed, depositions that assigned me a new role in the courtroom?

"I'm *not* sitting in judgment, Risa," I complained.

"Not in words, perhaps. But in attitude. Look look at you. You you you've never really forgiven me for run run running away—"

"Risa, let the boy alone."

"He's not a boy, Max. He never never never was a boy." She turned to me. "Why didn't I see that? You were all all always a little adult, always tallying, keeping score."

"What did you want me to do, look away? Shut my eyes?"

"Benoit, can't can't you forgive me even now?"

"There's nothing to forgive, Risa," I began. But her face was turned away.

And then it tumbled out. Fred, the black bishop in the Archdiocese of St. Joseph Stalin, had decided that Risa was running in the wrong race: the Caucasian one. This was the early stirring of the Black Revolution, and Deever, who was in dress, voice and temperament about as Negroid as J. Edgar Hoover, had told Risa, the great love of his middle years, that the struggle for equality meant, in the memorable phrase of *Reader's Digest*, "Going Your Own Way with Your Own Kind."

I thought for a moment that Risa was asking back in. But no, she and Max were merely managing that difficult business of friendship. Perhaps that was all their marriage had ever been. These days they were moved by the accumulation of loss, and when they sat, sometimes holding hands, sometimes apart while he napped and she sketched or read, they were rehearsing a death scene.

As the next few months proved, Risa never really dropped the torch for Deever; periodically they would reunite. I saw him shortly after this critique of my withdrawal symptoms at the opening of Risa's one-woman show. The trip to the Great Jones Street Gallery downtown via taxi took forever. We were slowed by patches of ice and stinging gusts of sleet. It was growing even colder, and there were times when traffic was invisible half a block ahead. In this harsh and dingy surrounding the taxi felt like a plane making its way through some particularly opaque cloud, an impression relieved from time to time by the sudden appearance of a pedestrian lurching against the visible wind. One of these figures was dressed in yards of black and appeared, for a moment, to be Eleanor Clair. I was about to check the driver's card to make sure that his name was not Charon when the figure turned around and reached out its hand to guide a small boy across Seventh Avenue, thereby exhibiting the magenta, snow-stung face of a middle-aged housewife. Loon, I told myself, but the case of mistaken identity was an interesting example of precognition for those who believe in ghosts. Personally, I have known too many to believe in them.

It was the same old fifties opening: everyone flushed and excited, every set of glassy eyes sliding over everyone's shoulders in the hope of finding a guest more compelling or useful in the background. The European refugees who arrived in threes and fives, never in even numbers, always with a house guest in tow, talked too loud in condemnation of either America's central heating or its commercial vulgarity; the girls who arrived in pairs wore chalky make-up and pale lipstick and tried to hint at past evenings of unimaginable depravity and suggested, instead, Redon's vases of cut flowers; the artists elaborately ignored the critics; the conversations were saturated with the cant of New Criticism and high gossip.

"Gang, I was out to see De Kooning last fall." This from a woman suffering from terminal celebrity-fucking. "You've seen his house? In the *Times?* All glass? Everything was migrating, flying south, and there are these enormous picture windows? And in the morning the lawn was *cov*ered with dead birds." A splendid still-life of the New York art scene, I thought, but did not articulate.

Actually, Risa was a lady with talent; I had forgotten that. The stuff she had learned from Chazal or picked up from courses emerged in her work, but she had no center, no light, no sun from which to derive her own sustenance. Whatever New York movements had passed in review were refracted on her canvases. Here were the abstract seizures of Pollock and the slashing calligraphy of Kline. She gave her audiences the witless power of oversized black-and-umber protests in sedulous imitation of Rothko; her formal abstracts were straight out of Motherwell down to the parasitic titles: *Homage to Zola; The Hiroshima Triptych; Kindertotenlieder.* Streaky declamations, formal abstractions, unrelieved bleaknesses; she could reproduce everyone except, of course, Risa. For a while, manifestly under Deever's influence, she had even executed works of top-heavy social significance, cannily using conté crayon and tempera: bludgeoned strikers, blurred, corrupt plutocrats worthy of Ben Shahn or Jack Levine. She was like some wry, brilliant impressionist who could mimic the entire cast of a movie, but who could no longer speak in her own voice.

The critics loved her. The show was a smash, received with such phrases as "refined painterliness," "crossed with turbulence and inspired accident," "resonant color sonorities" and all the other endorsements used in place of feelings, words too vigorous for the thoughts.

This was one occasion when my maligned silence would be much appreciated; either that or an encomium. Nobody asked. I was introduced to some harpy as Risa's son, to another, a man with a spade beard, as a portrait artist. "But why?" he boomed with what I took to be a Russian intonation. "De photograph has annihilated de portrait artist. All dis [indicating the walls of canvases], all dis is in defiance of Kodak. You are extinct, my friend. A dead star whose light is long gone."

Fred Deever swam into our tight orbit, and with unintentional mercy blocked the Russian and his companion. "Tell me, Ben," he said in his confidential bass, "what do you think of Risa now?"

"Well, she—"

"Marvelous feeling she has for the downtrodden," he said. "I don't care much for those splashy things, though."

"It's part of the—"

"She'll get over it in time, get down to bedrock. And how are you?"

"I seem to be—"

"We've had a difficult time, Risa and I. A prerevolutionary situation always creates a difficult social dynamic." At this the star arrived, anxious to sever Fred's party line.

"Ben, Ben, isn't it exciting?" Risa asked me. Her eyes danced and her skin was flushed. There was something youthful about her, something unseen since the days in London art class. She belonged in this aviary, worshiping whatever Baals the New York school was pushing. I congratulated her and pronounced the customary cabala familiar to anyone who frequents actors' dressing rooms, art galleries and publishers' parties.

"I'm sorry for the other day," she said. "I have no right to criticize."

"Yes, you do," I said. "To tell you the truth, I haven't been feeling very well recently."

"I'm sorry. I I I never thought to ask. Ennathing wrong? Enna enna ennathing physical?"

"No, I guess it's just Max. And thinking about being drafted. And—I don't know—other things."

"Ben, you haven't gotten into into into any more trouble, have you? With the police or anything?"

"No, Risa. I'm a very upright young animal these days. I respond to simple commands, I'm paper-trained and everything."

She let that by with a withering, assessing look. "Ben, you remember the business of that man what what what's his name? That you and Max tried to find?"

"And couldn't."

"And couldn't. I heard something from Mordecai about him. That maybe you you you really did see him, after all."

Jacqueline Clair, Dyanne, Sadie, Mordecai, Risa. The lethal telegraphy of gossip.

"Maybe. Nobody's sure."

"If he is alive, what will you do?"

"Find him if I can."

"How?"

"I don't know."

"What will you do if if if you do find him?"

"I don't know."

The Russian separated us, burbling at Risa, and I stood alone for a moment, contemplating an oil of unrelieved blackness. What would I do if I found Eleazar? My thoughts twitched like a fish on grass.

ITEM: "A number of Bessarabian Gypsies appeared. Two hundred men and eight hundred women and children. The Gypsies came on foot. Behind them came their wagons drawn by horses."

[—W. Grossman, *Die Hölle von Treblinka* (London: INC Publications, 1945)]

Afterwards they were made to undress for "baths" and then driven by guard dogs and blows into the gas chambers. We know that others came from Poland:

"Once a transport of seventy Gypsies from near Warsaw was brought in. These men, women and children were destitute. All they had was some soiled underwear and ragged clothes . . . Within a few hours all was quiet and nothing was left but their corpses."

[—Y. Wiernik, *A Year in Treblinka* (Gen. Jewish Workers Union of Poland, 1945)]

A group of Gypsies recaptured after trying to escape from the Warsaw ghetto were sent to Treblinka and killed by machine guns.

—Donald Kenrick and Grattan Puxon, *The Destiny of Europe's Gypsies* (New York: Basic Books, 1972)

"You don't look well, Ben."

Deever. Progressives always did have a keen eye for detail.

"It's terribly close in here with with with all these people," Risa complained over his shoulder. Her fingers dug into her lover's arm and the voice trembled with concern. I took her advice and went out on the street. New York was tied up and silent. The wind had died and the sleet had turned to snow-flakes the size of quarters. For a moment the Lower East Side looked like a jade frieze from the Sung dynasty. Angles were softened and the air was filled with crystals. Only a few other people were out, spouting steamy breaths and moving with cautious purpose over icy patches. It was difficult to perceive anything for any distance: a stage for illusions. I took out a much-folded letter from Dyanne, found an old, obscure address, and edged my way over to the apartment, up an icy stoop, and pressed the bell. No answer.

I worked my way down the steps onto the sidewalk and started home.

She appeared out of the white air like a memory coming to the surface of the brain. I said hello to her in French. She pulled her cloak further around her and looked sideways at me with a wounded, flinching attitude. I reminded her of who I was.

"Yes," she returned in French, "the Gypsy boy. Yes." But there was no illumination of recognition in her face; she was just going through cards in the file that was sutured to the top of her spinal column. "You were one of the ones who came after . . . my sister . . ."

"Yes. Do you still have the office?"

"My files are with me at home."

"Can I call you there? Or will you call me? If you find anything?"

"I will find nothing. What we had has vanished."

"All of it?"

"No, not all. But the files you wanted; most were taken or destroyed. Only a handful remain."

"Could I see them? Please?"

What an absurdity to stand here with the snow coming down my neck and soaking my hair. Had I even bothered to make a call, to write a letter, to attempt in any way to locate this poor ex-nun, this black figment, in the days and weeks—how long had it been?—since the death of Eleanor Clair and the resurrection of Eleazar Jassy?

The old lady looked at me without emotion. She walked very slowly away. I had no idea whether the gesture signaled abandonment or an invitation to follow her. But this seemed to me an afternoon to believe in portents, and I walked in her footsteps and drew alongside her. She made no response, no gesture. We walked in such quietude that you could hear the snow meeting itself on what used to be the sidewalk, a sound like soda or an apple bitten and held close to the ear. A set of wheels screamed against ice.

The building she lived in, south of Houston Street, was a peculiar place, half industrial and half residential, a stricken, settled pile—what Max would have been if he had been a building. It was shored up against the imminent visit of the wrecking ball. Workers had already destroyed the two neighboring structures; patched old wallpaper showed against the side of this age-stained structure, where beads of ice hung from a large drain spout like water from a runny nose. The anthropomorphism was accentuated by some windows illuminated with meager wattage and imperfectly closed off by shades half or three quarters drawn, like eyes on people with colds. The whole place offered the promise of double pneumonia, and the cold followed us into the narrow tiled lobby and up the stairs. I tripped on little warped steps that seemed too close together. Jacqueline turned to me and said, "You know what this was?" I kept climbing. "A shirt factory. They employed children. They made the stairs small so the little workers could go up to the machines."

Another thought to warm the visitor on his way up. Her flat was on the top floor, a place heated only by a coal-burning fireplace. The landlord had long ago extinguished the boiler in order to discourage his holdout tenants, but thus far, Jacqueline Clair said, only one aged couple had left. She and her sister had planned to stay until they got some sort of compensation, but now . . . the old lady just shrugged. "Time I left here anyway," she said.

"Where will you go?" She did not reply. Lights were clicked on and the place came to some sort of life. Its gray walls were festooned with black-and-white photographs in dime-store frames.

Jean Saint-Loup 1927–1943 Buchenwald. Ferdinand Leon Blanc 1927–1940 Belsen. Sister Annamaria Gerard 1922–1941 Belsen, along with five unnamed students captured with her. Etc., etc. Sisters. Brothers. Auschwitz. Dachau. Remember me, remember me.

The fireplace was ignited and immediately became the sun of the room. We pulled our chairs close to it. A bottle of wine appeared from nowhere along with glasses. Still nothing was said, but it took no special sense to feel Jacqueline's appraisal.

"The police are worthless," she said after a long interval.

"They never found who killed my sister. I think they never will. You know why?"

I didn't.

"I saw what they wrote on their report. They think because I don't speak English very well I can't read it. But I can. I can even read English upside down. On the paper it said 'Victim is of French citizenship, agitated and probably disturbed.' Well, they were right. On all three counts. But they won't find anything. Why should they?"

"What will you do?" Strange to be on the other end of that question.

"I don't know," she said. "I suppose go away. Back to the South of France. I have very little strength left now. I feel my age and the cold hurts me more than ever."

We sat quietly, sipping. The hot coal provided the only sound. I had a sudden recollection of the office, and looked around the room again. Here, too, there was no telephone. I wondered what had happened to the gun. Two aging sisters had lived in a shadowy, protected hole, and still they were found out and one of them had been murdered. A chance robbery, maybe. A junkie with his brain on fire, a prowler, a palmer of doorknobs. But I didn't believe it, and neither did Jacqueline Clair. She kept looking at me. I could have cartooned her then with bubbles rising above the head to a large balloon. And in that balloon? Ink, I guess. Just a large crosshatched mat of black.

I took out a 2B Mongol pencil and a little sketch pad and started to block in her features. I still have the drawing: it shows a weary, near-sighted face conditioned by facts and disciplined by too many years of moral training. The eyes have the cloudiness of incipient cataracts, and the mouth is marked by that feeling expressed by Zola when he concluded that anyone who did not want to see anything more disgusting during the day had better start by eating a toad for breakfast.

This old lady with her black habit and her acrid expressions and ambiguous attitudes could have taught a stone lessons in silence. Oceans rose and fell, epochs passed, dinosaurs were replaced by little furry animals, these in turn evolved into the two mammals that now sat opposite each other, and still no sounds were forthcoming. When even I grew weary of hearing nothing but the hiss of the anthracite and the whistle of wind in nostrils, Jacqueline Clair refilled her glass and mine and asked me whether I was religious. I told her no.

"Do you believe in God?"

My turn to say nothing.

"Most people your age," she went on, "and with your experience, have no religious sense. They think the concentration camps were a refutation of faith. Or a sign that the Antichrist had won."

I said I could see how people might feel that way.

"And you?"

"I don't think about it very often."

"Except at night."

"And even then not much."

A long, unbelieving stare. She rose and went to a portmanteau and rummaged around. She produced a folder, took a small snapshot out of it and handed it to me. It was a double exposure, two memories fighting for the same space.

One was a twenty-year-old, the other a grizzled soldier dressed in German uniform. He must have been the oldest corporal in the *Einsatzgruppen*. I knew the younger visage. "Yes," I said. "That's the way I remember him."

"All right," she replied with great rigidity. "Put away your paper and pencil and listen to me. Because you and I will never meet again."

"How do you know? I was thinking next year of visiting the South of France if I don't get draft—"

"We will *never* meet."

I expected her to sit down, but she seemed to have received an adrenal lift and walked around her little room, pausing every now and then to straighten a photograph or remove an imaginary speck of lint from her furniture.

"Benoit Kaufman, you know who this man is. *I* know who this man is. What happens from here on depends on you and on him. Because he is alive. Make no mistake."

"How do you know? How are you so sure?"

"The only records that were destroyed were his, or those pertaining to him. He wants no evidence of his past. Evidently he is an important man. Or wants to be."

"You're still in danger, then," I said.

"I doubt it." She closed her eyes and weighed the odds again. "No. Who would take a shaky old woman's word? The police think I'm senile. The governments have bigger fish. Eleazar Jassy is safe. So am I. But not you."

There was a throwaway line you could dine out on. Not that I hadn't thought about it. Jassy had killed before, though in different circumstances. If he could murder now, surely I, who had witnessed his crimes, was as valid a target as Eleanor Clair. Provided he knew I was alive.

"Does he know?" I heard my voice crack. "That I exist, even?"

"I think not," Jacqueline said. "You were just a number on the roster of orphans at the processing center. Then nothing. We never followed it up. We had other work to do."

"Then I have the advantage."

"It would seem that way. You never know, of course, what means he has of discovery."

I had a sudden need for air. The place was as enclosed as a fist and the atmosphere had the tropical oppression of a pet shop.

"Sit down," she said calmly. "Going away will accomplish nothing."

"I was just going to open a window."

"Sit down. In his zealotry, Jassy overlooked something."

She held up a little notebook. I sank back into my chair.

The entries were in some sort of code impossible for me to decipher, plus the names of a few towns. I handed it back to her.

"The part that concerns Jassy reads this way," she informed me. "Hasser, Endor, Paris; later Salant, Éduard, St. Albans, Queens. Import-Export. Married, no children. Wife, Patricia Sable, New York." Jacqueline looked up. "Does this mean anything?"

"No."

She leafed through a few heavily blotted pages. "He married sometime in the fifties under the name Hasser. Then he changed his name to Éduard Salant. In April 1958, the paper trail was lost. He pulled his money out of all bank accounts. We assumed he changed his name at least once more. And of course his address. But you have the name Salant to work with, and if you can locate his wife . . ."

"You want me to find him, don't you?" I could feel a constriction of the valves in my veins.

"If it satisfies you."

I stood up. "No," I told her, "not if it satisfies me. If it satisfies *you.*"

"Don't be a fool." She looked down at my hands. I tried to keep the fingers still.

"You want me to be some sort of trained predator," I said. "You sit there and unhood the falcon and lift him off."

She didn't move. "You think I'm mad, too." She gave me a stiff smile. "Maybe I am. Like Eleanor. Driven mad. Or maybe God robbed us of our minds that we might be made expressions of His own." She turned her head toward the bookshelf, but the stare seemed to remain on me like an Egyptian bas-relief whose eye looks forward even when the face is in profile. The corners of her cracked lips turned up. I had seen that look once before, on a shopping-bag lady who used to go across 72nd Street announcing that she was Helen of Troy.

My soaked black overcoat was leaning against the firescreen, steaming slightly. I leaned over to pick it up and she said, "All right. Go. But Eleazar Jassy, Hasser, Éduard Salant will stay with you as long as you live."

"Yes," I admitted. "I think you're right."

"I misjudged you. I *am* old. The police are right."

She helped me on with my overcoat, and that kindness hurt worst of all.

"Well, Benoit Kaufman. *Adieu.*"

"Good-by," I said in English. "I'm sorry for what I said to you."

"I, too." She opened the door and joined me in the frigid hallway.

"Go back in," I said. "You'll catch cold."

"Old people catch their death, not colds." She took hold of my arm. "Here, take this anyway." She gave me the notebook. I tried to refuse it and she thrust it into my coat pocket. "You know what the Jesuits say? About giving them a child for a handful of years, and after that the world can have him?"

"I've heard it."

"Do you believe it?"

"I hadn't thought. I suppose I do."

"Then the Antichrist must have the same power. Give the Antichrist a child and the world can have him forevermore. You understand?"

She didn't want an answer, or if she did I never had a chance to reply.

"Hitler was an Antichrist. Don't you see that? The Germans had you, child. Child you remain. My God, can't you see the way you talk, the way you think, even the way you don't dare to think—it's all from those years."

"Let me go." She had the clutch of a tarantula.

"Even the victim is part of the process, as necessary as oxygen to the fire. You participated, even against your will, against your choice." Her irregular teeth chattered. "No, don't pull away. You know you did. You will be a part of the Antichrist until *it* gets destroyed, or destroys you. You will be a sinner until you perform the final sin."

Madness establishes its own logic; for a dread second I could see flames under the cracks of the warped floor, and thought myself capable of the murder that might extinguish, for all time, that conflagration: the murder of Eleazar Jassy, or Jacqueline Clair, or Benoit Kaufman—it seemed to make no difference. Then I shook it off with the chill air.

Vengeance is why I stopped reading the Bible.

"And there came forth little children . . . and mocked him. And he turned back, and looked on them, and cursed them in the name of the Lord. And there came forth two she bears out of the wood and tore forty and two children of them.

"And he went from thence to Mount Carmel, and from thence he returned to Samaria."

So much for the miracles of Elisha.

Jacqueline would not release me.

"On the stage in Paris," she cackled, "they allow the actors to say a shocking thing."

"About what?"

"How lucky Christ was: 'Where he lived it was warm, it was dry! And they crucified quick.' You understand?"

I shook my head and took the stairs two at a time.

"You will, though."

The witch's words bounced down the stairs and spilled into the drifts.

It was even harder to get warm than to leave that place. I managed to get a cab uptown, but it had no heat. Even the apartment seemed cold and desolate. Max was sleeping again; Mordecai was sitting in the kitchen huddled around the stove.

"Mordecai's law," he said as I walked in. "The boiler will alvays blow on de coldest night of de yir. It's five above zero, you know det?"

"Ah, but that's only in the shade," I reminded him. Max didn't approve of my drinking; neither did Mordecai. I found a Scotch bottle, secreted it in my coat and took it to bed. In the morning things were better; the radiators hissed and Max was arguing down the hall with his old antagonist. This time the Yiddish was on the other tongue.

"*Der Yid hot nor geld tsu farlir, un tsayt krank tas zayn,*" Max was complaining. "A Jew has money only to lose, and time only to be sick."

"Listen," Mordecai counseled, "a doctor is not the Messiah. He cen't make you younger."

"I don't want him to make me younger. I want him to make me older!"

The Man Who Taught Blake Painting stared at me with great insect eyes. Get up, they said, and have a toad for breakfast.

I rose and looked down at the Drive. Ice floes edged down the river. Traffic was stalled on the West Side Highway. The whole world was frozen, not least of it that piece of sponge I used for a brain. The Clair notebook sat on the edge of my dresser, along with a collection of coins and pencils. I could have kidded myself before last night; Eleazar is somebody else's responsibility; who knows if he really exists? Two nuts say so, but who knows? Now there were shreds of evidence and it would be hard to look away. For a man of conscience, for a possessed Inspector Javert, maybe. Or Simon Wiesenthal. But we were not dealing here with your average obsessive-compulsive. We were dealing with the Gypsy rover, the one who looks for exits in the theater before he sits down.

I took down the balalaika and tried to stop thinking:

> *Na janav ko dad m'ro has,*
> *Niko mallen mange has;*
> *Miro gule dai merdyas,*
> *Pirani man pregelyas;*
>
> *Uva tu, oh hegedive*
> *Tut sal minding pash man.*
>
> I no longer know my father,
> And I lack friends;
> My mother is long dead,
> And my loved one departed angry;
> I play a song on my violin,
> To silence hunger and grief . . .

A bell interrupted my big number. Sullivan the doorman was mumbling something through the protective sheath of neutral grain spirits. The mail had arrived. I put on a bathrobe and stumbled down the hall. Sully, as we called him, now a good sixty-five and possessor of the finest exhibit of nose capillaries since W. C. Fields, wobbled as he stood, and regarded me with the woebegone expression of a man who has just dropped a full gin bottle on the sidewalk.

"Well, boy, it's here," he said in a paternal growl. "I remember my own years, long ago, guarding the world while others slept . . ." etc. I heard nothing more and never looked at Mordecai or Max. The letter was clearly labeled and no one doubted its contents. Still, I had hoped, because of my leg

injury and a few choice words said to the examiners at Whitehall Street, to be classified in some half-cracked category. Not
a chance. I was stamped fit for service, and a month later took
the celebrated one step forward and was caparisoned in gabar-
dine fatigues, olive drab, one each, the style that was so popular
in 1953.

So. If what was wanted was a sign, I had received it.

*Please excuse my son Benoit from his search and destroy
mission.* —GOD.

What the hell, if the Clair sisters were divine messengers,
why couldn't the United States government serve the same
role? Who was it said in an evil time everything is falsified by
simplicity and comparisons? I did. As I figured it, the signs
were telling me to lay off. To forget retribution. My conscience
turned around three times like a dog settling down, and went
to sleep.

Max and Risa saw me off on the plane when I was assigned
to Fort Lewis, Washington, for basic training. I had never been
west. "I'll sleep better knowing you're in uniform," Max said
through his cigar. His limp was pronounced even though he
tried to cover it with a bouncing gait. He handed me an
envelope with a hundred dollars in it. "You can buy your way
out of a lot," he told me. "I know. I was there." We found a
coffee shop where he discoursed on methods of passing inspec-
tions, how to keep the brass polished, where to hide valuables,
etc., until Risa disappeared to make a phone call.

Then he grabbed my arm. "Listen, Benoit," he said. "The
diabetes is got me, that and God knows what else. They won't
tell me. I doubt if they told her."

"I'm sorry, Max." Death seemed to embarrass us both. I
didn't know what to say.

"It doesn't matter." He waved to the waiter for some more
coffee, into which he dropped a cascade of saccharine from a
metal box. "Gift from a student," he said, wiggling his eyebrows in Groucho style to indicate a romance that I am sure
was wholly imaginary.

"Is there anything I can do?" I asked him.

"No. Nothing anybody can do. I'm not going this month, not even this year, maybe. I'm just telling you this so if you get some message when you're away, you'll know what's happening."

I sat there sipping my own coffee and wondering if this was the last time I would see the man who was neither father nor stranger, but something else, something better maybe, but someone to whom I could no longer talk.

"Benoit, you've seen enough in your lifetime," he said. "I have no real counsel for you. Just when you're in trouble or depressed, buy a book. Don't take it out on someone else. If you get assigned in the States, don't go to whorehouses. You're a nice-looking boy in uniform, you can get your own. You don't need hookers."

Risa was taking a long time; I wondered if this interlude was prearranged.

"All the years we knew you, we never inquired about . . . where you were, how it was for you before we met. Rough, I know. How rough is only a guess. Bad, I suppose."

"Yes."

"A thing like that can destroy after it's finished destroying. Like fallout. The only way to keep it from working on you now is to push on. Your work is good, very good. But in the last months you've been doing a lot of sulking, a lot of down time. Am I right?"

I nodded.

"I find myself thinking about you a lot. I'm proud of how far you've come. The portraits and everything."

I said, "Thank you," but I didn't know how to continue. "I'm no good at words yet, or feelings," I told him. "I can only draw what I see."

"The feelings will come," Max replied. "Right now they're still locked up and frozen. I remember what you looked like those first weeks. Sometimes I still see it. The eyes looking inside instead of out. No speech. Half fanatical. We often saw kids like that right after the war. Now you see them in slums. You never find out what happens to them."

"They get drafted," I said.

Max's face was pinched and colorless. He took out another pill and slid it under his tongue. "Nitroglycerine. For the heart. How do you like that? TNT to kill you or keep you. I use it in my class on the Moderns. To illustrate irony."

I had to turn away so that he wouldn't see my eyes.

"Ben, Ben," he said, blowing clouds of smoke at me. I pretended that it was the cigar fumes that were clouding my face. "If you don't watch it, you'll slide right back the way you did in the old days with the parole officers and the reform schools. You're a man now, not a boy. You're an orphan and you're a Gypsy and you were in hell and no power on earth can change any of that."

"I know."

"Some mornings you'll still wake up and wonder how anyone can live in a world that did what this one did to you and your people. I have no consolations for you. No religion, no politics even. We can't wait around for something to be revealed. We are not in an age of annunciations. You have a talent, use it. Don't slide, Benoit. You will if you're not careful."

At this, Risa came up and joined us. "Max Max Max has the *most* extraordinary way of of picking the wrong time for the the the wrong subject."

"I may not have another time," Max announced. "I'm dying, for God's sake."

"Well, I *know*, but but can't you lower your voice?"

He fixed her with a metal glare and returned to his quarry. "You draw well," he said. "But your stuff lacks the requisite hardness. Things still leave too deep an impression on you."

"Now, Max," Risa interjected, "isn't isn't that just what you're trying to do?"

At that he pushed back his chair and smiled at her. "There's hope for you," he said, "Risa, old horse, there really is hope for you."

A sergeant came around yelling the names of soldiers and hovered around our table, waiting for some body language to make sure I understood.

"One more thing," Max said, standing with me. "You're

going to hear a lot about how bad it is to be alone. Everything should go together in groups. Group writing. Group thinking. Group living. Group sex. The future will be full of it; the wind stinks of it. They're already shacking up by the dozen in California, the birthplace of the drive-in and the black list. But alone is good. Remember your title: *Private* Kaufman."

A few more embraces, reassurances, whinnies and I was off. From the tarmac I heard my name being called. "Private Kaufman, Private Kaufman." I and the entire company turned to look back at the gate. Mordecai stood there, dressed in formal attire, his jacket blowing in the backwash of the propellers. A silver item glittered in his hand.

I appealed to the sergeant. He nodded. I went back to the gate. Mordecai reached out a hand.

"Sorry I'm late. Subvay had a fire." He reached up and kissed me. "Don't vorry," he assured the audience. "Ve ain't *faygelehs.* Here. I vant you to hev." He held up a mezuzah on a chain. "All these yirs I never esked. Probably you're a Christian," he conjectured.

"I'm nothing."

"So? What do the nothings wear? I'll bring you one of those next time. Are you taking?"

I laughed and mimicked his tone: "Are you giving?"

"I'm giving."

"I'm taking."

And with a salute, administered left-handed, he began to walk backward. "Who would hev thought?" were his parting words. "De little scared boy, de little scareder man in London. Ve fooled dem all, not?"

"Not," I said, ostentatiously putting the chain around my neck, and climbed onto the aircraft. My seat said Private Kaufman. Max was right; a man could warm up to a title like that, go west with it, bring it home to meet the folks.

The mezuzah did its work. The plane went up and came down. So did all the others I took over the next two years. I was a good boy; this time when they said paint portraits, I painted portraits: generals, colonels, diplomats, wives of officers, children of West Pointers. If I was miserable, I scarcely even knew it. Besides, under the frightful grimace of that fifties world there were so many unhappier men.

In all that time, expanded now from its original state, like water into ice, only four incidents have value. (Five if you count the erosion of concern about Eleazar Jassy. He occurred in an occasional dream, that's all. As I write, there are fifty-nine Nazi war criminals kicking around this country. Only one has been brought to trial. This is with professionals on the scent. In those days I was an amateur at vengeance. I had forgotten my training. It's not like a bicycle or swimming. You have to keep in practice.)

Trouble occurred only once. A General Vance Ennis, admiring his portrait, from which I had carefully expunged all degeneracy, asked if I had ever thought of doing something "serious." I told him yes, I had often thought of deserting. There was an uproar ending with an adjutant telling me that the general did not like wise-asses and how would I like to be assigned to the infantry, even if the Korean War was over it could start up any minute, and in any case I could freeze my ass walking guard duty in Panmunjon, and did I remember the infiltration course with the tracers going over my head, it was not impossible for me to be permanently assigned to a unit undergoing perpetual training. It could have gone either way; I elected to tell the general that I was out of line and was full of chagrin.

This was one of the few words that betrayed my origins. The general repeated the pronunciation. "You *parlez français?*" he asked.

"*Un ou deux mots.*"

He tried me out with a burst of Army French, acquired, it turned out, during the occupation.

I replied in kind.

"Kaufman, we're going to do a little business," he said, then bellowed for his adjutant. I was dismissed, wondering. The puzzlement did not last long. In two weeks there came orders for one Private Benoit Kaufman, No Middle Initial, to report to Bremen, Germany, within ten days. Germany. I wondered, in my celebrated dispassionate, detached manner, what the place would be like. A group of us were bused to Munich, where I contemplated a city of the walking wounded. Many men were lame, one-legged, hobbling on crutches. The women, the middle-aged ones at least, were furtive and moved like fiddler crabs, with one hand advancing before their faces. I went to a beer hall alone and asked the man next to me in English what he did during the war. "Russian front," he said. The hand that held his cigarette was gloved and never moved; it was wood clear down to the wrist.

I asked others in the next days. They were all on the Russian front, or somewhere in Germany. Nobody had fought Americans. Nobody had any idea of what was happening in the camps. "People disappeared, that was all." "I knew nothing." The old story. The universal excuse.

But Rudolph Meiser knew better. He was a blond student, seventeen or eighteen, who tended bar and overheard me. When no one was listening, he said, "They lie. They know what happened. But all Germans are not like that. The young are different. Don't condemn a whole nation." It seemed urgent for him to convince me—who the hell was I? Some GI killing a few hours because I preferred them dead—that Deutschland must not be stigmatized. He kept it up, and when he got off duty produced two books from his satchel under the bar. Gifts. No amount of refusal would do. We parted friends, smashed. Where was he during the war? I didn't ask. He could not have been more than eight when it ended, anyway. A child.

I still have the volumes. *The Diary of a Man in Despair* and *Journal in the Night.* Both by Germans. The goods: men who didn't have to flee the beloved Führer.

You should read them sometime, Daniel. Because nobody else will.

"We talked about Furtwängler," says the Junker aristocrat Friedrich Percyval Reck-Malleczewen. "Evidently there is a way of conducting in a 'blond' manner." Of a massacre of 30,000 souls, he notes:

This was done in a single day, in the space of an hour, perhaps, and when machine-gun bullets gave out, flame

*throwers were used. And spectators hurried to the event
from all over the city, off-duty troops, young fellows with
the milk-complexion of the young—the children of men,
who also, nineteen or twenty years ago, were lying in cribs
and gaily bubbling and reaching for the bright-colored ring
hanging just above! Oh, degradation, oh, life without
honor, oh, thin shell that separates us from the lost souls
in whom Satan burns!*

No shell, Herr Malleczewen, although I could not believe
then that there was a German alive who could have written
that. And of course there wasn't. The diarist was put to death
behind barbed wire with a bullet in the nape of the neck,
February 23, 1945. We might have passed each other one
night.

"That little whore called history in Germany today, for sale
to the feeblest individual, exploited by those without honor."
This from Theodor Haecker, Catholic convert, philosopher,
diarist. Under arrest, of course, writing, like Malleczewen, in
the dark, in a cellar, moving his notes around so that they could
not be found, so that the arresting officers would not read:

*Their voices, my God, their voices! Again and again I am
overwhelmed by all that they betray. Their deadness is the
most frightful thing about them. The stinking corpse of a*
vox humana, *Death, disease and lies, and a solitude proud
of being deserted by God. It is not only in an objective
sense that the voice which is Deutschlandsender is inhu-
man; it is a mockery of the supernatural life and the
trinitarian God.*

Good men, decent sorts. Heroes, even. God knows the wages
demanded for such writings.

And yet neither of them could come to terms with Hitler.
Reck-Malleczewen, July 1936: "The Germans as they now are
need a master. And by this I most certainly do not mean that
forelocked Gypsy type we have been given to lead us in our hour
of need." And Theodor Haecker, 1940: "And you expect to

understand God. How silly that is! He places the world's destiny *in the hand of a Gypsy,* a knife grinder, a ham actor, a buffoon . . ." (Italics mine.)

Even those men in those dark times counted the Führer as Gypsy, not as a German, never as a German.

I expected rage to spill itself in some new way at these books, but a numbness set in instead. This condition is the real hell, this incapacity, this lack of passion, but in the beginning it always feels like grace.

General Ennis had conveyed me to Deutschland to paint not merely his French wife and their five children; I was also to render the French ambassador to Germany, then on a visit. But just before I was ordered back to the States, Mrs. General also asked me to sketch members of a Special Services troupe. I was driven in a jeep to a little theater where a bunch of half-familiar soldiers and girls were going through a Richard Rodgers production. On the back of the stage was a white banner inscribed with the device *Loud Is Good.* I thought I knew a couple of the players; they had been child actors in films. But one of the black men leaped from the stage and came at me even before I recognized him.

"Benny! The partially white man's burden!"

It was Otis, exuding the adrenal confidence of the carnival magician.

"You look different," he said. "Different and the same! As for Otis the Lotus, I'm Africa in fatigues, genius in ebony. I got a career, Ben. I'm a clown."

"You always were."

"Yeah, but now they pay money for it."

"Seventy-eight a month," I said. Like me, he had no stripes on his shirt.

"Sheeeyit, this ain't where the bread is. I perform nightly at the American bar, man. That's where I get my socks off, my knocks off, and my rocks off."

The boy who would do anything to get out and stay out was putting on an African mask so heavy it would take two to carry it, and both of them were Otis.

"This here is Private Ben Kaufman, ex-juvenile delinquent.

Now a toy soldier. *Sacré 'blew!"* He flashed a lot of candle-power at me. "Some born to watch and some to do." This kind of street jingle was to become his passport in the next few years; it had already extricated him from marching and maneuvers. "You're not angry any more," he remarked. "You was always the mad one. What happened?"

"I got older," I told him.

"Don't hand me no jive," he said. "We come from the same prep school. You just figured out what kine shit they was buyin' this year. Amazin' what sells, ain't it?"

There was no way to get through this glossy carapace. I could only listen and reminisce while I sketched him and his colleagues, and he rambled on about the days behind the walls, the low and narrow life of adolescents who were neither criminal nor upright, boys whith no moral allegiance. Sitting on the apron of the stage, Otis gesticulated constantly and I tried to catch him in a number of poses. The eyes of the Lotus swiveled, and he talked constantly with his hands and shoulders, kicking out, hunching, moving his chin around, rhyming, feinting jabs, inviting the insults that he would merchandise one day on CBS. There was a sibilance in his diction not due to large teeth, and a love of gossip, an adoration of the stars who were passing through on tour: Bette Davis, Marlene Dietrich. I remembered later that this was a boy raised by women; I had no idea what his inclinations were then. He only broadcast an enormous, unhappy drive, a need never to be alone.

"Come by, catch my act tonight. Sans loot," he said. "I'll mention your name in my routine. 'Man named Benoit stopped me on the way to the club tonight, wearing fatigues, bloused boots, asked me for fifty dollars for a cup of coffee. "Man," I told him, "coffee's only a dime." He says, "You don' 'spect me to go in dressed like an enlisted man, do you?" ' What say, Ben?"

I told him no, that I would be too busy finishing the sketches, but in the end I went to his club, sat in the bar and watched him, trying to forget my next assignment.

When I made ready to leave, Otis was forty-five minutes into his act and still warming up. The audience wouldn't let him go. I had laughed only twice, a certain sign of any comedian's commercial success.

"*Ciao*, soldier," said a girl next to me at the bar. This was the fanfare of the strumpet in Germany, but the come-on and the accent were both bogus. Her name was Inger Jonson, and she was part of Otis's troupe. She had also come to watch the act, I gathered. A blonde with long, straight glistening hair, a scoop-necked blue satin blouse and a long black peasant skirt. Lots of kohl on the eyelids. She carried a copy of *Seven Gothic Tales*. I had only heard of Isak Dinesen then. She raised the hair on the back of my neck. This was not fancy; I saw the same immediate stirring take place in men all down the bar. Their voices dropped to guttural exchanges and their faces broke into confidential erotic grins.

Hardly anything was said; she gave me a sexless, amiable mask to look at and I stammered some idiot reply. The notion that I could win her attention was beyond contemplation. After Otis finally quit the stage, to stampedes of delight and calls of "More!," Inger left me, acquired a guitar from some prop man and sat on a stool under a single spotlight. She was the next act, introduced as the Amerikaner folk singer and chanteuse.

Otis came to the bar, awaiting my approval. I don't know what I replied; my attention was rooted to the girl, as pale and supple as an ibis, now singing with premonitory magic, "O Sinner Man, where you gonna run to?" Not a bad voice; I imagined it as gold thread, an extension of her hair. She suggested the metal rings on the sides of immemorial caravans; the earrings of the girls, the necklaces worked by my uncle, the ornaments and sequins on the dresses of my aunts.

"She can't do nigger songs worth dick," Otis maintained. "*Mais elle est une* mighty fine *mignonne pièce d'asse.*"

I felt him regarding me from the side. He gave me his soul-brother locution: "Hey, mothuh, that's very bad news, that high-yaller stuff. Total opposite of you; she's like a negative of a picture in yo' haid. Stay away. Everybody in the company tried; nobody scored."

He tried another approach: "So the first cannibal says to the second cannibal, 'Ah cain't stand my mothuh-in-law.' And the second cannibal says, 'Den jus' eat de noodles.' "

Jesus, Otis could switch tracks in a hurry. So many personae, I thought, simultaneously regarding him and Inger, the way an instrumentalist watches a conductor and his music at the same time, and thinking, Is this the way a black man makes it? Reflecting in his life what Risa did in her paintings—pieces of everyone else's style? Is this what I have to do?

These speculations were overtaken by waves of ache, twists to my soul administered by the remote magnet who was now well into her act. Cigarette smoke hung in the blue air; everyone was hushed. She did a series of spirituals, and at one point tears gathered in her eyes and concentrated the light. I had no idea then that she could do this at will; every single performance she could produce them on the first verse of "Hush, little baby, doan you cry; you know your momma's born to die-ay-ay." As she finished, the spot irised down to a pinlight that concentrated on her gold hair, then went out, leaving the place in an instant of blackness. A gimmick finish, and it never failed. Inger was gone. No amount of applause could bring her back.

She might have been a vision, an impression she never tired of producing. Otis kept palavering: Learn good things, the bad will teach you by themselves. If you can tickle yourself, you can laugh when you please, etc. But I kept looking at the empty space the folk singer had filled. It was the last time I was to see her that year; my orders sent me back to Fort Lewis two days later, after I had spent eighteen straight hours sketching and painting my subjects. I only mention Inger because she was, in the fullness of castastrophe, to become my wife.

In the dingy fifties Fort Lewis was alive with returning prisoners of war, men exhausted by captivity, as thin and stark as wire sculpture. I was supposed to draw them for a series of Army newspapers and records; the Seattle *Post-Intelligencer* also hired me to do some work. The saddest, the ones I could never shake from my eye's mind, were under courts-martial, soldiers the Army, and now the civilians, called "turncoats." I was drawing one, a Sergeant Leland Oates, from the South somewhere, saying nothing, just moving the pencil across the page. The only other person in the room was a guard, an enlisted man with a totally unnecessary .45 pistol bulging ostentatiously in a holster. "Hell," Oates said, "here I am a prisoner all over again. I mean, wasn't it enough, two years in that hole? How the Christ can they judge me now?"

"I don't know," I said without lifting my eyes from the drawing.

"Everybody's a judge. Every goddamn person who had three hots and a flop all their lives is suddenly a judge."

Oates was held under charges of testifying that the United States had used germ warfare against North Korea. He had also given out that the General Staff was composed of warmongers. When this was announced, his wife had applied for divorce. Oates had come back to derision; even his mother had refused to see him. Multiply the story by a few hundred, change the details slightly, stick the enlisted men in the stockade, let the ranking officers go, and you have the *Zeitgeist* pretty well down.

The sergeant kept talking. "You can't judge a man till you've stood in his shoes. Look at you, Private. Where were you when I was in solitary, when I had malaria? When they killed lieutenants in my company in cold blood?"

"Warm and dry," I told him. Which is what he wanted to hear, and which was true. The impossibility of judging. A servile notion. A German ethic: Who can judge? Who can say? How much easier, as the drowning are supposed to be able to do, to close the eyes and welcome sleep. Zzzzzzzzzzzzzzzzzz.

In the middle of Oates's trial the telegram came.

YOUR FATHER IN NEW YORK HOSPITAL WITH MASSIVE CORONARY. RECOVERY UNEXPECTED. PLEASE COME. LOVE RISA.

The Red Cross lived for such emergencies; I was on the next plane out of Seattle. They flew prop aircraft in those days; it took fourteen bumpy hours to cross the country. We left the daylight behind, flew through rainbows that were perfect circles, and dived into night and stars. We set down in a New York that was as shiny and silent as the sky. It was 3:00 A.M.

I was admitted so quickly that there was no doubt as to
Max's condition. He lay in an oxygen tent, the chest and
stomach rising and falling as one, broadcasting a melancholy
so profound that Max's body seemed in mourning for itself. He
would awaken occasionally and regard me, sometimes with a
wink, to make sure I understood that he recognized the on-
looker. Of course with those eyebrows his wink was like somebody else's shrug.

You was always the mad one. All I wanted now was peace
for Max and for myself. The hours were composed of a hundred crises; every time the patient grimaced we thought it was
the end and witnesses were summoned from the corridor. But
he rallied and even spoke a few words. Light appeared over the
East River; in the intensive-care room the walls turned yellow.
For a few minutes I was the only one by Max's bedside. He
made some sort of motion with his face. His lips moved. I bent
close.

"You think Gepetto was a good father?" he asked.

"I don't know," I said. "You were."

"They blame human failings on the glands." This from out
of nowhere. The mind writhing, snapping at flies. "How do you
blame a social mistake? A catastrophe of minds, of genera-
tions?" His voice was light now, carrying like music. "You
make two dots on a paper, close one eye, then hold them out
about nine inches. Remember I showed you?"

I nodded vigorously.

"You look at the left one, the right one disappears. Everybody has a blind spot, remember? Everybody. But we had the
biggest. We thought if we cut ourselves the whole world bled.
In the movement I found poverty, youth and no gloom." He
had great difficulty saying this, but I could not stop him. "My
God, how can I make any of you understand what iniquity did
to us, why we believed?"

"It doesn't matter," I told him. "None of that matters in
this country."

"It was a time of garbage." I could hardly hear him. "We
were corpses on furlough. You're all right?"

"I'm fine."

"You don't look fine. Don't worry about me. This is a self-inflicted wound."

I don't know what his last words really were; these were his last to me. I left the room when the doctor said Max had stabilized and would be all right at least until nightfall. Breakfast downstairs took about half an hour, and when I came back he was dead. His daughter arrived about an hour later. Risa made all the arrangements.

There were a crowd of his old radical buddies at the funeral, along with a rabbi. That surprised me. It turned out the rabbi himself was an old Red, now backslid into the ancient faith. His eulogy was a collage of hypocrisies ending in "Judge not, lest ye be judged." Everybody wanted to get off the hook in the fifties, even Isaiah.

"You kent see de spark in flint, you kent see de soul in men." Mordecai buttonholed me as we walked from the grave. "This vos a fine soul. Ve locky to hev known him. Sixty-tree. A yongster. A shame. A vaste. Vot is God op to?"

The crowd dispersed at the gate. On some pretext I walked down the block, then reentered Mount Hebron with no other purpose than to stand for a moment undisturbed at the grave site. Why, I don't know. No soul resided here in this museum of superstition. Floes of granite. Jews allowed to be swallowed in earth, not eaten by flame. A tide of loss flowed around me and left me untouched. I felt like the stones that sat atop the graves. A witness without sensation, capable of neither hurt nor birth.

I wished in that futile mourning to recover the orchard of the first years, before capture, before the dust ground my people. "After the first death there is no other," Dylan Thomas assures me. Wrong. Oh, I thought, if I could capture even for an afternoon that time when things made proclamations, when flat water and unbroken snow were miracles, and the sound of hammer on copper and gold was the melody of the world.

The sidewalk outside the cemetery was broad and warm from memories of the noon sun. I felt in my uniform pockets for the crayon and charcoal sticks that were always there. Kneeling on the cement, I covered the rough square with my shadow and began to sketch Max. His face rose out of the stone, in that familiar scowl wrapped around a cigar. I sketched in fine detail. An audience gathered; coins scattered around me and jingled, catching bits of light.

"You drunk, sojer?" I blinked up and saw the dark outlines of a policeman. " 'At's public property."

I rose, dusted myself off and gave an excellent imitation of a man with a twenty-four-hour pass carrying a freight of boilermakers. "Go home and sleep it off, General," he said. I saluted him with mock inebriation. "Keep the change," I muttered and went home and snored in Max's bed.

It took a little longer than I expected to sleep it off. It took a career, a marriage and a life.

VII: LUST

Nietzsche tells me that to put away my own thoughts in order to pick up a book is a sin against the Holy Ghost. So, with all the others, add that.

From the service, work and displacement of thought by the same evasions over and over again. Every soldier had habitually read those books lying on his bunk; as a civilian I hid in them all again: Salinger because the entrances and exits of his children made me long for a family whom I might wittily harass or counsel upon their incessant and fortuitously timed breakdowns. Raymond Chandler, whose arena stank of power just out of reach, and of days in which walking in a circle could be considered progress. "I never saw any of them again—except the cops. No way has yet been invented to say good-by to them." It was better to read that than to think it. You could believe that the dregs of time had already been inhabited by someone else, someone back in forties Los Angeles, in a paperback society far from here.

The resumption of old ties was not difficult. Larry Lombard was a shotgun-sized homunculus with a vague resemblance to Lou Costello. He had a spray can on his desk labeled *Bullshit Repellent,* and a sign next to it that read, "I'd Like to Help You Out: Which Way Did You Come In?" His backyard pool displayed the legend: "OOL: Notice we have no P in our Pool." He still went to burlesque shows in Union City, New Jersey, and liked one-button sharkskin suits, white-on-white shirts and pinky rings. And he was the best artist's agent in New York. Within a year I had a loft on 29th Street and more work than I could handle. Much of it was buckeye: pictures of executives for the board room ("Paint more angels and make them gladder to see me" would have been their demand in the Quattrocento; now they just wanted everything larger: the canvas, the desk, everything except the fee); magazine spreads painted from photographs. Occasionally I got a crack at the famous: Jack Benny, who hummed and said little, because, he told me, his writers had not come up with any dialogue for the sitting; General Douglas MacArthur, who informed me that my military days were the capital, and all that came afterward, the interest; Albert Einstein, who insisted that he be posed at his office in Princeton. The desk held an opaque swell of material that reminded me somehow not of accumulated wisdom but of those primitive cultures who believed the earth was shaped like a mountain, like Babel or Ararat. "There is enough order in the universe," the professor said by way of excuse. His sort of mind could think past the thirties exile from Berlin, refuse the presidency of Israel, detach the flagrant insults and murders. It was too busy measuring the cold distance between stars. In his presence I felt as others did, smaller and paltry. It was more than the enormity of his brain that was enviable; it was that incalculable serenity, the gift of indifference to local matters. A spacious man; a god's-eye viewer.

I also drew, in the same week, Harold Howard Sanborn, who on a single afternoon in Morristown, New Jersey, had killed or grievously maimed twenty-two men, women and children with a surplus Army rifle.

I tried to find apertures in the mask of frozen contempt he exhibited in his cell. The gaze was closed off so that no one could peer back; his stare reminded me of the nictitating membrane birds drop across their eyes to protect them from high winds. It was Sanborn's mouth, pulled tight like the ends of a duffel bag, that suggested an inward cringing at whatever self he carried inside. That was all. He might have been a Nazi or a rising young dry cleaner.

As I sketched him I saw reconfirmed that no madman is totally mad in both eyes at the same time. What the mouth betrays, the forehead denies; even the nose is not quite on its own. Features tunnel inward; it is up to the painter to go as far as he can. With Sanborn I thought I saw glints of chaos way down, like looking into a well. But it could have been the

light and the crime. Who knows? The face is history, and
history is criminal. I painted what I saw. "Harold Howard
always kept his room clean," his mother kept mumbling to
reporters while Sanborn cowered in his cell.

I remember that evening dreaming about messy desks and
clean rooms and cluttered heads. About doing some "serious"
work. Instead, I shot the morning in my studio rereading *The
Long Goodbye*, skipping the plot, concentrating on the *pen-
sées* of Philip Marlowe.

I was to read the excerpt on blondes like a breviary in the
next years; just then it was an entertainment:

*There is the blonde who gives you the up-from-under look
and smells lovely and shimmers and hangs on your arm and
is always very very tired when you take her home. She makes
that helpless gesture and has that goddamned headache
and you would like to slug her except that you are glad you
found out about the headache before you invested too
much time and money and hope in her. Because the headache will always be there, a weapon that never wears out
and is as deadly as the bravo's rapier or Lucrezia's poison
vial.*

Lucky Marlowe; he found out early. But then, he moved like
a bishop, angled reliably across the board. I moved in knight-
fashion, one square straight, one slanted. Never in a line.
Never. I was thinking about blondes in that period because,
after carrying on with Myrna Strang, another of Marlowe's
perky blonde models who was always willing to go anywhere as
long as it was the Rainbow Room, I had begun to see Inger.
She had just cut her first major album, and her manager wanted
to use the charcoal half-caricature I had made in Germany.

I was not hard to trace; the day she called I invited her to
my studio. "Sometime," she said vaguely, and one afternoon
a month later, out of nowhere, she rang the downstairs bell.

We walked in the neighborhood first, threading in and out
of the wholesale florists, purchasing plants that were to die of
paint fumes in my studio a month later, talking aimlessly. I

hardly heard what she said; she spoke blonde. Her odor made the floral bouquets smell like spray cans. She showered me with pheromones. Upstairs she floated in my new studio like the heroine in some Cocteau movie.

"Did you ever think of doing anything serious?" she asked, and the question appeared fresh, canny, brilliantly put.

I showed her the new abstracts on wood that no one else had seen. She thought them "mangled." I found this acute, penetrating. Day bounced in her tresses; the room divided with light.

"I like your portraits better," she said. "You manage to catch things." She indicated a full-length canvas of Laurence Olivier. "How long did it take to do that?"

"All my life."

"Is that original?"

"It was once. When El Greco said it."

"Did Olivier pose for you here?"

With rue I admitted that it was done from memory. "It's a gift, a surprise from a producer. I spent an hour with him at the Players. He never knew. They told him I was a folk singer."

She laughed. It sounded exactly the way I expected her to laugh: like new aluminum foil.

"Don't I look like a folk singer?"

"No."

"What do I look like then?"

A long pause. "Delicious," she said.

I felt a shadow lift from my skin.

Slowly, slowly, I walked around her. We had dinner uptown, at some Armenian place. The subway, I jubilantly noted, was too loud for conversation, entitling me to look. I could see her hair in other men's expressions, and the liquefaction of her jumper.

"You stopped traffic," I said to her at the table.

"I stopped yours." She smiled and went right on eating.

No flattery, no tragedy would ever dim her appetite for food or wine. For a slender lady she must have had a liver the size of a yak's. I never once saw her drunk. Loose-tongued, always; inebriated, never. She began to speak of the men, on the road and in New York, the throng of egos onstage, the groupies in the audience, the superannuated swingers with expense accounts—the old Hollywood stories now exported to Nashville, San Francisco and all local stops.

Over coffee, quite dispassionately, she mentioned her dead husband, Jim Bob Turner. "Jesus, Jim Bob," she recalled and shook her head. "Jim Bob. That's a name for two dogs, not one man." Her summary, not mine. Turner was a pioneer of excess, the victim of an overdose of everything: travel, early recognition, heroin. Slightly behind Charlie Parker and way ahead of Janis Joplin.

"I loved his music," Inger said. "I never loved him." I should have watched that; instead, I believed not only her lyrics but her tunes. Whatever she hummed was truth.

Over coffee I said, "If I asked you to pose for me, would you think it was a come-on?"

"Of course," she said. "But I'd do it."

"Now?"

"If you want."

"Nude?"

"If you want."

I watched her legs and her backside all the way up the stairs; inside, I clocked the bounce of her breasts, even in those days unhaltered. And the movement of her thin arms. Around her there was a shimmer; like all the men, I had undressed Inger in musings. When I beheld her now there was no surprise, only affirmation.

When she walked across the room I stared until she told me to stop.

"I can't help it," I said. "Later I'll get used to you, but not now, not yet. I don't know why you're here."

"You mean, what I see in you?"

"I guess. Yes."

"Don't you think the light ever cries out for the darkness?"

A line like that enveloped me with its heat and mystery. Her album was still unreleased; I had no way of knowing that it was the lyric of a song about a Virginia coal mine.

|||

In time she began to spend more nights in my apartment than in her own. Which was just as well; her place on Barrow Street had the transitional quality of a hotel room. The walls were bare except for a few album covers nailed up with metal pushpins, and three guitars hung by their pegs. There wasn't even a bed. She slept on a mattress on the floor, like some waif in her songs.

The floor was her favorite place. She used to sit on mine while I painted. Love is a talkative passion; the days now seem fuller of conversation than of passion, although we made love nearly every afternoon and then sometimes long into the evenings. She had come from a family of hicks, farmers in Minnesota. She was still in flight from them and from anything else that smacked of the yokel.

People like Inger used to be the real New Yorkers; they set down roots like dandelions, on the cracks in the sidewalks. They attached themselves to neighborhoods three blocks square, smaller by far than the ones in which they grew up; became cronies of laundrymen and elevator operators, types they would have shunned back home; tried vainly to keep up with every new collagist who took the back off an old radio and called it "Limbo III"; stood on line an hour to see a French art film that would be on general release in a month and forgotten in a season; went to Lewisohn Stadium to hear music punctuated by the guttural roar of prop planes; exchanged atrocity stories about inflation; complained about the air that turned settled grit on the radiator covers and speckled the soup on terraces and postage-stamp gardens; bought a car to get out of the city on weekends, then spent an hour a day circling a block until the "No Parking 8 to 11 Tues–Thurs–Sats" sign could be successfully violated; watched their children play in boxes of wormy sand enjoyed the night before by the neighborhood dogs—and knew all the time that they were in the home of the spirit, the place they had read and dreamed about back in the flat little towns or over the dingy store, or, in Inger's case, down on the truck farm where she played a cigar-box guitar and prayed that Daddy would die and leave her money to go East.

Maybe these illusions are the real art: the images children

hustle out of short stories or films, or glimpse in the face of a driver asking directions at the gas pump, or detect in an accent from Somewhere Else, Anywhere Else. These are the emotions we remember, the ones we are faithful to, even when our hopes have been mocked by facts that are dingy or vicious.

It took a while before I was willing to speak of my origins, though this was the epoch in which unhappy childhoods were swapped like friendship rings. It was the way people got acquainted then, and sometimes it turned into a rivalry: the more miserable the formative years, the greater the score. It was a game I had learned long ago not to play. I went slowly and left out a lot of things. But I told Inger more than I had told anyone else about the early days in Rumania. They were not unhappy at all; why had I held them back even from Max and Risa? Why had I never told the story of the Gypsy Adam and Eve, for instance, who before sinning gave off their own light? After the Fall they lost their luminosity and two bright bodies were created, the sun and the moon.

One afternoon as Inger sat leaning against the wall, her wide blue-tweed skirt forming a scoop for the chrome yellow that fell from the skylight, I recalled a story often told on the caravan: A young Gypsy presented himself at court and asked for the hand of the king's daughter. This so outraged the king that he threw me (I always assumed the heroic role in this tale) in jail. There I languished until the appearance of Mautya, Queen of the Fairies, protector of the poor and disinherited. Mautya showed me a box and a long stick. "Pull out some of my hairs," she said, "and stretch them on the box. Now pull out more and stretch them on the stick." This was how I made the first violin and bow. I begged the jailer for one more audience with His Imperial Majesty. My new music made the guard wonder, and he brought me before the king, who wept—a thing he had never done before. So I obtained the hand of the girl, dwelt in a castle, and composed all Gypsy airs. The people in the story are gone, but the violin and his children still live, and still make people cry as if they were kings.

Tears sparkled warmly. Genuine this once, I hope, looking back. Ah hell, whatever she was or was not, Inger had no part in it. She was an invention, a production, as elaborate and bogus as a television special. I needed a woman who was nothing of myself, no sadness, no shadow, nothing dark, not even the pudenda; a Norse figure originating from some country where ice froze the sorrows of life and the citizens were radiant with health and had an uninterrupted past of sagas and castles and thoughts of white gold.

My job ceased its meaning. Portraiture became a matter of filling in blanks. I *was* always facile; the kind of rendering necessary to make a face appear on canvas or rice paper was the true minimal art. All that was omitted was insight, distinction and style. I worked instead on Inger.

Whenever she went on the road the worst appeared in visions: plane crashes, car wrecks. No, these were second-worst; the most wretched nights came when she called me from some hotel room and music or laughter scratched the background.

I thought of the thousand variants on Jim Bob, whose pale, harrowed face stared from an album she had never removed from the wall. I couldn't find anything in it to loathe, except for its testimony of rivalry. He was blonde like Inger, and his eyes were as pale. She had married herself. Mirror, mirror.

There were times when I wanted to take the first plane out of La Guardia, to find her in Cincinnati on a college tour, or out on the banks of the Monongahela River collecting material, or in Los Angeles cutting a master disc. Work and some remaining shred of dignity kept me in New York, but I never stopped thinking of her. Photographs, sketches, impressions of her lay everywhere. She left a musk in the sheets that no laundry could expunge.

During that first year, when we had the illusion of living together, Inger and I were actually apart more than half the time. When she arrived from a western swing I was always at Idlewild or at Penn Station, carrying some trinket or flowers. The taxi was always warming up at the curb, the ride home was always annealing and comic, full of gropings and idiot comedy about audiences so dumb they believed Joe Hill was a song about a mountain, and who thought "The Frozen Logger" was so funny it was all they could do to keep from laughing out loud.

But I could never let hell enough alone. Resentful of her trips, I demanded details about the performance, about where she stayed, who she stayed with. She would turn in her tracks like a hunted animal.

"You mean who I *slept* with?"

"Not necessarily."

"You don't want to get into my pants. You want to get into my *lug*gage. Why don't you hire a goddamn private detective?"

"I just wanted to know who you were with."

"I was with friends. Which is more than you were with."

The proper answer to this was silence, to break the circle. Naturally, I chose these occasions to speak. "How do you know who I was with?"

"Because you have no friends."

"It's better to be alone than with geeks."

"You envy every human contact I make because you can't make any. If you're not painting somebody you have no relationship with them."

"That's not true."

"You ought to hear what Tony Colocus says about you."

"Tony Colocus' idea of wit is to tell kids not to eat yellow snow. Or to make posters of rhinoceri humping."

"What gives you the right to be such a goddamned snob? That's not art *you're* doing."

"What is it then?"

A long, furious gathering of strength for the ultimate putdown: "Craft!"

I never knew whether to laugh or cry at that point. Through her voice I heard the bitching of the Slaters, the only friends she had who displayed something other than instruments, photographs or bullfight posters on their walls. I would never fail to tell her so.

"Well, the Slaters are right about you," she said. " Sissie is a very perceptive woman. She even looks brilliant."

"She looks like a girl who married a mime. She looks as if she mates by touching fingertips. So does he."

"Bernard is a very dear, very giving person. Just because he has a pierced ear everybody thinks . . . God, you are the biggest character assassin in New York!"

"That covers a lot of ground. Then again, so does Bernie."

"There's only one thing uglier than jealousy."

"What?" The straight man now shouting.

"You! Take a look at yourself."

The first few times I did: the old stiff, excited mask, a man punched off center.

Variants of this exchange were sounded periodically, the heat always followed by deep, seething silences—what she called a shared widowhood. Neither of us dared to leave. A need to hurt was followed by the wish to assuage the wound with a laugh: something about a theater she played in so far in the Maine backwoods that the manager was a bear; or the junkie who hadn't had a bite for weeks, so she bit him. For my part, I would paint her charts of old signs that I would have to pull up from the buried past, marks I recalled with enormous difficulty, transfigured by memory, symbols painted on Rumanian walls and doors:

+ Here they give nothing.

⊙ Generous people, friendly to Gypsies.

⚨ Here Gypsies are regarded as thieves.

ɯ We have already robbed this place.

△ You can tell fortunes with cards.

⊖ Mistress is dissolute.

≠ Master likes women.

⚢ Marriage in the air.

After an interval of an hour, maybe two, of drinking or sulking, there was what Inger called drunking and silking; things would be healed in a reproducible drama. I would kiss her wet face, she would hold me, hold the member she called the Japanese soldier with its red-helmeted, featureless face, and end with her head in my lap. Giving head, they called it then; I suppose they still do. A misnomer. She gave nothing; nor did I. It was all exchange or atonement. Watching her storybook hair, my hands raking it as it brushed across flesh with the

delicacy of a suggestion, sensing her lips traversing the en-
chafed blood, I would often pull her upward to hear the soft,
moist popping sound and kiss her and want to take her on the
bed, but she would pull away and put herself again on me to
stay with long, slow, grave movements until I could no longer
stand the sweet delay; yes, certainly, an old story, but why did
it cause such indebtedness? Why did the sense of obligation
increase with the moans, with the fountain in the cave, the
assertion of self in the home of speech, the swallowed silver and
the clinging to the diminished finger? "Shall you turn cockwise
on a tufted axle?" Dylan Thomas asks. Answer available on
request, mailed in plain brown human. O Christ, the furnace
of those days; how we burned in each other's demands, and
how light we felt between catastrophes.

All the same, the clashes could soak every thought. I came
to her apartment one day to find Inger seated in a chair,
staring. At what I could not tell. She scarcely talked. Kissing
her was like embracing a towel. I asked what the matter was.

"You wouldn't know."

"Not until you tell me."

"Even then you wouldn't know."

"Try me."

She shifted uneasily. "Get out of here. Give me back the key
to my apartment."

I bounced it on the table. Her eyes were not focusing well,
but there was no evidence of drugs around, no wine, no joints,
nothing. Whatever moved her was not induced by those
sources. This was an inside job.

"Will you get *out!*"

I answered in a voice of theatrical calm. "Does it matter
whether I leave now or in five minutes?"

"As long as you *go.* "

"Just for laughs, you mind telling me what I've done?"

A dark, unmelodic hum.

We sat in the place with its emergency-room illumination
emanating from a fluorescent light fixture. She looked like
some figure out of Lautrec or Marsh, vessels suddenly visible
on the eyelids and disfiguring green shadows on the skin. There

were plenty of pencils scattered about the place: I had to combat the urge to draw her even then.

"Did you ever wish someone dead?" she asked me.

"Often and often."

"And have them die?"

"I never had the luck."

ITEM: Professor Clauberg sterilized between 120 and 140 Gypsy girls who had been brought to the camp from Auschwitz. This was probably done by an injection into the uterus. The mothers of the girls signed forms of consent after being promised release. Several died and the survivors were not freed but transported to another camp. One twelve-year-old girl operated upon did not even have her abdominal wound sewn up after surgery. She died after several days of agony.

> —E. Buchmann, *Die Frauen von*
> *Ravensbrück* (Berlin: Kongress, 1959)

—*We could do it at night.*

—*We could never do it.*

—*I can. The air shaft is small. And there is an axe on the wall. One blow is all it takes.*

—*Little Fish, you could not even lift that axe, much less murder with it.*

—*I can. Watch me.*

—*Hold him! He is crazy.*

—*I'm not. He will cut up all of us if we don't stop him.*

—*Be grateful that is not your blood on the floor, Benoit.*

—*It is my blood! The blood of my people.*

—*Will you listen to that? You have no people, Little Fish, only yourself.*

—*Some day, Eleazar, I will be too big to hold down.*

—*You will never get bigger if you don't keep still. I'll see to that.*

Inger turned and looked at me slowly. I recall the feeling as anesthesia lifting, but it was to go no farther. The downstairs bell rang imperatively. Inger rose and pushed the intercom: it was the Slaters.

Sissie glided into the room. She looked like money; she would always look like money. She was thin and long-boned with the suggestion of Southern fields grown picturesque and sloping and infertile. Her kind of etiolated style would always be in. There would always be dresses to fit her, and she would photograph well until she was an old lady. Even then she would be the kind of figure to elicit the comment, "She must have been beautiful when she was young." And the remark would not be wholly wrong.

She was all in denim, one beat ahead of the sixties and two beats ahead of Bloomingdale's. Her hair was mid-length and black, shot with premature gray that intimated, falsely, the intelligence of experience. Her husband was in matching denims. He was thin only in the hair and suggested an indulgent mother, large, starchy meals, good breeding and a sense that life, albeit short and bittersweet, could also be tiresome.

The guests' effect on Inger was electric.

"Dinner!" Sissie sang. She unveiled a large selection of sliced ham and salami from some neighborhood delicatessen several cold cuts below Zabar's. Inger's face exhibited none of the previous weights. She was not a woman abruptly cheered up; she was a different self, merry and conversational. Sissie was shrewd enough to feel whatever residue was in the room.

Inger read her face. "Just tired, is all. Too much rehearsal."

"Honestly, you raggle-taggle showfolk." Bernie poured himself a concoction of chocolate syrup and soda. "I don't know *how* you survive. My idea of going on the road is the Brooklyn Academy of Music."

"Bernie's going to star there," Sissie announced.

"Well, it's just for the kiddies. I sort of get up on my tippy-twinkletoes and show them the history of mime, from the Greeks right up through Barrault and Marceau. I feel . . ."

Here the listener's brain was kind enough to introduce its time-honored method, known in television as continuing with the picture portion while the station experienced difficulty with the audio. Bernie went on with his illustrated history. I heard no sound emanating from him, an experience usually felt when an industrial client, seated for a portrait, bombinated on the poetry of big business. As he spoke I had a peripheral sense of Inger in animated chatter. There was not a scintilla of disturbance in her posture, her voice or expression. The mystery of the earlier squall deepened.

We resumed with the audio portion quickly enough when her name was mentioned. Inger and Sissie went into the kitchen to put the food on plates. Bernie turned on the radio; "Covering noise," he said, and lowered his voice. "About our friend. I know it's *ab*solutely none of my business and tell me to shut up if you must. *But...*" He waited for the interruption. None came. He had all my attention now. "Inger's a wonderful girl, but she's sick. You know that."

"Sick how?"

"You mean sick *where.*" He tapped his temple. "You should know that if you're planning to marry or anything."

"You want to go into detail?" I asked him. "Or is this the whole act?"

"You don't have to *bristle,*" he said. "I'm only trying to open your eyes, is all."

"I'm sorry." I opened a beer for myself and offered him some. He held up his egg cream. "Lips that touch liquor are usually mine." He sat down in a black wing chair. "But Mr. Slater is hung today. *Well* hung, mind you, but *hung.* God." He exhaled thin, expressive streams of smoke through his thin, expressive nostrils.

"I didn't mean to jump on you," I told him.

Bernard dismissed my temerity with an indulgent wave. "It's only conjecture, you understand. But an educated one. I think she's MD. Manic you-know-what. Only *tons* of D and damn little *M. Damn* little."

The women came back as he spoke, and that was the end of his bulletin.

The rest of the meal was concerned with the Slaters' analysis, all four years of it. They were going through some therapy imported from San Francisco and now threw up every morning to begin their day, then sat in various boxes and screamed. What Bernard and Sissie Slater did in bed only Aubrey Beardsley, I suspect, could limn. I jettisoned everything he said about

Inger: the baby, the bath water, the bassinet, the rubber ducky, everything. But he knew, the bastard really knew. And his listener was as willfully ignorant as a child who plugs up its ears at the sound of rain.

When the Slaters left, Inger put on her new single. It was a setting of Blake: "Terror in the house does roar. But Pity stands behind the door." She got down her guitar and harmonized with herself.

It was seven-thirty on her electric clock. A liquid hour in New York. I went into the kitchen to call my answering service. The window was open and her place smelled of other people's dinner. Inger had a blackboard near the phone and I started writing the messages in chalk. I heard her coming in; she wore the guitar around her neck on a long lanyard, and that was all she wore. She shaded her eyes in the fluorescence like a sailor looking for land. She snapped off the light, but there was more than enough illumination from the other room and from the little window. The guitar rang with a hollow sound when she set it on the counter.

Colors were muted, and the sounds at that moment were very distant. The songs from the mixed radios were indistinguishable. Inger bore a vague aroma of soap, talcum and Norell. And something else, like ashes, something oestrous maybe. Or old furies. The kiss lasted longer than I wanted it to. She began to unbutton my shirt and stopped.

"Needing something is a dreadful feeling," she said. "Needing somebody is the worst feeling there is." Another lyric. She felt hot and as burdensome as love itself as she sank, very slowly. I knew, with the body's eyes and not the mind's, that this would not wind down, that the need was far greater on the Kaufman shore. She breathed on the live coal, and I believed or hoped just then that we would become each other turn by turn. That we could farm our griefs, that I would lose the numbness, that she would lose the shadow. Lunacy. But it passed for clarity that night and a thousand others that followed. Plastered on gin and elation, I went out very late that night into the hall, naked, running into an elderly couple who were kind enough to avert their eyes. "We're getting married,"

I explained, and down the incinerator jettisoned the garbage, the album cover from off the wall and my watch. I was never to own another one.

The word "promising" had attached itself to Inger in those days, and I had been illustrating theater pieces for the *Herald Tribune* and the Sunday *News*. Ed Sullivan announced our engagement and Inger's picture made the *Trib*. I heard from a few old classmates and from the Dean and Dyanne and from Otis, rehearsing off-Broadway in an interracial production of *The Emperor Jones*—so free of bias, he said, that the title role was taken by a white. I also heard from one other, a man whom I had forgotten entirely, and who was to determine the way I would end on earth.

I spoke with all of them briefly, or answered their letters with an invitation. I thought to catch up with everyone before the ceremony, staged at the ludicrously ostentatious home of the Lombards on the Larchmont shore. We were given the A treatment: caterers, striped canvas canopies, long shadows on the lawn. Veuve Cliquot in jeroboams and Nebuchadnezzars, crowds of well-wishers and witnesses and a man from the Ethical Culture Society. There were Inger's fellow folk singers who strolled and strummed, already high on something; Sadie surprised me by showing up on Mordecai's arm with her traditional aphorism: "When you're in love the whole world's Jewish"; Dyanne was carried along in her mother's wake. She was very pregnant, flushed and lovely, probably the healthiest and best woman there, and she seemed wholly irrelevant, a stranger from another country. I hardly understood her when she kissed me and hoped for good years. Inger's parents came directly from the bus terminal, her mother a wasted, sallow creature who might have stepped from Walker Evans' contact sheets; her father a large florid rube, still blond, with hands no larger than Mickey Mantle's glove. He said grace in Swedish, and gave us three hundred-dollar bills. With them a grunt escaped: "Maybe you can control her. I don't know." A wifely tug on the arm, shaken off like a brewery horse dismissing a nit. "We could never control her. And her husband couldn't even control himself." The smoky, dulled eyes concentrated on this latest threat to his runaway daughter. I tried to stare him down, but he wouldn't respond. Control, I tried to suggest, was not what I had in mind.

"Your life." He shrugged. "Just pray and try to live good."

Those were his last intelligible words. He and the War Department, as he called his wife, refused hard liquor or champagne but sipped the lethal Boston Fishhouse Punch and later passed out on beach chairs. Everybody was crocked by midafternoon.

Tony Colocos told me that marriage was like coffee; you had to brew it fresh every goddamn day. Then he gave me a card, *Anthony Colocos' Tool Works. Does Yours?*, along with a poster indicating that he had outgrown pictures of rhinoceri humping. This had pigs humping. The legend in Bodoni Bold read: *Makin' Bacon.* Thereupon Tony retired, his future in the pantheon of Pop Art secure.

Otis showed up late; he was the only black except for the waiters, and made much of that, putting a towel around his arm and taking orders for drinks which he never brought.

"Howdo, I'm your local *schvartzer,*" he said to Mordecai, who bowed and replied, "End I em likewise, de frandly neighborhood 'onkie."

"I'm on the wing, brother," Otis proclaimed. "I'm up for parts in two commercials. I get either one, I'm off to the Coast. I'm gonna make Sidney Poitier look like Regis Toomey, you watch."

His advertisement for himself was interrupted by the appearance of Joe Tower, hugely changed from the days at Mondale, pockmarked, the boy hidden in scars and fat.

"Joe, what have you been doing since we last saw you?" I asked.

"Eating," Otis ventured.

No smile from Joe. He said very little, just shook hands all around and took me aside. "I figure you're doing very good. Big place."

"My agent's."

"Ten percent, right?"

"Yeah, but he has a lot of other clients, Joe."

"Okay. You're not rich. Can you lend me five hundred?"

"Jesus, Joe, I don't think—"

"Listen, Ben. I can't tell you everything now. I can get a lot of bread if you give me a little now. Otherwise I'm dead—I mean really dead."

"How much trouble are you in, Joe?"

"The worst."

I gave him the money Inger's father had pressed in my hand. He took it, went away for a few minutes and found me again to present a badly wrapped shoe box of great heft.

I stashed it by a bunch of luggage and other presents under a tree. The wedding started a few minutes later, and if Joe was present in the little crowd, I missed him.

After the ceremony we went back into the house and, pie-eyed, opened presents. A cornucopia; manifestations of the America I had never quite apprehended: if G.E. had managed to invent a counterclockwise electric grandmother, I'm sure we would have received that, too. There were things that mashed and chopped and toasted food, and things that put it back together; blankets that heated and machines that froze; services for eight and candlesticks for two and government bonds for one. Only a couple of the gifts were solely for me: Max's $1,000 bond purchased in his final month, and Joe Tower's little surprise, secreted in a Lloyd and Haig shoe box.

Smith and Wesson were making a very good phallus in those days. It was of medium length and looked about as clean as a subway platform and it could come six times. Bullets were in the revolver; the safety catch was on. Evidence, I ceaselessly thought from that moment; Joe has stashed this with innocent parties, and God knows who it has killed or is supposed to kill or why. Probably the police are looking for it, or the Mafia. Somebody. All the Marlowe fantasies, all the ragged stuffing of police memories began to come out of my head. "I never saw any of them again—except the cops. No way has yet been invented to say good-by to them."

You say this person who came to see you, you hadn't seen him since you were kids. In a juvenile home?

Yes.

And he just left this sidearm with you. No explanation? And you didn't ask?

I would have no backchat for that. Drown it in the Hudson, whispered the soft voice of the rabbit; when Joe comes back to reclaim it, give him hell. No, he has already had enough of that arena, the serpent said.

The gun lay there grinning, daring me to do something. I did something. I put the lid back on the box. I rewrapped the whole thing and stuck it in the trunk under an old and greasy Army blanket.

The afternoon was spent in a fever of celebration and saline advice. We went home in a small parade of honking cars to a new apartment on Central Park West, overlooking the Park and the rent. All the gifts came upstairs—except for the shoe box. That remained locked in the trunk.

The car was garaged much of the time, used only on weekends. I forgot about the gun for long stretches. The only time it came urgently to mind was during the process of moving to a larger apartment in the same building to make room for the baby we expected in the summer. We had just finished the parquet floors in some sort of spar varnish joyously prodding us with intimations of spilled formula and ammonic diapers, and were lying before the fireplace. The phone rang and I pulled myself away, the Japanese soldier at attention and bouncing. The inquiring voice was expressionless and sounded of cigarettes and neutral grain spirits. There was a hollow, irregular noise around it—the subway, probably.

"Ben?"

"Yeah."

"Joe Tower. Listen. You still have that thing I gave you?"

"Yes."

"Bring it to me, I'll give you your money back, plus one G."

"One G." Joe learning to sit up and talk like Alan Ladd.

"I don't want the money. Just tell me where I can meet you."

"White Rose Tavern. Forty-fourth and Eighth. Can you do it in half an hour?"

"I guess."

"Bring it in the shoe box, okay?"

"Yeah."

Now play this scene sporadically in the next year. The phone call always at the most inopportune time, though not always *in flagrante;* the excuse to Inger; the hasty cab ride downtown, always at some bar. And the no-show. I would stand around, sipping my beer, wondering if I heard right, was it this White Rose or another? Was it a put-on? Am I being watched? And always, two or three weeks later, Joe calling full of apologies, promising money and a new meeting place.

Back would go the goddamn thing in the trunk. I had other and deeper concerns. In Inger's seventh month we lost the baby, lost it in a sudden cascade of screams and fitful cramps. I sat beside her in the ambulance and at the hospital while both of us wept. A miscarriage, you can try again, said the doctors, and we nodded and felt like amputees.

I came home and gathered all the baby stuff and took it over to the old family apartment. No one was there, and I sat in a corner of my old family room in the dark with the lights off and drank, thinking of Inger's body and how soon I could get back to it. She still occupied all of the territory normally reserved for reflection. I was not thinking of trying again in the procreative sense, only of trying again. She lay on our bed pale and bereft and voiceless. But in my brain her lyric soprano sang over the metal strings, and she gave out such light that I could have read by her body. The real woman was another and more grievous matter. In the next months Inger frequently gave way to seizures of bleak depression. She would be found some afternoons in bed, incapable of doing anything but staring, sometimes at nothing, sometimes at an old television movie that she scarcely saw.

Often she would not let me touch her. Then, with urgent and always astonishing power she would reach for some impossible sexual peak that made the soul clap its hands and the body shrug its shoulders—and then she would succumb to whatever feelings immobilized her.

"What does it feel like?" I used to ask her at the beginning.

"I don't know—bad," is all she could tell me.

"You want to see somebody? A doctor?"

"No."

"Maybe you ought to think about going on tour. Before we try again."

"My voice isn't up to it, Ben. Or my head."

The words "child" or "baby" had become off-limits. No jokes about it any more, no references. The wails of children down the hall seemed an affront. We had the stereo on all the time.

Or else we were on the floor, on the couch, in the shower, devouring each other. Sometimes I would read to her, but in fact I had fallen out of the habit of reading even to myself, and more often we would listen to records of people—her friends, mostly—telling us in song of the woes of vanished laborers, ancient lords and English peasant girls who perished in a fever of love for the noble and unattainable.

We tried again. This time we walked gingerly around the apartment. We never went anywhere except by cab. We grew superstitious. Inger remembered some old folk tale about the hair of a horse braided around the wrist, and we took a carriage ride in Central Park and gave the driver five dollars to let us clip the tail of his animal. I recalled the song my aunt sang, cracking an egg when her own baby was coming:

> *Anro, anro hin olkes*
> *Te e pera hin obles*
> *Ara cavo sastovestes*
> *Devla, devla, tut akharel . . .*

The egg, the little egg is round
All is round
Little child, come in health
God, God is calling you . . .

When was this? I don't know. The years bleed into each other. I can understand now as I never understood before how Henry Adams could so meticulously describe his education: "Failure" . . . "Chaos" . . . "Twenty years after"—dropping two decades without a backward glance. They were the years of his marriage. But O God, for that second pregnancy she had the shy and swollen magnificence of a Van Eyck, walking around the apartment naked with her stomach large and smooth, the baby or babies—the doctors thought they heard a multiple fetal heartbeat—carried well forward and kicking sometimes, and the blond down catching the light, the good, sculpted legs growing slightly wider at the calves. We were indoor nudists those months, complete nature freaks, sleeping North to South, following the Yoga asanas, practicing the prana-yama breaths, forsaking red meat, saying "OM" a lot.

One afternoon Inger was out for too long. I began to worry about her, called her friends, then asked the doorman if he had seen her walking. Nothing. It began to get sullen outside; I hoped she had enough money for a cab, wherever she was. At six the rain came in big drops and the wind showed the white underside of the leaves in the park. The windows rattled. She showed up soaked and cheerful, her arms full of packages. "I couldn't stay still," she explained. "I had to dust something or buy something. So I went out and dusted Saks."

I helped her out of her clothes. She was soaked and smelled of downtown. But after she was showered and powdered and fireplaced Inger posed for a nude portrait, almost completed and in sedulous imitation of Matisse's odalisques. She seemed radiant again, and as expectant as a child, the concerns gone, the lines ironed out. The restorative power of money, I thought. Her occasional royalties, my commissions. We had invested cannily. Everybody was making money then.

Two days later money was all we had. In the next years almost all of it was gone.

Inger stood under a light, looking past me at a candle, humming some childhood hymn. The drops hit the floor with an imperceptible sound. There were three or four of them before I noticed the incarnadine warning between her bare feet.

As gently as I could I told her to lie down. But she could read my face and, a moment later, the blood on the floor and now on the inside of her thigh.

"Jesus God, no!" she cried and covered her mouth with her hand, as if she could cancel death.

They were very quick at St. Luke's. The ambulance arrived within five minutes and they sped us to the hospital.

In the hall you do nothing. Only listen for the sound of recognizable distress. Blood soaked the gowns of the nurses. The normal world turned inside out. Whirs of machinery. I tried to put off the tide, thinking anything. The work due, the shredded magazine on my lap. Music. The colors of this metal evening. Joe's gun.

—*There is no time for an anesthetic.*
—*Still, Doctor, this is a child.*
—*Begin. No, first get rid of the boy.*
—*Let me go! What will you do to her?*
The screams muffled in cloth. A hail of despair. The grip of predators tearing at the cage of the face. I will never wash the blood from my eyes.

They tried to save the child by all the many means. Perhaps now it could have risen, gasping, to an incubated rescue. But the fact is that it stopped breathing within an hour after birth. Something to do with RH incompatibility. Among other things, among other things. Nameless, breathless, an isolated hope. An extension in time, severed. And with her any chance, so they told us later, of having our own children.

For a long time afterward we barely talked. Such catastrophes sometimes weld lovers; more often they cleave them. I despised whatever flaws I had given the baby, whatever incapacities to endure. I don't know if Inger thought about her own genes; she certainly despised mine. Fingers through the hair was about all she allowed, and I was too wracked to ask for more. There was no consolation in love and none in music or reading.

"Philosophy, philosophy," Max used to counsel when he was wounded in the old days. But it was his favorite, Santayana, who told me that there was no more hideous centipede than life in general.

Inger's voice went, and with it my spirit.

In time the old Adam returned, but Inger was hardly ever receptive, and who could blame her? An assistant editor at *McCall's* came down to the studio one afternoon to negotiate with me about a gallery of prominent American women. She was fashionably haggard and wore a wide hat and had a surprisingly full blouse. We had drinks in the studio, and after the requisite waltz she hung her clothes, like a model, on the screen. And the Japanese soldier would not even come to parade rest, much less attention. I felt wholly unmanned: the head, the heart, the whole erotic self still chained to the hearth.

This was only to be broken by Inger herself. I came home one afternoon to an empty apartment, with the obligatory note written in white tempera on a piece of canvas board. *B. I have to go away for a few days with Sissie. Call you. Love. Me.*

Which might have been bought wholesale except that two days later Sissie called to ask how things were. I made some vague reply that Inger would be back tonight, and that evening Sissie and Bernard came up and told me that my wife had gone off to Connecticut with a man named Luke Turner—Jim Bob's old washtub bass player.

"Is there some special kick you get out of telling me this?" I asked them.

"You would have found out sooner or later," Sissie said. "You might as well know now."

"We thought someone might get hurt," Bernie added, "if you didn't know the circumstances."

"This way everything's fine," I replied.

"Hostile, *ho*stile," he said.

"Shut up, Bernie." Sissie tried to exclude him by joining me on the couch. She touched my arm unprovocatively and said, "Look, Ben. Inger and Jim Bob had a terrible marriage. I guess you know that."

"We don't talk about it," I told her.

"For heaven's sake, what *do* you talk about?" asked Bernard.

"We don't speak. We fuck all the time."

"Witty," he said. "Wit-tee."

"Bernie, why don't you go? Why don't you just go?" his wife snapped.

Bernard stirred himself. "I dislike argument," he said. "It's always vulgar and often convincing." And with that, the road-company Wilde mimed his way out, tossing a last unpleasant look at his wife.

She took a breath and began. "Inger was married to a wrongo. Did you ever hear any of his records?"

"There's a couple here, but I never put them on."

"Afraid you might hate him?"

"Afraid I might like him."

Sissie gave me a sidelong nod. "You wouldn't. Nobody did —not even Inger. I mean, at first she was crazy about him. Because he was Calvin Cool. Didn't give a shit whether she lived or died. Naturally, she began to chase him. Are you listening to me?"

"Yes."

"Well, then, grunt or something every once in a while. Let me know you're here. Did you use to do this to Inger?"

"Do what?"

"Sit there and take pictures with your eyes. So . . . after they got married she found out A) he didn't have half her talent. All he could do was that caterwauling voice on country-and-Western. Made a five-hundred-dollar Martin sound like a cigar box and rubber bands."

"And B?"

"He was a doper. Shot, swallowed, sniffed everything there was. Used to pass out onstage, at parties, on the subway, any-where."

"Where was Inger all this time?"

"With him. She looked like a pile of laundry after he was finished with a tour. She used to clean up after him, mop up when he was sick. Which was always. Then one day she'd had it. Just bloody had it. We were at a party, and he was stoned out of his head and slapped her around at a dinner table and she cried and said she wished he was dead."

"And?"

"And they went home and he piled into bed with a bottle of rye and God knows what else, and in the middle of the night he rolled over on her and she pushed him away and in the morning she rolled over on him and he felt funny and cold and she got her wish. He was dead. Choked on his own vomit. How do you like it so far?"

"God, Sissie, I never knew."

"So. What you're married to is 105 pounds of guilt. She still thinks if she wishes evil for anybody, it comes true."

"Has she left for good, do you think?"

"My guess is when she stops feeling bad about you she'll come back—if you still want her."

"I still want her. Only, I don't know, why didn't she ever say something?"

"Do you say things? She says you hold back a hell of a lot."

"She's right."

"You two obviously don't talk to each other. By God, you *do* fuck all the time, don't you?"

"We used to."

"There are other things besides screwing, Ben."

"So I'm told."

"You ought to take something. Yoga, Zen, *some*thing for your karma. I mean, look at Bernie and me. We don't have any sexual hold on each other. We're together out of spiritual need. It's a beautiful thing."

I tried to turn her off, like a television set, but she wouldn't fade.

"If you and I were to have an encounter now," she said, "Bernie wouldn't feel the slightest pang. It would just be part of the great chain of being."

I looked directly into her eyes for the first time. They were as glossy and blank as a doll's. She put her hands on my neck. "Would you like to be part of that chain?"

It was like making love to a pond. She kept chirping *shanti* until it was over, and then wanted to know if it had helped.

"Yes," I lied. "Thank you."

"Would you like to do it again?"

"No."

"I don't mean right now. Later. I'll call up Bernie and the other mimes and they can come over and watch. They like to watch."

"Sissie," I stood up. "Will you please get your karma out of here?"

"Very well." A hurt tone. She dressed rapidly and in silence. At the door she bestowed a sad, shallow kiss.

"You're twisted and unhappy and terribly neurotic," she said. "I like that in a man." And she was gone.

Bernie can come over and watch. Max was right. Group sex, group thinking, group everything. The gang bang as Spirit of the Age.

A week later, Sissie proved a prophet about one thing. Inger did return. We tried to make it work. We tried to make it play. We tried everything, we thought. But we must have left some things out. Yet there were evenings when the greenness of spirit would return like a season in the earth and we would be warm and trouble-free for months. And then something would happen, some remark or an involuntary reminiscence, and Inger would lie immobile in bed in the mornings, unable to do anything, to smile even. Her mouth narrowed into a position of permanent bitterness. The seizures intensified. She refused offers to sing anywhere. Her old manager came to see her once. I heard his sorrowing voice through the door.

"Try one concert," he begged. "One. Make a recording in a studio. A single. Try."

"My voice is gone," Inger informed him. "There are new people now. Go ask Joan Baez. You want another blonde, try Mary Travers. I'm finished as a singer. I'm finished as a woman. Don't ask me again."

The only thing she wanted from life was separate beds, then separate rooms. Just for a while, she assured me.

I slept in the abandoned nursery most nights. Or walked around the apartment, over the sensual ruins. Or went out to the West End Bar until I closed it and clambered back to paint until the sun came up and I could rest. Day and night changed places. That way we would see little of each other. Meals were pacific but remote. After a long time I tried to tell my agent Larry about it. "How can I understand women when no two of them are alike?" I asked him.

"Keed, no *one* woman is alike," he said. "My prescription is bimbos."

"I don't want bimbos. I want Inger."

"Tough to be stuck on any woman, Ben. A wife is worst.

Like having your scrotum stapled to the kitchen table."

"I can't say it's that comfortable, Larry."

"Then take what you can get. You want numbers? Addresses?"

"The hooks are in too deep. It doesn't seem to work the same way with anybody else."

He left an address book anyway. It lay unexamined for a long time. I still owed whatever light leaked into my soul to Inger's inaccessible presence; I could neither take her nor leave her. The perfume, the soap she used still drove me nuts. I used to burn incense so that I could expunge her traces. I railed against her, banged on her door like Stanley Kowalski. One evening, rent by booze and sore in my joints, I shouted through the door that the room was her cunt and that nothing erect would be allowed through it, that she had become the frigid snow queen Otis had warned about in the Army years before.

"Erect things come through here, don't you worry," she yelled.

"Not mine!"

"No, not yours."

"Better ones?"

"Different, anyway."

"You want to go away with Luke Turner, is that what you want?"

"Sometimes."

"You mind telling me what fucking virtues he has, what makes him preferable?"

This served to open the door. She looked out, her housecoat loose, her hair tangled and dim. A breast looked at me. She covered herself.

"I'll tell you what makes him preferable," Inger said. "He . . . isn't . . . you."

The bell interrupted this. The doorman honked something and I yelled into the intercom: "We don't want to see anybody," and slammed down the little receiver. I turned to address my wife and she shut her door—her body—with a quiet and terminal click.

Scotches later I remembered the bell and curious, confronted the doorman. He had a note: Mr. Tower had called. He was at 144 West Eighty-fourth. The street was known in that period as Murder Mile because of a series of fatal stabbings, muggings and OD'd hopheads collected in a few published months by the 20th Precinct. Joe lived in a single-room-occupancy building. A group of bent and and smoldering men were in front, scattered like butts in an ashtray.

Jaundiced halls fought with the Chinese-red lobby. An old black man sat at the desk. Tower was on the eighth floor, he said, with a Jamaican intonation. I started to ascend the bent, broken stairs, but this was one place in which the steps were out of order and the elevator was running. I caught it on the second floor. Joe's door was open and the radio was blaring a ball game. He was calling encouragement to Yogi Berra and coughing furiously, but there was something out of phase with the announcements of Mel Allen and the shouts of Tower. He was a few beats behind the action and his pale skin glistened. He offered his hand. It was as dry and cold as a toad.

"You wanted me?" I said.

He looked at me and coughed. "Why wouldn't you let me up, Ben?"

"I was having an argument with my wife."

"Wife?"

"Yeah, the one from the wedding, remember?"

"Yeah. So long ago that was. How is she?"

"Sick."

"Me, too."

"What's the matter? Cold?"

"I got a bad case of revenge," he said. "You bring that thing I gave you?"

I handed him the box. He removed the gun.

"Thanks," he said. "I was afraid you woulda thrown it away." He took it out and gestured with it, still trying to be Alan Ladd. But he looked like the sparrow I remembered from the Home.

"Can I do anything, Joe?"

"Stay a while. Keep me company."

I sat on a hard chair next to his bed. We listened to the

Yanks blow a three-run lead in the ninth. The game went into extra innings. Joe's conversation was desultory; I only got pieces and suggestions about delivery of hardware—guns, I guessed—to some men from Toronto. He passed out after a while. I pulled the blanket down. His chest was taped up and slightly stained. He opened his eyes.

"What happened, Joe?"

"I cut myself shaving."

"Stop talking like a goddamn movie. What's wrong with your stomach?"

"They can't take the bullets out just yet."

"You belong in a hospital."

"I go to the hospital today, I'm in jail tomorrow."

"You don't go to the hospital now, you're in the morgue tomorrow. What the hell, Joe, I can talk Warner Brothers as good as the next crook."

"Go away, Ben."

"Let me call St. Luke's."

"Don't call nothing." He pointed the gun at me, then started to cough and put the thing down on the couch. I stayed where I was. A loud, absurd finish in a blank place exerted a dangerous appeal.

Joe lost touch again. He breathed heavily. I thought about what he had said. *Was* jail preferable to lying here half alive? I filled up some glasses with water and left everything, including the gun, in easy reach. A key chain lay on the bureau. I took it and locked the door on my way out.

The lady from *McCall's* was home. Heartless now, the Japanese soldier functioned routinely; the night dissolved. The morning Hudson looked malignant and dark, and the lobby of Joe's building had the smell of shoals. I opened the door of 8H fearing the worst. The bed affirmed it. I felt all over for a pulse, and then called the emergency number listed under the glass cover of his end table. I left the keys on the bed, started out, returned, put the gun back in the shoe box and left with it in my hands.

Many times that night and the nights afterward I played as children will with the gun at my heart or head. Thoughts of

suicide are very comforting. With them one has got through
many a bad night. *Ja,* Herr Nietzsche. I could finish the job
that you Germans could not.

ITEM: Nothing else in the long catalogue of German crimes sur-
passed the slaughter of the Gypsies. . . . Every variety of murder
was tried on them: more than any other group they were forced
to serve as guinea pigs for "scientific" experiments, and at
Ravensbrück, while some Germans might be sterilized as a form
of individual punishment, only the Gypsies were subjected to
such treatment as a group, one after another—even the youngest girls.

Why? What were these poor people's crimes? If they were
so culturally inferior, whose fault was it but the Germans', who
had ruled most of them for centuries, doing nothing for them
before they began the slaughter. The Germans—a shameful
breed who knew only how to kill the defenseless.

—Germaine Tillion, *Ravensbrück*
(Editions du Seuil, Paris, 1973)

The road is better than the inn, my father and uncles
sang. Yes, but suppose you have not only forgotten the inn
but lost the road? Suppose it is getting dark and cold and
there are only stones and brambles underfoot and dark bare
trees ahead and no previous paths to follow? You could always, of course, pull the trigger. No trouble following that
route. And yet, and yet . . .

Maybe it was the booze. I began to see Death a lot that
summer. I saw him in the eyes of J. Robert Oppenheimer when
I painted him, coloring the stare bright with pain and the fear
of something worse: the contemplation of nuclear waste and
secular hounding and God knows what residual fear of divine
retribution. I watched him bring down Gary Cooper, his eyes
hiding the leather mask. "I'm not lookin' for trouble," he told
me, blinking in that funny way, "but if trouble's lookin' fer me,
I won't be hard ta find."

And the seamy face of Auden: "You're not American, are
you?" he asked.

"I am now. I wasn't born here."

"Ah."

The "ah" said volumes.

"What a face," I remarked to his old companion. "It looks the way Comedy might look if the mask was taken off."

"Yes, well," the man said. "You must realize that Wystan's been working on that face for years."

Auden talked about the crowds of Americans without faces, and I tried to say something about the lack of mystery in American life, and about Yeats and Tarot decks, and he said I read too much. An acute comment. I had resumed the use of my old anesthesia. I had five books going at once: in both johns, in the headboard, at the kitchen table, on the couch. Sometimes I would read while I pushed the gun barrel against my hot chest, hoping to stanch the troubled memories. That was one trigger I seemed unable to hold back now.

—Shut the boy's mouth.

—You are a little idiot, Benoit.

—But these are our own people!

—Our own people? You think they wouldn't do the same to you if they could? There are no more people. Only prisoners.

—We can't let them be butchered, Eleazar.

—We can't prevent it.

—I can mix up their records. Lose a file.

—You worked that for the last time. You're lucky still to be alive.

—We have to try something.

—We have to cooperate. Tell them where to find the Andis family. The Tzawous.

—No!

—They will find them sooner or later. This way we get credit. We live.

—And they die.

—And we live.

Terror clung like salt to their mouths twisted in some grin I could not understand. A rictus of pity. They clattered over the boards leading to the wooden barracks with the black metal roofs, armbands sewn to their clothes. The old men had already been shot. Two girls walked with sticks, their arms and legs black with beatings. Carol, who had splashed in the Sinet River with me and drunk the sweet water walked in an odd, lallygagging way while the wet wind blew her mother's shawl. The shining eyes perceived nothing; she was blind.

This while sober, I think. Drunk was another matter. So many ways of being drunk besides Scotch. Cocaine wonderfully concentrated the mind on trivial occurrences. And the black book of Larry; these encounters led one even farther away from thought.

Screwing. I made a little chart of home games and away games—the home games fewer, the stadium and players in ill repair. On the bedroom circuit, vague fits and disturbances. Promiscuity was the small change of despair: insane nights in the percales of strangers, peculiar athleticism, coming again and again with no exhaustion and no satiation, no peace.

And the dreams, the dreams. It came to me that Freud was locked somewhere in the nineteenth century with tunnels and silos, and that our dreams were still obedient to his archaic metaphors. Whereas in waking hours you could see fucking and sucking in the movies, you could go from the cocktail party to the sack without an intervening kiss.

Larry's women were listed in mirror writing or in a simple substitution code: G for A and so on. With various notations: number of climaxes, variants of locale, posture, etc. An old story, on either side of the bed. I met a weather lady who kept a book like mine, only thicker, with ratings of the men she had been with. I saw the scrawl of isobars and high-pressure areas listed next to Kaufman, Benoit, on one page. The meaning was never vouchsafed.

There were other catalogs. It was at this time that I began to clip newspapers and underline books about Gypsies. An obsession resuscitated after the years of numbness. There was a lot of talk then about the Holocaust, that sorry, hot, inadequate euphemism. All wrong. The Hebrew proficiency at hating in Samuel and Kings was gone, bled away, bred out. The *goyim* had it now, had possessed it for centuries. The Jews had lost the knack. This epoch needed Grosz, not Chagall; Weill, not Copeland.

At home the collisions accelerated. Inger went off, came back, went off. One night in a downpour I drove down to Bucks County to pick her up in a motel. Luke Turner had abandoned her. On the long drive home I asked whether we ought to split, or whether it was worth one last try: no marriage counselor, no advice from friends, something we might do ourselves, something that might save us *from* ourselves.

"What?" she asked, looking away from me out the dark window.

"A child."

"Ben, don't."

"I don't mean a baby. A child."

"We've been over that. I don't want to adopt."

"We don't have to. We'll take a foster child. Somebody from a home. Somebody nobody wants."

"Foster children get taken back."

"Eventually."

"That's the point, isn't it? That we won't get too attached, that the child won't stay?"

"I don't know what the point is. I just thought maybe we could help him and he could help us, is all. Or she."

The windshield wipers banged metronomically against her silence.

After about sixty miles Inger spoke. "A little Benoit," she said. I expected this to be followed by a diatribe, but all she said was "I will if you will."

I don't know Inger's criteria, Daniel. I wanted you of all the others because the record said that you had been suffering from insomnia from the age of four, when you told the doctor that during the sleepless nights you "lay awake and thought about the past." That amused the social worker, but it knocked me out.

Larry made all the arrangements; you hardly spoke at all at first, just listened while I read everything aloud. When you began to warm up, you had none of the expected questions, nothing about your real mother in the TB sanitarium, or about the man who had abandoned her, or why the sky was blue or the sun yellow. You wanted to know if men came from a different planet from women, and if centaurs were insects because they had six limbs, and if mermaids could go to the bathroom. Yes to all these.

You grew at a regular—which is to say terrifying—rate. Inger and I had some rough spots, but for a while I could scarcely wait to get home from the studio, and her depressions were manageable. We even slept together for brief periods.

Your memory of this will be better than mine—and different. Perhaps now you can see what was happening while you looked up to see the towering, difficult strangers who seemed so arbitrarily happy or frowning. Our lunacies had nothing to do with you. You repaired us, for a while, as best you could. Your report cards were our passport to the main currents of American thought; your chatter and gossip were our currency.

I don't know when chaos and old night resumed; a few years later after you were in school around the block, I guess, studying *Media for the Child.* You made Super-8 movies of dinosaurs and other celebrities. I worried about the collapse of the afternoon newspapers. Inger couldn't get out of bed again; no ministrations helped. I called a psychologist, a friend of Risa's. The squat, admirable lady came in under the guise of a subject having her portrait painted, and quickly gave the whole show away. They spent days together in that room. In the end Dr. Leise told me that Inger was deep in some sort of trough; there were drugs she prescribed, and shock therapy if those didn't work. We tried the chemicals. After a while the patient became mobile enough to get out of bed. But you and I had to make the trip, hand in hand, to school and from it, and learn the location of the produce in the aisles of the supermarkets.

With the rest of your generation, you became a watcher. You and your friends were hooked on TV: the smaller the set, the greater its hypnotic effect. Everything was minimized, localized—emotions, history, art. Yet you were kind; so much kinder than I would have been in your place, so much more decent than I had learned to be to Max or Risa.

Do you remember our trips to the galleries? I tried to see the work as a child might. The controlled accidents, the indistinct lines and modish assaults, the engorged Ace comic icons; the broken machines and impotent software seemed a testimony to sterility, though whether it was the artists', the patrons' or the onlookers' was arguable. I only knew that I could not enter it. You consoled me, assured me that the objects meant nothing to you either. It was you who looked after me then, took me to musicals and circuses, to museums and parks, who tried to help me grow.

We had long, philosophical rambles on the Drive, and I was not the only speaker. You reminded me of things I had forgotten: how adults smell to children—oceans of tobacco, admixtures of deodorant and sweat and starch from the Chinese laundry. Of how a child's eye is fixed below an adult's, and knows the underside of things—tables, bookcases, kitchen shelves, life. You would hear Inger and me arguing and run to your room, and then an hour later when she was in the bedroom and I in my study, I would ask you to come in and you would say, "No, you're still yelling at each other," and I would shake my head but of course it was you that saw correctly.

So this was no time of renewal after all, but we stayed together. The focus, the source: a child. Plus the residue of affection and the glue of habit. I am no longer clear on dates or events. Things began to have a brighter feel; sounds had edges like knives, I remember that. And hues, even on people's faces, looked as if they had come out of tubes.

We seldom went anywhere; after the shock treatments Inger wanted to stay at home all the time. I only watched one of her sessions: the tongue gagged, the fingers curling into fists, the once-lovely body seeking its prenatal ball, the face, formerly the repository of so much beauty and tenderness and odd culpability, now stretched beyond its limits, like water leaping out of itself at the ledge of a fall, the mouth and the eyes anagrams of each other, an infinity of aspects and pains.

—No way exists to help your people.
—You can lie. Say you already did the operation. No one will know.
—You know nothing. You are a child.
—And you are a doctor!
—That means nothing here. If I don't take from the women the organs, they will take from me the organs. Do you understand?
—He understands, Doctor.
—I don't understand, Doctor!
—Take him away, Eleazar.
—She can't breathe with all the things you have on her.
—She can breathe.
—Eleazer, let me go.
—Remove him.
—Out, Benoit. Stop pulling!

ITEM: The mass of Gypsies still resemble eternally primitive African or Asiatic peoples. Interbreeding with this morally and spiritually inferior people will necessarily mean a decrease in the value of the offspring. On the other hand, interbreeding is favored by the fact that the young Gypsy men are especially sexually aggressive while the Gypsy girls are sexually unrestrained . . . It is not possible to fight this danger merely by guarding them in central camps. Their transfer to a foreign country too is hardly possible. Since they have no means of subsistence they cannot be deprived of it. The only effective way I can see of relieving the population of the Burgenland from this nuisance . . . is the universal sterilization of all Gypsies . . .

> —Dr. Meissner, General Public
> Prosecutor, Grasz. Letter written in
> 1940

She sat by the window looking out, an ivory chess queen staring straight ahead for hours. Except for an occasional restaurant, or for a weekend on a lake in Connecticut, we stayed put. You and I went canoeing sometimes; then you went off to camp in the summers and played ball on the streets when you could. I leaned out the window frequently, Max-style, showering the sidewalks with coins, thinking about him, imitating him, chewing on the White Owl that choked me when I inhaled, speaking to his ghost, reading his books to nail down my own mind with black letters and ideas.

Like Max, I dragged you off for my own moral adventures; to the Speakouts in the Village, where black men assailed the cancer of the white race and flagellated an audience hypnotized by fury; went on marches with banners inscribed with devices of liberty; once even took you South on a freedom ride, and in Georgia, when the white men gathered dangerously at the door of the men's room, we left the restaurant and peed on the Coca-Cola sign outside and newsmen took pictures and said that this was more of a sacrilege than the entire ride.

Protest became a way of life at some point in there, and you were always along, quizzical, moved less by events than by the comments of your friends, while I wandered through fogs of unrest, angry less at Washington or the Pentagon than at the world. The truth is, I would have stood forever at the sidelines, unmoved by editorials or by reports of terror in Southeast Asian towns. It was only when we went to that rally in Union Square —the echoes of that place unending—and we heard the medic speak that I was jarred. I saw your eyes when he described one of the pilots transporting wounded children, reporting over his radio: "Jesus, they're glowing in the dark." "Burned to varying degrees by white phosphorus," the medic told us. "They came in two and three to a stretcher. Several were blinded. All were still burning." I did not know whether to let you hear this. You dug in and decided for me. "Five died that night," the speaker went on. "The remainder will carry the scars all the days of their lives. An adult had set off the explosion in a crowd of children, thinking it was a smoke grenade." The listeners responded with a guttural roar of outrage, but I found the noise hard to bear, malicious; atrocity was what they came to hear. And I? What did I come for? "Like so much of the misery," the doctor concluded, "intentional and accidental, in Vietnam, that grenade was made in the U.S.A. Children everywhere comprise mankind's unrepresented constituency. They

do not deserve to be dead or blinded, two to a stretcher in a
world of our creation."

I looked at the child at my side and for the first time since
my own childhood was able to pray that he might be spared
not only the wounds but the wounding.

Then abruptly the speaker started to talk about the "Nazi
tactics of this American government," and on the dais red-
white-and-blue swastikas appeared, and signs, "Amerika, the
General Motors of Death" and the Gypsy liturgy froze in my
throat. I stood up and, embarrassed, could not find a way to
agree with either the music or the lyrics, and was shouted down
when I tried to talk of moral distinctions, attempted to find the
words to explain what the Germans were, how they operated,
but was not allowed to say that if all evils ran together like
pigments, if there was to be no such thing as history, we could
easily lose the little remnants of decency that remained. I left
with my head down, feeling a fool, an adolescent blusher,
hoping that one day you might enter what I could not. Benoit
Kaufman in America, I realized anew, was like some sperm cell,
driven, uncomprehending, banging its head with wild futility
against the side of the egg.

Soon afterward I fell ill for about a month with a grippe that
I could not shake. Many hours in bed, sipping liquids and
watching soaps. Light-headed. A kid again. But when Larry
summoned me downtown to the Yale Club I could scarcely
make it to the curb. I went because there was some urgency
in his voice. I half expected to hear of another magazine fold-
ing, a new professional disaster, but he kept the chatter light
until the appetizer was consumed. Then he said, "I was down
at the studio, looking at your stuff. You're overdue. The Mets
want their pictures in time to print the program."

"I know. I've been sick."

"You've been worse than that. Your stuff is different."

"I've been experimenting with it."

"You mean it's been experimenting with you. That's not
your stuff, Ben."

"What do you mean, not mine? I don't have any ghosts. I
never will."

"I mean it's not your style. Blurry. Colors too violent. Listen, they're still buying. I can still sell your fucking *doo*dles, for Chrissake. I'm not worried about your income, I'm worried about you."

"What's the matter with me?"

"I don't know, Ben. But I can guess, can't you?"

He pointed to my glass. "How many of those do you put away in a day?" he asked. "And when do you start?"

"I don't know." I tried to calculate, but nothing came to mind.

Larry raised his voice. "What time is it? What day is it? What year is it? You don't know that either. You drink a lot, and you start early. Very early. I've caught you stinking at eight o'clock in the morning when you bring your kid to school."

"I don't remember that."

"You don't remember anything any more. Except how to draw and how to drink. Look at yourself. Here—" He took one of the table knives and pointed its flat side at me. "Look at your eyes. Look at the capillaries on your nose."

The silver caught the light and focused it in my eyes. I blinked away the glare and saw a rubicund blowzy caricature posing as a lunch guest.

"You're an alcoholic, Ben. You've been one for years. Only now you can't get away with it. Your liver probably looks like Brillo."

"Who asked you to speak to me about this?"

"What do you care?"

"Inger?"

"Daniel."

I tried to think. Ideas shattered like windows. "What am I going to do?"

Larry knew. He took me out of the restaurant and we caught a cab and wound up in the office of some specialist who wrote me a prescription on the spot. If the pills didn't work, he said, we would try a place up the Hudson where I could dry out and still be close to the city.

I went home and tried to compose some sort of apologia, some kind of logic for my behavior to Inger, to you.

I found her wailing in my study, throwing stuff around.

"Thank God Daniel's going to camp," I said, or thought I said. She turned as I came in, her mouth a round O.

"Well, try calling them now!" she yelled.

"Call who?"

"Your girls. Your bloody harem!"

Had one of them called here? Surely Larry wouldn't say anything—

"I found your goddamn notebook."

"What notebook? I don't have a notebook"—having just returned the address book to its owner.

"The one in code. Probably with ratings. Good fucks, bad fucks, leather, daisy chains, *soixante-neuf*—God knows what."

Pointless to deny the adultery. But the notebook in code? Was I still drunk? Was she raving?

I looked down at the floor at the scraps of paper. Inger had found the book given to me by Jacqueline Clair, the one with whatever shreds and clues remained of Eleazar Jassy.

"That's not even my writing," I said. "Can't you see how old that paper is? That's not my book. It belongs to an old lady."

"Liar!"

"It does. What did you do with the paper?"

"I threw it out the window."

I stared out at the Park. It was not a windy day but the scraps were scattering in the wake of cars. I ran out, took the elevator downstairs and traversed the streets and the greens. I gathered what I could and went home and we had yet another scene and in the end I committed myself to the Senasqua Retreat above Croton. There was no possibility of another day, even another hour of this.

My life, *that* life was done, and agony would have to shop elsewhere. So I thought, so I thought.

Man walks with one foot on the curb and one on the street. Friend: "Come on home, you're drunk." Drunk: "Thank God, I thought I was a cripple."

Friend to drunk after they see *The Lost Weekend:* "I'll never drink again." Drunk: "I'll never see another movie again."

Etc. The alcoholic as jester. This is the way they did it at

Senasqua: ridicule, movies of yourself plastered, japes. Plus the mnemonic training:

S. O. B. E. R.

S: Self-knowledge leads to
O: Openness
B: Bravery
E: Excellence and
R: Reformation.

We wore S.O.B.E.R. pins and psyched each other. It was an animal existence, but then we were animals, foulers, howlers, lechers, reprobates, drunks.

The oldest was seventy-two, the youngest fourteen. We were of different shapes and sizes; you could see that in the morning, standing in formations in our whites, like a row of irregular teeth. But we were identical in one respect: we were sick, and we were scared. More than the testimonies of our friends or families, the blood samples, the results of the stress tests, the proclamations of the looking glass had done it. Unbearable evidence.

Pointless to chronicle the backsliding, malingering, fatuous optimism, the scrambled weeks, the erosion of feeling and recollection, the sense that even your hands are strangers, your organs visitors, and what is that broomstick in the trousers and where has it been? John Berryman reminds me:

> All what help I found left me intact
> safe with a quart of feral help a day.
>
> DT's convulsions. Hospitals galore.
> Projectile vomiting hours, intravenous,
> back in the nearest bar the seventh day. . . .
>
> I am *hurting*, daily, & when I jerk
> A few scales seem to fall away from my eyes
> until with perfect clarity enough
>
> seems to be visible to keep me sane
> & sober toward the bed where I will die.

Gradually I got used to a world of balanced landscapes and quieter, less freaky sounds. The questions of the inquisitors no longer flayed; I was pierced by deeper things again.

"Why are you angry, Mr. Kaufman?"

"I'm not angry."

"I think you are. I think that's why you drink."

I thank that's why I drank. I thunk; that's why I drunk. Yes, Doctor, I was angry; yes, rage moved me more than it had ever moved Inger. It knotted the muscles of my guts again, and in the mornings I began to awaken with fists. I knew I could no longer suppress the heat. It would have to die, like poor Berryman's. Maybe in much the same way.

Toward the end of my stay I found it possible to tolerate the day room, where pool balls clicked perpetually in the background and the yammering television set unreeled reruns of mice bombarding wabbits and Lucy fixing the plumbing. One evening I walked through the room on my way to dinner and heard something odd, something that jangled in the head. I looked up and saw an electronic Otis, arms akimbo, yelling "Humongous!" to the camera, and breaking up our little Senasqua audience. He was the star of a show about a black family, and that was his word, a neologism coined to mean big, and directed toward his fat mother or a large car or any oversized object. The kids of America had grabbed it, and there were Otis T-shirts and dolls. I alone had failed to notice. He appeared on a talk show later that week with Muhammad Ali, the two of them scattering jingles like pennies.

It was the cold sight of my old fellow inmate that made me feel strong enough to leave. This would be the last institution in which I would be contained. No more internments, no more homes, no more hospitals and no more marriage. On that, at least, Inger and I could agree. Before making an exit, I would stop once at the touchstones that comprised my life. That witness to who knows how many ironies would wait for me, the six bullets still in its chamber. I had hold of enough of this world to know its worth and mine. I had finally acquired the calmness, the requisite hardness, the ability to go home in every sense. There was no hurry now that I had discerned the purpose of Joe's present.

"I had a dream yesterday. We were blue-haired and lived our lives over TV dinners in a Florida motel," Inger was saying. My first day back, over wine and a damnable glass of iced tea.

"Were we fighting?" I asked.

She looked pretty again; not restored, she would never be restored, but better off somehow, older and pacific, distanced from trouble, away from me.

"The music of your face—" I began.

"Don't," she said, and put her hand on mine. "I'm so sorry. I can imagine what you've been through."

"No, you can't. But it's not your doing. It never was."

"You think you'll marry again someday?"

"No," I said. "You?"

"Yes."

"Luke Turner?"

"That was never anything, Ben. Just a dumb gesture, you know?"

"I do now."

"I want to take care of somebody. And I want somebody to take care of me."

"I know." I couldn't look at her. "I'm sorry I couldn't do that."

"Not your fault. I drove you to drink."

"So? I drove you crazy."

"I was crazy before."

"I was drunk before."

"But tomorrow morning you'll be sober. And I'll still be crazy."

"You look so much better. You must be better inside."

"It is. Sometimes."

"Do you ever play your guitar any more?"

"No. But I'm going to start. Maybe I'll meet some nice guy who sings harmony . . ."

Tears gathered in her eyes and mine. On such notes the long cacophony ended. We said our farewells like two kids holding on to a toy and a dollar bill, trying to let go at exactly the same time. You and your trust fund went home, Daniel. Back to Erie, Pennsylvania; the one good thing we had shared now phasing back into a separate life and scaring the hell out of both of us. What damage had we done, what good had our honorable intentions performed—if indeed they were honorable? Your reassurances have not sat well; Inger and I worried each other on the phone for a long time afterward.

Your mother stood in the front yard, twisting her apron and thanking us over and over. "A nice couple," she kept saying. "A pity you couldn't have your own. Daniel thinks the world of you."

"And we think the world of him," Inger said.

"He's smart. Maybe too smart for me now, Mrs. Kaufman."

"No," I told her. "He'll take care of you. He'll keep you well."

"Almost thirteen now." She put her hands on your hair. "All those years of growing I missed."

"There's plenty more," I said. Frost tells me home is the place where, when you have to go there, they have to take you in. Well, you were in. People occasionally believed that you really were our son, that the auburn was a mix of Inger's blondness and my black strands. But now I saw the resemblance between you and your mother and how little you had ever belonged to us. Had we taken too much from you? Had we given you enough? A family like ours in constant dissolution, raging, racked by sins. Better than an institution, I console myself on dark nights. Maybe, maybe. I left you with our traditional family joke: "What was the Snark?"

"A Boojum!" you yelled. You were still yelling it when we left. I watched you in the rear-view mirror until the dust and the trees obscured you. I would never see you again, I knew.

The divorce, after all that time, was anticlimactic. I felt no liberation at all, only a blankness. New York began to close on me like an iris that winter, and on a sudden whim I flew to Los Angeles. There, through Larry and Celebrity Service, Otis was located at Universal City. I drove out in a rented car past the signs: Pray in Car, Topless Mother of 8, Topless Billiards, Waterbed Hotel, a movie entitled *The Man Who Came at Dinner*, and wondered whether it was true that the world would look like Los Angeles one day. And would we know it? Maybe the world was like Los Angeles now.

Otis was leaving the gates of the studio when I found him. He was with some rangy white man I took for a grip, a page right out of *Pumping Iron*. Otis froze, looked at me and gave an impulsive wiry embrace. He proffered a copy of his paperback original, an autobiography entitled, typically, *The Testimony of the Spade*. It was in comic-book form and entirely omitted the Home. "Fiction, of course," he said. He took me to a delicatessen where an entourage dissolved in laughter every time he said "humongous." The only straight man was an uncomfortable-looking accountant who seated himself next to me. In hoarse tones he whispered between pastrami bites, "I tell you, this man is a black Jerry Lewis, the most talented faggot since Clifton Webb. Says one word and he's a hero. His autograph costs five dollars. I incorporated him yesterday. America."

"Draw my picture," Otis demanded. "Everybody takes my picture, but nobody draws it."

The accountant produced a notebook with lined paper. I used his felt-tipped pen and drew a caricature of Otis now— hair styled and teeth capped, outfitted by Lew Mangram, shod by Frye boots and sporting a gold medallion—and superimposed him on the Otis I recalled, looking out from behind accordion-gated windows. He smiled a lot when I handed it to him, and yelled "humongous!" and his crowd applauded, but I could see what it did to him. This was Homo Hollywood; he had a present, and if they picked up his option, a future, but no past, thank you, no memory.

No old friends. And no old words. Dyn-o-mite, laid back, humongous—those were the ones he lived by.

That night Otis swept me along with his groupies to a party in the Hills. Everybody was high on something; I told him I was off the sauce, so he offered hash, coke, anything. I smiled back emptily and asked for soda. It was not until very late that he turned on me.

"It's none of your business what I do in bed."

"Or out of it," I assured him.

"I know what they say when I'm gone. '*Schvartzer, faygeleh,* nigger, junkie, quiffo, cocksucker, queer.*' " His face contained the child and the old man, but not the present tense. "You think it's easy, you mother?"

"Don't Mau Mau me, Otis. This is Benny from the Home. It's no easier on this side of the net."

"Then why do you look like I'm a hit-and-run driver and you de onliest witness?"

"I make you uncomfortable, is that it?"

He lowered his voice. "Yes, you do, Ben. You look too thin, too worn. Too much gray in your hair. You make me feel funny and old. I'm sorry."

"I'm on my way out, Otis."

"They think I'm in my twenties. What do you think of that?"

"Fine with me."

"How old am I, Ben?"

"Does it matter?"

"It do here. But it don't matter what color you is, long as you got green somewhere on you, dig?"

In the appropriate chiaroscuro Otis had a cubistic look, merry and infinitely unsatisfied, five or six faces in one. He shook slightly, like a motor. Behind him you could sense the mama and the aunts, the abandonment of the father, the sensitivity and perhaps brilliance choked but not suffocated on the Bedford Stuyvesant streets, the stealing of childhood from the child, all the pride and energy let out in effeminacy and manic performance, and a constant thirst for adulation. Another American portrait.

"Ben. You know, even when you were in that place you looked like you were outside looking in. On everything. You look like that now."

I said good-by to him for the last time and he walked me past the yammering, weaving crowd who touched him as he went by.

At the door he said, "What you lookin' at, Ben? Come on, sketch me a sketch."

"I was just thinking about the price you paid for this."

"Humongous." He flashed an Armstrong grin.

"I didn't mean the real estate."

"Neither did I. Hu-mongous!" he shouted, and waves of hilarity broke behind him as he shut the door.

I had a short list of people, and Otis was crossed off. The rest were back in New York. I needed to neutralize the pastel and Day-Glo rock of L.A. Two hours later I was in the air, and the next morning found me sleepless and hungry in the old apartment.

More ancient than the city, gnarled as the pine he used to shape, Mordecai sat in Max's old chair examining me with still-shiny eyes and an intelligence that age had not dented.

"You know I never knew you drenk," he said, "until vun day you came in sober."

"How are you, Mordecai?"

"Listen, ever since dying came in fashion, life hasn't been safe. How should I be?"

"I worry about you. You need anything?"

"Yes, abot minus tventy yirs. And what can I do for you, boychick? All de time gone by, England, New York, Max dead, you so sad-looking, Sadie dead, me alive, who vould think?"

"I didn't know about Sadie? When?"

"Long ago. You were *shikker* in dose days. All de time. What did you know? Dyanne called. No answer."

"I'm sorry."

"No need. You look so sed. Diworce, I heard. Booze. Sickness." He framed his chin with his hands. "Only one God and so many enemies."

I made him a glass of tea, and we sat and chatted for a while. I asked him if he ever had visitors, if he was truly provided for.

"Don't vorry. I got frands. Also Social Security, plos de apotment. Denks for payin' de rent, bot not necessary. Look!"

He showed me a bankbook with forty-two thousand dollars in it, scrimped over the years. "Sadie's vill, also Max's. I told you, don't vorry. I got de necessities. *Tsum shtarbn darf men keyn luakh nit hobn.* You don't need a kelender to die."

In a while, Risa stopped by with groceries and hugged me, and we talked until dark about all the expected things: Max, the old days and the new. I asked her about her work.

"I'm I'm I'm *quite* notorious, ectually," she said. "I see you you don't read *New York* magazine."

I told her that at Senasqua they had tried to get rid of our masochistic impulses.

"There was an article on me and my work. Said I was was the Ahlma, mind you, the Ahlma Mahler of the Old and New Left. Because of Lauritz and Champeter and Deever—and of course Max."

The first two names did not register.

"Oh, there's so so *lit*tle you knew. They were all my friends, all ebsolutely wonderful men. God, those were good times. Then in in the sixties, the students were *so* exciting."

Could it be that this horsy old lady with the irregular teeth and the unnaturally chestnut hair, this anthology of borrowed styles and attitudes, my foster mother, was really a secret sex symbol?

She could gauge my astonishment.

"Oh, Benoit, you missed so much. You you never really knew me, did you? And I never knew you."

"You did pretty well in the old days."

"No, that was instinct, not not knowledge. Max used to say, let let let the boy alone, but I always used to tell him that was the worst, the totally *worst* thing we could do. Because you you came out of hell, and that was where you would go if we let you alone. It was like a homing instinct, wasn't it?"

"I don't know, Risa. Hell has never seemed like something I had to look for."

When I got ready to leave, I told her I was making a few visits to old friends, to sort of get acclimated. I asked her about Dyanne. Mordecai, stirring from his nap, rummaged around and found an envelope with the address in Westchester. I called her and Dyanne invited me to come out the next day. I stayed over with Mordecai and Risa, and in the morning we had a long sentimental breakfast and then I went downtown, bought a souvenir album of Casals and, like a commuter with half a day off, took the 11:55 to Briarcliff. So Mordecai had survived and Risa had prospered. It would be all right to leave, to end with everyone well. I was almost anxious to get it done, and got off the train smiling, unreeling fantasies about the pistol.

Dyanne met me at the station. I don't know what I expected; certainly not what I saw. Everybody else had aged; like Merlin in *The Once and Future King*, Dyanne had apparently been living her life backwards. She looked like an undergraduate. Her body had stopped growing at the right time; the waist was still tiny, and from what the faded jeans revealed, she still had the hips and legs of a *jeune fille en fleur*.

"Wheat germ," she confided in the car. "And I go to a gym three days a week. Also I'm very unhappy. Curbs the appetite."

"Also you're very frank to somebody you haven't seen in so long."

"Also I'm very happy to see you looking so—"

"Don't say it. I know what I look like."

"Well, you look sad, but you look alive. The last time I saw you, you looked like something out of *The Possessed.*"

"When did you last see me? I don't remember."

"You wouldn't. I was on my way from Grand Central to Bendel's. You were coming out of a bar on Madison. It was ten A.M."

"And I was stinking?"

"Even then. Well, you had your reasons." She pulled the car up to a large fieldstone house with a horseshoe driveway. The grass looked like the top of a pool table.

"You've heard everything, then," I said.

"From Risa, mostly. And Mordecai and . . . I don't know, around."

She had the kind of place that makes hostesses say they had a decorator, but they worked with him. The interior shone with calculation and order. Too much rosewood and leather. The bookshelf in the living room was filled with her old textbooks and some best sellers. I found the turntable and put on the Casals: Dvořák. She sat on the overstuffed couch and patted a cushion beside her, but I sat in an Eames chair across the room.

"I've been meaning to call you," I said.

"For about a millennium."

"I had my hand on the phone lots of times. I just couldn't do it."

"Why?"

"Nobody likes to be reminded of past mistakes."

"Am I your past mistake?"

"I think so sometimes."

"I hear you were working on some serious stuff when you were . . . away."

"Drying out? It's okay, you can say it. I don't drink any more. Or smoke."

"And two out of three ain't bad?"

I didn't know whether to pick up that card. I let it sit for a while and we were still, listening to the cello reach for the high C's. I asked her if she ever played.

"I *shlep* the kids to lessons. Leonard Bernstein's cleaning lady gets closer to music than I do."

"I'm sorry. You were good."

"Ear of the beholder." She smiled. "I have other interests, anyway."

"Like what?"

"I run the damn town, Ben. I'm on every committee there is; you can't run for mayor or stage a musical without coming here for permission. When the Tokyo String Quartet plays at the high school they stay here. I raised seventy-five thousand dollars last year for the Urban League and the United Fund. You want to see my plaques? They're downstairs. They cover two walls."

The sun was in my eyes. I squinted at the framed photographs on the Steinway.

She pulled the shade down but never stopped talking. "I was in est. I go to Yoga once a week. We have a subscription to Lincoln Center. My daughters take every lesson there is— riding, ballet, piano."

I looked at the pictures again. The girls had the carriage of young women.

"I'm surrounded by people my own age and income. I have everything I want," she said, and bit her lip. "You ought to do my picture now. You always liked to draw caricatures of American archetypes."

I sought to change the pitying drift. "I envy you your daughters," I said.

"Yes. Well. For them it'll be different." She stared at the wall. "Maybe. God, I bought it all. Twice I bought it. All the stuff about the station wagon, the crabgrass, the briquettes. Then I got mad and I bought the nuclear-family-as-the-first-fascism line. I marched. I spoke. I yelled. And here I am. No different. Just older."

"You've been angry for years and years, haven't you?" I asked. "Why didn't you leave?"

"I did, Ben. And I came back. Why didn't *you* leave?"

"I don't know," I told her. "I guess I thought . . . I thought I could undo the damage that was done to me long ago. I was wrong."

Dyanne stood up and smoothed her hair and shook off something. "You want anything?" she asked.

I shook my head. "Only what I can't have."

"Like Scotch?"

"Like you."

"I'm not hard to have. They call me passion's plaything around here."

"Is that right? Peyton Place on the Hudson?"

There were tears in her eyes. I was sure they still brimmed at Excedrin commercials. We looked at each other. *"Nu?"* she asked finally, in the distinct tones of Upper Broadway.

She dropped her eyes. I felt as abashed with her then as if both of us were kids again.

"Taste is a one-room house consisting of the mouth," Chazal tells me. "Hearing has the boudoir of the ear, the eyes have the parlor of the cornea, and smell has the long hall of the nose. But the poorest lodged is touch, who lives on the naked plains of the skin like a vagabond in the streets." A Gypsy. Time took the afternoon off, but this was a trick of touch; the bodies were different, and the minds and the circumstances. This was not an affair but an adieu. I think Dyanne sensed that. When she asked me what I was going to do now, I would not tell her.

When I asked her the source of her unhappiness, she replied by humming and asking me to make love again before the kids came home.

We were lying on the bed talking about one of Sadie's meals when Dyanne sat up suddenly. Her breasts still had the kind of sauciness that women are supposed to lose in their early thirties. She had lost nothing, nothing at all. Maybe misery agreed with her. It does with some people. There was a mannerism from the past playing about her mouth. Something rang in the mind. A Gestalt therapist would have had a lovely session with us that afternoon.

"For a long time," I said, "I didn't think about the Clairs. Now I can't keep them away. You know I followed up all their leads."

"The letter was useless, then?"

"What letter?"

"You know, the one about the cities."

"I didn't get any letter."

"You must have. About two years ago? I sent it to your apartment."

Maybe it was during one of the arguments, when Inger used to rip up my stuff. Or maybe I was drunk—when wasn't I drunk?—and confused it with junk mail. It could have gone in the fireplace or the garbage. It might still be around, under something or behind the old highboy. Inger and I had recovered many a Bloomingdale's bill back there. Neither of us were neat freaks.

"What did it say?" I wanted to know.

"You really never got it? I thought you just didn't care any more. Let me try to remember."

When we got dressed she sat down on the couch, and this time I sat next to her.

"I didn't make a copy," she said. "There was something about her illness. She had cancer; I guess she's dead by now. And then the rest was about, you know—"

"Eleazar. Jassy."

"She had figured out some sort of answer. From your notebook. Does that make sense to you?"

"Yes. But there's no notebook any more. Just some pieces of paper."

I went to the hall closet and got my wallet from my jacket and shook out the handful of little folded pages that remained. "There's nothing on them but foreign names." I showed her. She shuffled the lined sheets.

"Oranjestad, Kralendijk . . . something illegible, something else illegible." She examined the other papers. "Andros Town. Point-à-Pitre, Fort de France, Frederiksted, I can't read the rest of it. *What* have you been doing with this, skin diving?"

"It met with an accident."

"Jacqueline's penmanship was very wobbly," Dyanne said. "I couldn't follow all of it. But she had figured out the names. They're cities in the Caribbean."

"And?"

"And they all have airstrips. And there's only one airline that flies to all of them. Virgo. You know it?"

"We never went to the Caribbean. Our idea of an out-of-town trip was the Bronx Zoo."

"You wouldn't know this airline anyway. Strictly freight. I checked a couple of years ago when I got the letter. It's based in the U.S. Virgins. That's why the name."

She shrugged her shoulders.

"Is that it?" I asked.

"What do you want from a suburban housewife, fingerprints?"

"No. You did fine. Only—"

"Only you don't know how to proceed. You could start with a phone call."

"To Virgo?"

"Ask to speak to whatever name you last had for him."

"Éduard Salant. Suppose he recognizes my voice?"

"Then hang up. Never mind. I'll call."

She went to the study and dialed Virgin Islands Information and then the number. Virgo was on St. John. I expected the whole process to be like a tedious transatlantic call, but she was connected in about a minute. I went to the bedroom and picked up the extension. "Virgo Air Freight. Good morning."

"Good morning. May I speak to Éduard Salant, please."

A pause. "There is no one here by that name." A soft black island intonation.

"This is Bubkes Imports. May I speak to the president of your company, please?"

"Mr. Mellilo is not in. He is expected back Monday. Whom shall I say called?"

"Bubkes. I'll call next week."

"Thank you." Click.

We met in the living room. "Does that sound promising?" she asked.

"No."

"He could have changed his name again. And maybe he's not the president. Maybe he's a pilot or a salesman or something."

"Or maybe he's moved on."

"Is it worth looking into?"

"No."

"Well." Dyanne sat down hard. "It was worth a try. You know what *bubkes* means in Yiddish?"

"No."

"Beans."

That was what I deserved for picking up a cold trail. Cold *bubkes.*

Dyanne offered to drive me to the station, but I told her I wanted to walk to clear my head.

At the door she said, "Ben, I'm sorry you didn't get what you wanted. Or did you?"

"Meaning what?" I asked. No reply, which was a reply.

"Maybe I did," I said.

"Don't kid yourself. It wouldn't always be like this. Habit is a great sterilizer. We would have bored each other to death by now."

"Do you believe that?" I said.

"Go away." Her voice shook again, and I went down the front steps and down the block without looking back until I reached the corner. Dyanne was still standing there.

"Out of sight out of mind," I called to her. "You go out of my sight, and I'll go out of my mind."

She waved and smiled and I returned the signals, walking backward until a row of Norwegian pines blocked her from view.

That night I dreamed about her. Not with any sexual connotation; there is a theory that the mind, like a computer, clears itself for the next day's totals. Maybe, maybe. I watched the conversation in recognitive fragments, like watching the little screens on airplanes, where the image occurs a few seconds earlier than the one on your own screen. Mr. Mellilo is not in. Mr. Mellilo is not. Mr. Mellilo.

The island accent, perhaps. The intonation. An alarm system. Something wrong with what I heard. An echo. It rankled in the morning. I too dialed the Virgin Islands. This time it took longer. That was all right; time was all I had.

"Virgo Air Freight. Good morning."

"Bubkes Imports, good morning," I told the voice. "May I speak to Mr. Mellilo."

"Not in until Monday morning, sir. May I take a message?"

"No, I'll write him. May I have the correct spelling of the name, please?"

"Certainly. Mr. Jonas Melalo. M-E-L-A-L-O."

The hair rose on the back of my neck. His kind of contemptuous wit. The word laughter hiding in the word slaughter. Still, I could not be sure until I got to St. John. It would be worth the trip: something else to keep the little revolver off the streets while it was waiting for me.

ITEM: Several [Gypsies], given the rank of work foreman, formed an authority within the camp. They improved their position by stealing, sometimes from each other. A large-built man from this group was for a time Kapo of the Punishment Company and those sent to the company had to bribe him not to beat them. There were also small Gypsy children, some born in a concentration camp and many of them orphans. They kept the parade ground and streets clean, starting work as soon as the other prisoners left the camp in the morning. . . . Selections and

mass killings appear to have begun in 1943: Eighty pregnant
women . . . were exterminated on arrival.

—Donald Kenrick and Grattan Puxon,
The Destiny of Europe's Gypsies (New
York: Basic Books, 1972)

—*Come, Benoit. The soldiers will be here soon. Come with us
on the truck.*
—*No.*
—*Fool. I could have killed you. Or had you killed. Instead you
were spared.*
—*I was useful to you.*
—*Yes. You were useful.*
—*And now I'm not.*
—*No.*
—*Why don't you kill me, then? Have you run out of gas or
rope?*
—*We have grown up here, Little Fish. We have a few
things in common, you and I. One was that we lived
through it all. How long will you remember that? Are you
coming?*
—*No. I am not afraid of the English soldiers, Eleazar.*
—*Call me what the others called me.*
—*Melalo?*
—*Yes. It suits me. Come, Benoit, come on the truck.*
—*No.*
—*Adieu then.*
—*Au 'voir.*

ITEM: The queen . . . gave birth to a demon, Melalo, who had the
appearance of a bird with two heads and whose plumage was
a dirty green colour. (Melalo is the most dreaded demon of the
Gypsies.) With sharp claws he tears out hearts and lacerates
bodies; with a blow of his wing he stuns his victim and, when
the latter recovers from his swoon, he has lost his reason. He
stirs up rage and frenzy, murder and rape.

—J. Clebert, *The Gypsies* (London:
Vista, 1963)

I took the little list out of my pocket, crossed off Dyanne's name and inscribed a new entry: *Eleazar Jassy.* It looked strange in my handwriting, but it also looked credible and extant. Revenge is a kind of wild justice, Francis Bacon tells me. The justice was for others to judge; the wild I could testify to myself. On the subways, posters of the Caribbean shouted at me from the walls. I spent a trip downtown wondering how one took a pistol past the X-ray security machines in airports. It was not until Rockefeller Center that I saw quite clearly how it could be done.

VIII: WRATH

ABOVE GATE 21 A BILLBOARD TOLD ME TO CLIMB ABOARD a cruise ship and shuck my cares. Tan girls in LaCoste blouses sported on deck in the arms of handsome Protestants with unseasonable tans. "Follow your lead in Caribbean Eden," it yelled in Day-Glo magenta. "See your travel agent for details." I saw my travel agent for details. Boats to the tropics were interested in examining your checkbook, as I suspected, not your briefcase.

No one knew I was going except Larry, and he only threw my line back: why didn't I travel in season when there were more bimbos than I could shake a stick at, if that was my idea of a good time? I told him I was going down with some stewardess I had met at Reno Sweeney's, and he said going down *with* or down *on*, and I gave him a large hollow laugh and he advanced me two thousand dollars. It was a simple as that.

The Dutch boat starred a Gypsy trio whose music and genealogy were as authentic as the soprano's eyelashes. The off-season manifest listed participating Kiwanis and urologist conventions. At my table were the professionally unaffiliated: an obese nurse's aide who got seasick while we were undulating in harbor and retired to her stateroom, never to be seen again; and Mr. and Mrs. Selwyn Doré. She was somewhere between fifty and Social Security, with a metallic blond wig, wide Revlon-carmine lips, two circles of rouge, and skin the color and texture of parchment. Her husband was a vulpine cadaver so thin, she liked to cackle, that you had to look twice to see him. On the first evening of the voyage, I told them my profession, and in wine and Bols they revealed theirs. They were cardsharps on the way to Aruba to fleece the sheep. I tested them out; they were as thorough as any urologist aboard. Two hundred dollars were surgically removed from my wallet without benefit of anesthetic. For a time thereafter I stayed in my cabin reading and going over the clippings in my scrapbook.

It occurred to me toward daylight the next day that I had never unpacked the pistol or fired it, and that this long carom might end in one of the botched confrontations beloved by the *Daily News*, in which a gun jams and the cop becomes a victim, or a malefactor a corpse. I unpacked the thing and examined its chamber. All the bullets were still there; brass and oil made the gun look efficient and conscienceless.

I went up on deck and strolled to the stern. One of the bus boys had just thrown out some garbage. Gulls screamed after it in the thin pink light. A few of the birds settled on the rail and quarreled over offal, ignoring me. I came within two of three yards of one of the larger ones and rested the barrel of the pistol on my left wrist.

The little silver sight was leveled at the bird's gray wing. Perhaps it was the ocean's cacophony or the wind or the steady roll of the engines. I heard nothing, only saw the explosion of feathers and blood.

"What do you do?" The Dutch voice came from behind me. I turned to see two officers standing close-by. They were on watch and walking toward the stern; the shot must have astounded them. They looked ready to jump me.

"I just—I was practicing," I said lamely.

"No firearms are allowed aboard this ship," the younger one said. The larger, blond man held out his big red hand. "If you please?" he said. "Quickly. That is a dangerous thing."

"I'm sorry," I replied. "This is my property, gentlemen. I assure you—"

"The whim of the tourist is worthless on board this ship. You will hand over the weapon, please, before the passengers see you."

I gave it to the young man. He handled it as if it were evidence in a murder trial, gingerly, holding the gun by the tip of the barrel upside down.

"You might put the safety on if you're going to carry it around like that," I said.

The older officer took it from his companion. By now some other officers in the same starchy whites had assembled behind us. Exit time. I gave them a big salute and opened the door out of which I had emerged ten minutes before and took the steps two at a time to B deck. Several stewards saw me and pointed and buzzed among themselves. I had heard about the velocity of shipboard gossip, but this struck me as a bit too rapid—until I entered my stateroom and looked in the mirror. The white ducks and linen shirt I had just put on were dotted with seagull blood, and there were red spatter prints on my face and hair. I was changing clothes when a knock sounded peremptorily at the door.

"The captain wishes to see you." It was the voice of the blond officer.

There was no point in making any more trouble. I followed him quietly.

"Mr. Kaufman," the captain said when we were alone, "this is most irregular." He was a tall man, given to ambiguous smiles after each sentence. There was about as much iron-gray hair on the back of his hands as on his head.

"By all rights I should confine you to quarters if what Mr. Willems says is true."

"It's true, Captain," I confessed.

"Guilty with an explanation?"

"The gun is a surprise for a friend. I just wanted to see if it would shoot straight. So I took aim this morning at a bird. That's all."

"The name of this friend?"

"If I told you, it wouldn't be a surprise, would it, Captain?"

He breathed through his nose and contemplated the problem. "I hate incidents," he said finally.

"I too."

"Have you a suggestion?"

"Keelhauling?" I volunteered.

"Mr. Kaufman, you don't appreciate the seriousness of this violation of tradition and law."

"I'm sorry," I said. "Why don't you keep it under lock and key and return it to me when I debark?"

"I will have to report this."

"Why? It can only lead to trouble, investigation, that sort of thing."

He let his temples work on this for a minute.

"Captain, I won't say anything if you won't."

"I will think about it," he said.

I left under escort. Mr. Willems took me silently to my cabin. As I entered it I could hear him talking ominously in Dutch to some other officers. The voices echoed down the metal corridor and vanished.

In the afternoon there was a good deal of nudging and whispering when I was around. Clearly, the story had gained currency.

At dinner the conversation was desultory and everybody seemed anxious to get out of the room. Ringo Kaufman was in town, the law this side of the Pecos, the man who shoots down guano-slingers without a backward glance.

By evening only the cardplayers would talk to me. Mrs. Doré gave me the latest shipboard version of the now-infamous gun incident: I had pulled a pistol on the first mate in an argument about his wife, and he had wrested it away from me. I was now under a kind of house arrest. I told the Dorés the truth, but I could see doubt playing about their features.

She smiled. "True or not," she said, "you may as well face it. We're the only ones who'll talk to you for the rest of the trip. Cards?"

We played everything from casino to blackjack. Invariably I won at the beginning, teetered in the middle, and wound up poorer at the finish. When my funds were appreciably diminished, I begged off.

"Tell you what," she said, "I'll play you for something other than cash."

"Like what?"

"Like that gun the captain took away."

"Now, dear," said Mr. Doré in a ghastly bass. "What would we do with a gun?"

"I could think of a few things," she replied cloudily. "However, why don't we play for something else, Mr. Kaufman?"

"Like what?" I asked.

"Your talent."

"I beg your pardon?"

"If we win, paint one of us. If we lose, we'll pay your fee How much do you get for a picture?"

"Depends," I said. "Anywhere from a few hundred to thousands."

"Say one thousand?"

"All right."

"What game?"

There was only one game I thought they could not rig. "How about dice?" I offered.

"We haven't got dice."

"There are some in the game room," I told her. They sent for the steward and he brought us a pair.

"High roll?" Mr. Doré asked.

"Fine."

I took them, blew on them and came up with a seven. I should have suggested craps. Too late.

The mem-sahib popped the cubes in her empty tumbler, rattled them loudly and upended the glass. Five and six.

"I won! I won!" she said, and whistled for another gin.

"Sorry, old man," said Mr. Doré. "It was legitimate. Truly."

"Never mind," I consoled him. "It'll help to pass the time."

"Tomorrow, then? After breakfast?"

"All right."

He regarded his wife. "Oils, I think, don't you?"

"I haven't any," I told him.

"Ah, but we do." He smiled triumphantly. "Eugenia's an amateur painter."

I told him I could imagine some of the amateurs she had painted, and withdrew to the promenade deck. Nobody came near me. When most of the passengers were gone I strolled about in the night, looking up at the star-dogged moon and down at the general bioluminescence of the sea.

Sleep was nowhere to be found. Since leaving Senasqua I had experienced almost no longing for alcohol, but just then I wanted it with irrational thirst. Why not? sang the waves, what point to staying sober now? But there was some overmastering pride, or fear of losing the sense of time and purpose I had so recently acquired.

Mrs. Doré's oils were of the dime-store persuasion, lacking subtlety and finish. I took my time sketching her; fatigue scattered my thoughts and shook my fingers.

The weather blew us about that day and the next. It rained fitfully and turned cold. When we looked at the black water it hurt the backs of our eyes. The crew was short with each other and with the passengers. There was a lot of bitching on deck. The boat lurched and rolled too much, despite the stabilizers, and there were fewer attendants at the meals. People liked to gather around us in the palm court to compare the painting and the subject.

"Exactly like her," one man said at my back.

"Misses entirely. No soul," somebody whispered.

There were arguments and, although I did not look up, I thought I heard sounds of someone being jostled.

That evening at dinner an officer asked to see me privately. "The captain requests you do your work in private," he reported.

"Why?"

"It seems to disturb the passengers."

"You mean it seems to disturb the captain."

"I'm merely following a command, sir."

I packed up the gear and went downstairs. We finished the trip in the Doré stateroom, except for those thrashing hours when I attempted the impossible: to shut my eyes for a bit. On the last day I completed the oil to an extravagance of praise. I sensed, and the Dorés knew, that it was my last painting. She had gambled for my talent and, such as it was, had won it.

"It seems a shame." She kept admiring the canvas on which she had been relieved of ten years. "I have the painting *and* the money. Can't we give you something?"

"Sleep is all I want," I said. "Just sleep."

Her husband rummaged through a forest of bottles and found a little glass container. He shook out a couple of torpedo-shaped red pills. "The Doré drugstore," he said. "We relieve people of everything: money, jewelry, insomnia."

In all the bad years I had never taken chloral hydrate, always relied on liquor. Now I popped two little red bombs in my mouth and went back to my own bunk. The chemistry took effect immediately. I unreeled a festival of hallucinations: a portrait of a ship painted badly on an ocean of aggressive colors; Mrs. Doré gaming for the bones of the crew. When I awoke there was a rime of salt around my mouth. I was thirsty when I checked out and thirsty when the captain called me in and thirsty when he returned the gun wrapped in a towel of his steamship line and bound with rope. I thanked him and apologized for the difficulty.

"This was not a good voyage," he replied. "You are bad luck. You have booked return passage?"

"No."

"Do us both a favor and find some other way to come back."

"I'm not coming back."

"Better still."

I never saw the Dorés. Doubtless they used pills themselves and slept through the debarking. The man who rowed the little tender to shore was large, black and surly, and looked like something from last night's dream. An outsize wave slapped the boat and soaked a couple of us. He grinned wickedly. "Welcome to Paradise, mon," he said.

It was the colors that threw the first challenge. Pelicans speared the Caribbean water and came up with groupers shining in their elastic beaks. Pale and hot-red hibiscus hung down from rock fences, and banana quits, little yellow birds, quarreled with gray-green lizards. Sugar-apple trees gave the unsaturated air a vague perfume. Eden, maybe, but to a city boy raised in an atmosphere redolent of delicatessen and exhaust, a place full of rectangles and shadows, this flat island had a blank, melancholy aspect. An arena where slaves had once rebelled and died, a dangerous place for retirees, a breeder of white alcoholics ready to bleach out their brains in the Caribbean sun.

Cruz Bay has a rank of cabstands and a square of dirt beaten flat and a dive place where you can rent scuba equipment.

Across the square sits a couple of glassy tourist shops and a handful of duty-free liquor stores and municipal buildings. Five minutes' walk and you're out of the island's only metropolis, until you get to Caneel Bay five miles away. I bought a straw hat and a mask, and hired a taxi for the day. The driver's name was Tracy, and for a while I wore the hat down around my nose to hide my features. He was sure to be questioned by the police afterward. Then I thought what foolishness this was; I was still thinking like a man with a calendar. I started to relax. Tracy drove to the long brown edge of Trunk Bay and napped while I splashed out over the fire coral where hawkshell turtles and schools of parrot fish undulated like blue-and-yellow pennants.

I don't know how long I was out there: the misnamed silent world crackled and hummed; my fingertips withered and a chill played down my back. I came out too rapidly and without looking down. One of the sea urchins that look so pleasant on bookshelves and so malignant when in operation, thrusting out long black porcupine spikes, managed to meet my foot halfway, embedding the tips in the sole. Tracy drove me back. "Spikes not poison, mon," he said. "Give it two, tree weeks, all gone."

But I could not wait three weeks, and the calcium points felt venomous. On the way, the foot pulsing, I thought that in this Eden the sea urchin was the serpent. But no, that was not true. It was an innocent thing, after all, protecting its turf. Yet there was a serpent on the premises: the creature's name was Benoit.

It was Sunday night and the last ferries were taking visitors back to St. Thomas. I made a great show of limping up the hill to visit friends. Then, out of sight, I hobbled down to the Cruz Bay beach, parked myself under a coconut tree and watched the little boats jostling in the tide and soft wind. The sun reddened the outer islands and gave them shadows and dimension, and then eased them into the dark. There were only a few lights and the far-off sounds of reggae music. A police truck went by slowly with two black cops in the back giving the street a sleepy scrutiny. It disappeared up the hill to town.

I put the satchel under my head. The stars looked wet. It took me an hour to think myself away from the foot and into sleep. Booze would have done the job in ten minutes.

The morning sun came with a quick ingratiating heat. Sleep had been dreamless, a white night. Nothing in the little town was moving except some chickens. I lay looking up at pale-yellow hibiscus visited by brown hummingbirds with diamond-shaped green iridescent crowns. Lizards came out to lick dew off stones. The bay was still: I could hear the reptiles scatter dryly when I got up and plunged in the water. I swam out to one of the cabin cruisers anchored close to shore. It was wide open; a portable radio and kitchen utensils lay where anyone could reach them. It all reminded me of the innocence in New York a childhood ago when people left their cars open. After bathing in the warm salt water, I swam back, set up a little pocket mirror on a palm tree and shaved as closely as I could with hand soap and salt water. There was still no one out, although sounds emanated from the hill in town. I dressed in a blue shirt and tie and cord suit, and put my wet trunks in the towel, cut open the rope around the Smith & Wesson and checked its contents. For one chill moment I thought the captain might have removed the bullets; I had no extras. But there were still five in the chambers. More than enough. The gun went into the little sailcloth carry-all, along with the straw hat. A paved road separated the beach from a wooded area leading up to a gray cement block house. I pushed the luggage between some rocks and covered it with dried palm fronds. If they blew away, if somebody found the suitcase, and needed underwear and books, good luck to him.

I found Virgo Air Freight in the telephone directory near the taxi rank. There was no listing for Melalo. The first ferry of tourists came rattling in at nine. When it tied up, I mixed with the group of tourists and climbed the hill to town. Virgo was at the end of a narrow street of little shops and grocery stores. It occupied what must have been a store in a sleepier time. There was a waiting room of fairly new vintage, furnished with tube aluminum and plastic chairs, a low railing, and in back of that a young black secretary typing and answering phones. Behind her was an office with a green door marked "Private," and another, a john, marked "Employees Only." No other employees were visible. I went to the railing.

"Mr. Kaufman to see Mr. Melalo."

"He's not in yet." The eyes appraised me quickly. American. Suit. Money. The usual. "Do you have an appointment?"

"No." I gave her a card with my name on it. "It's about shipping some building supplies. When do you expect him?"

"He usually gets in about now. Would you like to wait?"

"Outside in the sun," I told her, and settled on a white rock near the building to watch the little beach wagons toiling around the one-way streets. Tourists shuffled through the open drugstore buying sunglasses and Bain de Soleil. Black men came into the bar and started drinking rum and beer and palavering. Kids ran out and populated the schoolyard and picked up a game of cricket. Chickens held an election in someone's backyard. Goats clopped around and dogs napped in the heat. A nice place to grow up, except that there was no work to help you grow up and no future except the green heat of Eden and rum in the mornings, and beer and arguments in the afternoons. Unless you operated a store. Or taught school. Or owned Virgo Air Freight.

Two black men went by me into the office and shut the door. In a few minutes one of them came out and walked down the hill toward the beach. After a short wait the secretary emerged.

"Mr. Melalo will see you now," she announced. I followed her in.

A gray-haired Negro sat behind the desk looking at me through mirrored sunglasses. He wore an open-necked white short-sleeved shirt. His office was very spare, only a brown desk made out of a door, supported by matching metal filing cabinets. No pens, no blotter, just an abalone shell serving as an ashtray with one large white ash in it, and an open box of Havanas. Melalo was smoking one, and it about matched his skin. That took me aback for a minute. He looked a native of the islands, a case of mistaken identity.

"May I help you?" he asked. It was the voice that could not be masked.

—*Eleazar, I cannot bear to hear the way you scream at them.*
—*Then don't listen.*

—But they're being punished for nothing!
—No, not for nothing. For being Gypsies.
—But you and I are Gypsies.
—We are being punished too.
—What have we done, then?
—What have we not done, then?

ITEM: [Gypsies] were deeply anti-social, according to the National
Socialist thinkers. It was advisable, therefore, to rid Germany
and Europe of this alien presence, which carried everywhere the
poison of treason, as proven by this collective guilt complex
which they could not shake off and which remained stuck to
them during their endless wanderings. The Gypsies, responsible
for the first flood, will bring on the second. The Gypsy legend,
the story handed down from generation to generation, says that
this tribe, condemned to wander indefinitely and unable to
settle in the Americas, will herald the end of time, when it
begins to settle down permanently.
> —Jean-Michel Angebert, *The Occult and
> the Third Reich* (New York:
> Macmillan, 1974)

He motioned me to a chair.

"I would like to speak to you about shipping freight," I said.

He held out the cigar box. "What sort of freight is it?
Building materials, my secretary said."

But the skin was dark, much darker than mine, much darker
than the sun would make it even if he lay in it each day.

"Well, it's a bit more than that," I said. I lit my cigar slowly
and watched him over the smoke. "A matter of some discretion."

He rose, shut the door and locked it, and returned to his seat.
I could see him casing me, trying to remember something. He
was a bit restive, but betrayed no physical language of recognition.

"So," he said. "Now. What is it? Contraband?"

"Things like this." I dipped into the bag and handed him
my scrapbook.

He exchanged his shades for a pair of clear reading glasses.

I saw his face plainly; even with the mustache and the Negroid features his identity was no longer in doubt. He read one item slowly and completely, thumbed through the other pages, then looked up at me over the glasses.

"What is it that you want?" he asked.

"Can it be that I've changed so much?"

He peered at me very intently but without fear. "You're a Gypsy?"

"Like you."

"I am a black man, Mr. Kaufman. It says so on my records. What is it that you want?"

"Maybe if I tell you my first name," I offered. "Benoit."

He pushed back against his chair, and his mouth got small and full of lines.

"You did come through, then" was all he said.

"I came through."

How to negotiate this? he seemed to say, gesturing, reaching out to me across the desk. He relaxed his posture and opened his mouth in a wide smile. Several teeth gleamed gold.

"Well!" he said. "A celebration then. A reunion! *Kai jas ame, Romale?*" Where are we going, Roms? A traditional question. He started to rise.

"Stay where you are," I told him. I removed the gun from the bag.

He sank back in his seat, but not in any kind of terror. Interest was all; curiosity. "What do you want, Benoit?" he asked.

"To see you."

"So? You see me. What else?"

"To hear you."

"I don't know what to say." He moved his hands in an impotent gesture.

"You used to talk a lot. Tell me what happened after you drove away."

"What didn't I do? Please put that away. We can talk like gentlemen."

"We're neither of us gentlemen. Tell me what you did."

His eyes looked at the ceiling and back at me. They seemed amused. "We took the truck as far as we could. We made our way to France. I worked there for a while."

"Worked at what?"

"Hod-carrying, road-building, anything I could find."

The telephone rang. I could hear the secretary pick it up and say something indistinct. A buzzer sounded.

"Tell her you're too busy to talk," I said.

He barked some instructions into the receiver; for an instant he seemed tempted to say something else. I shook my head.

"You were in France."

He nodded.

"It must have been difficult to work without papers. The Allies were looking for you."

"I had papers," he said. Even now a smile escaped from the corners of his mouth.

"You bought them?"

"Yes."

"With what?"

"With what do you think? Money."

"Where did you get money?"

He slammed down his palms on the desk. "I stole, is that what you want to hear? I smuggled. It was hard, it was impossible, but I did it."

"Doubtless you had connections."

"Some."

He looked at the ash on his cigar. The gun no longer seemed to interest him.

"I knew a lawyer once, an Alsatian," Eleazar said abstractly. "He used to put a wire in his cigar just before his opponent began summing up for the jury. Pretty soon everybody's eyes would be on the ash. It just got longer and longer, and nobody was paying any attention to what the other lawyer was saying. Misdirection." He pushed his chair back a bit.

"That's as far as you go," I warned him. "Tell me more."

He shrugged.

"I came to America. I prospered like everyone else. Like you. That's all. Tell me about yourself."

I talked a little about being adopted and about what I did for a living.

"Maybe I saw your work. I used to read a lot of magazines

when I was in New York. Now nothing but television. The sun rots your brain. Makes you lazy. You got married?"

"And divorced."

"I, too. Twice."

He turned the cigar around in his fingers. "Havana. Cigar heaven. You think Cuba and the United States will ever get together?"

"Go on," I demanded. "Tell me how you lived in New York."

"I worked. I took flying lessons. I got a job with an airline, and they liked my style. I flew things that other people were afraid to fly."

"Like what? Gold? Dope?"

"Sometimes. I saved enough to buy a share in a freight company. Two years ago I bought out my partners. That's all. Not very glamorous, but it pays well."

The phone rang again.

"Too busy to take any more calls," I instructed him. He repeated the words and hung up.

"You left things out," I said.

"Lots of things," he agreed. "You want to know about this." He pointed to the skin on his bare arms. "An old trick: melanin. I have to take it frequently. The hair I have curled by a barber in St. Thomas. The lips were made larger by a tattoo artist. Nothing special."

He smiled at me and showed his teeth again. He pointed to them. "Gold," he said. "I became an island black. I even do the accent." This last was said with a singing, arhythmic locution.

"You could fool me," I said. "You must have had a lot of practice." I shifted my feet. I must have winced.

"Leg bothering you?" he asked. "You want to lie down? You can keep the gun. I just want to make sure you're not in pain."

I shook my head.

"You always limp?" he asked.

"One way or another, always. Why did you become black?" I indicated my own skin. "Wasn't this dark enough for you?"

"It was necessary for me to disappear. Most fugitives go

underground, vanish into another country. I vanished into another race. They didn't know where to find me. I got away." "Until now."

"Until now." He smiled again, a great open expression, the kind that had smiled away the obscenities and God knew what else since. It was not hard to remember his ability to ingratiate himself even in the worst situations.

"How did you find me?" he asked. "Accident?"

"Not really." I told him about the indefinite glimpse of him in another time, another country. And about the odd business of the Clair sisters.

"Did you kill Eleanor Clair?" I asked. "It doesn't matter. I just want to know."

"What do you mean it doesn't matter? Of course it matters. I never killed this nun of yours."

I aimed the pistol over my wrist again, as I had done with the gull.

"I didn't kill her, Benoit."

"You had her killed."

He shrugged. "A minnow then," he said, "a minnow now. You want everything to be right again, the caravan rolling through the Transylvanian forest. Songs. Your sisters virgins, your brothers strong. Your father alive. Impossible, Benoit. Draw the picture; don't try to live it."

"The only pictures I see are the ones in the camp. Children's charcoal scrawls. Little figures badly drawn, standing on dirt with the chimneys in the background. No butterflies. No birds. No trees."

"Come, Little Fish. Let's go outside into the sun."

I just sat there.

"You truly want to shoot me?" he asked.

"I've been thinking about it for a long time."

"Too long." He started to get up and I put both hands on the gun and aimed it and he sat down again. "You're a goddamn fool," he said, the charm draining out of his manner. "You always were a goddamn fool."

"I know it," I said.

"You want to kill me because of some things that happened

in another world. If you want to kill the real killers, go hunt Nazis. There are hundreds of them walking around. You want names? I'll give you names, addresses."

"There's only one name I wanted, Eleazar. Yours. Why did you choose the name Melalo?"

"It suits me. I have a bad character."

"And you're proud of it."

He nodded. Some men are proud that they sleep badly or have short tempers.

"It helped me get through the world."

"Not everybody needs a bad character to survive."

"Were you so virtuous then? You were years younger than I, that's all. You had some talent. You were little. You were useful. In my place, who knows what you would have done? Maybe worse. Impossible to judge."

"An old line, 'impossible to judge.' The Germans were aces at using it."

"And later the Americans."

"Yes, later the Americans."

The phone rang again. I could hear the secretary's voice faintly through the door—which meant that she could hear ours. It depended how eager she was to eavesdrop, how dedicated she was to her boss. Maybe she understood what was going on behind the door, maybe not.

"Is it all right if I go for coffee now?" she shouted.

I nodded vigorously. He said it was all right. I could hear the movement of feet; then we were alone. If I was to kill him, it would have to be soon.

Eleazar talked deliberately, without tone. He made no sudden movements. We were still six or seven feet apart, he had no weapon and there was nothing to read in his face or posture.

"You talk like a *Gajo*," I told him, "an outsider. Gypsies hate the courts of the state, but we have no trouble judging each other."

"Ah, the *kriss*." He looked sorry for me. "Elders gathering round to weigh the crime and decide the penalty. Good for Romanies, Benoit. Not for us. We're neither of us gypsies any more. What color was your wife?"

"White."

"The hair, I mean. Blond?"

"Yes."

"Hah! Yellow hair. Me too, both of them. Some Gypsies we were, running from the caravan as fast as we could. Your wife had big boobs?"

"No."

"Both mine had grapefruits. Chests mean nothing to Romanies, you remember? Women going around with babies suckling, washing their breasts in the fountains? Only the legs covered, out of sight. So what do I choose? Stick legs and big tits. A real American. Come on, Benoit, don't give me Gypsy talk. You don't even *look* like a Gypsy any more. Only the skin. I know what your trouble is: you still think there's something terrible about surviving."

Oh, the old cant: survival guilt, I thought. Even he has picked it up.

"No." I tried to blink away the pain of the spikes. "It's worse than that. The day we were rounded up and sent in a file into the first of the camps, the day they beat the old men and took the babies from the mothers, I wondered, 'What have we done wrong? What misdeed have I committed?' There was no father to tell me, no mother who was smart enough. And you? What help were you to me, who looked up to you? I wanted to know why *us*? What had we done? Particularly the kids. How had we sinned? If we felt guilt it was at the capture, not at the survival. The child who is arrested, beaten, taken from his family, he wonders what transgressions . . ." The pain seemed insupportable. I tried to concentrate on his face, to stay conscious as the bright flat sunlight fell across my eyes.

—*You kill well, Gypsy.*

—*Why did he say that, Eleazar?*

—*That is my business, Benoit.*

—*Killing is your business, you mean?*

—*Keep still or you will be my business next. You understand?*

—*I don't understand anything.*

—*You understand this, don't you? A knife will make you bleed.*

A rope will stop your breath. A bullet will break your head.
That is all you have to understand.

I hardly saw him in the glare. He was an outline, a vibrating silhouette, wavering, still uncertain of his peril, of whether I was out of control.

ITEM: A doctor came for several days, possibly a week, and all day long, while he was in camp, he was busy sterilizing Gypsy children by X-ray, without using any anesthetics. After sterilization the children used to come out crying, asking their mothers what had been done to them. . . .

> —Testimony of Gustawa Winkowska,
> from A. Mitscherlich and F. Mielke,
> *Doctors of Infamy* (New York: Henry
> Schumamn, 1949)

"Eleazar." I heard myself speak. "My children died as infants. I don't know what they did to us in there. They ate our past, they burned our future."

"How should I know what they did?" he asked. "They taught me well, is all I know."

"Taught you what?"

"You look like a dead fish on the water. You want me to get you something?"

"Taught you what?"

"God damn you. You don't even know how to hold that thing. Taught me about what power was. That the only immorality is not to have it. We had no power as Gypsies. But I had power as a Kapo."

"The power to kill."

"The power to eat. That's all power is, Benoit. To eat food, to eat money, to eat people, to eat countries. You think the Yid wants revenge? No. Power. Israel wants power because power is all the world responds to. You want to kill me for power? My heart would fear for it; my head would understand. But you don't want to kill me for power."

"No."

"Imbecile. Even now you don't know who won the war, Little Fish. Look at me and try to comprehend this. The Germans won the war. You hear? *The Germans won the war.* The men who operated the gas chambers, the guards who commanded us, who made us kill, they're all walking around, old men or middle-aged, safe, warm, forgetful, happy. The doctors who worked the X-ray machines still practice. The bureaucrats still function. Every now and then they arrest someone. Applause. Meantime Dr. Mengele, who stole the eyes of the Gypsy corpses, is loose. You remember Emma Kraus, who killed the women in E Block?"

"Yes."

"She thrives. I heard she was in France two years ago, selling jewelry."

"Who lost the war, then?" I asked him. My God, the foot seemed ready to burst through the shoe.

"You did." He smiled. I could see him rise. "The dead, too. They lost. And the torn, the wounded. The powerless."

His shadow came across my face and his movements were so swift that even on whatever instant replay the mind furnishes in times of violence I can recall no transition between the time the shell ashtray rested on the desk and the instant it lacerated my hand, releasing it from what must have been a tenuous and unwilling hold.

I tried to rise and Eleazar pushed me back. Involuntarily I leaned heavily on the injured foot and was half blinded with pain. He reached down for the gun and I grabbed at his arm and he came at me with open hands for my throat. He was a powerful figure, used to bulling his way up all these years.

Outside there were the sounds of the children in some post-game exuberance and the irrelevant cackle of chickens, and of some seaplane sputtering in the harbor. My head throbbed, and there was no time at all, only space. I was in the tormented air of the camps again, and yet here in the singing air of St. John, the potential murderer now fighting for breath. I was the confused Romany of St. Luke's banging poor Simms' head against the fence, and I heard Eleazar's head against the wall, then against the side of the desk. The sun came in like a declaration. I kept saying something, or perhaps he did, but it was extinguished. Hard breathing covered the distant cacophonies and I thought of how difficult it must be for Eleazar now, but the breathing was my own. I released my hands from his neck and he sank down to the shining floor like something in water. His face looked black beneath the artificial brownness. There was no movement at all. I looked for the last time at that face, so altered from its youth and so identifiable through all the artifices of disguise. O God, Eleazar, O God. All the sins are as nothing now.

I limped out in the street and washed my face in the sea. Gypsies, how can we ever call our shattered selves whole again? A hive of memory buzzed in the dry air.

Welcome to Paradise, mon.

Beyond calculation, I thought—I think now—the "Holocaust." Yet the people survive, a nation rises from the flames and bones and screams, even if the rest of the world would prefer it dead, the salt run in its soil, its citizens gone, vanished, assimilated, made over in somebody else's image, preferably somewhere else—Madagascar, maybe. If we are moved by that history, what are we to say to a people totally annihilated or scattered, with no testament or psalms to calibrate the deep well of the past, no compensatory country, no telethons, no bond rallies, no touring orchestras, no Einstein, no Bernstein, no Jessel, no Anti-Defamation League, no suburban pledges, no stand-up comics, no mysterious alphabet, no Moses, no Joshua, no prophets except the ones in the store windows who tell fortunes for a dollar. A people whose number was up in this century when the cities seized the land around them and forbade the caravan, when wanderers without jobs were locked outside the social contract. People who did not even have the privilege of starving when there were Germans and their friends to hasten history on its way.

ITEM: Something protected us, kept us from seeing. But Anne had no such protection, to the last. I can still see her standing at the door and looking down the street as a herd of naked Gypsy girls was driven by, to the crematory, and Anne watched them going and cried. And she cried also when we marched past the children who had already been waiting half a day in the rain in front of the gas chambers, because it was not yet their turn. And Annie nudged me and said: "Look, look. Their eyes. . . ."

She cried. And you cannot imagine how soon most of us came to the end of our tears.

—E. Schnabel, *Anne Frank: A Portrait in Courage* (New York: Harcourt, Brace & World, 1958)

Half an hour later I boarded the ferry to the larger island of St. Thomas, half expecting to be stopped and searched and taken in. But the journey was rapid and the big jet left from that lethal airport without incident. I landed in New York and took the next available 747 for Paris. They must have been searching for me by then, but the rustling at my back was nothing but tourists. I bought a few clothes at a rag shop and put them on in the men's room of a restaurant on the rue Casimir de la Vigne. Thumbing a ride took longer than I anticipated, but by nightfall I was in Normandy and slept in a hayfield.

I wander now, a solitary, pointed out by nannies as a madman, the last of the caravan. I think of you constantly, Daniel, and pray that in some way I am in part your Max. I would like to believe that. I miss the rest: the Jews who gave me back myself. Max, Dyanne, Mordecai. They all knew something; they had some connection that would always be denied the Gypsy remnant. They understood, they understood. I miss Risa's whinnying and even her rubber-stamp paintings, and her oracular lover. I miss Otis's chatter, Otis no longer like me with his nose pressed up against the window; inside now, warm and dry, but at what cost. And Joe Tower, and Sadie and Larry and Inger—oh, Inger maybe most of all. Americans, they knew how to adjust, accommodate. I never did, I never could. At times I miss Eleazar, or the hunt for Eleazar. I suppose through all the sins I wondered if there was any purpose to my life except the ending of his.

Painting was certainly not my vocation, nor even portraiture;

in any case the facility is gone. Nor marriage, nor fatherhood; seeding the garden of family life was denied by Germans or by an accident of genes. Nor, like the other refugees, sitting on the long mourners' bench. Enough of that forever. I limp through the tongues of Europe and hide on the broad and comfortable cement of the old cities with a sheaf of faked papers. I eat in old cafés, keep my books in libraries, and strike up conversations with thieves and shopkeepers, children and whores. I watch for the police, and they, I imagine, for me. It hardly matters. I sleep off the road and in open cars. I blow my nose on newspapers and shower in the public baths. I stay in cities mostly, where the exhaust fans from buildings keep me warm on chilly nights. The law, in its majestic equality, forbids the rich as well as the poor to sleep under the bridges, Anatole France tells me. Wherever I am, I sleep poorly and read my scrapbook a lot. Irony supports me and stays my hand when I feel moved to hand death another Romany.

ITEM: Shortly before he came to power, Hitler had sought out a Gypsy fortune-teller and asked her to predict his future. She came to Munich, saw Hitler and predicted great power for him. But she also predicted a sudden fall, more rapid than his rise. He got very angry and thought he could break the evil powers of the Gypsy people by exterminating them.

—P. Scize, *La Tribu Prophétique* (Paris: Table Ronde, 1953)

ITEM: Already in January of this year, it was foretold me by a Gypsy fortune teller that I would be brought to trial, and that I would not live beyond my fifty-sixth year. The first prophecy has already been fulfilled, and I am sure that the second cannot be altered.

—Testimony of Adolf Eichmann from M. Pearlman, *The Capture and Trial of Adolf Eichmann* (New York: Simon & Schuster, n.d.)

The Gypsies foretold the German future; the Germans foretold ours. I write that occasionally on the sidewalks where I make my living, drawing in chalk as I did as a child: murals, cityscapes, the faces of film stars or passers-by willing to pose. The coins clatter in my hat and on my blanket. *Merci. Grazie. Thank you. Gracias.* But never *Danke schön.*

I write in my head a history of the unborn, destroyed by X-rays, scattered in smoke over the slate roofs and forests, burned and hacked and buried in the black earth. My own unborn sons and daughters chorus in the nights of the cities. Last month in Bucharest. Last week in Normandy. Yesterday, in St. James's Park, I lay on the grass re-creating the recuperative nonsense of the Snark: *But the worst of it was,/He had wholly forgotten his name.*

His name, his name. Different on the passport now. Different even then: Benoit Kaufman. Of course my name was not really Kaufman; that was Max's name, and Risa's. I was an adoptee, mute and half alive when they lifted me up and took me in. They never asked, never knew who I was. The boy mattered, not his label. But the name had always mattered to me, and there were times when it was all that mattered. My surname was Jassy. Eleazar the Kapo, the collaborator with the Germans, the killer of Gypsies, the man I had sought to destroy all this time? My older brother. *Mon semblable, mon frère.*

And what was accomplished by his murder? Did I truly extinguish the evil that is supposed to reside in my own skin? Or I have I fed it? Or merely reduced the dwindling lives of my people? Or avenged a whole line of martyrs? Or kept wounds open too long after the fact? How long can a Gypsy bleed? *The Guinness Book of Records* is no help.

Sometimes I visit the angry, chilly places—the death camps that have become museums—and there I still hear chords once chanted by the Gypsies:

> *U bar dikhila xoymi, oprundus,*
> *sviymi vastinsa bari armyasa.*
> *Liska ozistar sesi garadu*
> *mangila pali ti inkil ziyasa.*

The upright stone stares angrily
with clenched fists and a great curse.
From within a hidden voice
tries to send out a song.

At night, when sleep is elusive, I sometimes think that the
looking was the finding, that the life of seven sins was the
avoidance of the eighth, the deadliest sin: the sin of forgetting.
And then, Daniel, I think that this thing, this notebook, this
reminiscence, this bloody, dog-eared letter of avarice and sloth
and pride and lust and envy and gluttony, and most of all of
wrath—that this is the song.

STEFAN KANFER is a native New Yorker educated in the city's public and private schools and colleges. Of Rumanian descent, he has long been involved in the investigation and rehabilitation of Nazi victims. He served in Intelligence in the U.S. Army, and after attending graduate school began a career in journalism, a profession he still practices as a contributor to most national publications and as the editor of *Time*'s book review section. Mr. Kanfer has written for television and film, and his articles on language have appeared in many textbooks and anthologies. He is the author of *A Journal of the Plague Years*, a book about the witch hunts of the fifties.